ree Cheers for the
ipyard Girls

author, title and ll is the author of the Shipyard Girls series, which is set
east of England during World War II.

former journalist who worked for all the national news-
iding them with hard-hitting news stories and in-depth
ncy also wrote amazing and inspirational true life stories
t every woman's magazine in the country.

e first started writing the Shipyard Girls series, Nancy
ck to her hometown of Sunderland, Tyne and Wear,
er husband, Paul, and their English bull mastiff, Rosie –
short walk away from the beautiful award-winning
oker and Seaburn, within a mile of where the books

ject is particularly close to Nancy's heart as she comes
line of shipbuilders, who were well known in the area.

Also available by Nancy Revell

Three Cheers for the
Shipyard Girls

Nancy
Revell

PENGUIN BOOKS

PENGUIN BOOKS

UK | USA | Canada | Ireland | Australia
India | New Zealand | South Africa

Penguin Books is part of the Penguin Random House group of companies
whose addresses can be found at global.penguinrandomhouse.com

Published in Penguin Books 2022
003

Copyright © Nancy Revell, 2022

The moral right of the author has been asserted

Set in 10.4/15 pt Palatino LT Pro
Typeset by Jouve (UK), Milton Keynes
Printed and bound in Great Britain by Clays Ltd, Elcograf S.p.A.

The authorised representative in the EEA is Penguin Random House Ireland,
Morrison Chambers, 32 Nassau Street, Dublin D02 YH68

A CIP catalogue record for this book is available from the British Library

ISBN: 978-1-529-15681-2

www.greenpenguin.co.uk

Penguin Random House is committed to a sustainable future for
our business, our readers and our planet. This book is made from
Forest Stewardship Council® certified paper.

To my wonderful Readers,

This final book in the series is dedicated to you all.

Were it not for you buying the books, writing reviews, leaving feedback, and keeping me buoyed up with all your lovely messages, cards and letters, *The Shipyard Girls* series would never have been the success it is.

Thank you!

With Love,
Nancy x

Acknowledgements

Although I have dedicated this final instalment of *The Ship-yard Girls* series 'To my wonderful Readers', I want to reiterate those words of gratitude, and thank you all again for relaying to me your love for the series, and particularly the characters, who, you tell me, have become your friends, as they have mine. I've loved hearing of your frustration at my tendency to end some of the books on cliff-hangers, your heartfelt demands that certain characters find love, and others end up at the bottom of the North Sea! Your words over the years have fired me on and enthused me with the determination to make each book better than the last. To do my best. Thank you for your lovely, warm words of support, the beautiful – often handmade – cards, messages, flowers and presents, which I have been gifted over the past six years.

I'd also like to say a big 'Thank You' to all those other individuals, businesses, media outlets and libraries who have supported *The Shipyard Girls* series throughout:

The lovely staff at Fulwell Post Office, postmaster John Wilson, Liz Skelton, Richard Jewitt and Olivia Blyth, Waterstones in Sunderland, the Sunderland Antiquarian Society, namely Norm Kirtlan, Philip Curtis and Linda King, (whose mam, nicknamed 'Tan', was a WW2 welder making 'scoops' for the mine sweepers at a foundry in Sunderland), researcher Meg Hartford (whose aunty, Martha Tinsley Graham, was a riveter during WW2), Jackie Caffrey, of Nostalgic Memories of Sunderland in Writing, the amazingly supportive Beverley Ann Hopper, of The Book Lovers, journalist Katy Wheeler at the *Sunderland Echo*, Simon Grundy at Sun FM, Julie Pendleton from Nova Radio (North East), Pauline Martin at The Word, the National Centre for the Written Word, Pat Johnston and everyone at the Hendon Community Library (Sunderland), and BBC Radio Newcastle producer Jane Downs and presenter Gilly Hope (whose great nan, Francis Dagg, was a WW2 shipyard worker), and all the fabulous book bloggers who have reviewed the series – special thanks to Amanda Oughton, of Ginger Book Geek, who was one of the first to jump on board and sing the praises of my Shipyard Girls on her brilliant blog.

To artist Rosanne Robertson, Soroptimist International of Sunderland, in particular Suzanne Brown, Kathleen Tuddenham, Megan Blacklock, Hilary Clavering and Marjorie Wilkinson, Kevin Johnson, Sunderland City Council, and Louise Bradford, owner and director of Creo Communications, for their continuing work to make the country's first ever commemoration to Britain's real shipyard women a reality.

To Ian Mole for bringing the series to life with his *Shipyard Girls Walking Tour*.

To my lovely editor and publishing director Emily Griffin and copy editor Caroline Johnson and all the professional and hardworking 'Team Nancy' at Cornerstone/Penguin Random House.

To Gina Wilson for her continuing love, care, insights and guidance.

To my mum Audrey Walton (née Revell), whose childhood

and memories of living in Tatham Street have been such an inspiration for this series.

To my sister, Jane Elias, brother-in-law Sion, their truly lovely children, Ivor, Matilda and Flynn, and my husband, Paul Simmonds – for listening to me, encouraging me and for the love you give.

Thank you all.

Do not look back and grieve over the past, for it is gone; and do not be troubled about the future, for it has not yet come. Live in the present, and make it so beautiful that it will be worth remembering.

Ida Scott Taylor (1820 – 1915)

Prologue

Mrs Evans pulled the long brass rod by the side of the front door and heard the muffled ring of the bell from inside the house.

She took a deep breath to quell the swell of anger and adrenaline.

It was freezing cold, and a thick layer of snow had just settled on the town. A group of children were playing out on the street, building snowmen. Their joy and laughter sounded so innocent.

Mrs Evans felt the bile of deep-seated vitriol rise as her daughter's face flashed into her mind's eyes.

Innocent. Like her daughter. She looked down at the stone step she was standing on. *Before she stepped over this threshold.*

Now it was she – the mother – who was about to cross into this house of evil. The ever-present gnawing hunger for retribution felt all-consuming. How she wished with all her heart that she could act upon that deeply embedded craving for vengeance.

If it was just herself left in this godforsaken world, she truly believed she could. But not with her husband, Gibson,

1

waiting for her at home. He had already lost a daughter. He could not also lose a wife. She could only do what she had come to do – pass on the burden of knowledge about the maleficence manifesting itself in this house.

Mrs Evans heard the turn of the handle and watched as the door was opened. The immediate rush of air that escaped was warm and infused with the smells of Yuletide – pine and cinnamon, and a touch of nutmeg.

A pompous-looking man with scraped-back hair, brilliantined firmly into place, stared down the length of his nose at her.

'Can I help you?' His voice had only a hint of a north-east accent.

'Yes.' Mrs Evans held his gaze as he appraised her. 'I'm here to see the mistress of the house. Mrs Havelock. Mrs Henrietta Havelock.'

The man, who Mrs Evans presumed was the butler, hesitated, as though unsure whether to shoo this woman away or show her in. She had a worn shawl wrapped around her shoulders and was dressed from head to toe in black. A widow, he guessed. And a poor one at that. But not destitute. Not quite poor enough for him to shut the door on her.

Mrs Evans straightened her back and hardened her look.

'I'm presuming the mistress of the house is in – it being Christmas Day,' Mrs Evans said. A statement, not a question.

'She is,' the butler said, 'but whether she is available is another matter.'

A blast of icy air swept over Mrs Evans and into the house.

Over the butler's shoulder, she had a partial view of a huge, beautifully decorated Christmas tree that dominated the grand hallway of the Havelock residence. As in the previous five years, Mrs Evans and her husband had not put up a tree this year. They would never celebrate another Christmas again.

'Well, I'll have to go and see the mistress and find out if she is available to see unexpected guests. I'm *presuming* you are not expected, otherwise you would have said – and *I* would have been told.' A statement, not a question.

Mrs Evans was wondering whether to push past him into the house and demand to see Mrs Havelock when she heard rustling and quick, dainty footsteps clip-clopping on the tiled hallway.

'Is that Miriam and Margaret?' the excited, well-spoken voice sounded out.

The butler turned slightly.

'No, ma'am, it's not. There's a woman here asking to see you.'

'Really? I'm not expecting anyone. Who is it?'

Mrs Evans watched as her daughter's former mistress put a hand on the butler's arm and gently forced him to stand aside.

Another blast of biting-cold air swirled inside, causing Henrietta to usher Mrs Evans into the house immediately.

'Goodness me, you'll turn to ice stood out there. Come in!' Henrietta threw the butler a look of reproach. 'I don't know what's got into Eddy here, letting you stand out in such Arctic conditions. Never mind at Christmas. Peace and goodwill to all men . . .' Another scornful look.

Mrs Evans stepped across the threshold and into a house she had only ever heard about from her daughter.

She smelled the Christmas dinner cooking – goose.

'Thank you, Mrs Havelock,' Mrs Evans said, looking at

the diminutive frame of the mistress of the house. She was exactly as Gracie had described. Theatrical in her dress, wearing a long, hooped taffeta skirt; the alabaster white of her skin contrasting with the deep-purple fabric, heavily made-up face, cobalt blue eye shadow and small, scarlet lips. Doll-like.

'Please, call me Henrietta.' She extended a hand in greeting. 'Everyone calls me Henrietta.'

'Nice to meet you, Henrietta.' The two shook hands. 'I'm Mrs Evans.' A pause. 'Gracie's mother. Gracie Evans. Your former maid. She left your employ over six years ago?'

Henrietta's face lit up. 'Of course, I remember. Gracie. My little Gracie. How is she?'

She looked towards the door of the lounge.

'Come, come,' she cajoled, taking Mrs Evans by the arm and guiding her to the front room. 'My, you're freezing. Come and get warm and tell me all about Gracie. How's she doing? Oh, I do miss her.'

So, Henrietta doesn't know.

Mrs Evans allowed herself to be drawn into the sitting room, with its blazing fire and plush furniture.

'Eddy, bring us something to drink. I'll have my usual.' She turned to Mrs Evans. 'What can I get you? If you don't drink spirits, we have eggnog?'

Mrs Evans shook her head. Henrietta's chirpy demeanour and the sudden heat had made her feel dizzy.

'Sit, please sit, Mrs Evans.' Henrietta gestured towards the armchair.

Feeling as though she might faint if she remained standing, Mrs Evans reluctantly sat down. She had wanted to simply stand tall, tell Henrietta what she had come to tell her and go.

4

'My dear, you look as white as a sheet. Are you all right?' Henrietta asked, sitting down on the adjacent sofa and leaning forward so that she was almost able to touch her former maid's mother.

'I'm fine,' Mrs Evans said. 'I won't take up much of your time.' She paused. She had promised herself not to cry or get emotional. Which was hard. She still wasn't able to even think about Gracie without crying – never mind talk about her.

Just then she heard a deep voice shouting out:

'Eddy!'

Henrietta jumped up. 'Excuse me a moment.'

Mrs Evans heard Henrietta telling her husband he'd have to be patient as Eddy couldn't be in two places at once and that Eddy would see to his needs after he'd brought her a drink.

Hurrying back into the room, Henrietta settled back down on the sofa just as Eddy appeared with her vodka. He placed it on the side table and strode out of the room, eager to tend to his master.

On hearing the voice of Charles Havelock, Mrs Evans's jaw had clenched in cold anger, and any tears that might have been threatening were nipped firmly in the bud. She sat up straight and looked at Henrietta.

'I've come to tell you that Gracie's dead,' she said simply.

Henrietta, who had just taken a sip from the thick cut-crystal tumbler, swallowed hard and stared at Mrs Evans.

'Gracie's dead?' Her disbelief was evident in her tone.

Mrs Evans nodded. 'She died quite some time ago. Four and a half years, to be exact. May 1914. I thought you might have heard about it or seen it in the notification of deaths in the local paper?'

5

Henrietta shook her head.

It was clear to Mrs Evans that not only was Gracie's former mistress not lying, but she was shocked. And upset. She could see her eyes were filling with tears.

'I don't understand,' Henrietta stuttered. 'What happened? Was she ill? Was she in an accident?' Her pale hand went to her rouged cheek. 'Oh, Gracie. My poor little Gracie.'

It went through Mrs Evans's mind that she should have felt affronted – Henrietta was calling Gracie *her* little Gracie – but she didn't. Gracie had told her how the mistress of the house had always referred to her as '*my* little Gracie'. How Henrietta had been kind and caring – loving, even – to Gracie. She had wondered if it was because her own daughters were never around; had never been around much, by the sounds of it.

'The thing is,' Mrs Evans said, 'Gracie wasn't just *your* little Gracie, nor was she just *my* little Gracie.'

She waited a beat. There was no need. She had Henrietta's full attention.

'My daughter was also *Mr Havelock's* little Gracie.' She paused. 'For a while, anyway.' Another pause. 'When it suited him. Or, from what I was able to gather, when he was back home from his long trips abroad.'

Henrietta looked puzzled.

'There are some who would use the term "taken advantage of",' Mrs Evans explained, 'but that's not an expression I would use.' Her lips were taut with the pull of the anger that sat with her day in and day out. 'I like to call a spade a spade and the word I would use would be "violated".'

Henrietta still looked confused. Her hand was still holding her tumbler, clasping it tightly.

'What are you saying, Mrs Evans?'

6

'I'm saying that your husband violated my daughter in the worst way possible.'

Henrietta's hand went to her mouth as though she were about to suppress a scream.

'Are you saying my husband *raped* little Gracie?' she asked, her voice a hoarse whisper.

'I am,' Mrs Evans said. 'And not just the once but on several occasions.' She felt the guilt buoy up next to the anger. How she had berated herself for not realising. For not seeing the signs. If she had been a better mother, Gracie would have confided in her. When she'd found out, she had asked her daughter why she hadn't. And when she did, she had cried angry tears late into the night, going over Gracie's words to her, explaining how happy they had been that she had a job in the 'big house' – how lucky she was to be working as the mistress's maid.

'And I doubt very much that my Gracie was the first – or the last,' Mrs Evans added.

Henrietta sat. Shocked into silence.

'I suppose it was inevitable that Gracie ended up in the family way,' Mrs Evans continued. 'She tried to hide it – and succeeded for a good while. You know how small she was. Looked so much younger than her age. So, at first, I thought she was just growing up. A bit of a late developer.'

Henrietta continued to listen.

'But, of course, she couldn't hide it for ever. I think she was hoping she'd lose it and that she wouldn't have to tell me or her father.' Mrs Evans had a flash of her husband when he'd found out the truth. She'd had to physically stop him coming here and venting his fury on the man who had defiled his daughter. She had often wished she hadn't.

7

'But she didn't. The baby was determined to make it into the world, and Gracie gave birth to a little baby boy.'

'Oh my goodness.' Henrietta had put her drink down on the side table and was now leaning forward, hands knotted, hanging on every word that was coming from Mrs Evans's mouth.

'Which, of course, she immediately gave up for adoption,' Mrs Evans said. 'I say "*of course*", as clearly Gracie did not want a constant reminder of that man.' She nodded towards the door – to where she'd heard the agitated voice. 'And what he'd done to her.'

'And Gracie?' Henrietta asked, not wanting to hear how she had died, but needing to.

Mrs Evans blinked back her own tears.

'Two months after she'd handed the baby over, Gibson and I came back from the market to find Gracie hanging from the bannisters. She'd made a noose for herself out of some old rope and ended it all.'

Mrs Evans breathed in.

'A noose which should have been tied around *his* neck –' another nod towards the door '– not my daughter's.'

Both Henrietta's hands went to her mouth. 'No, no, no, no – not Gracie – my lovely little Gracie.' Tears started to drip down her face.

Mrs Evans stood. She had done what she had come here to do. What she had wanted to do for a long time. What she should have done immediately after Gracie died.

Now that Henrietta knew the truth, Mrs Evans just wanted to get out of this house. To leave it behind for ever. And go back to her home. Back to her husband. Back to their memories of their daughter. Gibson, she knew, would be worried. He had not been happy about her coming here – had wanted to accompany her, but she had refused. This, she had told him, was something she wanted to do on her own. One mother to another.

'I'm going now.' Mrs Evans looked down at Henrietta, sitting rigidly. 'I wanted you to know what kind of a man – *monster* – you are married to.'

She walked to the door and turned.

'It's probably too late for any of the maids you've had since Gracie, but as of today, if what happened to my Gracie happens to another maid here in this house, then it will be on your conscience.'

And with that, Mrs Evans walked out of the room. She let herself out quickly and quietly and hurried down the front steps.

A wave of nausea hit her as she reached the bottom step and she had to stand for a moment, swallowing hard.

When she felt able to walk without retching, she made her way down the driveway.

She wrapped her shawl around herself and crunched through the snow and gravel, not once looking back at the house that had taken her daughter from her.

Chapter One

New Year's Day 1945

'I love the start of a new year!' Dorothy exclaimed, banging her tray down on the table. Her voice was raised as the canteen was noisier than usual. The atrocious weather had brought just about every worker at Thompson's shipyard inside for a respite from the bitter cold and howling winds.

'Why's that, Dor?' Gloria asked, taking a hunk of bread and dipping it into her bowl of stew. She was starving. The colder the weather, the hungrier she always felt.

'Well, it's like yer get to start all over again, isn't it?' Angie chipped in. She and Dorothy had been discussing it as they'd hurried to work that morning. They were both still feeling a little high from seeing in the New Year with their sweethearts. They'd gathered with a large crowd outside the Town Hall and cheered and kissed and tossed their hats into the air as the shipyard horns and church bells had sounded out.

'Well, it's certainly going to be a new beginning for *you* this year, isn't it, Angie?' Rosie said, looking at her squad sitting round what had become firmly established as the 'women welders' table'.

'What do yer mean, it's gonna be a new beginning for me?' Angie asked, taking a bite of her sandwich. Her face, like those of her workmates, was flushed red after spending the morning out in the freezing cold, then coming into the slightly overbearing warmth of the canteen.

'Because you're engaged – you're gonna become a married woman,' Martha, the group's gentle giant, laughed.

'Yep, new life – even a new name,' Polly agreed.

'Who says I'm gonna get hitched this year?' Angie demanded.

Everyone automatically looked at Dorothy, who had the decency to blush.

'Dor! I said not to say anything until me 'n Quentin had agreed a date,' Angie reprimanded.

'I'm afraid it was my fault,' confessed Hannah, the group's 'little bird', who now worked in the drawing office. 'Olly and I were asking Dorothy if she thought you'd get married before or after the war ended.' She glanced at Olly, who nervously nudged his wire-rimmed spectacles up the bridge of his nose.

Angie smiled at the pair, who had met at the yard and were now pretty much inseparable. She was too happy to be angry. Since Quentin had proposed to her at the Christmas Extravaganza, she'd been walking on air.

'Well, we're quite keen on getting married in May,' Angie said. 'Even if the war's not ended by then, it'll be almost as good as. Quentin said his work's already started to drop off, so he can probably get a week off.'

They all knew Angie's beau, Quentin Foxton-Clarke, worked in the War Office in London.

'It'll give them time to meet the parents – and for them to get over the shock,' Dorothy explained in all earnestness.

Gloria shook her head. 'Just because Angie 'n Quentin

come from different backgrounds, it doesn't mean their parents aren't gonna be as pleased as punch for them.'

Dorothy let out a spluttering cough. 'What planet are you living on, Glor? Angie'll be the first to admit that Quentin's mother and father will not approve of the match.'

Angie agreed. 'Quentin's said so himself. There's no use him pretending – in their opinion, I'm as far from "marriage material" as it's possible to get.'

She looked at everyone's concerned faces.

'But don't worry,' she reassured. 'In Quentin's words, he'd be "frightfully worried" if I was.'

'Because?' Martha asked.

'Because his parents,' Dorothy jumped in, 'would have poor Quentin marrying some awful horsey, stuck-up snob who's only interested in his money and his social standing.'

Everyone looked at Angie, who nodded.

'It's true.'

'And what about *your* parents?' Polly asked.

'I dinnit knar what my mam 'n dad'll say, to be honest,' Angie admitted. 'When we were just courting, I'd have bet a week's wages on them saying that he was just after one thing 'n he'd toss me aside like a used rag when he was ready to settle down. But now he's proposed . . .' She shrugged her shoulders.

'Do you think they'll like him?' Olly asked.

'Oh no,' Angie said. 'He's posh, so they'll hate him.'

'But they won't hate his money,' Dorothy butted in.

They all looked at Angie for her reaction.

'Dorothy's right.'

'Oh dear, I don't know which sounds worse, you meeting his parents or him meeting yours,' said Hannah, who was from Prague and hadn't seen her own parents since they'd sent her to England to stay with her aunty Rina shortly before the outbreak of war.

'It's definitely a toss-up, isn't it, Ange?' Dorothy put her arm around her friend and squeezed. 'But we've decided that after each meeting of the parents, Angie and Quentin are going to meet up with us and tell us all about it, haven't we?'

'That's if everyone wants to?' Angie asked tentatively.

'*Of course*,' the women chorused.

'We'll be all ears,' Gloria said. 'Wanting to hear every cough 'n spit.'

'And hopefully seeing the funny side of it all,' Dorothy added with more optimism than she felt. Her own experience of taking her boyfriend, Bobby Armstrong, to meet her parents had been disastrous. So bad that she hadn't spoken to them since.

When the klaxon sounded out the end of the lunch break, the women made their way back out into the yard. The weather was still cold and windy, and they were all tired from having been up late, seeing in the start of the New Year, but none of that mattered, for victory was just around the corner. British bombers had just attacked Berlin, America's Third Army had broken the siege of Bastogne in Belgium, and the Hungarian provisional government had just declared war on Germany.

It was a good start to the New Year. A very good start indeed.

*

In the admin offices, Helen gave her personal assistant, Marie-Anne McCarthy, instructions for the rest of the afternoon.

Helen had to suppress a smile on seeing Marie-Anne's exuberance on being handed the reins. There was nothing more her flame-haired assistant enjoyed than stepping into the boss's shoes for a few hours.

As Helen hurried out of the main building, the wind and cold hit her – along with the deafening clanking and clashing of the shipyard. Waving up at Davey, the young timekeeper, she trotted across to her green sports car. She'd been up until the early hours, seeing in the New Year with Matthew Royce, manager of Doxford's shipyard, at a do at the Town Hall. She should be tired, but she felt wide awake, energised and very excited, for she was going to pick up her grandmother from the hospital.

After more than two decades of being locked up in the Sunderland Borough asylum at Ryhope, Henrietta was coming home. Not to her former home, where her estranged husband, Charles Havelock, still lived. There was no way she could be anywhere near the man who had been responsible for incarcerating her – and who had just spent the past few months trying to poison her. No, Henrietta was coming to Helen's home on Park Avenue in Roker where she lived with her mother, Henrietta's daughter, Miriam Crawford.

Driving along Dame Dorothy Street, Helen knew her present feelings of excitement and anticipation were also in part because she had arranged to meet Dr John Parker there.

The man she loved.

Her mood, though, started to drop as reality pushed through.

A love that was destined never to be.

An image of John kneeling and proposing to Dr Claire Eris

15

outside the Ryhope Hospital while the Christmas Extravaganza took place inside flashed into Helen's mind.

It should have been *her* sitting on the bench with John on bended knee – *her* kissing him, telling him that she wanted him, wanted to be his wife, wanted to be with him for the rest of her life.

Driving across the Wearmouth Bridge, Helen glanced to her left.

Every time she crossed the Meccano-like green bridge that connected the north side of the town to the south, she looked out at the Wear. It was always such a hive of activity, crammed full of vessels, naval and merchant, some being built, some simply being repaired before being sent back to war. There was the old faithful passenger ferry, *W.F. Vint*, making its way across the water, and a half a dozen fishing boats tied up by the docks. All overshadowed by an avenue of huge metal cranes.

Helen never failed to feel a swell of pride that she was part of the town's shipbuilding industry. Her pride was greater still as it was clear that the war would soon be won, and that it was largely due to the hundreds of cargo vessels the Wear had birthed. Thompson & Sons shipyard on North Sands had built nigh on forty Merchant Navy ships since the start of the war. Ships that had transported food and fuel, men and munitions to battles all over the world. It had been something they had all discussed with great verve last night.

The New Year's Eve party had mainly been attended by those connected to the town's shipyards and engineering firms. She had heard at least a couple of the directors from the town's nine yards reciting part of Churchill's speech about how, were it not for the Merchant Navy and its vessels, Britain would be in a 'parlous state'.

Thinking back to how the evening had developed, Helen blushed as she recalled explaining to Matthew that the brief kiss they had shared at the Christmas Extravaganza party was a one-off – that she had been caught up in the emotion of the day. Which was not really a lie. After all, she had just seen John proposing to Claire. Broken-hearted, when Matthew's lips had brushed hers while they danced, she had allowed herself to pretend he was John.

But yesterday, on the stroke of midnight, she had kissed Matthew, and had done so knowing exactly who it was. It had meant nothing. It was New Year's Eve. It was tradition. Kissing was a way of welcoming in the New Year, wasn't it?

Although, in the stone-cold sober light of day, she wished she hadn't done it. It would only encourage him in his pursuit of her. She'd have to tell him straight.

How could she court another man when her heart was taken up with John?

Driving through town, Helen saw two beautiful shire horses pulling the Vaux dray. She dropped down a gear and slowed down. After they turned off to the brewery, she continued on, driving up Durham Road, before pulling into the Sunderland Royal Infirmary.

Hurrying through the entrance, she walked quickly down the main corridor to the ward where she knew her grandmother would be waiting to be discharged.

Walking through the swing doors, she stopped dead in her tracks on seeing John.

As always, her heart hammered when her eyes met his.

17

He turned slightly to show her that Dr Bernard, her grand-mother's suitor from the extravaganza, was also there, chatting away to Henrietta.

'Helen, you're here! Come over,' Henrietta called out on seeing her granddaughter.

Helen smiled at the nurse, who was looking a little flustered as it was against the rules to have so many visitors at one time. As two of those visitors were doctors, though, she'd held back from enforcing the rules.

'You remember Dr Bernard, don't you?' Henrietta said as soon as Helen reached her and gave her a kiss on the cheek. 'From Christmas Day?'

'Of course,' Helen said, shaking the doctor's hand. *How could she forget?* Not only did Dr Bernard have the most impressive handlebar moustache, he and her grandmother had been loath to part when it was time for Henrietta to be returned to the Royal.

'Your dear aunty . . .' Dr Bernard said, shaking Helen's hand and turning his attention back to Henrietta, '. . . dropped her glove when she left the party – a party which I have to say was the most marvellous event, *absolutely marvellous* – so I thought I would bring said glove today and wish her a Happy New Year in person. And I am so glad I did, as I hear she is now well enough to go home.'

Dr Bernard twiddled the end of his light grey moustache and smiled at Henrietta.

'Helen . . .' John stepped forward and gave her a chaste kiss on the cheek. 'Can I have a quick word?'

'Of course,' said Helen.

'Take your time,' Henrietta commanded. 'Dr Bernard here will keep me entertained.' She patted the chair next to her. Dr Bernard seated himself, needing no further encouragement.

'Is everything all right?' Helen asked as they walked out of the ward. 'You look awfully serious.'

Dr Parker looked along the corridor. Seeing a couple of chairs to one side, he gestured for them to sit down.

'No, no,' he said. 'Everything's fine.' They both sat down. 'More than fine, actually.'

He turned to Helen, brushing his sandy-blond hair away from his face. 'I wanted to tell you some good news.'

'Go on. Sounds intriguing,' Helen said, knowing what he was about to say, but not wanting him to realise that she knew all about the 'good news' he was about to impart. *Had seen it with her own eyes.*

'I proposed to Claire, and she said yes,' Dr Parker said, trying to sound happy about it. He *was* happy about it, wasn't he?

Helen worked hard to manufacture the kind of look people made when they told you they were getting married.

'That's wonderful news, John,' she said, surprised at how convincing she sounded. 'Congratulations!' She went to give him a kiss on the cheek, but he turned slightly, and she ended up half kissing him on the lips.

'*Sorry!*' They both apologised at the same time.

Helen got up, afraid she might kiss him again, and that this time it would be properly.

'So, have you set a date yet?' she asked as they both started walking slowly back to the ward.

'No, no, not yet,' Dr Parker said. He hesitated when they reached the swing doors.

'Well, be sure to tell me when you do,' Helen continued,

sounding convincingly sincere. 'Give me plenty of time to buy a hat.' *More like enough time to think of an excuse not to go.*

Dr Parker forced a smile. Helen seemed genuinely pleased. He really did have to get it out of his thick skull that there could ever be anything between them. It was not healthy. He was an engaged man. And Helen saw him as a friend – *just* a friend. And nothing more. She had even told him so.

'Well,' he said, holding the door open. 'Let's get Henrietta home . . . I'll just sign her discharge papers.'

He nodded to the nurse, who had them ready.

'And here are the papers sanctioning Grandmama's release from the asylum,' Helen said, opening her handbag and giving John the necessary documentation.

As she did so, her hand touched John's and she felt a slight electric shock.

They both laughed.

'*Static.*'

Once again, they spoke in unison.

Chapter Two

At four o'clock, Rosie pushed up her welding mask and moved her squad around, tapping each of the women on the back and giving them the signal to down tools. Today they were finishing early. No one needed telling twice, and within minutes they'd put their tools away, packed their haversacks and were walking from the dry dock where they had been working all day on the yard's latest commission for the Ministry of War Transport. As they crossed the yard to the timekeeper's cabin, they got their clocking-off cards ready. Seeing Hannah and Olly coming out of the main doors of the drawing office, they waved across to them, gesturing for them to hurry and catch them up.

'Is everyone still up for that drink?' Dorothy asked as they reached the main gates.

Everyone nodded.

'Just the one, though,' Polly said through a yawn. 'I'm kippered.'

'Same here,' said Gloria, heaving her haversack onto her other shoulder. 'Us married women with young children can't do the late nights like we used to.' Gloria and her soon-to-be husband, Jack Crawford, had only just managed to stay up until midnight before carrying a sleeping Hope to her cot and collapsing into bed themselves. 'Isn't that right, Polly?'

Polly nodded and yawned again. 'It's a sad state of affairs when your mam has more stamina than you – and ends up staying up into the early hours.' Like Gloria, Polly had also hit the sack shortly after the turn of midnight, although her sleep had been fitful as her baby boy, Artie, now sixteen months old, had kept waking up.

'Were Beryl 'n her hittin' the brandy?' Angie asked. Beryl was Agnes's neighbour and best friend.

'She was – *along with Dr Billingham*,' Polly said, raising her eyebrows.

'Really!' Dorothy exclaimed, leading the way across from Thompson's to the yard's nearest watering hole.

'Are they courting?' Hannah asked, pulling up her hood and holding it in place to combat the force of the wind, which had whipped up even more during the course of the afternoon.

'Just friends,' Polly said, arching an eyebrow. Dr Billingham, a divorcee, had saved the day when Polly had gone into labour prematurely, and ever since his visits to the Elliot household had become more frequent.

'Ahh, warmth!' Angie rubbed her hands together as they all bundled into the Admiral.

'And practically empty,' Rosie said, pulling off her red headscarf. She was glad she'd sanctioned an early finish. They would at least be able to get a table and chat without shouting before the pub filled up with the inevitable hordes of shipwrights, platers, riveters and caulkers all eager to continue the New Year celebrations.

Once they were all sitting down with their drinks, Gloria raised her glass. 'A toast!'

'To a Happy New Year!' Dorothy jumped in.

'And one which brings our men back home,' Gloria added, looking across at Polly.

Gloria knew that just as she would not be able to rest until her youngest son, Gordon, was back, Polly, too, would not be happy until her husband Tommy was safely returned to her.

'Hear! Hear!' the women chorused.

They all sipped their drinks.

'Helen not coming?' Polly asked.

'No, she's gone to get Henrietta from the hospital,' Gloria said. 'She's been officially discharged from both hospitals – the Royal *and* the asylum.'

'That's marvellous news,' said Hannah, looking at her workmates. They had all been appalled at the injustice of Henrietta's wrongful imprisonment in the local mental hospital. 'And there'll be no repercussions?' They were all well aware of the axe Charles Havelock wielded over their heads should Henrietta's true identity be revealed.

'As long as she remains Henrietta *Girling*,' Gloria said. 'Some spinster great-aunty from way back when. Which, by the sounds of it, Henrietta is more than happy with.'

'I'll bet! *More than happy* not to be in any way associated with that horrible husband of hers,' Dorothy said.

'And at least they won't have to worry about anyone recognising her,' Martha chipped in. Henrietta had been given a new, more conservative look that was nothing like her previous theatrical way of dressing. Even her red hair had been toned down.

'Certainly not now Kate's worked her magic,' Rosie added.

Kate was Rosie's old school friend who had lived on the streets for a while, but had since turned her life around and was now esteemed in the town for her seamstressing skills and her amazing designs.

'Actually, there's something else I need to tell you all,' Gloria said.

'Sounds ominous,' said Dorothy.

'A little,' Gloria admitted. 'It looks like Dr Parker and Dr Eris are going to tie the knot.'

'Really?' Polly said. 'But he loves Helen!'

'Yeah, and Helen loves him,' Martha added, equally crestfallen.

'That might well be,' Gloria said, 'but unfortunately Dr Parker doesn't know that – nor can he.'

'Because of *us*,' Martha stated, her tone tinged with anger.

'But that doesn't mean *you're* to blame,' Rosie said, glancing at Martha, Dorothy and Angie.

'Yeah, it's that conniving cow that's to blame.' Angie spat the words out.

They were all quiet for a moment, thinking of their secrets, which were preventing Helen from being with the man she loved.

'Is there anything we can do?' Polly asked.

'There must be something,' Dorothy said, exasperated.

'For Dr Parker's sake too,' Olly said. 'I wouldn't have thought a marriage based on deceit bodes well for a happy future.'

They all murmured their agreement and sipped their drinks, their delight at hearing about Henrietta's discharge dampened by news of Dr Parker's proposal.

'But, on a more positive note,' Gloria said, wanting to lift the mood, 'I thought I'd tell you all before a certain someone starts badgering me –' she looked at Dorothy '– that, as suggested, Jack and I are going to get married on Valentine's Day.'

'Yeah!' Dorothy raised a triumphant arm in the air, causing the barman to look over and shake his head.

'That's wonderful news,' Hannah said, looking at Olly, who nodded his agreement.

'Congratulations, Glor,' Martha smiled.

'But,' Gloria stressed, 'it really is going to be a very small affair. Just the registry office and a few drinks in the Tatham afterwards.'

'Sounds perfect,' Rosie said, understanding Gloria's need for a low-key affair. Not just because this was a second marriage for both her and Jack, but because they wanted as few people as possible to know, reducing the chances that Jack's ex, Miriam Crawford, would hear about it and cause an upset.

'A *small* affair,' Gloria repeated, turning the attention to their newly engaged workmate. 'Unlike Angie's wedding, which, I think it's safe to say, we're all hoping will be a very *grand* affair.'

Angie blushed.

'Too right!' Dorothy said. 'The bigger the better.'

'Well, this is already starting off to be a happy New Year,' Hannah said. 'Two weddings in the first five months.' She looked at Dorothy. 'Does all this marriage talk not make you think about changing your mind?'

Dorothy had surprised them all just before Christmas when she'd told them that she'd decided she didn't want to follow convention by getting married and starting a family, much as she was head over heels in love with Gloria's son. Since she'd been courting Bobby and had heard about all the

25

different countries he had visited during his time with the navy, she'd developed a yearning to see the world.

'No, I'm probably surer than ever. But that doesn't mean I'm not mad about other people's weddings,' she said, looking at Angie and then at Gloria.

'So,' Rosie said, 'I'm guessing you're both going to be popping into the Maison Nouvelle to see Kate?'

Gloria shook her head. 'I have the perfect dress earmarked and happily hanging in my wardrobe. But I can't wait to see what Kate will conjure up for Angie.'

Everyone looked at Angie, who again blushed, unused to being the centre of attention.

'So, have you thought about the design?' Polly asked, thinking of the most amazing dress Kate had designed and made for her wedding to Tommy.

'Not really,' Angie said.

Wanting to divert the conversation away from her wedding plans, Angie took a quick sip of her port and asked, 'But what I have been thinking about is, what are we all gonna do once the war is won? The yard's obviously not gonna want to keep us on, are they?'

'I wouldn't have thought you'd *want* to be kept on?' Rosie asked. She was glad Angie had broached the subject as she was keen to know what all her squad had planned. 'You don't want to carry on working at the yard after you're married, do you?'

Dorothy spluttered to get her words out quickly enough. 'Unlikely! Angie will be living the country life in a stately manor.'

Not wanting the conversation to turn back to her, Angie looked around at her workmates.

'What about you Martha? What are you gonna dee?'

Everyone looked at Martha, whose face suddenly dropped.

'I don't know,' she said. Her heart sank just at the thought of leaving the place she had come to love. A place that had become her life. And, moreover, a place where she felt she belonged. Something she'd never felt in her whole life.

Rosie saw the sadness in Martha at the thought of leaving Thompson's. She wanted to reassure her that she could continue to work at the yard, but didn't want to raise her hopes. Especially as it had been made clear that as soon as the men were back, the women would be given their cards.

'Let's worry about that when the time comes, eh?' Rosie said. 'Let's just win this war first.'

The women agreed and finished their drinks. Since the pub was now almost full to bursting, they took their empty glasses to the bar and headed out.

As they ambled down to the ferry landing, Gloria dropped back to speak to Rosie.

'I'm guessing you'll be staying on?' she asked.

'Definitely,' said Rosie.

They watched as Polly, Dorothy, Angie, Martha, Hannah and Olly paid their penny fares to Stan the ferry master. It was dark, but due to the blackout regulations being phased out, there was now a lamp hanging from the funnel and they could clearly see the old man's weather-beaten face.

'You're not thinking of leaving and having children – "breeding and baking", as Dorothy likes to put it?' Gloria asked, looking at Rosie as she rummaged in her haversack for her purse.

Rosie shook her head. 'I don't think that's the life for me.

For starters, I can't bake to save my life, and as for breeding, well, I've got Charlotte – and she's more than a handful.'

They both paid their fares and stepped onto the ferry.

'Yes, but Charlotte's yer sister – she's sixteen now, nearly seventeen, 'n it sounds as if she won't have any problem getting into university, so it won't be long before she's up 'n away. The house will probably feel empty when she goes.' Gloria had certainly felt a huge hole in her life when Bobby and Gordon had left to join the navy when they were Charlotte's age.

'I think it would be different if I didn't work,' Rosie said.

Gloria looked at Rosie and tried to read her friend's face. They had all wondered after Rosie had married Peter if she would want to start a family. As Peter had been over in France working as an undercover agent for the Special Operations Executive, that was clearly not a possibility. But now he was back, and had been since June last year, they had all anticipated Rosie coming in to work one day and telling them she was expecting.

But it was now six months down the line, and no such announcement had been made.

As they all stood huddled together in the small cabin of the battered old steam paddler, trying to shelter from the icy winds that were battering *W.F. Vint* as she made her way across the Wear, the chatter once again turned to what life would be like after Hitler's defeat. Rosie listened while musing that for her, the end of the war would be a double-edged sword – great joy and relief that finally good had triumphed over evil, but also personal loss as she would no longer have her squad of women welders with her every day. As the ferry bumped against the jetty, they all bustled off and started the trek up Low Street to the main road, any talk now impossible due to a sudden downpour of stinging hailstones. Rosie just hoped this final furlong towards victory would be one filled with a lightness of being they all very much deserved. And that there would be no more unwanted surprises hiding in the wings.

Chapter Three

Mr Havelock heard the rat-a-tat-tat of the hailstones against the sash windows of his study. He reached over to the flat-bottomed ship's decanter and poured himself another Rémy. Apart from the rattling windows and the sound of the wind coming down the chimney, causing the open fire to flutter, the house was quiet. He had given his manservant, Eddy, and housekeeper, Agatha, the evening off because he wanted to be left on his own to think.

He needed to work out a plan.

Helen had unearthed the original admissions form that clearly stated that the person who was admitted to the asylum on Boxing Day 1919 was his wife, Catherine Henrietta Havelock. If made public, it would be his undoing.

The authentic documentation had bought Henrietta her freedom. Her real identity, though, would still be unknown, providing he kept shtum about the women welders' secrets. If he didn't, Helen would make sure everyone got to know exactly what he'd done to Henrietta – as well as what he'd done to little Gracie and Pearl, and all the other maids.

He took out a cigar from his breast pocket and clipped the end.

There had to be a way out of this stalemate. A way for him to become the ultimate victor.

He lit his cigar, turning it slowly so that it burned evenly. He puffed, filling the study with swirls of grey smoke.

He would think of something. Some way of ensuring he came out as top dog.

As he swigged the dregs of his brandy, a smile crept across his face, causing even deeper lines to form in his leathery skin.

Stubbing out his cigar, he pulled out an address book from the top drawer of his desk and flicked it open.

Picking up the receiver of the black Bakelite phone, he dialled the number he'd been looking for.

'Bob? Is that Bob Thurley?'

He waited for the affirmation.

'Good. I need to employ your services again, Bob. When can we meet?'

Chapter Four

As Helen and Henrietta drove away from the hospital, they were waved off by Dr Bernard and Dr Parker. Helen glanced in her rear-view mirror and caught a quick glimpse of John before turning right out of the main entrance. Her spirits dropped as they always did whenever she said goodbye to him. More so of late, as she was never sure when she would see him again. She looked across at her grandmother and forced herself to buck up. This was a huge day for them both and she wanted to enjoy it.

'So, Grandmama, it looks like you have an admirer in Dr Bernard,' Helen smiled as she drove slowly towards town. It was now after six and the temperature had dropped to below zero, causing the roads to become covered in patches of black ice.

'As you, too, have an admirer in Dr Parker,' Henrietta parried.

Helen was quiet. The time had come to be honest with her grandmother, though it would have to wait until they were safely home.

Five minutes later, Helen was pulling up outside the three-storey red-brick house that stood on the corner of Park Avenue.

'Home sweet home!' she declared.

'It looks magnificent,' Henrietta said.

Helen laughed.

'Grandmama, it's so dark you can barely see it.'

'My dear Helen, anything is going to be magnificent after being stuck on that ward for the past two weeks.'

'But it did the trick,' Helen said. 'They've got you back on your feet, and from what John said, you're in pretty good health – all things considered.'

'And now that I'm out of there, I'm hoping you will be able to tell me exactly *why* I ended up being so ill. I might be old, but I'm not senile. Not yet, anyway. And I know you've been keeping something from me.'

And with that, Henrietta opened the car door and swung her legs out.

Helen got out, hurried round to the passenger side and took her grandmother's arm.

'The truth,' Henrietta demanded. 'From now on, no more secrets. About anything? Agreed?'

Helen sighed. 'Agreed . . . Now come on, let's get you in before we both freeze to death.'

Unlike Miriam, who had apparently got sick of waiting and had gone to the Grand, Mrs Westley, the housekeeper, was there to welcome Henrietta.

Mrs Westley had happily agreed to do more hours to ensure that Henrietta was well looked after. Now, she showed her new charge to her room on the first floor, which had once been where Jack, Miriam's soon-to-be ex-husband, had slept. Not that she said as much.

After the housekeeper had helped Henrietta unpack the few possessions she'd brought with her, she bustled off to the kitchen to make them both a pot of tea before leaving Helen with her 'great-aunty'.

Mrs Westley had her doubts about Henrietta's purported kinship to Helen and Miriam and thought it likely the old lady was more closely related – much more – not that she would ever voice her suspicions, not even to her own family. Mrs Westley had been with the Crawfords for many years, and she was determined that should be the case for many more to come – especially now that Helen had taken charge and her wages had been increased along with her hours.

When Helen and her grandmother were settled in front of the open fire in the front reception room with their cups of tea, it was Henrietta who spoke first.

'So, now we are alone,' she said, 'the first thing I want you to be totally truthful about is what's going on with you and Dr Parker. You are both clearly in love. Any fool can see that.'

Helen smiled, feeling a clash of emotions. Happiness on hearing that Dr Parker was 'clearly in love', followed by a heavy forlornness that their love could never be realised. She took a sip of her steaming-hot tea and savoured it for a moment.

'OK,' she said. 'The truth.'

Henrietta listened intently as Helen told her how she had been right in her deduction that Dr Parker did in fact have feelings for her – just as she did for him. But, as she had already mentioned previously, she could never admit that she loved him, for if she did, others would suffer.

Henrietta raised her hand, as though stopping traffic.

'I need you to start from the beginning and tell me how you met Dr Parker in the first place. And how it is that you didn't start courting him straight away. It is important I hear this love story from the very beginning.'

Helen glanced up at the clock on the mantelpiece. It had gone seven o'clock. 'It's rather a long story. And you've had a long day, Grandmama. I imagine you'll be wanting to climb into a nice warm bed soon.' Helen knew that Mrs Westley always made sure there was a hot-water bottle in every bed before she left for the day.

'Poppycock,' Henrietta said. 'I can sleep all I want when I'm six feet under.' She took a mouthful of tea and settled back into her armchair. 'I'm all ears.'

And so Helen told her grandmother how she had first met Dr Parker when he had been caring for her father during his time at the Royal Infirmary. Jack had been in a coma, having nearly drowned after the ship he'd been travelling in was torpedoed.

It felt somewhat cathartic relaying how she had then met Dr Parker again, this time at the Ryhope Military Emergency Hospital when he had helped her through a traumatic time after being duped by a surgeon working at the Ryhope. Theodore Harvey-Smith had lied and told her he wanted her to be his wife, when all along he was already married with two children and another on the way. He had skedaddled back down south to his family just as Helen had discovered she was pregnant.

Henrietta blinked back tears as her granddaughter told her how she had miscarried at four months, and how Dr Parker had saved her life, getting her to hospital in the nick of time to stop her haemorrhaging to death.

Henrietta shuffled closer to Helen and held her hand, feeling the pain she still carried, wanting to relieve her of it, but knowing she couldn't.

'When I started to recover,' Helen explained, 'when I

eventually started to surface from this horrible, cloying grief, I realised I was in love with John.' She sighed. 'But I never told him. Never thought he would want to be with a woman with my sordid history.'

At this point Henrietta tutted, showing her disapproval. 'There's nothing sordid about it. You simply made a mistake. Life's all about making mistakes. You were a naïve young girl looking for some love,' she said.

'When I finally realised that John did actually love me – it was too late.'

'Because he had met someone else and that someone else had something on you,' Henrietta mused, recalling what Helen had told her during one of her visits to the asylum.

Helen looked at her grandmother and knew it was safe now to tell her about Dr Eris and the hold she had over her. It would possibly have caused problems if Dr Eris had still been her doctor, but not now. Not now that her grandmother never had to step foot in the asylum ever again.

'That's right,' Helen continued. 'About two years ago, Dr Eris started work at the asylum. As soon as I met her, I knew she had John in her sights, and sure enough, before long they'd started seeing each other.' Helen sighed. 'It was just at the time I'd got the nerve – and the confidence – to tell John how I felt.'

Helen reached into her handbag and pulled out her packet of Pall Malls. *If only she'd acted sooner.*

'So,' Henrietta guessed, 'it is Dr Eris who has got something on you. Something that's stopping you telling Dr Parker how you feel?'

Helen nodded and lit her cigarette.

'So, what is it that she has on you?' Henrietta asked, concerned.

Seeing the fire had started to dwindle, Helen got up and added another log, prodded it with the iron poker and sat back down.

'I'm afraid it's you, Grandmama,' Helen said. 'Dr Eris has made it plain that if I tell John that I love him, she will tell the world that you are the wife of Charles Havelock – not some spinster great-aunty – and that he had you locked up, unnecessarily, and under a false name. She says if I declare my love for John, she will blacken the Havelock name and reputation.'

Henrietta let out a burst of laughter. 'Then tell the world. What's stopping you?' She eyed Helen. 'You're not trying to protect me, are you?'

'No, no,' Helen said, then laughed. If she had to pick a character trait she loved the most about her grandmother, it would be her couldn't-care-less attitude. *How she wished Henrietta had been in her life when she was growing up.*

'No, I wasn't trying to protect you, Grandmama. Not because I don't care, but because I actually think you'd enjoy seeing your husband vilified for what he's done. I know I would.' She took a deep breath. 'No, I'm afraid it's more complicated than that.'

'Go on,' Henrietta encouraged her.

'Well, you see, Grandfather has told me that if the truth comes out about you – and what he has done to you, never mind anything else – he will hold me responsible and will make good his threats to reveal the secrets of those close to me.'

Helen blew out smoke.

'The women welders? Your friends?' Henrietta asked. 'The ones I met at the extravaganza?'

'That's right – *my friends*,' Helen confirmed. It still felt a novelty calling them that, but they were. Over these past few years, they'd become the best friends she'd ever had.

'And may I ask what these secrets are that would ruin so many people's lives?' Henrietta asked. 'They must be serious.'

'They are,' Helen conceded. 'They are indeed.'

Henrietta listened as Helen told her about Martha's true parentage, how her real mother was the infamous child murderer who had poisoned nearly all her children, about Dorothy's mother, who was a bigamist, and Angie's mam, who risked being thrashed within an inch of her life if her husband found out she was having an affair.

'So, you see, I've let Dr Eris think that I'm worried about the family name being brought into disrepute—'

'When in reality, what is at risk is far greater,' Henrietta concluded.

'Exactly,' Helen said, standing up and putting her arm out.

Henrietta took it and stood up too. 'You've sacrificed your love for the sake of your friends.'

They made their way out of the living room and up the stairs.

'It's a noble thing you've done,' Henrietta said, puffing slightly as they reached the top of the stairs. 'But still, it feels so wrong that your love for Dr Parker has been thwarted.'

'Perhaps,' Helen said. 'Or perhaps it really goes to show that John and I aren't meant to be together.'

Henrietta bit back a reply. She gave her granddaughter a kiss goodnight and got ready for bed. In normal circumstances, she would have been revelling in her first night spent away from the asylum. Her first night of freedom in twenty-five years. But Henrietta barely noticed the soft bed linen, the puffed-up pillows and warm bed. Instead, her mind was taken up with thoughts of Charles. A man who seemed to hurt everyone he came into contact with – and who was now strangling the life out of her granddaughter's chances of love.

Chapter Five

'I'll have another G & T.' Miriam pushed her empty glass towards the bartender. 'And my friend here will have another glass of Chablis.'

Turning away from the bar and surveying the busy lounge of the Grand, Miriam declared, 'It's going to be a good year. I can feel it in my bones.'

Amelia chuckled. 'I think that's the gin you can feel.'

'No, really.' Miriam looked at her friend in earnest. '*It is.*'

Amelia eyed her. 'I thought your spirits might not be so high this evening, seeing as you now have the added burden of a great-aunty living under your roof?'

Miriam waved her hand dismissively. 'Mrs Westley will look after her, and Helen – when she's not working, that is. My daughter seems to have developed a bit of a soft spot for the old woman.' She paused, as though in thought. 'Besides, if it all gets a bit too much, I can simply come here and live. I could have my own suite, which is actually very appealing.'

'Now that would be an idea!' Amelia said, her eyes lighting up.

The barman put their drinks on the polished wooden counter and added the cost to their growing tab. What the two women had spent over the course of the past two nights would have kept his daughter and her family going for a week, with a little left over.

Turning and picking up her drink, Miriam smiled on seeing the slice of lemon bobbing in it.

'A sure sign this war is soon to end,' she said, fishing it out and popping it into her mouth.

'So, come on, tell me why you seem so sure this is going to be such a remarkably good year,' Amelia asked. She was quite surprised Miriam was in such good spirits since she was expecting her divorce from Jack to be finalised in just a matter of days.

'Well, for starters,' Miriam said, reading her friend's mind, 'I'll be a free woman who can do as I wish.'

Amelia spluttered as she took a sip of her wine. 'Miriam, darling, you do that anyway!'

Miriam laughed. A little too loudly, causing a few drinkers to glance in her direction.

'Or should I say, I can be more open about embracing my new freedom.'

She took another sip of her drink.

'And don't forget,' she threw Amelia a look, 'I am set to inherit a fortune.'

Amelia raised her glass. She knew all about her friend's future windfall. Miriam mentioned it regularly. When the old man did finally pop his clogs – which had to be soon, he must be at least eighty – the pair of them were going to have the time of their lives. They had already talked endlessly about their future plans and the adventures they would have.

'So,' Amelia said with a playful smile, 'where will we go first? How about Morocco? I've heard it's going to be *the* place to go when this wretched war ends.'

'Sounds good to me,' said Miriam, raising her glass.

'I'll drink to that. Chin-chin!'

Chapter Six

Friday 19 January

When the klaxon sounded out at 5.30 p.m., the shipyard workers at Thompson's were quick off the mark to hotfoot it out of the yard. Tools were downed and packed up by the time the drone of the horn had ended, and heavy, steel-toecapped boots sounded out on the concrete as hundreds of men and dozens of women marched to the timekeeper's cabin, their hands stretched out, holding their white boards as though begging to be rescued, which in a way they were. Rescued from a week of the vilest, most unforgiving weather – bouts of blinding snow and swooping winds, and a raw cold that no amount of warm clothes and thick winter coats could keep out.

Hurrying off the ferry, Polly waved goodbye to the rest of the women welders and was joined by Bobby, after he'd given Dorothy a quick kiss. As they battled the elements back to Tatham Street – to Polly's home and where Bobby had been lodging since his return from war – they chatted briefly about Gloria and Jack's wedding, which was now just over three weeks away, but, as Gloria had said more than once, couldn't come soon enough.

As usual, when they stepped over the threshold of the Elliot household, a Victorian mid-terrace, they entered bedlam. The dogs, Tramp and Pup, were the first to greet them. In a flurry of excitement, snuffles and drooling chops, evidence that they'd just had a feed, they demanded a pat before skidding on the floor tiles back down the hallway.

On walking into the kitchen-cum-living-room, they were hit by the mouth-watering aromas of Agnes's renowned rabbit and black pudding stew, and greeted by a harassed-looking Bel trying to feed the twins, Gabrielle and Stephen, who seemed more interested in watching their six-year-old sister, Lucille, trying to make Artie stand on two feet for longer than a second.

Bel's husband, Joe Elliot, and his former zone commander, Major Black, who was in his wheelchair puffing on a cigar, offered them a hearty welcome. Joe had recently been taken on by the Major as a recruitment officer for the army after the standing down of the Home Guard.

Seeing that his mammy was home, baby Artie dropped down on all fours and speed-crawled over to her. Hauling him up with tired arms that had been doing overhead welds most of the day, Polly kissed her boy's rosy cheeks and with her last bit of strength held him in the air, making him squeal with glee. Polly could smell Artie's clothes had been freshly laundered and smiled her thanks to her sister-in-law.

Deprived of her playmate, Lucille turned her attention to the twins, giving them a little tickle and pulling funny faces, making the pair gurgle and giggle, before announcing she was going out to play in the street with her friends.

'I want you back in half an hour for your tea,' Bel ordered.

Seeing the time, Major Black announced he was off.

Agnes, who had been chatting to Beryl in the scullery,

43

shouted for him to wait. Grabbing a round of sandwiches she'd made earlier, she gave them to him, and saw him out.

After the Major's departure, Bobby sat down with Joe and the two started chatting about the latest war news, a mixture of the good – Soviet troops had taken Warsaw – and the bad – reports were coming in of those who had died as prisoners of war in Japanese camps.

Hearing the front door open and then slam shut, they all turned to see Bel's ma, Pearl Lawson, appear in the doorway. Her entrance caused Bobby to get up mid-conversation and head up to his room to get ready for his date with Dorothy, and Joe to suddenly remember that there had been a delivery of coal that needed shovelling into the bunker. Beryl, too, slipped out the back door, mumbling that her daughters, Audrey and Iris, would be back from their shift at the GPO and she'd best get their tea ready.

'Hi, Ma, fancy a cuppa?' Bel asked.

'Twist my arm,' Pearl said, patting the dogs, who had bounded towards her. She was glad the kitchen had become less crowded as now she could sit at the table. She looked at Polly, coming out of the back bedroom with Artie clinging to her like a baby baboon. She was holding a bottle of formula and brushing away a loose strand of hair from her eyes.

'Dear me, yer look worn out, Pol,' Pearl said. 'Doesn't she, Isabelle? As grey as them metal sheets she spends her days welding.'

Polly opened her mouth, but didn't say anything. Pearl was right, although she didn't have to be so brutally honest.

Pearl's gaze turned to the twins. 'How's the babs?'

'Too busy nosing at everyone else to eat their tea,' Bel complained.

44

'They'll eat when they're hungry,' Pearl said. 'Yer fuss too much.'

'How's Bill?' Agnes asked, coming out of the scullery and giving the supper a gentle stir.

'Happy as a dog with two tails,' said Pearl.

Agnes smiled. So was Pearl since she had met Bill – and even more so since they had got married and she had been made joint licensee of the Tatham Arms.

'To what do we owe the honour?' Bel asked, eyeing her mother. She tried to maintain their barbed way of communicating, but it was really just an act. The two had become closer after Pearl had revealed that she had been raped by Charles Havelock and that he was Bel's real father. Knowing that her daughter would go and confront Mr Havelock, Pearl had tracked down the parents of another young maid called Gracie, who had also fallen prey to Mr Havelock, and had used the threat of them bearing witness to his crimes to support Bel in her stand-off with Charles.

Bel caught her mother glancing across at the stew simmering on the range.

It was a look Agnes also caught. 'You going to join us for a bit of stew?'

'Ah, I couldn't impose,' Pearl said. 'Gotta get back behind the bar at six. Only popped round to see Isabelle 'n the grandbairns.'

Bel rolled her eyes to the ceiling at the familiar scene, which played itself out at least once a week.

'I'll pop some in a bowl and you and Bill can have it later,' Agnes said, walking over to the sideboard.

'Gan on then, but only if yer let us get yer 'n yer fella a drink when yer both in the pub next.'

Agnes held back from telling Pearl – yet again – that Dr Billingham was merely a friend. It was clearly a battle she wasn't going to win.

As Agnes set about carefully ladling the stew into the bowl, Pearl started flicking through the *Sunderland Echo* that had been left on the table.

Watching her ma quickly turn pages until she reached the Marriages, Births and Deaths section towards the back of the paper, Bel sighed. This was the only part of the local rag that her ma ever read. She had a good idea why.

'Talk about morbid, Ma.'

Pearl looked up at her daughter and then back down at the paper. 'There's nowt wrong with wanting to know who's popped their clogs.' She wondered if Bel guessed that the real reason she checked the death notices was in the hope of seeing the name Charles Havelock. One day his name would be there, and when that day came, she would make sure she'd go and dance on his grave. Mind you, she'd have to get there early, as there'd probably be a queue.

Bel looked at her mother and saw a change pass over her. Her face had become serious, and she'd straightened her back. She continued to observe her as she quickly closed the paper, folded it in half and placed it back on the table.

'Eee, is that the time?' she said, pulling up her sleeve and staring at her watch. 'I best get going.' She stood up, grabbed her handbag off the floor and pulled her coat from the back of the chair.

Bel looked at her ma with a puzzled expression on her face. 'You all right, Ma?'

'Course I am.' Her eye caught the twins, and she pointed

a finger in their direction. 'Yer wanna feed them poor bairns. They look hungry.' She made to leave the room.

'Ma, aren't you forgetting something?' Bel asked. Her mother looked at her, confusion on her face. Her mind was clearly a million miles away.

Bel glanced at Polly, whose slight frown showed she also thought something was amiss.

'*Your stew*,' Bel said, with a laugh. She got up and took the bowl Agnes had covered with greaseproof paper and tied with string. She grabbed a wicker basket by the side of the range, placed the bowl in it, and covered it with a tea towel.

'Eee, I'd forget my head if it was loose,' Pearl said, taking the basket from her.

'Thanks, Agnes,' she shouted through to the scullery, before hurrying out of the room, down the hallway and through the front door.

Bel watched her ma cross the road to the Tatham. She looked at the time. It was only ten to six. Ten minutes before opening time. A cold gust of wind blew through, into the house, and Bel shut the door.

Retreating into the warmth of the house, she was just about to have another try at feeding the twins when she stopped on seeing the *Sunderland Echo*. She shook out the newspaper and started thumbing through the pages until she reached the page her ma had been reading. She ran a finger down the first column in the section headed 'Deaths'.

And that's when she saw it:

Evans – January 7th, following a short illness, Gibson James Evans, dearly beloved husband to Cecilia Evans and father to Grace. Father and daughter together again.

47

Bel sat down in the chair. Mr Evans. Gibson. *Little Gracie's father.*

Judging by the look on her ma's face, Bel was right in her suspicion that she had kept in contact with Mr and Mrs Evans. As Bel got up to tend to the twins, she considered why her ma wouldn't have mentioned her ongoing friendship with Gracie's parents. After that Christmas Day – when she and her ma had gone head-to-head with Charles Havelock and threatened to tell the world about what he had done to Pearl and Gracie, and God only knew how many others, not to mention his wrongful incarceration of his wife in the local asylum – they had never talked about Charles Havelock, or anything to do with him. It was as though they feared just speaking his name would risk infecting them all.

The man had already contaminated their lives enough.

*

After dropping the stew off with Bill, Pearl did an about-turn and headed straight out of the door again. She thought back to when she had gone to see Mr and Mrs Evans after she and Bel had had their showdown with Charles Havelock. When she had explained that her daughter had struck a deal and swapped their silence about his crimes for the return of Jack to his home town, it was evident the couple were disappointed that the man who had caused the death of their only child would continue to live without punishment. They had made it very clear to Pearl that should the time come when they could shout the truth from the treetops, they would be in good voice.

Thereafter they had stayed in touch. Every few weeks Pearl would pop in for a quick cuppa, encouraged by the fact that Mr and Mrs Evans were always welcoming and always seemed pleased to see her. They loved to hear about Bel. Just as Pearl loved to tell them how proud she was of her. There was always a sense of expectation, though, that one day Pearl would come and tell them their testimony was needed, and the gag that had been put in place when Bel had done her deal with Mr Havelock could be removed.

The last time Pearl had been to see Mr and Mrs Evans, a couple of weeks ago, just after the New Year, they had both seemed well. They weren't exactly spring chickens any more, but Mr Evans hadn't looked anywhere near death's door. Pearl battled against the windstorm as she hurried down Tatham Street, passing the last few houses that had been bombed in one of the worst air raids the town had endured. *Poor Mrs Evans. What would she do without her husband?* The pair were always together. Had always been together. Now she would be on her own.

As Pearl walked under the railway bridge that transported coal to the Hendon docks, she had a slight respite from the foul weather. Hearing the sound of an engine, she turned and saw a bus heading in her direction.

'Small mercies,' she muttered as she caught a glimpse of the destination. Hurrying to the bus stop, she stuck out her hand.

After paying her fare, she sat down on the first seat she came to and got out her cigarettes. The bus was half-full with a smattering of overall-clad workers and mothers with their children. Its tired engine groaned into action and the single-decker started along Suffolk Street. As she sparked up a cigarette, the wind suddenly pounded the window, giving her a jolt and causing her to look out at yet more bombed buildings.

Squinting through the smoke of the cigarette she had lodged in the corner of her mouth, Pearl watched as a skinny young blonde jumped on at the next stop. She was not quite a woman but also no longer a girl. She felt her body stiffen. It was like looking into a mirror image of the past. The poorly dressed, pinched-faced girl looked the spit of Pearl at that age. And Gracie too. Mrs Evans had shown her a photograph. It was proof that they'd all looked the same – all the maids who had worked in the Havelock residence.

Getting off the bus opposite the entrance to the Barley Mow Park at the top end of Villette Road, Pearl kept her head down as she felt the start of the rain. She turned down Hunter Terrace. After a hundred yards she'd reached Mrs Evans's front door. She banged hard. She wasn't quite sure why, but she felt a sense of urgency. *Was she worried that the older woman might decide to cut short her own life? With her husband now gone, she might see no reason to carry on.*

Pearl knocked again.

Would she blame her? Would it be such a terrible thing? Perhaps she would finally have some peace. Finally be with the daughter she had adored. Whose death she had never recovered from.

Another loud knock.

She supposed it depended if Mrs Evans believed in an afterlife.

Finally, the door opened.

'Mrs Evans,' Pearl said, relieved. The older woman had told her many times to call her by her first name, but it had never felt right.

'Pearl, come in.' Mrs Evans immediately ushered in her unexpected visitor.

Pearl stepped over the polished brass front doorstep. Mrs Evans did not have much money, but her modest terraced cottage was what was described in these parts as 'nipping clean'.

'Yer should 'ave told us about Mr Evans,' Pearl said.

Mrs Evans sighed.

'Give me your coat,' she said, putting her hand out.

Pearl complied and Mrs Evans hung the shabby winter coat on the hook rack by the door.

'Go and warm yourself in front of the fire and I'll get us a cuppa,' the old woman said.

A few minutes later, they were sitting, their faces rosy with the heat from the open fire and the hot tea.

'So, what happened?' Pearl asked. 'He didn't seem ill when I saw yer both last.'

'Heart attack,' Mrs Evans said simply. She took a sip of tea. 'I think his heart would have given up the ghost when Gracie died were it not for me.' She got up and went to the sideboard to fetch a bottle of whisky. She poured out two glasses and handed one to Pearl.

'To Gibson and Gracie,' Mrs Evans said.

'Aye,' Pearl said, raising her glass, 'to Mr Evans and little Gracie.'

They both drank in silence for a while.

'How yer gonna manage without him?' Pearl asked.

'I'll cope,' Mrs Evans said. 'I've got a lot to sort out.'

Pearl looked at the old woman. She did not have the air of a grieving widow. Her hair, which she knew had turned grey the day Mrs Evans had found her daughter hanging from the bannisters, was neatly tied up in a bun. Her posture was not stooped under the weight of her grief. Quite the reverse. She was sat bolt upright.

'I'm guessing yer've got the funeral to sort?' Pearl asked.

She couldn't think of anything else. The Evans were poor. They'd only had the one child. There would be no will, no possessions to divide up.

'There's the funeral,' Mrs Evans said. 'And there's one or two other things to be dealt with.'

Pearl thought Gracie's mam sounded a little evasive, but didn't push. It was none of her business.

'Can I do anything to help?' Pearl asked. 'You can have use of the Tatham for the wake, if yer want.'

Mrs Evans shook her head. 'There'll be no wake. I just want him buried next to Gracie. That's all. It's all he would have wanted.'

Pearl understood. Wakes were about the celebration of a life well lived. Mr Evans, she knew, had never lived life. He had only grieved the life that had been taken from him.

Chapter Seven

Lily, her orange hair in curlers and smoking her first Gauloise of the day, walked down the staircase of the beautiful three-storey townhouse on the stretch of road known as West Lawn. The house, which was owned by Lily, now functioned as a high-class bordello only at weekends. A change brought about so that Charlotte, who had become like a surrogate daughter to Lily, could come and go as she pleased during the week.

Eyeing Kate pulling on her woollen coat in the hallway, Lily asked, 'Where are you off to so early on a Sunday morning?' Smoke billowed out of her mouth as she spoke. Kate looked at Lily, still in her long Chinese-patterned silk dressing gown, over which she was wearing a long cashmere cardigan. 'You're too late for early-morning Communion. Or are you going to the family service?' It still astonished Lily and everyone else at the bordello that Kate went to church. After the life she had endured at the hands of the nuns at Nazareth House, a so-called children's 'care' home, they were amazed she hadn't been put off God for life.

'I'm going to meet Helen and Henrietta at Maison Nouvelle,' Kate reminded her.

'Oh, Gawd! Course you are. You said so last night,' Lily recalled, slipping back into her cockney accent. 'Memory like a bleedin' sieve.' She watched as Kate adjusted her black felt hat so that it sat neatly on the side of her head and put on her kid gloves. 'Shame I couldn't pop in to meet her. The woman intrigues me.' Lily knew that Kate was gradually creating a new wardrobe – or, rather, a new look – for Henrietta, to lessen the chances of her being recognised. Although it didn't sound as though there was any great rush as Helen's grandmother had yet to venture out the front door.

Thoughts of Henrietta inevitably led to thoughts of Charles Havelock, and the threat he still posed to the bordello, and everyone connected to it. Lily knew that if the old man was ever free from the fear of having his wrongdoings exposed, one of the first phone calls he'd make would be to the Sunderland Borough Police. It was one of the reasons she was so anxious to make her business legitimate.

'Kate,' Lily said, walking over to the mahogany side table and tapping her cigarette into a cut-crystal ashtray, 'I've been wanting to ask you if you might like to accompany Maisie and Vivian to London – when they put a stop to these dreadful doodlebugs, that is?'

'Why?' Kate asked, her tone defensive.

'Why?' Lily repeated. 'Why would a budding hautecouture designer not want to go to the capital? To the epicentre of fashion and culture?'

Kate remained silent.

'*Ma chère*,' Lily said, not hiding her exasperation. 'You can't spend the best years of your life scurrying from bordello to boutique.'

'Why not?' Kate bit back.

'Because,' Lily gasped, 'you're an artist, my dear child, a wonderful creative genius and you need to get out in the world, immerse yourself in the sights, sounds and smells of the big city, draw on all our great capital has to offer – the museums, the galleries, the fashion.'

Lily had talked to George, her fiancé, Maisie, who managed the Gentlemen's Club, and her 'head girl', Vivian, and they had all agreed: Kate was destined for greater success. Just as they also knew she would need a little cajoling, a gentle push – and that Lily was the person to do it.

'I have my magazines,' Kate said, picking up a small stack of them from the stand by the door. She hugged them to her chest as though to prove her point. 'I know exactly what is happening in the world of fashion.'

'*Ma chère*, you need to start spreading your wings!' She flung her arms out to emphasise her point, causing ash to go everywhere. 'Look at Henrietta Havelock – even *she* has started a new life after being locked up in an asylum for decades. If she can make a new start, so can you.'

Lily took another drag on her cigarette, not caring where the ash went, so intent was she on convincing Kate that she was right. 'You've become a big fish in a little pond – it's now time to start swimming in the sea.'

She pulled a small fan out of her cardigan pocket, snapped it open and started fanning herself to combat another hot flush.

'It's frightening to take the plunge, but once you've done it, you'll wonder why you didn't make the leap sooner,' she said.

Kate glanced down at her watch. 'I've got to go. I don't want to be late.'

Lily watched as Kate slipped out the front door. She sighed. It was time her little fledgling flew the nest, much as it would break her heart to see her go.

Chapter Eight

'You look fabulous, darling,' Henrietta exclaimed, standing back and admiring her granddaughter in her deep green dress, which complemented her hourglass figure and drew attention to her striking green eyes.

'Thank you, Grandmama.' Helen looked at Henrietta in her new tailored grey skirt and cream cashmere jumper. 'As do you. Are you sure you don't want to come?'

Henrietta shook her head. 'No, no, darling. You go and let your hair down. And tell Jack and Gloria congratulations from me and may they have a long and happy marriage.'

Helen smiled. 'I will.'

It would have been easy to assume that her grandmother did not think it appropriate to go to the wedding of her daughter's ex-husband, but Helen knew it had more to do with the fact that Henrietta was not quite ready to face the outside world just yet.

'I look forward to being regaled with all the details,' Henrietta said, walking Helen to the front door.

'Let's just hope my dear mama doesn't try and cause trouble, or pull some kind of stunt,' Helen said.

'Oh, my dear, I'm sure she won't,' Henrietta said with more confidence than she actually felt. 'Oh . . . and, Helen, darling,' Henrietta's tone became conspiratorial, 'you won't forget about that favour I asked, will you?'

Helen shook her head. 'No, I won't. I'll speak to Pearl.'

Henrietta had been on at Helen to track down Gracie's mother since being discharged from hospital. Helen had insisted she wait until she was fully recovered and back on her feet. Last night, Henrietta had declared herself well enough and, knowing that Pearl would be able to put her in touch with Mrs Evans, she had made Helen promise that she would ask her former maid to facilitate a meeting.

Helen stepped in front of the mirror and tied a headscarf over her raven-coloured hair, which had been set in victory rolls. She hoped it would give her some protection from the wet and windy weather.

'And you won't be too lonely on your own?' she asked, unhooking her long angora winter coat from the coat stand and slipping it on.

'Not at all, darling,' Henrietta said. 'Actually, I'm expecting a visit from Dr Bernard. Gin rummy followed by a book review of Virginia Woolf's *Mrs Dalloway*. By far her best work.'

Helen opened the door.

'Ah, talk of the devil,' she said as her grandmother's suitor opened the creaking Arts and Crafts iron gate and started up the short pathway. On seeing Henrietta and Helen, he immediately removed his trilby.

'Good afternoon, ladies.' He stopped in his tracks. 'And may I be so bold as to say you are both a sight for sore eyes.'

Helen laughed as she hurried down the short flight of steps. She gave Dr Bernard a quick kiss on the cheek. He had become a regular visitor at the house since Henrietta's discharge from hospital.

'Enjoy your gin rummy,' she said.

'And you your wedding,' he said. He twisted the ends of his long moustache. 'You know what they say about weddings?' He didn't wait for an answer, but exchanged mischievous looks with Henrietta. 'Perfect place to find your match. Perhaps even your future husband.'

Helen shook her head and threw them a disparaging look.

'I'll see you later.' Helen continued down the path and through the gate. As she turned to close it, she had to smile on seeing Dr Bernard greeting Henrietta with a gentlemanly kiss on the hand. Her grandmother clearly didn't need to attend a wedding to find *her* match.

When Helen arrived at the registry office on John's Street in town, she was relieved to see that her mother was nowhere in sight.

As a newly married couple passed her on their way out, Helen spotted her father, Gloria and Hope waiting in the small reception area. Jack was in his best suit, Gloria was wearing a sky-blue dress and Hope looked as pretty as a picture in a beautiful ivory bridesmaid's dress.

'Heleeeen!' Hope's eyes lit up at seeing her big sister and she ran towards her.

'Who's looking like a little angel?' Helen said as she hauled her three-and-a-half-year-old sibling onto her hip.

'If only she were acting like one,' Gloria quipped.

Helen looked at Hope's rosy face and brushed her thick black hair away from her eyes. The pair were often mistaken for mother and daughter. 'Have you been misbehaving?'

Hope shook her head vehemently.

'Just a few demonic temper tantrums,' Jack said. 'Nothing I haven't had to deal with before.'

Helen laughed. 'My understanding is that I was the perfect daughter – sugar and spice and all things nice.'

Jack chuckled. 'I see a lot of yer in Hope. You're both – how'd I describe it? – yer both very *spirited*.'

A blast of cold air turned their attention towards the main entrance and in came the women welders with their significant others – Dorothy and Bobby, Rosie with Peter and Charlotte, Angie and Quentin, then Hannah and Olly. They were followed by Polly, Martha and then Bel and Joe.

Bobby and Dorothy hurried over to Gloria as Jack went to greet the rest of their guests.

'How you feeling, Mam?' Bobby bent over to kiss his mother on the cheek.

'Honestly?' she said, looking at Bobby and then at Dorothy. 'I'll be glad when it's all over and done with.'

Dorothy tutted and Bobby nodded. They both understood, though. For Gloria and Jack this really was simply a registration of their marriage, a necessary formality to give them – and especially Hope – the respectability they needed to ensure a quiet life. Gloria had endured some horrid namecalling and had even been spat at because she was living in sin with a married man. It wouldn't have been long before Hope, as her illegitimate daughter, would also have become a target for those with hate in their hearts.

'Bobbieee!'

Everyone looked to see Hope, who had just realised her big brother was there, stretch out her chubby little arms, demanding he take her.

'It's good to know who the favourite is,' Helen said, handing over her little sister, secretly relieved. Hope was getting bigger by the day.

'That might be because . . .' Bobby said, taking hold of Hope and reaching into his pocket, '. . . I always come armed with something sweet.' He produced a lollipop.

Hope squealed with delight.

'Are you all right looking after her while we get this done?' Gloria said, her eyes straying nervously to the entrance.

'Of course we are,' Dorothy said. 'I am her godmother, after all.' She looked around at the other women chatting and shaking off their coats. 'And all her aunties are here to lend a hand too.'

Gloria smiled, recalling for a moment the day of Hope's birth at Thompson's in the middle of an air raid. They'd all helped bring her daughter safely into the world.

Seeing one of the clerks open up the frosted-glass door to the registry office, signalling it was time, Gloria breathed a sigh of relief.

'Thank goodness for that,' she said to Jack, shooting another anxious look at the main entrance.

Rosie had been listening to Peter field questions from Hannah about his time in France, and what he had heard about other parts of occupied Europe, when she glanced over at Gloria and saw the worried expression on her face. Knowing it was not a case of pre-wedding jitters, she went over to her.

'You still worried a certain someone might turn up?' she asked, not wanting to mention Miriam by name.

Gloria nodded. 'She'll have known we'd want to tie the knot as soon as the decree absolute came through. She could

easily have rung the registry office 'n found out we were getting married today.'

Rosie gave her friend's arm a gentle squeeze. 'Forget
about her. It's your day today. Yours and Jack's.' She looked
over to see Bobby and Dorothy with Hope, who was happily
sucking on her lolly. 'And Hope's.'

'I know,' Gloria said, but her unease remained.

Five minutes later, everyone was seated and Gloria and
Jack were standing at the front, looking at the middle-aged,
smartly dressed registrar. He had placed a large leather-
bound book on the table that stood between them. It was
open and ready for when the witnesses were required to sign
it. He'd guessed this would be a low-key affair as both par-
ties were divorcees, which had been confirmed by his clerk
when he'd conveyed the couple's request for a simple service.
Just the basics, which suited him fine, especially as today
had been busier than normal considering it was midweek –
something he was in no doubt was due to the fact that it was
St Valentine's Day.

'Good afternoon, everyone.' He smiled at Gloria and
Jack and then at their handful of guests. 'First of all, I have
to explain that the place where we are now gathered has
been duly sanctioned according to law for the celebration
of marriages.'

He gave a quick, rehearsed smile before beginning:
'Today we are gathered to witness the marriage of Jack and
Gloria and to support them with our presence and to share
in their joy.'

Everyone was sitting quietly, listening to the registrar's
preamble. Peter squeezed Rosie, showing her he was thinking

of their wedding at the registry office in Guildford three years ago, before he'd left for a life behind enemy lines.

Bel glanced at Joe, recalling how they'd fallen in love after he had returned from war, how she'd fought her feelings for him, but thankfully had failed, and a few months after sharing their first kiss they had got married in this very room.

Polly's mind had naturally gone to her Christmas wedding to Tommy. The feeling she'd had standing next to him in front of the vicar at St Ignatius Church more than two years ago would never leave her.

The registrar glanced down at the small book he was holding and then looked up again.

'I will begin the ceremony by asking if any person knows of any lawful impediment why Jack and Gloria may not be joined in matrimony.' He paused. 'If they should, declare it now.'

The registrar was surprised at the deathly silence and sombre atmosphere. Normally at this point in the ceremony there were a few chuckles, sometimes even a few jokey comments. But not today. Quite the reverse.

Looking down at his book again, more out of habit than necessity – he could probably recite the order of ceremony in his sleep – he took a breath, ready to start the exchanging of the vows. He was just about to begin when the door swung open.

Naturally, everyone turned.

There were a few sharp intakes of breath.

It was Miriam.

She was dressed up to the nines, make-up perfectly applied, wearing a little black dress. Her bobbed blonde hair contrasting with a small black headpiece with a net veil. Her attire more suited to a funeral than a wedding.

She remained standing in the doorway.

'Don't mind me!' she said, waving to Jack and Gloria, a wide smile on her face. 'The invite must have got lost in the post.'

Helen was staring at her mother. She made to get up and felt Martha's hand firmly on her arm. 'Leave her,' she whispered. 'It's what she wants.'

Everyone continued to stare in disbelief as Miriam tottered in her heels to a chair near the back and sat down.

'I'm guessing you've done the bit about anyone objecting?' she asked, a devilish smile on her red lips.

The registrar nodded, half expecting the woman, whom he knew to be Jack's ex-wife, the daughter of Charles Havelock, to declare that she did, in fact, know of some 'lawful impediment' that would put a stop to the marriage.

He continued to look at Miriam.

'Honestly,' she said, crossing her legs and adjusting her hat slightly, 'I always find that part of the wedding rather ridiculous, don't you?'

Everyone's eyes were glued to Miriam, wondering – or, rather, dreading – what would come out of this despicable woman's mouth next.

Bel glared at the woman who was her half-sister, disbelieving that they were in any way related. She then turned her attention to Joe, who read the question in her eyes. He shook his head. Like Martha, he knew that this was exactly what Miriam wanted. A scene. Drama. The best-case scenario for her would be that the ceremony ended up in some kind of fracas and the wedding was called off.

The registrar looked at Jack, whose face was full of fury, and then at Gloria, whose eyes were starting to well up. He'd seen some strange scenes in this room over the years, but this was a new one.

'Please, *do* carry on!' Miriam's voice was loud and clear. It was as though she was the one in charge of the ceremony, which in a way she was.

'Are we all right to continue?' the registrar asked Gloria and Jack. His voice was low, but not low enough for Miriam not to hear.

'Of course, please don't mind me!' Miriam's sickly sincere voice resounded around the high-ceilinged room.

Jack looked at Gloria, who took hold of his hand and held it tightly.

'We're fine,' she said. 'Please carry on.'

'Are you, Jack Crawford, free lawfully to marry Gloria Elizabeth Armstrong?'

Before Jack had a chance to reply, Miriam's high-pitched voice sounded out once again.

'He is! I brought the decree absolute with me just in case there was any doubt!' She waved the documentation in the air.

The registrar looked up at Miriam, who mouthed 'Sorry' and tapped her hand as though she were a naughty schoolgirl. If this had been anyone other than the daughter of Charles Havelock, he would have had her removed. But she knew, and he knew, that it would not be worth the consequences should he get on her bad side.

The registrar looked at Jack.

'I am,' he said through gritted teeth.

The registrar repeated the question to Gloria, secretly crossing his fingers that Miriam would not cause any further disruption.

'Are you, Gloria Elizabeth Armstrong, free lawfully to marry Jack Crawford?'

'I am,' Gloria said straight away, without waiting a beat.

'And now if we can move on to the making of the promises.' The registrar had started to sweat a little. He wondered how fast he could go without it seeming rude or ridiculous.

'Do you Jack Crawford take thee Gloria Elizabeth Armstrong to be your lawfully wedded wife?'

Jack's reply was drowned by a loud sneeze.

'Terribly sorry!' Miriam called out.

The registrar decided to ignore it and simply soldier on. He'd heard the reply even if no one else had.

'And do you Gloria Elizabeth Armstrong take thee Jack Crawford to be your lawfully wedded husband?'

Gloria's reply was obliterated by Miriam blowing her nose.

The women all stared at each other. They seemed on the verge of lynching Miriam. They looked to Rosie, who gave them a hard scowl and a curt shake of the head.

Again, satisfied that he had heard Gloria's reply, the registrar decided to charge on. At this point in the ceremony he would normally say a few words on the meaning of the ring, about it being a symbol of eternity, that there would be no end to their marriage, or their happiness, but, seeing the looks on the faces of the bride and groom, he decided to simply cut to the chase.

'And now if we can proceed with the giving of the ring, please,' the registrar said, his words spoken so quickly as to be almost incoherent.

There was no hesitation on Jack's part. He quickly took a thin gold band out of the inside pocket of his jacket and reached out for Gloria's hand, which was clammy and shaking ever so slightly. He gave Gloria a look that he hoped said to her, 'Hang in there, we're nearly done.'

Knowing what he had to say, Jack glanced at the registrar and then back at his bride, before declaring:

'I give you this ring as a token of our love and marriage.'

As soon as he had spoken the words, Jack slipped it on.

'You may now kiss the bride!' the registrar announced, his voice betraying his relief that this debacle of a ceremony was now nearing its end.

Suddenly, there was the loud scraping of a chair and Miriam stood up.

'Sorry!' Her voice sounded anything but apologetic. 'Forgive me, but I have to take my leave. A prior engagement. Awfully sorry!'

And with that, she picked up her handbag and sashayed out of the room. If looks could have killed she would have been dead on the floor before she reached the main corridor.

The registrar again looked to the couple.

Neither appeared as though they were in the mood to kiss.

'What comes next?' Gloria asked under her breath.

'Just the signatures,' the registrar said apologetically, knowing he should have expelled the Havelock woman from the ceremony before she'd had a chance to sit down. He'd heard whispers that their divorce had been far from amicable.

Helen and Bobby got up and stepped forward to sign the ledger to show that the marriage of their parents had been formally witnessed.

The charge in the air had disappeared, replaced by an overriding sense of relief that Miriam had left the building and Gloria and Jack had finally got married.

There was still, however, a residue of anger and frustration. Yet again, Miriam had managed to taint their happiness.

A day most couples remembered with a lifting of their hearts would, for Gloria and Jack, be forever pushed into the recesses of their memories in the hope that it could be forgotten.

Waiting outside the registry office, ready to take a photograph of the newly-weds, was the women welders' friend Georgina Pickering, formerly a private investigator and now a reporter for the local newspaper.

Georgina had seen Miriam appear. She had watched as she had practically skipped down the steps and, with a bounce in her gait, walked over to a chauffeur-driven black Jaguar. She knew that Miriam would not have been there to make amends to the bride and groom – far from it.

At that moment, she realised it was unlikely she would get the shot she was after – a natural photograph of everyone piling out, laughing and joking, the happy couple being showered with confetti. So, when the bride and groom and their guests emerged from the registry office a short while later, Georgina immediately took charge, ordering them all to stand close together at the top of the steps, with Jack and Gloria in the middle. She then demanded to see their biggest and best smiles, even if they might have murder in mind.

Her words made them all smile naturally, and Georgina succeeded in getting a photograph that was the best one possible, considering the circumstances she could only guess had gone before.

Chapter Nine

'Oh my God! I can't believe she just did that!' Dorothy hissed to Angie as they started to walk down John Street.

'Me neither!' Angie said. 'I just wanted to grab her by the scruff of the neck and drag her out of there.'

'Which was why she sat a few rows back.' Polly had appeared next to them as they turned left onto Borough Road. 'She knew she was taking a risk.'

'She's lucky she managed to leave in one piece,' Angie said, her anger still bubbling away. She couldn't imagine how she would react were anyone to do that at her wedding to Quentin.

'Yes, I think Gloria showed amazing restraint,' Dorothy said.

'I think Helen struggled to hold herself back,' Martha chipped in. She was walking behind with Hannah.

'Or rather, had to be held back,' Polly added. She had seen their gentle giant put a hand on her arm and the look of fury on Helen's face.

'I just can't believe anyone could be so spiteful,' Hannah said.

'She knew she couldn't stop them getting married,' Dorothy said. 'So she did the next best thing.

'Ruined their wedding day,' Angie huffed.

'Well, she might have managed to ruin the ceremony, but she's not going to spoil the rest of their day.'

'Do you think Gloria's all right?' Hannah asked.

They all looked ahead. Gloria was walking in front of them with Rosie on one side and Helen on the other.

'She'll be fine,' Dorothy declared. 'She's got us, hasn't she?'

When they reached the Tatham, Bobby took Hope over to the Elliots. Agnes had agreed to have Hope for the night so that at least Jack and Gloria could be on their own for their first night together as a married couple.

Pulling open the pub's front door, Jack stood back.

'Before yer all go in, I just want to say a big thank you for holding your tongues and your tempers back there in the registry office. I know exactly what yer all probably wanted to say and do – but thanks for not giving in to the urge, 'cos if yer had, I don't think I'd be standing here now with my new wife next to me.'

Gloria took hold of Jack's hand and smiled at them all. 'And can I just say that the wedding part of today might not have been particularly pleasant, but I want to make sure the rest of the day is. So, there's to be no mention of that awful woman, or what she's done – from now on in it's about having a good time.'

Rosie looked at Gloria and not for the first time admired her quiet strength of character. 'I couldn't agree more,' she seconded.

'Now, get yourselves in 'n get warm,' Jack said. 'We'll just be two minutes.'

When everyone had piled into the pub, Jack pulled Gloria close and kissed her.

They stood for a moment, oblivious to the biting cold, and kissed.

They held each other tight.

'That's to make up for the kiss I missed out on earlier,' Jack said.

Gloria smiled. Miriam might have wrecked their wedding ceremony, but nothing she could ever do would come close to marring the love they had for each other. And that was all that mattered.

Jack opened the door and waved her through. 'After you, Mrs Crawford.'

Shaking off their coats in the hallway, Gloria felt herself relax. She knew Miriam would not dare to come anywhere near the Tatham. Not if she valued her life.

As they walked into the main lounge area, they were greeted by a huge roar of 'Congratulations!'

'Oh, my goodness,' Gloria said. 'I didn't realise we'd invited so many people.'

For a moment they stopped dead in their tracks, taken aback by the crowd of people who had come to celebrate their marriage. The bonhomie and jolly faces just about diminished most of the bad aftertaste left by Miriam's impromptu appearance.

The crowd parted, allowing them to make their way to the bar, where there was a beautifully decorated wedding cake. There was also a pint of Vaux beer, Jack's favourite, and a glass of port, Gloria's favourite, waiting for them.

Pearl and Bill were standing behind the bar.

'Congratulations,' Bill beamed, sticking out his hand.

'And dinnit even think of paying for any of yer drinks, 'cos everyone's had a whip-round and there's a jar stuffed full,' Pearl said.

'Enough to drink the pub dry,' Bill added.

They picked up their drinks and turned to face their family and friends.

'Thank you!' Jack shouted out, raising his glass. 'For the whip-round Bill's just told us you've had – and for the amazing wedding cake. But most of all, thank you for coming and making this day extra special for us both.'

He looked at Gloria.

His new wife's eyes were glistening with emotion.

After making their way round the guests, shaking hands and having a quick chat, Gloria left Jack with Peter. This was the first opportunity the two had had to talk properly since Peter's return as much of his time was spent travelling to and from London. Gloria knew Jack wanted to thank Peter for helping her get shot of her ex-husband, Vinnie, by strong-arming him into signing the divorce papers and forcing him to rejoin the navy. Peter had also made it clear that Vinnie was never to return to his home town, even after the war ended. If he did, he'd find himself behind bars for brutalising Gloria.

Heading over to see Helen and the rest of her workmates, Gloria knew they would be indulging in lots of wedding talk, which she was eager to join in now that hers was just about done and dusted.

'Here comes the bride!' Angie announced, seeing Gloria heading towards them.

'It'll be your turn soon,' Gloria said, looking round for Angie's future husband and finding him standing by the bar, chatting to Bobby and Olly.

Angie looked nervous.

'And it'll be fantastic!' Gloria enthused.

'Yeah, it will,' Martha agreed.

'I think the look you're seeing on Angie's face is more to do with what comes before the wedding than with the day itself,' Dorothy explained.

'Ahh,' Rosie said, 'the dreaded *meeting of the parents*.'

Angie nodded.

'They're going to do it next time Quentin's up,' Dorothy said.

'That's good. Get it over 'n done with,' Gloria said, falling into her role as mother hen. 'And then yer can get on with enjoying it all. Have you sorted out the church?'

The conversation came alive as they all discussed every aspect of Angie and Quentin's wedding – and, of course, there was much discussion as to what kind of dress everyone thought Angie should have.

When Helen went to get another round of drinks in, Gloria went with her.

'Yer know how thankful yer dad 'n I are to yer, don't you?' Gloria said as they reached the crowded bar.

'For helping with the divorce?' Helen asked, seeing Pearl pulling a pint and remembering she had to get her on her own later and fulfil her promise to Henrietta.

'Not just *helping*,' Gloria said, as they reached the bar. 'For sorting it all out. If you hadn't, God only knows how long it would have taken. I honestly think *a certain someone* would have dragged it out for years.' Gloria was keeping her promise by not mentioning Miriam by name.

'I do too,' said Helen. 'But really it was a joint effort.' As she tried to catch the young barmaid's attention, Helen saw her father's divorce solicitor, Mr Emery, coming into the pub.

She waved him over. 'Come and meet Gloria!' Helen raised her voice to be heard over the chatter and laughter.

By the time Mr Emery had weaved his way through the guests, Helen had managed to order a round.

'I'm so glad you could come,' said Helen.

'Lovely to meet you, Mr Emery,' said Gloria.

'And you too, Mrs Crawford.'

Gloria grimaced. Every time she heard that name she thought of Miriam. 'I think it might take me a little while to get used to the name.'

'You'll have to make it your own,' Mr Emery said, although from what he'd learnt about Miriam Crawford, he could totally understand why Gloria might feel the way she did. 'And thank you for inviting me. Not everyone wants a divorce lawyer at their wedding.'

They all laughed.

'Well, if it weren't for you 'n Helen . . .' Gloria dropped her voice '. . . *and Georgina*, we'd certainly not be here this afternoon celebrating.'

Their drinks arrived.

'I took the liberty of getting you a pint,' Helen said, handing Mr Emery a beer.

'Oh, look who's here.' Gloria gave Helen an anxious look.

Helen followed Gloria's gaze and her heartbeat quickened.

'Ah, it's John . . . and Claire.' Helen forced a smile. 'I wasn't sure they'd make it.' *Had been hoping they wouldn't.*

Spotting Helen at the bar, Dr Parker and Dr Eris headed over to them.

Helen plastered a smile on her face and introduced everyone.

'Congratulations, I hear, are in order for yer too,' Gloria said. 'Helen told me yer also taking the plunge.'

'I guess we are,' Dr Parker said. He felt Helen's eyes on him but found himself unable to return her look.

'Have yer set a date yet?' Gloria asked.

'We're looking at sometime in May – probably the first or second Saturday,' Dr Eris said. Seeing Helen's eyes flicker down to her left hand, she showed her the diamond engagement ring.

'Oh, it's lovely.' Helen forced the words out.

'And between you and me . . .' Dr Eris leant towards Helen as the men started to chat about the latest war news, '. . . we'll be looking to move to London once the war's over. If John wants to further his career in prosthetics, that's the place to be.' Dr Eris was actually telling a bit of a white lie. She had merely suggested it to John; it was in no way a done deal.

'And, of course, they've got plenty of mental hospitals in and around the city for me to apply to . . .'

Helen looked at Dr Eris. She watched her speaking but wasn't really hearing the words.

John was moving to London.

Helen felt the knife in her heart.

London.

Not only was the man she loved going to marry someone else, but he was also going to move to the other end of the country. They wouldn't even be able to maintain a friendship.

Even that was being taken away from her.

Suddenly she couldn't bear it any more. She needed to get out. She could see the women welders looking over at her, their eyes full of concern. They had seen Dr Parker's arrival with Dr Eris, had watched as Dr Eris had showed off her ring.

'Excuse me, I'll be back in a minute,' Helen said, picking up her handbag and quickly manoeuvring her way through the throng to the door.

She needed air.

As she made it out into the hallway, she inhaled, forcing herself to breathe. It felt as if she couldn't get enough air into her lungs.

'Yer alreet there, pet?'

Helen turned to see Pearl sitting on the bottom step of the staircase that led to the living accommodation above the pub.

Helen nodded but didn't feel able to speak.

Pearl lit a fag off the one she was smoking and handed it to her.

Helen took it – and as she did so, her hand shook.

'Man trouble?' Pearl said.

Helen didn't answer.

'Aye, thought so – it's always man trouble. More bother than they're worth.'

Helen looked at Pearl and suddenly laughed. Doing so seemed to dispel the darkness and the feeling of suffocation.

'What's so funny?' Pearl asked.

'You,' said Helen. 'You've found a man that's worth the bother.'

Pearl chuckled, aware of her hypocrisy. 'I knar, pet, but I had to kiss a fair few frogs before I met Bill.'

They both smoked in silence.

'Actually, I've a favour to ask,' said Helen.

'Oh, aye,' Pearl said, warily.

'It concerns Henrietta.'

Pearl's face dropped.

'If it's owt to do with her old man, I'll stop yer there.'

Helen shook her head. 'No, it isn't. And I wouldn't ask you if it was.' She was aware of the lifetime of pain and suffering Pearl had endured because of Charles Havelock. 'Henrietta wants to go and see Gracie's parents and she's asked me to ask you to see if that might be possible.'

Pearl eyed Helen suspiciously. 'Why?'

Helen blew out smoke and sighed. 'I'm not entirely sure. I think she wants to apologise for what happened to Gracie.'

'It wasn't her fault,' Pearl said simply.

'I agree,' said Helen. 'But I think Grandmama still feels she is in some way to blame.'

Pearl stubbed out her cigarette.

'I'll ask, but there's only Mrs Evans now – Mr Evans passed a few weeks back.'

'Oh, I'm sorry to hear that.'

Pearl stood up.

'But if she doesn't want to rake over the past, Henrietta will just have to accept it.'

'I know,' Helen said. 'And thanks.'

The women had all watched Helen talking to Dr Parker and Dr Eris. They didn't need to say anything, but it hurt them to see Helen like this. She had become their friend, something none of them could have imagined when they'd started at the yard. Helen had gone from being their nemesis to someone they knew they could trust with their lives. She had proved herself several times over – she'd gone to Gloria's rescue when she was being beaten by Vinnie, she'd saved Gloria and Hope on the night of the Tatham Street air raid, and, most recently, she had forsaken her chance of love with Dr Parker in order to keep their secrets under wraps.

'I feel so sorry for Helen,' Hannah empathised.

'It makes me feel angry,' Dorothy seethed. The flush in her face proved her point.

'Me too,' said Angie.

'And me,' agreed Martha.

'I think we can safely say, we're all pretty mad,' Rosie said. 'The question is, what can we do about it?'

Gloria joined them.

'Do about what?' she asked.

'Helen and Dr Parker,' Hannah informed her.

Everyone was quiet for a moment.

'When it boils down to it,' Dorothy surmised, looking at Angie and Martha, 'it's *us* that's really stopping them from being together. *We're* the problem.'

'Yeah, Dor's right,' Angie said, crestfallen.

'So,' Martha concluded, 'we've got to stop our secrets from being secrets.'

'Easier said than done,' Dorothy pointed out. 'I'm not sure how my mum can suddenly *not* be a bigamist.'

'Or the woman who gave birth to me *not* be a murderer,' said Martha.

'And my dad might end up *being* a murderer if he finds out about my mam,' Angie added dejectedly.

'I still don't understand,' Polly queried, 'how Mr Havelock will benefit from telling the world about your mams? It's not saving his skin.'

'But the threat of it is,' Rosie said.

'And,' Gloria added, 'from what I've gathered from Helen

about the man, it'd bring him satisfaction that he wasn't the only one going down with the sinking ship. It sounds like his life's been built on the suffering of others 'n the pleasure he's got from that.'

'A proper textbook sadist,' Dorothy theorised.

There was a moment's quiet.

'That man really is the epitome of evil, isn't he?' said Hannah, shaking her head.

'Yer can say that again,' Angie agreed.

'Is there really nothing we can do?' Polly asked.

'Perhaps we can somehow scupper Dr Eris and Dr Parker's relationship so it ends naturally – of its own accord – and it has nothing to do with Helen,' Dorothy suggested.

They all thought, but they didn't look particularly convinced that in reality it would work, especially in the limited time they had.

'Perhaps we're looking at this the wrong way,' mused Georgina.

Everyone looked at their friend, knowing that she still felt a residue of guilt for being the one who had unearthed their secrets in the first place.

'We're looking inward when we should be looking outward,' she reflected.

'Yer speaking in riddles, Georgie,' Angie said. She had taken to shortening her name – something Georgina didn't mind. In fact, it made her feel even more part of the gang.

'What I mean,' Georgina clarified, 'is that perhaps we should be looking at what secrets *Dr Claire Eris* might have. She's bound to have at least one skeleton in the cupboard, don't you think?'

Dorothy's eyes widened. 'Of course!'

'Don't screech, Dor,' Angie reprimanded. 'We dinnit want people hearing what we're talking about.'

'Or perhaps I should rephrase that,' Georgina said, looking around at the women's faces. 'Perhaps *I* should take a look into Dr Eris's past? It is what I do for a living, after all.'

'*Did* for a living,' Martha said. 'I didn't think you worked as a private eye any more?'

Georgina laughed. 'I don't. But being a journalist isn't that much different.'

The women eyed each other.

'Well,' Gloria said. 'I can't imagine it'd do any harm.'

'Agreed, then?' Georgina asked.

The women nodded.

'Agreed,' they all chorused.

Dorothy looked at Angie and both their faces lit up.

'And if you need any help . . .' Dorothy said, thinking of all the exciting stories Georgina had told them about her PI work.

'Yeah, yer just need to ask,' Angie stressed enthusiastically.

'*Oh, my goodness, it's time!*' Rosie suddenly interrupted, looking up at the clock above the bar.

'Time for what?' Gloria said.

'The toast.' Rosie took hold of Gloria's arm. 'Come on, I need you to be standing next to your husband.'

'*You're* deeing the toast?' Angie asked in disbelief.

Martha also looked surprised. 'I thought it had to be a man?'

Rosie looked at her squad, whom she was more used to seeing with dirt-smeared faces and wearing denim overalls than in their best dresses, with make-up on and their hair loose.

She shook her head. 'Just like you used to think that it was only men who could weld?'

She heard Dorothy laugh out loud as she turned and headed to the bar.

'Can I have all your attention, please?' Rosie shouted above the growing chatter. She had a glass of port in her hand.

'I'd like to make a toast to the happy couple,' she declared. 'But before I do so, I'd just like to say a few words about Jack and Gloria.'

There was a murmur of surprise from the guests – not only that it was Rosie, a woman, making the toast, but that she was clearly going to make some kind of speech.

'I personally have much to thank Jack for,' Rosie began, 'because many years ago he took a chance on me and argued the case with his superiors about employing me as an apprentice welder.' She looked at Jack and smiled. There was a ripple of chatter from the older workers from the yard who remembered the hoo-ha over Jack's decision.

'But I also think it's safe to say that we are all indebted to Jack for his work with Churchill's British shipbuilding mission.' No one needed reminding that Jack had travelled to America with the managing director of Thompson's to oversee the mass production of the new emergency war ships needed to replace the many cargo vessels being lost to German U-boats.

'I don't think there's any doubt that if those ships had not been built, we wouldn't be on the verge of winning the war like we are now.'

There was a robust ripple of agreement and a few calls of 'Hear! Hear!'

'And as many of you know,' Helen reminded them, 'Jack

nearly lost his life on that trip.' Not wanting the mood to become sombre, she quickly added, 'Thank goodness he didn't, as we wouldn't all be here having a merry ol' knees-up!'

Hearty chuckles and raised glasses followed.

'I'd also like to thank his new wife, Gloria,' continued Rosie, 'for being an invaluable part of my squad at Thompson's. Not only did Gloria choose one of the hardest and most dangerous jobs to help the war effort – but she has also been my right-hand woman, a pillar of strength and support, and the glue that has kept my squad together. I really don't know what I – and the rest of my squad – would have done without you, Gloria. So, thank you!'

Everyone raised their glasses to Gloria.

Rosie saw Polly, Dorothy, Angie, Martha and Hannah's faces beaming back at her – their expressions proud and a little emotional.

Turning her attention to Gloria and Jack, who she knew would not be comfortable being the centre of such praise and attention, she was pleased to see that they looked touched by her words.

'So, a toast to two people who really do deserve a "Happy Ever After". Congratulations to you both. Here's to a long and happy marriage!'

Rosie raised her glass of port in the air.

'A long and happy marriage!' the guests toasted.

As Helen raised her glass and joined in the toast, she felt overwhelmed by a mix of conflicting feelings. She was so incredibly happy for her father and Gloria – and little Hope too – but she was also incredibly sad that she had been deprived of her chance of a happy marriage to the man she loved. She glanced across at Dr Parker and Dr Eris and felt the familiar piercing pain in her heart – made worse still by the fact they looked so well suited, *and so bloody in love.*

'You OK?' Polly asked quietly so the rest of the women couldn't hear. She had seen Helen looking at the future Mr and Mrs Parker.

Blinking hard, Helen hoped her eyes hadn't become bloodshot with the sting of tears she was desperately trying to hold back.

'Yes, I'm fine,' she said, taking a big slug of vodka and lemonade, forcing her feelings down.

'It's been a day and a half, hasn't it? What with your mam turning up like that at the registry office. And then Dr Parker and Dr Eris coming.' Polly looked at Helen's very beautiful but incredibly jaded face. 'We didn't think they would.'

'I knew John would want to come,' Helen said, taking a deep breath, forcing herself to get a grip. 'He was Dad's doctor when he was in a coma.' She let out a genuine burst of laughter. 'Although I sometimes wonder if John likes to see Dad purely to check him out after his amnesia. He keeps saying he wants to write a paper on it.'

They each took a sip of their drink.

'I also knew that Claire wouldn't let John come on his own,' Helen said with bitterness. 'She'll have forced herself to come here and endure it. You watch, though – they won't stay much longer. As soon as the cake's been cut, she'll be dragging him out that door and off to somewhere posh to make up for having to slum it.'

'We saw her showing off her ring,' Polly said.

Helen let out a mirthless laugh 'I know this sounds terribly bitchy, but I wanted to grab hold of Angie and get her to wave her diamond ring in front of Claire's smug face – it would have put hers in the shade.'

Polly chuckled.

Sensing people's voices dropping and their attention turning to the bar, they saw that Jack and Gloria were preparing to cut the cake.

'Our beautiful wedding cake,' Gloria announced, 'was made by the two women who run the café on High Street East.' She looked over to Vera and Rina, who appeared stunned at suddenly being in the spotlight. 'They really do make the best cakes and pastries in the whole of the north-east!'

'And the best bacon butties!' Jack chimed in, making everyone laugh.

As Jack and Gloria made the first incision, Polly nudged Helen. 'Look, Matthew's here.'

They both turned to see Matthew brushing back his thick dark hair from his face, his eyes scouring the pub for Helen. Finding her, he started threading his way through the crowd.

'Sorry I'm late,' he said, giving Helen a kiss on both cheeks. He looked at Polly and the rest of the women. 'Afternoon all.'

They smiled back, never quite sure whether to call him Matthew or Mr Royce, so they tended not to call him anything.

'I'm afraid I got held up at the office,' Matthew apologised to Helen, straightening his tie and pulling down his cuffs.

Helen thought he looked flushed. 'You look like you've run all the way here.'

Matthew laughed again. 'Not in this weather. Even the old gal struggled to get through some of the roads.'

'Marie-Anne said you were letting everyone off early today?'

'Ah, yes, Marie-Anne, your *personal assistant*.' Matthew

83

always liked to joke about the title Helen had given her right-hand woman. 'Well, yes, I did, but I had a load of invoices to go through with *my* personal assistant.'

Helen raised her eyebrows. 'Have you promoted Dahlia?'

'I have, but only for a quiet life. She said it was demeaning being called a secretary when Marie-Anne was a personal assistant.' He took a deep breath and looked at Helen – *those eyes, that body*. He had to force himself not to stare at her rather daring plunging neckline.

'It's lovely to see you, Helen,' he said, his voice soft.

'You make it sound like we've not seen each other for ages,' Helen jibed.

'I know I saw you on Saturday for *Meadowbank*'s launch, but that was very fleeting. You'd gone before I had the chance to drag you off into town for a bite to eat. Then I thought I might catch you at Pickersgill's for the Royal Navy landing-craft launch on Sunday. I saw your grandfather there.'

Exactly why I didn't go.

'I was a little launched out,' Helen lied.

'I wondered if you were avoiding me after New Year's Eve?' Matthew dropped his voice. He didn't need to say *after we shared a kiss*. Their second over the festive period.

'If I was trying to avoid you,' Helen said, 'I would not have invited you to my father and Gloria's wedding reception.'

'Not important enough to be invited to the wedding itself, though,' Matthew said, trying not to sound put out. If Helen had invited him to the actual ceremony, it would have been a sign that she might want them to court properly – and not just have a flirt and a kiss every now and again.

'As I explained,' Helen said, 'it was really just close family and friends.' An image of her mother's theatrics suddenly sprang to mind, followed by relief that she hadn't invited him as her plus-one.

'Mmm,' Matthew said.

'Besides,' said Helen, 'it's a good job I didn't as you would have been tied up working on your invoices.'

Matthew was just about to bat back a reply when Hannah appeared with two plates of cake and gave them to Helen and Matthew.

'Thank you, Hannah,' said Helen. 'Have you met Matthew before?'

Hannah shook her head, and the introductions were made.

'I keep wanting to ask you,' Helen said to Hannah, 'how's your aunty been? Are you still at loggerheads?' Hannah had told the women that she and Olly wanted to go over to Europe after the war to find her parents, but her aunty Rina was far from happy about it. 'Is she still standing firm in her insistence you stay put?'

Hannah sighed. 'She is. I also feel she's trying hard to believe that she can still tell me what to do, which she can't. I'm twenty-three now. I'm an adult.'

Helen nodded her agreement, although she was on Rina's side. Going off to Europe, even after the war was over, was risky.

After Hannah left, Matthew watched her as she carried on distributing slices of cake to the guests.

Helen read his thoughts. 'I know, she only looks about sixteen, doesn't she?'

Matthew chortled his agreement as he left to get them their drinks and top up the kitty with a generous donation.

When he returned, he handed Helen her vodka and lemonade.

'Oh, you've got a little bit of cake, just there . . .' Matthew touched the corner of Helen's mouth and gently brushed away the offending crumb. But instead of taking his hand away, he kept it there. His fingers finding the back of her neck, he pulled her face towards his own and kissed her.

Helen felt Matthew's soft lips on hers. The vodka she had drunk a little too quickly before his arrival had given her head a fuzzy, slightly confused feeling. She gave in and kissed him back.

The kiss only lasted a few seconds, but it gave Matthew the green light he'd been waiting for.

'Miss Helen Crawford,' he whispered into her ear, 'will you finally allow me to take you out on a proper date?'

Helen turned her face and looked him in the eye.

When she'd first met Matthew, she'd thought him a bit of a callow charmer – a 'love them and leave them' Casanova – but over time she'd got to know him. She'd consistently knocked him back when he tried to woo her, but in the process she'd discovered he was funny and interesting, and surprisingly open-minded. It was also definitely a confidence boost having someone so attentive and so admiring of her – so determined to win her over. And there was no denying he was incredibly good-looking. And he certainly knew how to kiss a woman. So why not? Why shouldn't she have some fun? Date other men? *Was she going to mourn a love she couldn't have for the rest of her life?*

'OK,' she relented. 'One date. Somewhere fancy.'

Matthew threw back his head and laughed. 'But of course. I wouldn't dream of taking you anywhere else.'

Dr Parker averted his eyes on seeing Helen and Matthew kiss. Well, now there was no denying they were an item. He had suspected that they were for a while. But why had Helen kept on denying there'd been something going on between the two of them?

Why did it bother him so? He looked at Claire as she chatted to Dr Billingham. He heard the word 'firestorm' and knew they were discussing the mass bombing of Dresden by the RAF. They'd been talking about it just before they came here. Claire had been quite emotional about the tens of thousands of lives lost. They had both agreed that although they both desperately wanted the war to end, the killing of so many innocent civilians just did not sit right.

Dr Parker wanted to kick himself. *He loved Claire.* Loved her empathy and the way she cared so much for her patients. She'd even risked her job for Henrietta, defying Charles Havelock's demand that she put Helen's grandmother back on her heavy and totally unnecessary medication. And then when Henrietta had been poisoned, Claire had worked flat out to find an antidote. She'd helped save Henrietta's life.

There was his future wife. The woman he would spend the rest of his life with.

He took a large mouthful of frothy beer.

Was he fixated on what he couldn't have?

Perhaps it *was* a good idea to move to London. Claire had mentioned it a few times since he had proposed, and it made sense for their careers. When she had first mentioned it, his instinct had been to buck against the suggestion. *Was that because he wanted to stay near Helen?*

He looked again as Matthew slid his arm around Helen's waist.

'A penny for your thoughts?'

87

Dr Parker turned to see Claire standing next to him. Had she seen him looking?

'I'd say it was about time,' she said, her eyes flicking in the direction of Helen and Matthew.

'Time for what?' Dr Parker asked.

'Time those two got together,' Dr Eris said. 'They've been skirting around their attraction for each other for some time now, don't you think?'

Dr Parker allowed himself another quick look. 'You think this has just happened?'

'I'd say so,' Dr Eris said. 'I think she's played the long game. Or should I say, she's played hard to get. The treat them mean, keep them keen philosophy.'

'You think so?'

'Darling,' Dr Eris kissed his ear softly, 'it's my job. I read people for a living. And if being a matchmaker was my job, I'd say they are very well suited – in all ways.'

'Really?'

'Of course,' Dr Eris said. 'It's obvious. They're both in the same business, come from similar backgrounds – they even look alike. Both dark and drop-dead gorgeous.' Dr Eris laughed. 'If they had American accents, they could easily be mistaken for Hollywood royalty.'

'Yes, I suppose you're right,' Dr Parker said. *How stupid to even think that Helen might have feelings for him.*

Dr Parker looked at his watch. He had a sudden urge to leave.

'Well, it's time for me to fulfil my side of the bargain. Let's head off to that little restaurant you've heard such good reports of.'

Dr Eris was tempted to stay longer. This wedding had

turned out to be much more enjoyable than she could ever have anticipated. She couldn't have planned it better had she tried.

'That sounds like a wonderful idea,' she said, kissing him on the lips.

She hoped Helen was watching.

*

When the bell for last orders sounded out, Jack and Gloria had already gone home, Dr Parker and Dr Eris had also long since departed, and Helen had just been to say her farewells before leaving with Matthew. The rest of the women had decided to stay until the final curtain.

'So, it looks like Helen's getting it together with Matthew,' Polly said.

'It certainly does,' Martha said. She had been quite shocked to see the pair share a quick kiss in public.

'Gloria said Helen told her that she'd agreed to go on a date with Matthew. That it was time she moved on from Dr Parker,' Rosie said.

'So, what do yer think?' Angie said, looking around at her workmates' faces.

'Should we still try and work out a way to get her and Dr Parker together? Or not?' Hannah asked.

'I think we should,' Dorothy said.

'It does somehow seem wrong that they're not together,' Georgina chipped in.

'Gloria also said that Helen was wondering if perhaps the reason she was so mad on Dr Parker was because she couldn't have him,' Rosie interjected, playing devil's advocate.

'That's ridiculous!' Dorothy exclaimed. 'The only reason they aren't together is because of Dr Conniving Claire Eris.'

'So, should we stick our noses in?' Georgina asked.

'I'm wondering,' Rosie mused, 'if this is more a case where *we* want to see Helen and John together, but perhaps they *aren't* meant for each other.'

'Perhaps Matthew *is* the one for her?' Martha ventured, although she didn't sound convinced herself.

'Why don't we hold off until we see how things go with this date – see if Helen likes Matthew,' Polly suggested.

There was a general mumbling. It was hard to tell whether they all agreed with Polly's proposal or not.

Georgina kept her counsel. Her interest in Dr Eris had been whetted. Someone who was capable of blackmailing another woman in order to get herself a husband was a complex character. And complex characters usually had a past.

Chapter Ten

Friday 23 February

Over the next nine days, gales reaching 80 to 100 mph swept across the whole of the country, causing severe damage to homes and businesses. Sunderland suffered the added hardship of hail, snow and frost, and a failed electricity supply in the early hours of Thursday morning. The Havelock residence had been in full swing to ensure the fires were burning throughout the house and candles were at the ready should they suffer another impromptu blackout.

For most people, though, the news reports crackling through their radios courtesy of the BBC Home Service more than compensated for the hardships the weather was inflicting. Every day there was news of another Allied triumph, another successful sinking of a U-boat, or an air raid attack that was bombing the Axis powers into submission. Today the headlines announced that Turkey had just declared war on Germany, and the Battle of Poznań in Poland had ended in Soviet victory. Since its defeat in the Battle of the Bulge, the German Army had been retreating into Germany itself. Even Hitler's own newspaper, the *Völkischer Beobachter*, had reported: *Every German must accept the fact that this is the final showdown. About one third of Germany has become a bombed area, and sometimes looks like a scene immediately behind the front line.*

As the grandfather clock in the hallway of the Havelock mansion struck one o'clock, Eddy knocked on the oak door to the master's study.

'Yes!' Mr Havelock's voice bellowed out.

Eddy opened the door.

'Mr Robert Thurley here to see you, sir,' he announced, moving aside to allow the former detective, now private eye, to enter the room.

'Ah, Bob, come in, come in!'

Bob Thurley walked into the room, unsure of the kind of welcome he would receive. Last time he had been at this mausoleum, the old man had been cantankerous and far from courteous.

'Good to see you again!' Mr Havelock said, gesturing towards the Biedermeier tub chair positioned on the opposite side of his large desk. 'Sit!'

Mr Havelock looked over at Eddy, still loitering in the doorway, waiting to be dismissed.

'Get Mr Thurley a brandy,' he ordered. 'I'm sure he needs something to warm his cockles in this damnable weather.'

Bob immediately relaxed. The old man must be in a good mood. He didn't normally offer him a drink, never mind take it upon himself to force one on him – although he'd still been instructed to use the tradesman's entrance.

'I have to apologise for the delay in my being able to come here and see you,' Bob said, lowering his considerable bulk into the chair. 'I was needed down south on government business, which was impossible to get out of. I hope you understand?' As a former detective who had worked for both the Sunderland Borough Police as well as the Metropolitan Police, this might well have been true. As it was, Bob's time had really been taken up with bringing black-market produce up from London.

'Of course, when your country needs you . . .' Mr Havelock said, letting his voice tail off. It had become harder of late to hide his disappointment that this green and pleasant land would never enjoy a fascist government. Not in his lifetime, anyway.

Bob looked at Mr Havelock. He'd discerned something in the tone of his voice he was not quite able to decipher. Not that it mattered. He obviously didn't hold it against Bob that he'd had to cancel his initial meeting. Or that it had then been postponed for several weeks.

Eddy arrived and handed Bob his drink, leaving as quickly and as quietly as he had come.

Bob raised his glass. 'Cheers. To victory.'

Mr Havelock paused for a second before raising his bulbous glass of Rémy.

'Yes, of course, old boy, to victory.' *His victory.*

They each took a good mouthful.

'So,' Mr Havelock began, smacking his lips. 'First of all, I have to reiterate that you did a splendid job for me last time, which is why I have you back here.' Mr Havelock had decided to butter Bob up this time. Previously, he had been rather severe with the slovenly private eye, but for this one last job he wanted him firing on all cylinders and eager to please. The amount he would receive should ensure he did a thorough job, but he knew the man would go that extra mile if he liked his employer. With that in mind, he'd resolved to be on his best behaviour, hard though it might be.

'Thank you, Mr Havelock,' said Bob. He took a handkerchief out of his pocket and wiped his forehead. It was bitter

93

outside, but the heat from the fire had hit him as soon as he'd walked into the room, and it now felt like being in the tropics.

'The Gentlemen's Club certainly threw up a few surprises,' Bob added, thinking back to the investigation he'd done almost a year and a half ago, when he'd found out the house next door to it was a high-class knocking shop. His discovery had put a rare smile on Charles Havelock's face, and he had been well paid for his efforts.

As Bob loosened his navy blue tie slightly, he kept his fingers crossed that this job would be equally profitable.

'So,' Mr Havelock said. 'Let me get started.'

Bob took another quick swig of brandy, pulled out his small notebook, the same kind he'd always used when he was a copper, and with pen poised, ready to make notes, he listened as Mr Havelock began to explain exactly what it was he wanted Bob to do.

As Bob walked away from the house, his heavy footsteps scrunching in the loose gravel of the driveway, he saw a car turning in off the main road. Curious, he moved to the side so that his back was touching the hedging that separated the Havelock residence from the grounds of the neighbouring mansion.

A jolly-looking chap waved his thanks as he slowly pulled into the driveway. Bob couldn't help but stand and admire the unusual light green MG T-Type sports car, as well as wonder why a man with such considerable weight on him would choose to squeeze himself into such a small car.

As Bob carried on his way, he decided if he ever won the pools, he would buy a big spacious Bentley or Rolls-Royce for himself.

Casting another look back, he saw the ruddy-cheeked man hauling himself out of the driver's side before leaning back in to grab a briefcase from the passenger seat. Whoever Mr Havelock's next visitor was, he was clearly there for business rather than pleasure.

Which made Bob wonder what it was the old man was up to.

'Good afternoon, old chap.' Mr Havelock welcomed the family solicitor, Rupert Gourley, into his study, repeating his demand to Eddy to fetch a brandy. Normally, he wouldn't have had two meetings in one day, never mind one after the other, but time was marching on, and he needed everything squared up.

He topped up his own drink from the decanter on his desk.

'Take a seat.' Mr Havelock nodded towards the chair, at the same time flicking open his box of cigars and taking one.

Knowing Mr Havelock would not get down to business until Eddy had brought his drink, Rupert started to chat about the war. He often wondered of late what they'd all converse about after the war ended.

'I was just reading this morning that today is the two thousandth day since the start of this war,' Rupert said, watching as Mr Havelock went through the ritual of smelling his torpedo-shaped Cuban cigar, then clipping the end.

'Is that so,' Mr Havelock feigned interest.

'It won't be long now, though,' Rupert continued, as his client flicked open his silver lighter and slowly rotated the cigar, taking the odd puff. 'The end is near. Very near.'

Mr Havelock's friend Oswald Mosley had been saying

the same thing just the other day when they'd been speaking on the phone, only the manner in which it had been said had been very different.

Mr Havelock breathed a sigh of relief when Eddy appeared with Rupert's brandy.

'Righty-ho! Now we're settled, I can tell you exactly what it is I want you to do for this old man.'

'*Old!* Ha! People like you, Mr Havelock, don't get old – like a good wine, you merely improve with age.' Rupert said what he knew his client wanted to hear.

Mr Havelock basked momentarily in the compliment. He certainly didn't feel old in his mind. It was just such a shame his body wasn't following suit.

As they settled down to business, Rupert opened up his briefcase and got out Mr Havelock's Last Will and Testament, which he had been asked to bring. He had been informed by the old man that he wanted to make some 'tweaks'.

As they chatted, both taking the occasional sip of their brandy, Rupert had to hold back his surprise at his client's so-called 'tweaks'. He was certainly of sound mind, so legally there would be no loopholes or any room for contention, but, ethically, well, that was a different matter.

He had heard through the grapevine that there had been some familial unrest and that Charles and his granddaughter Helen Crawford were not as close as they once were, but the changes he was being asked to make now were quite drastic. Everyone in Rupert's circle knew you'd be a foolish man or woman to cross Charles Havelock, and that many had learnt this lesson the hard way, but he hadn't thought it would extend to Charles's own flesh and blood. It was certainly a change of heart Rupert would never have forecasted.

But there was nothing as strange as folk. His years working as a lawyer had taught him that.

Observing the old man, he could see the lines of blue veins plainly beneath the thin skin on his temples. Age was finally catching up with Charles Havelock, although you'd never think it the way he talked. Even sitting here and making out his new will, he spoke as though he were immortal.

As he finished off his drink and went over his notes to check he had written everything down correctly, he wondered what had caused Mr Havelock's change of heart. And also, his mind skipping back to his arrival, who had been there before him. Whoever it was had obviously been there a while, as the seat had still been warm when Rupert sat down.

His job, however, was not to wonder, but to do as he was told. Which, of course, he would. He was being paid enough, after all.

'And there is just one more request I have,' Mr Havelock said, 'which requires very little work on your behalf, but I need to be absolutely sure that you will carry out my wishes to the letter as and when the time comes.'

Mr Havelock took another puff on his cigar.

'And obviously, you will be handsomely paid for it. Very handsomely.'

Rupert's face lit up.

Money, Mr Havelock thought, really could get you anything.

*

While the master of the house was holed up in the study with Rupert, there was another pull on the doorbell.

'It's like Clapham Junction in here today,' Eddy complained.

Agatha brushed past him.

'Don't worry yourself, I'll get it. It'll be the new cleaner. Or rather, the person who I'm hoping will be our new cleaner.'

Eddy allowed her to pass and open the door.

'Hello, Mrs Bevan. Please come in,' Agatha said, ushering the woman in.

Eddy wandered off, shaking his head. He'd never heard Agatha sound so welcoming to a tradesperson – and a cleaner at that.

'Will this weather never ease up!' Agatha said as Mrs Bevan stepped across the threshold, shaking off her headscarf as she did so.

Agatha noticed that the woman's thick brown hair had the slightest hint of red in it. As she showed her towards the kitchen, she touched her own grey hair and wondered if the new cleaner's colour was natural.

As they sat down at the kitchen table, Agatha poured them each a cup of tea. She looked around for Eddy and was glad he wasn't about. For the first time in the thirty-odd years they had worked together in this house, there was friction between them. Eddy hadn't said it outright, but he suspected that it was Agatha who had somehow got word to the hospital that Henrietta had been poisoned. It was eating away at them both. He could not understand how she could have scuppered the master's attempts at finally getting shot of Henrietta – and Agatha could not understand how Eddy could have gone through with it.

'So, tell me a little about yourself,' Agatha asked. This was meant to be an interview, but she had already decided Mrs

Bevan had got the job. She knew, having read her letter, which had been delivered just after the last cleaner had suddenly left, that she would be perfect for the job. She had impeccable references from a solicitor in town, was a widow, so wouldn't be tired out cooking and looking after a husband when she wasn't working, and she lived just a short distance away, so there would be no excuses that bad weather had prevented her from getting to work. And, more than anything, it would save Agatha from putting an ad in the local paper and going through the tedium of interviewing a load of applicants.

'Well,' Agatha said, having only half listened to the woman's summary of what sounded like a very ordinary life, 'I think you seem perfect for the job. I will just have to get the master to sanction your employ, and if that goes as it should, when do you think you could start?' Agatha raised her eyebrows, adding, 'I was hoping you might say tomorrow.' She crossed her fingers. She had been forced to spend hours cleaning the silver yesterday and did not want to have to do two jobs for the same money longer than necessary.

'That won't be a problem. I can certainly start tomorrow,' Mrs Bevan said.

Hearing the front door close, Agatha scraped back her chair and stood up.

'That's the master's last visitor of the day gone. If we go now, you can say a quick hello and once's he's given you the nod, we'll sort out your hours.'

Agatha caught a slightly apprehensive look on Mrs Bevan's face and wondered if the master's reputation had gone before him. He might make out he was a courteous do-gooder to the town's bigwigs, but to those in the lower ranks he could be downright rude and quite nasty.

'Don't worry, his bark's worse than his bite,' Agatha reassured. *Who was she kidding? His bite was far, far worse.*

As they made to leave the kitchen, Eddy appeared from the servants' quarters.

'Ah, Eddy, meet our new cleaner, Mrs Bevan.'

Eddy stretched out his hand.

'Pleased to meet you, Mrs Bevan.'

'Please, call me Tan. It's what everyone calls me.'

'Tan? I don't think I've heard that one before.'

'Just a nickname that stuck,' Mrs Bevan said.

Agatha turned to lead the way back to the main part of the house.

'We don't know each other, do we?' Eddy asked.

Mrs Bevan forced herself to look him in the eye.

'No. What makes you think that?' she asked.

'Oh, it's nothing,' Eddy said, looking at the new cleaner more intently. 'It's just that your face seems familiar. I thought we might have met before?'

'No,' Mrs Bevan said, 'I think I would have remembered if we had.'

'Come on,' Agatha said impatiently. 'Before the master goes up for his afternoon nap.'

A few minutes later, Agatha was knocking on the master's study.

'Yes!'

Agatha turned to Mrs Bevan, who was nervously straightening her skirt.

'Just wait there a moment,' she whispered.

Opening the door, which had been left ajar, Agatha stepped into the master's inner sanctum. She caught him putting some documents away in his safe. She waited until he had shut the small metal door and twiddled the combination lock.

'Yes?' He turned to Agatha.

'I've the new cleaner here for you to meet,' Agatha said.

Mr Havelock surveyed his housekeeper. Since the debacle that was Henrietta's poisoning, he had noticed a change in the woman. It was subtle. Nothing he could pick her up on, just a slight difference in her manner.

'And?' he demanded.

'And,' Agatha looked him in the eye, 'as is usual whenever there's a potential new member of staff—'

'*Servant!*' Mr Havelock barked. 'A potential new *servant*. Let's call a spade a spade, eh?'

Agatha watched as his thin lips curled into what was meant to resemble a smile.

'As is usual,' she repeated, 'whenever there's a potential new *servant* to be taken on, I bring them to you to ensure you are happy to go ahead with their employment.'

Suddenly tired from having two back-to-back meetings, Mr Havelock walked over to his chair and slumped into it.

'Well, bring her in!' he ordered.

Agatha turned, half expecting to see the back of Mrs Bevan as she made a run for it. If she had been in her shoes, and her age, she might well have done. Would certainly have been sprinting out of the house if she knew the truth about her new employer. But, thankfully for her, anyway, Mrs Bevan was still there. Agatha gave her what she hoped was a reassuring smile. At least, Agatha thought, she was dressed smartly enough to pass muster. And she had a straight posture – stomach in, shoulders back. Any hint of a slouch would have her sent packing by the master.

Mrs Bevan walked into the room and stood a few yards away from the chair at the front of the desk.

Mr Havelock scrutinised her without saying a word, as though she were cattle in a farmers' market. He turned his attention to Agatha.

'What? You couldn't have got someone younger?' He had meant the question to be rhetorical, but Agatha answered back.

'No, sir, all the young ones are doing valuable war work. *Servant* jobs are now the domain of the older folk.'

Mr Havelock took one more look at Mrs Bevan.

'If she can start tomorrow, she's got the job,' he said. 'And let's hope she does better with the silver than you.'

He then shooed the two women away.

Agatha turned. Mrs Bevan took a last look at her new employer and followed the housekeeper out of the smoky study.

'Do you still want the job?' Agatha asked tentatively as they walked across the tiled hallway to the front door.

'Oh, yes,' Mrs Bevan said, clearly unperturbed by the master's boorishness. 'I most certainly do.'

'Oh, thank goodness for that,' Agatha said, her relief plain to see. 'I'll see you tomorrow. About ten o'clock. We can go through your hours then and I can show you the ropes.'

Mrs Bevan nodded and walked down the short flight of stone steps.

This time she did not need to stop for fear of being sick.

She had changed since that day.

And not necessarily for the better.

*

Hearing the front door close, Mr Havelock got up and put another log on the fire. He looked at himself in the mirror. He smiled at his reflection. He had enjoyed a successful life. Not just as a sales negotiator for one of the world's leading shipbuilding companies, as well as a successful businessman and admired philanthropist – he was also proud of the fact that he had an unblemished record in regard to his personal battles. During his eighty-odd years on this planet, not one person had ever got the better of him, and boy oh boy, there had been those who had tried. *Tried and lived to regret it.*

He turned and looked out of the window, watching the new cleaner disappear around the corner. He sighed. Gone were the days of pretty blonde maids. But still, he'd had his fill, hadn't he?

He walked back to his chair, eased himself into it and poured another drink.

There might well have been those who had crossed him, but none had got away with it – not until recently, anyway. Not until his granddaughter had decided to stick her oar in. She was the only blot on his copybook.

And he was damned if he was leaving this world without erasing that stain.

She might be happy with the trade-off. She had got what she wanted after all – her father's return and her grandmother's freedom – *and* on top of it all, she had orchestrated it so that her workmates' secrets were kept under wraps.

But *he* wasn't happy. Not by a long shot.

Helen, he knew, thought he had not fared too badly out of their deal. He had, after all, kept his past misdemeanours from being exposed. And even though Henrietta was now living in the real world, she was doing so under an assumed name. No one knew who she really was. His reputation had certainly remained unsullied. But, still, there was no getting away from it – Helen had one over him. *She* had dictated to him how the game would play out.

He smiled to himself as he took another sip of his drink and closed his eyes, imagining the future he was in the process of making into reality.

This was to be his last battle, and he was determined to be the victor, come hell or high water.

And after today, he was well on his way to a rather dramatic triumph.

Chapter Eleven

A week later

Thursday 1 March

'We're back!' Pearl's voice sounded out down the hallway as her granddaughter, Lucille, pulled off her woollen hat, scarf and gloves.

'Mammy! Mammy!' Lucille called out as she continued to disrobe, shaking off her winter coat before sitting on the tiled floor and pulling off her wet boots.

'We had hot chocolate,' she shouted, huffing air with the exertion of freeing herself of her tight footwear. 'And Aunty Maisie bought me a new dolly!'

Lucille looked up to her grandmother to make sure she still had her new toy. Jumping to her feet, she took the pink plastic doll from her grandmother and raced into the kitchen to show her mam.

When Pearl walked into the warmth of the main living area, she saw Bel inspecting her daughter's new treasure. Seeing Pearl standing in the doorway, she shook her head.

'I wish Maisie wouldn't spoil her. She's going to expect a present every time she takes her out,' Bel said, watching as her daughter hurried into the scullery to show her other grandma her cherished present.

'Aye, she will, but our Maisie *wants* to buy the bairn a present every time they gan out, so there's no harm done, is there?' Pearl argued.

Bel eyed her mother. She should know better now than to expect her mother to ever agree with her. Or, rather, to expect her to criticise her favoured daughter in any way.

'You not taking your coat off?' Bel asked. 'Cuppa?'

Pearl shook her head. 'No, I'm gonna get straight off. Things to do. People to see.'

Bel surveyed her mother. 'That sounds a bit vague. Where you off to?'

'Just off to see an auld friend,' Pearl said.

'I didn't think you had any old friends,' Bel said, her curiosity piqued.

Pearl turned to go. 'Ah, well, it just shows – yer dinnit knar everything about yer auld ma.'

Agnes appeared from the scullery.

'Wait up, Pearl, I'll come out with you,' she said, ruffling Lucille's hair.

She walked past the cot and had a quick look at the twins lying next to each other, fast asleep, before giving her attention to Bel. 'I won't be long. Just need to get a few extra bits and pieces for the tea.'

Pearl and Agnes walked down the long hallway, buttoning up their coats before stepping outside.

'Where you off to?' asked Agnes.

'Villette Road,' said Pearl.

'I'll walk with you, I'm going in that direction.'

As they left the house and started to walk down Tatham Street, Pearl glanced across at Agnes. 'Is there summat on yer mind?'

'Actually,' Agnes said, 'there is.'

'Summat up with Isabelle?' Pearl asked. Chances were if Agnes wanted to chat to her, it would be about her daughter. Much as Pearl was loath to admit it, Agnes had probably been more of a mother to Bel when she was a child than she ever had.

'I think Bel's still hankering after a baby.' Agnes just came out and said it.

'Ah, for Gawd's sake – hasn't she gorra her hands full as it is with the twins 'n LuLu?'

'That may well be,' Agnes agreed, 'but I think she's still desperate to have a baby with our Joe.'

Passing the sweet shop, Agnes looked in and waved at the owners, Maud and Mavis.

'Well, if it's not happened now . . .' Pearl said. 'How long have they been married?'

'Coming up to three and a half years,' Agnes answered.

Pearl walked in silence.

'Why can't she just be happy with what she's got?' Pearl said.

'You can't help the way you feel,' Agnes defended Bel. 'And I can understand her wanting to have a child with Joe.'

'Joe's not pestering to have another bab, is he?' Pearl asked sharply.

'No, he's not,' Agnes bit back. 'Joe's the most easy-going husband a wife could want for. It's Bel who's desperate to have another child.'

Agnes looked at Pearl. She'd got to know her these past few years since she'd tipped up out of the blue, and she knew that Pearl's ire was because Bel was hurting. Pearl would never admit it, but she loved her daughter dearly. Knowing

Bel wanted something it seemed unlikely she could have maddened her.

'I'm telling you because I just wanted to give you a heads-up,' Agnes said, slowing down when they reached the butcher's.

'Aye, good to know,' said Pearl, her anger replaced by jealousy that her daughter had chosen to confide in Agnes over herself. Not that she should be surprised. She and Isabelle did not have that kind of relationship.

'You off anywhere nice?' Agnes asked. She was curious after hearing how evasive Pearl had been with Bel.

Pearl glanced at Agnes, wondering how much to tell her. It had now been a fortnight since Gloria and Jack's wedding, when Helen had asked if she would find out whether Mrs Evans would be willing to meet with Henrietta. She'd put it off long enough.

'Doing a favour for Helen Crawford, believe it or not,' Pearl said, keeping it vague.

Now Agnes was even more curious. It had to be in some way connected with the Havelocks, which would be why Pearl had wanted to keep it from Bel. Pearl might have failed abysmally as a mother, but when it came to Charles Havelock, she was fiercely protective of her daughter. Agnes knew that Pearl didn't even want to pollute the air Bel breathed with the mere mention of the man.

*

When Pearl reached Mrs Evans's house, she took one last drag of her cigarette and tossed it into the gutter. She knocked on the door, and heard Mrs Evans's footsteps hurrying to answer.

'Ah, Pearl, this is a surprise. Come in,' she said, standing aside.

'Sorry to come unannounced,' Pearl said, stepping over the threshold.

'You don't have to have an appointment to see me. The door's always open. Besides, you couldn't have timed it better, I've just got in and was about to make a brew.'

Pearl looked at Mrs Evans and thought she seemed different. Her manner was different. She had expected to find her sad and subdued, dressed all in black, still bereft at the loss of the husband she had adored. Especially as it was barely eight weeks or so since he'd passed away. Pearl had thought Mrs Evans would mourn her husband until her dying day – just as she mourned poor Gracie.

'Go in and get warm, and I'll get us a cuppa,' Mrs Evans said, hanging up both their coats.

When she took off her headscarf, Pearl's chin practically hit the floor.

'Eee, yer've dyed yer hair.' The words were out before she could rein them in.

Mrs Evans touched her hair self-consciously. 'Yes, I dyed it a few weeks ago. I went for a job and thought I'd stand a better chance if I didn't look like I had one foot in the grave.'

Pearl continued to stare. Mrs Evans looked like a different woman.

'Go, get yourself sat down.' Mrs Evans gestured to the front room.

Five minutes later, Pearl and Mrs Evans were sitting drinking tea in front of the electric fire.

'So, what's this new job yer got yerself?' Pearl asked.

'Oh, just a little cleaning job,' Mrs Evans said.

'Are yer short of dosh?' Pearl just came straight out and said it. "Cos if yer are, me 'n Bill can help yer out.'

Mrs Evans smiled. Pearl might be as rough as a badger's backside, as the saying went, but underneath her brassy, hard-nosed exterior was a kind-hearted person. Charles Havelock might have blighted her life, but he had not extinguished her humanity.

'The job's not because I need the money, Pearl,' Mrs Evans explained.

Pearl took a sip of her tea and waited for her to shed more light on why she was working as a cleaner, but Mrs Evans was not forthcoming. Instead, she asked, 'So, tell me why you're here. My sixth sense tells me this isn't just a social call?'

Pearl sighed. 'Am I that readable?'

'You just seem a little on edge,' Mrs Evans said, glad to have successfully steered the conversation away from her new job.

'I've come to relay a request,' Pearl said. 'And please just say no if it's not something yer wanna dee.'

'Of course,' Mrs Evans said. 'Go on, I'm intrigued.'

Pearl took a deep breath.

'Henrietta Havelock wants to come 'n see yer,' she said, having decided to just come out and say it.

Mrs Evans's eyes widened. 'Really? Well, that *is* a turn-up for the books. I thought she was still up at the asylum?'

'No,' Pearl said. 'She's out. She got out at the start of the New Year. I didn't want to mention it before, yer knar, like, with Mr Evans just passing 'n everything.'

Mrs Evans was listening intently. 'Go on.'

'Well, it appears that Helen Crawford—'

'The granddaughter?'

'That's right. Well, Helen somehow wangled it so that Henrietta was allowed to go and live with her in the big house in Roker.'

'Allowed?'

'Aye, I knar,' Pearl said bitterly. 'The man himself apparently sanctioned it – or rather, didn't object.'

'Really? That surprises me.'

'Aye, and there's a bit more to it,' Pearl said.

'Go on,' Mrs Evans said, pouring them another cup.

She then sat back and listened as Pearl related to her how Charles Havelock had tried to poison his own wife with a foreign plant he'd brought back from some far-flung country he'd visited years ago and which he had donated to the Winter Gardens.

'Someone got a message to one of Helen's mates,' Pearl finished the story. 'And they were able to find some kind of antidote to save her in the nick of time.'

'And she's all right now?' Mrs Evans asked.

'Fit as a lop, by the sounds of it,' Pearl said, relating what she had heard from Polly.

'So, the granddaughter asked you to ask me if Henrietta could come and see me?' Mrs Evans said.

Pearl nodded, taking a slurp of her tea.

'Did she say why she wants to see me?' Mrs Evans asked, her mind going into overdrive.

'I think she might want to apologise for what happened to Gracie.' Pearl dropped her voice, something she always did whenever she talked about Mrs Evans's daughter.

'She's not got anything to apologise for,' said Mrs Evans.

Pearl agreed, but didn't say anything.

'So, what do yer reckon?' Pearl asked.

'Oh, most definitely yes,' Mrs Evans said. 'I would *very much* like to meet with Henrietta.'

After Pearl had gone, Mrs Evans made herself another cup of tea and sat in the quietness of her front room. Her mind went back twenty-five years, to when she had seen Henrietta for the first and last time.

When she had heard that Mrs Havelock had died of some tropical disease out in India not long after her visit, she had thought it an odd coincidence. Henrietta had found out what her husband was doing to the young girls in her employ and a month or so later she was dead. At the time it had flashed through her mind that Charles had killed her, but she'd dismissed it. Perhaps if Henrietta had died at home, she might have given that theory more credence.

Then, when Pearl had come knocking the Christmas before last and told her and Gibson that Henrietta was alive and had been committed to the asylum in Ryhope, everything had made sense. Henrietta must have said something to Charles that day and in return had been silenced by the cosh of a bogus mental illness.

No doubt she would find out exactly what happened when Henrietta came to visit.

Pearl felt unsettled as she turned right and started walking back down Villette Road, passing the Hendon branch library with its signature porthole windows.

Her visit had not gone as expected.

Mrs Evans was not acting in a way she would have anticipated.

She was certainly not adhering to the normal behaviour of a bereaved wife.

Something wasn't right.

She'd even seemed eager to meet with Henrietta.

There had been something a little unhinged about her. Her husband's passing had changed her.

It was almost as though his death had liberated her – but from what?

Pearl wasn't sure.

But whatever it was, it did not feel like a good kind of liberation.

That much she did know.

Chapter Twelve

Two weeks later

Tuesday 13 March

Over the past few weeks winter had finally relinquished its brutal grip and spring had gingerly started to nudge its way to the fore. It made working on the edge of the River Wear, just a quarter of a mile before its waters joined the North Sea, much more pleasant. Of course, there was still a nip in the fresh, blustery north-east air, and most mornings the townsfolk were greeted by the sight of a thin covering of frost when they pulled back their curtains, but it was nothing compared to the punishing weather of the last few months.

The mood amongst the workers at Thompson's was like the weather, warm and sunny, and was bolstered by the news that a German submarine had been sunk near Hamburg and another scuttled south of Ireland. RAF bombers had also dropped over five thousand bombs onto Essen, effectively destroying the city, and this morning, reports were coming through of the Soviet army taking Küstrin in western Poland, a significant occupation as the town was so close to the border with Germany.

As the workers at Thompson's gathered for the launch of what they knew would be one of their last commissions of the war, the anticipation of victory could almost be felt in the air.

For the women welders, the ship's christening was particularly special as the yard's head honcho, Harold, had given the honour of launching the ship to Helen, who was clearly being primed to take over his job when he finally retired, something he had promised he would do once the war was won.

The entire workforce at Thompson's had downed tools and gathered by the far single-berth slipway, where the 10,000-ton cargo vessel was proudly awaiting her baptism.

Rosie, Gloria, Polly, Dorothy, Angie, Martha and Hannah had managed to push their way to a prime spot near the temporary platform that had been erected within spitting distance of the ship's bow.

'I know it sounds daft, but I feel nervous for her,' said Polly.

'I do too,' said Martha.

'I knar – remember when Marie-Anne did it?' Angie said.

'Sick with nerves, wasn't she, in case the bottle didn't smash,' Hannah chipped in.

'I told Helen to imagine she was chucking the bottle at someone she didn't like,' Gloria said, keeping her eyes trained on her stepdaughter, and her fingers crossed everything went to plan.

'No guesses who that'd be!' Angie guffawed.

There was a slight shifting of bodies as workers stood aside for a small group of dignitaries making their way to the makeshift podium.

'I think you spoke too soon,' said Hannah.

'Oh. My. God,' Dorothy declared.

They all fell silent as they watched Mr Havelock, with Miriam by his side, the mayor, and a few other shipyard managers, who included Matthew Royce, make their way up the steps to the wooden platform.

'What are *they* doing here?' Gloria hissed. 'I thought there was an unspoken agreement that they would avoid each other wherever possible.'

'If there was,' Rosie said, watching as Helen was forced to acknowledge her grandfather and her mother, 'it's an agreement which has just been broken.'

'Well, that's going to totally ruin the day for Helen,' said Polly.

'Something I'll bet you was their intention,' Rosie uttered with annoyance.

The women were still staring when Marie-Anne and Dahlia suddenly appeared, hurrying up the steps to join Helen and the rest of the men.

'Why's Dahlia there?' Dorothy practically spat the words out. She was not Dahlia's number-one fan. They all knew she hated the fact that Dahlia, who had earned herself the nickname of 'the Swedish seductress', had gone on a few dates with Bobby.

'Yeah, she's nowt to dee with Thompson's,' Angie said, linking her arm with Dorothy's to show her solidarity.

'I believe,' Rosie said, 'that Dahlia has demanded that she be given the same privileges as Marie-Anne.'

'*Demanded*?' Martha said, surprised.

'It would appear so,' Rosie continued. 'And, as Helen always takes Marie-Anne to the launches at Doxford's, Matthew has been cajoled into taking Dahlia to any launches here.'

Helen had told Rosie about Matthew's secretary – now his personal assistant – when they were chatting about the launch. They had both agreed that Dahlia wouldn't have got her own way had Royce senior still been in charge.

'Look at her,' Dorothy glowered. 'You'd think she was on the catwalk.'

The women, dressed in their usual work attire of oil-stained overalls and leather boots, their hair covered by head-scarves, all stared at Dahlia, who, it had to be said, did in fact look like a catwalk model with her long corn-coloured hair, even longer legs and perfect porcelain skin. Matthew was introducing her to Mr Havelock, the mayor and the rest of the men who had been invited to share a bird's-eye view of the launch.

'God, you can practically see them all drooling from here,' Dorothy said.

'She looks like she's loving it,' Polly said, sympathising with Dorothy. They had all seen the way Dahlia had enjoyed flirting with Bobby at the Christmas Extravaganza.

'Looks to me like she's stealing the show,' said Hannah.

'She'll be yanking the bottle out of Helen's hand, given half a chance, and doing the launch herself,' Dorothy hissed.

Gloria looked at Miriam and could see she was riled by being upstaged by a younger and far prettier model. It gave Gloria a modicum of satisfaction. As did the fact that Miriam had just staggered a little to her left. She'd clearly been at the gin beforehand.

Everyone stopped talking when they heard the loud tapping noise come through the speakers as Helen tested the microphone. This was followed by an annoying hissing noise, which seemed to further quieten everyone down.

Rosie noticed that Helen had stepped forward and was keeping her back to the VIPs – particularly her grandfather and mother.

'Good,' Helen said, her tone light and joking. 'It's working!'

There was a smattering of chuckles.

'We have all come here today to launch *Empire Joy*.' Helen's voice sang out to the hundreds of workers who were gathered around the launching berth or sitting, legs dangling from the staithes. 'Commissioned, as I am sure you are all well aware, by the Ministry of War Transport.' Helen took a deep breath. 'And what an appropriate name for a ship. Especially at this point in time, don't you think?'

Helen's wide smile seemed to be infectious, as the workers all cheered and sounded out their agreement. Hannah looked around and could see that the pride Helen clearly felt at being part of the creation of another ship was reflected in the soot-smeared faces surrounding her.

There was the flash of a bulb as Roger, one of the *Sunderland Echo* photographers, and also on-off boyfriend of Marie-Anne, took a photograph.

'Eee, she's dead confident, isn't she?' Angie said in awe.

'Either that or she's putting on a good show,' Dorothy said, glancing across at Bobby, who was standing further back with his gang of riveters. He saw her and smiled.

'I think it's because she's passionate about what she's saying,' Gloria chipped in. She, too, had sought out the man she loved. Jack was standing not far from the platform so as to get the best view of his daughter's big day. Gloria knew he'd be feeling as proud as Punch. Just as she also knew he would be trying to blot Miriam from his vision.

'Before we send *Empire Joy* down the ways, I wanted to

share with you some figures which have just come through from the Wear Shipbuilders' Association,' Helen announced.

A quietness descended on the yard. Some of the younger apprentices were shushed by their elders.

'Sunderland shipyards,' Helen's clear, well-spoken voice sounded out across the yard, 'have produced *a million and a half gross tons* of shipping between September 1939 and September 1944.'

She paused, allowing the huge achievement of the entire town to sink in.

'The number of new vessels built by the town's nine yards has now hit two hundred and forty-five – *and a half.*'

There were a few chuckles and general chatter as it had been the talk of the town when an oil tanker that had been damaged needed a new fore end.

'And this total does not include naval vessels or those repaired,' Helen added. 'As a town we have produced more than a quarter of the ships built so far during the course of this war,' she declared proudly.

Rosie watched as Matthew Royce, who was standing just behind Helen, raised his hands and clapped loudly. Seconds later, the whole shipyard followed his lead and the yard echoed with the sounds of whistling and cheers.

'What do yer think of Royce Junior?' Gloria asked Rosie, seeing her watching Helen's beau. The pair had been courting for a month and Helen claimed to be very happy with her new fella.

'Mmm,' Rosie said, observing how Dahlia, who was standing behind Matthew with Marie-Anne, had not taken her eyes off her boss. 'I'm not sure, to be honest. On the surface, he seems pretty much perfect.'

'Too good to be true?' Gloria speculated.

'Or are we just getting too cynical in our old age?' Rosie said.

Gloria laughed loudly. 'I think it's life that makes for cynicism, rather than age.'

The clapping and cheers died down and Helen continued.

'To quote the report,' Helen continued, ' "these figures give some indication of the great effort by the Wear shipbuilding firms and the people in keeping open the nation's ocean lifelines." '

Helen was handed the bottle of champagne, which had been wrapped in loose netting and was attached to a length of rope.

The words she said next were spoken with great passion.

'I hope you all feel as proud as I do today. For it is all of you who have built the ships that have helped to win this war. Make no mistake.'

And with that, Helen drew back her arm and swung the bottle at the bow of the ship. It smashed into an explosion of white spray. As it did so, the workers below yanked out the blocks of woods that had been holding *Empire Joy* back from where she belonged.

Everyone who was anyone at the launch had been invited back to the administration office at Thompson's, which had been emptied of workers. The desks had been pushed together to accommodate the buffet, and the sorting table was where the drinks were being dispensed. There was a choice of tea, port or whisky. Most of the people there were men, and so, not surprisingly, the beverage of choice was mostly whisky. Helen had asked a couple of the comptometer operators if they would serve the tea and drinks, and two of the typists if they would act as waitresses for the afternoon, to which they had agreed with unreserved enthusiasm as Helen had told them they could set aside some of the sandwiches and slices of cold pie to take home for their tea. She'd also told them that they could partake of a glass of port, but only the one. The rest of the admin staff had been given the afternoon off.

'So, Helen's got herself attached to the Royce boy?' Mr Havelock was speaking to Miriam, but his eyes were firmly focused on his granddaughter and Matthew Royce standing chatting to the mayor in the far corner of the room. 'They make quite the couple, don't they?'

Miriam took a sip of her drink and followed her father's line of vision.

'They do,' she said, pushing down the green-eyed monster. Her daughter's good looks and, even more, her youth, always rankled her. Although today she had realised there was an upside to having a daughter who outshone you, and that was being able to bask in her reflected glory. Her speech at the launch had gone down a storm – short and sweet and passionate. The workers loved her, which was some feat, considering the general consensus was that women did not have a place in the yards or the boardroom.

Miriam had spent much of the afternoon being showered with praise for producing such a wonderful daughter and being told it was clear the apple had not fallen far from the tree – especially in the looks department.

'Do you think he'll want to make an honest woman of her?' Mr Havelock probed.

Miriam dramatically spluttered on her drink. 'Not if he knows the truth, he won't.'

Mr Havelock looked at his daughter, encouraging her to go on.

'About that surgeon, *Theodore*.' Miriam kept her voice down. As much as she enjoyed the overspill from her daughter's high praise, she did not want to be tarred with the same brush if it became public knowledge that Helen had become pregnant out of wedlock – and the baby had been a married man's. *Thank God Helen had had a miscarriage.*

'Of course, of course,' Mr Havelock said. 'How could I forget?'

Mr Havelock took a sip of the cheap whisky and looked again at Helen and the Royce boy.

He and Helen had drawn swords, but so far the two had really just fenced. Now he'd seen a gap in her defence and it would be foolish of him not to take the opportunity to lunge forward and give her a short, sharp stab. Nothing fatal, of course, but enough to wound.

Matthew looked around, suddenly conscious that Helen had drifted away not just from his side, but from the launch party.

'Matthew, would you like another drink?' Dahlia asked, sidling up to him.

'No, no, thank you, Dahlia,' Matthew answered without looking at his secretary.

He continued to survey the room. Catching sight of Charles Havelock talking to his daughter, Miriam, he thought Helen might be with them, but she wasn't.

'Don't worry about me,' Matthew said, still not looking at his secretary. 'You go and enjoy yourself with the Irish girl.'

Dahlia felt like poking him in the ribs to make him look at her.

'Honestly, Matthew,' she purred, fluttering her eyelashes at him in a coquettish manner. 'The Irish girl has a name, you know.'

Matthew laughed, finally looking at Dahlia and her blue eyes, which always reminded him of sparkling sapphires. 'I know. I only say it because it annoys you.'

He looked around again and caught a glimpse of Helen through the partially opened venetian blinds in her office.

'There she is . . .' he muttered to himself as he left Dahlia.

When he reached Helen's office, he was surprised to see that the door was closed. He knocked and walked straight in.

'There you are!' he said. 'What are you doing hiding away in here?'

Helen didn't answer. She couldn't tell him it was because she couldn't bear to be within spitting distance of her grandfather for fear of what she might say – or do. Nor that she was wishing that John could have been here today to see her launching the ship.

'Didn't your mother teach you any manners?' Helen said, giving Winston the office cat one last stroke before gently picking him up from the top of her desk, where he had been parading, and putting him back in his basket.

'Why you keep that flea-bitten moggie in here is beyond me,' he said, wrinkling his nose.

Helen watched as he turned and shut the door behind him.

'You sound like my mother, Matthew.'

'Well,' he said, walking over, 'perhaps your mother has a point.'

Moving around the desk, he put his arm round Helen's waist and pulled her towards him. He started kissing Helen and she kissed him back.

'So, why don't we go for an early meal this evening and then perhaps you can come back to mine for a little nightcap?' Matthew whispered in her ear.

'Mmm,' Helen said, enjoying the feel of his arms around her and his kisses. 'A meal would be nice,' she said, as his mouth found her neck. 'But no nightcap.'

Matthew stopped kissing and looked at Helen. He was still holding her close.

'We've been courting for a month now,' Matthew argued. 'I don't think it would be unseemly for you to come back to mine and partake of a small sherry to end the evening?'

Helen stepped back and reached down for her handbag.

'A sherry might not be *unseemly*,' she said, 'but I think you'd want me to partake in more than a small sherry.' She reached into her handbag and took out her lipstick and compact.

Matthew laughed loudly. When Helen chatted and joked, she came across as a woman of the world, but when they had been on their own these past four weeks, she had been more like a Vestal Virgin. They had kissed, but whenever he had tried to go further, he had been slapped back, quite literally on occasion.

'Come on, I don't want people talking,' she said, quickly reapplying her signature Victory Red.

'If they're talking, it's only because they are jealous,' Matthew said, watching Helen snap her compact shut and drop it into her bag.

'I have a reputation to keep up,' Helen said, 'something you men don't have to worry about.' She walked over to the door to the office and opened it wide.

'Which is why every day I thank my lucky stars I was born

124

a man.' He laughed as he walked over to Helen, kissing her quickly before they went back to the party. *Perhaps that was why she was playing hard to get.*

As they both made their way over to Pickersgill's managing director to ask about their next launch, Matthew let Helen walk ahead of him. She did have the most amazing figure, which he hoped one day he would be able to enjoy in full – and not just admire from afar.

Chapter Thirteen

As soon as *Empire Joy* hit the water, Rosie left Gloria in charge of her squad and, as planned, hurried to the main gates to meet Peter and Charlotte. Peter had been given a little grey Austin 10 so that he could travel down south whenever needed by his commander at the SOE. Today it was being used to drive them over to the south side to the Holme Café in the centre of town. It was their favourite tea room and was next door to the Maison Nouvelle, which was another reason they'd chosen to go there as Charlotte was booked in to see Kate, having shot up this past year and outgrown most of her wardrobe.

Walking into the small café, Rosie was relieved to see that they'd managed to get there before the inevitable rush that followed a launch. They ordered tea for two, a hot chocolate for Charlotte, and three slices of cake, which arrived just before the first burst of customers bustled into the café.

'So, did you enjoy the launch?' Rosie asked Charlotte. She raised her china cup to her mouth and blew on her tea before taking a sip.

Charlotte nodded, giving her big sister and Peter a cheeky grin. 'Especially as it meant I got to have an afternoon off school.'

'Just remember the trade-off, though,' Rosie said.

'Yes,' Charlotte sighed, 'a five-hundred-word essay describing the launch.'

'So, what will you write about? What sticks in your mind the most?' Peter asked.

Watching Charlotte take a big bite of her Victoria sponge, Rosie said, 'And that does not include coming here and being treated.'

'The part where the ship hits the water.' Charlotte's words were muffled as she swallowed her cake. 'I always worry it'll hit the south dock.'

Rosie chuckled. 'I think that's everyone's worry.' The Wear was notoriously narrow in parts, with many difficult bends, making broadside launches tricky and dependent on the thick chains that stopped the ships crashing into the opposite side of the river, as well as on the skilled guidance of the tugboat skippers.

'Anything else which you thought was memorable?' Peter asked.

'Helen's speech was pretty good.' Charlotte gave Rosie and Peter another mischievous smile. 'And, of course, I'll have to mention the tall, dark and handsome Matthew Royce.'

Rosie rolled her eyes and suppressed a smile.

'How lucky is Helen!' Charlotte said, before taking another bite of cake.

'Or rather "How lucky is Matthew",' Rosie countered.

As Charlotte finished the last of her cake, she started to shift around on her chair a little nervously.

'Do you need the toilet?' Rosie asked, eyeing her younger sister.

Charlotte shook her head. 'No, why do you ask?'

'You just seem uncomfortable,' Rosie pointed out.

Charlotte sighed. Her sister could read her like a book sometimes.

'Actually, I wanted to ask you both a question,' she said, her attention swinging from Rosie to Peter and back to Rosie again.

'Sounds intriguing,' said Peter.

They waited.

'Well, go on, what's the question?' Rosie prodded.

'Well . . . um . . . I was wondering if you might be needing my room any time soon?' Charlotte asked hesitantly.

Rosie and Peter looked at each other, puzzled.

'You know,' Charlotte said, wiping her mouth with a napkin. 'For a nursery?'

Rosie shook her head at her sister's audacity.

Peter looked at Rosie, trying to keep the look of concern from his face.

'No, you can keep your room,' said Rosie.

A look of frustration crossed Charlotte's face. This was not the reply she was after.

Again, her eyes darted from Rosie to Peter.

'I mean, I can always go and live with Lily, you know – I wouldn't want you to think you needed to worry about me if you decided to . . . you know . . . if you decided . . .'

'Go on, spit it out, Charlie – if we decided to *what*?' Rosie asked, poker-faced.

Charlotte took a deep intake of breath.

'If you decided to have a baby.' She finally spat it out.

Rosie tried to read her sister's face. 'The room's yours for as long as you want it.' She stared intently at Charlotte. 'But if this is a subtle way of asking if you can go and live with Lily, then the answer is no.'

'No, it's not . . . I think what I'm really trying to say . . .' she took a deep breath '. . . is that if you were wanting to start a family and were worried about me for any reason whatsoever – which I could understand because of that stage I went through of being all clingy and insecure . . .' Another pause. She looked at Peter, who had been in France when she'd turned into a human limpet. She could tell that Rosie had told him all about it. 'I suppose I just want you to know that I would be fine with it – more than fine with it – I think it would be great having a niece or nephew.' She had been nervous about broaching the subject, but was glad she'd taken the plunge and had just come right out and said it. It was something Lily had told her to do if anything was playing on her mind. *Better out than in*, she'd often tell her.

'Well,' Peter said, smiling at Charlotte, 'that's a lovely thing to say. And it's also good for us to know that you feel that stage of your life when you felt . . .' he stopped, thinking of the right words to use, '. . . when, from what I heard, you felt a little *adrift* in life, well, it's good to hear that you're now past that – that you feel happier, more secure.'

'I do,' Charlotte said. 'Probably even more so since you came back,' she added a little sheepishly. She and Peter were still getting to know each other, and they weren't ones for great displays of affection, but she liked Peter. A lot.

'That's so good to hear,' Rosie said, fighting back a mix of emotions. 'But we won't be needing your room.' She smiled. 'Peter and I are more than happy just the way we are.'

Charlotte looked at her sister. 'OK, but just so you know – either way it's fine by me.'

Rosie let out a short laugh. 'Well, Charlie, we're happy you've given us the go-ahead if that's what we want to do.' She looked at her watch. 'Now go! Kate will be waiting. It's gone three.'

Grabbing her satchel, Charlotte jumped up.

'You'll come and get me when you're finished?' she asked, pushing her chair back under the table.

'Of course,' Rosie said. 'Go!'

Charlotte squeezed herself past the other seated customers and hurried out of the café.

'She's still a bit insecure, isn't she?' Peter said.

Rosie nodded. 'She is, but it'll go in time.'

Peter took a sip of his tea, put his cup back carefully in the saucer and looked at Rosie.

'Do you think she wants a niece or nephew?' Peter asked. 'I couldn't tell.'

'I honestly think she meant what she said – that she's happy either way.'

'Just as well,' Peter said, taking Rosie's hand and squeezing it. 'Are you all right?' he asked gently.

'Of course I am,' Rosie said. Her smile showed the love she held for her husband. 'I've known I'll never be able to be a mother for a long, long time now. It's not as if it's anything new, is it?' Her words were spoken without a trace of bitterness.

'It's not,' Peter conceded, 'but you weren't married back then – it was probably the last thing on your mind. But now you *are* married, it might be something you've thought about. Felt sad about, even?'

'Yes, I know,' Rosie said, 'but I really am happy the way we are. Just you, me and Charlotte – for as long as we have her.'

They were quiet for a moment.

'Perhaps we should be honest with her,' Peter said. 'She's growing up fast. And what she just said there showed a certain degree of maturity . . . And . . . if we're going to be honest with her about you not having children, then I think we have to be honest with her about everything.'

Rosie took a sip of her tea. 'You're sounding like Lily now. Ever since she told Charlie about me – and my work, my other job – she's been on at me to tell her the full story.'

Lily had told Charlotte about how her uncle Raymond, now thankfully deceased, had raped Rosie on the night of their parents' funeral, and threatened to do the same to Charlotte if she did not acquiesce to his perverted demands. And how, in order to keep her little sister safe and give her the best chance in life, Rosie had worked as one of Lily's girls to earn the money to send her to boarding school.

'Much as I don't exactly relish being compared to Lily, however fond of her I am,' Peter said, 'I do, however, agree with her. Charlotte will have to know the whole truth sooner rather than later. And, like Lily said the other day, it will be good to tell her well before she flies the nest. Give her plenty of time to digest what really happened to your parents.'

'I just worry how it might affect her,' Rosie said.

'Well, we're here to catch her if she falls,' Peter reassured.

Rosie took Peter's hand. There wasn't a day that went by when she didn't thank her lucky stars Peter was part of her life. Not only that she had met him, and that he had fallen as heavily in love with her as she had with him, but that he was here now, and not still buried under a bombed building in France, like the rest of his unit.

'I love you, Peter Miller,' she said tenderly.

Chapter Fourteen

Eleven days later

Saturday 24 March

As Helen drove slowly down the Ryhope Road, she glanced at Henrietta in the passenger seat. She appeared surprisingly relaxed and was looking out, quite enrapt, at the passing buildings and street life. She had asked Helen to slow down as they passed the rather magnificent synagogue with its beautiful stained-glass windows and oversized, arched entrance. Helen had realised, on her grandmother's return to the real world, just how many buildings had gone up in the town since her incarceration. The synagogue, which she knew to be the one Hannah and Rina attended, was one of them.

'Did you know,' Henrietta said, 'that the exterior is an art deco interpretation of Byzantine style?'

Helen shook her head. 'No, that's interesting, Grandmama.' She had learnt that one of her grandmother's loves, along with books and fashion, was architecture.

'So, you'll be all right?' she asked anxiously as she turned off the Ryhope Road into Villette Road. She wondered if her grandmother's intense interest in the passing sights was shielding her nerves about her imminent meeting with Mrs Evans.

Indicating, she waited for a tram to pass, before turning right into Hunter Terrace.

'I'll be fine, Helen. You worry too much,' Henrietta reassured her.

Helen parked up outside number 22, the address given to her by Pearl.

'I think it's only natural that I'm a little concerned,' Helen said. 'I feel you might be walking into the lion's den.' *Going to see the mother of the young girl who was raped by your husband and made pregnant, who then gave up the baby and hanged herself, certainly did not bode well for a pleasant afternoon of tea for two.*

'A lion's den holds no fear for me, darling,' Henrietta said. 'If I get mauled, then so be it. I'm just so glad I have the chance to come here.'

Helen got out of the car to help her grandmother.

'I'll be back in an hour,' she said. 'If you want to leave earlier, ring the Tatham. I've put the number on a piece of paper in your handbag. I can be here within minutes.'

Henrietta patted her granddaughter's hand.

'Rest assured I will, although I'm certain there will be no need. Now stop fussing and go and enjoy yourself at Joe Elliot's party.' Bel's husband Joe had been awarded a medal for his service in North Africa and there was to be a celebration at the Tatham.

Helen walked back round the car to the driver's side, all the time watching as her grandmother walked to the front door and knocked. As soon as the door opened and Helen saw Mrs Evans, she stopped dead in her tracks and stared at the small, rotund woman. *She knew her. Recognised the face.* Although she was sure her hair had been grey – but she could be mistaken. On both occasions it had been partially covered by a headscarf.

As Helen continued to scrutinise Mrs Evans, the older woman looked over at her and held her gaze for a brief moment, before turning and closing the door.

It *was* her.

It was the cleaner from Mr Emery's.

Helen got into her car and pulled away. Her mind flashed back to her visits to Mr Emery's solicitor's office just off the Hendon Road in the town's east end. She had seen Mrs Evans there on each occasion. *How strange. Such a coincidence.* Or was it? *If Mr Emery employed Mrs Evans as his cleaner, did that mean he, too, had known Gracie?*

Helen did a three-point turn and headed back down the street. She did the maths in her head. *If Gracie had lived, she would be in her mid forties. Around the same age as Mr Emery. Had the two known each other?*

Indicating right, Helen pulled out and drove down Villette Road.

Was that why Mr Emery had been the only solicitor willing to take on her father's divorce? The only one who would go up against the daughter of the revered Charles Havelock?

*

Mrs Evans stopped and stared for the briefest of moments at Charles Havelock's granddaughter. Helen Crawford was a stunning woman with her jet black hair and piercing green eyes. Mrs Evans had thought on seeing her up close for the first time at Ethan's offices last year that she must have inherited her father's looks as she was nothing like her mother or grandfather with their fair hair and blue eyes. Now, as she welcomed Henrietta into her home, she realised that the girl was actually very like her grandmother. You could certainly see that the two were related.

'Come in.' Mrs Evans shut the door while Henrietta's granddaughter was still staring at her. By the look on her face, she must have recognised her. She'd have to make sure Helen didn't see her if she ever visited her grandfather. She couldn't risk her true identity being revealed. Not until the time was right, anyway.

Turning her attention to her guest, she took her coat and let Henrietta stand for a moment in the hallway, from where she could clearly see the bannisters from which Gracie had hanged herself. Mrs Evans watched as Henrietta's gaze travelled up the stairs. She could still hear the scream – *her* scream – that had filled the house and had the neighbours banging on the door to see what was wrong. She could still see Gibson's desperate attempts to free their beautiful dead daughter from her noose, the frantic look – the desperate hope that he might be able to resurrect his beloved Gracie.

*

When Helen reached the Tatham, her mind was still churning over what she had learnt about Mrs Evans's connection to Mr Emery. She wished she had invited him here today. She would have been able to quiz him about the relationship. Helen's gut told her that Mrs Evans was more than just an employee.

Walking into the lounge area of the pub, Helen immediately spotted Rosie and the rest of the women at a table in the corner. They were such a distinctive, mixed bunch it was hard not to notice them.

As soon as she reached them, they all stopped talking and looked at her expectantly.

'Have you dropped her off?' Gloria asked.

Helen nodded. 'I have.'

'Was everything OK?' said Rosie.

The women stared at Helen, awaiting her response. They all knew that not only was this Henrietta's first outing in the three months since she'd been discharged from the hospital – but that her reason for leaving the safety of her new home was to see Gracie's mam. Not exactly a social call.

'Everything *seemed* all right. As far as I could tell,' Helen said, checking her watch. 'I suppose I'll find out soon enough. I've got an hour before I go and pick her up.'

'Fingers crossed,' Dorothy said.

'Yeah, fingers crossed,' Angie repeated.

The women murmured their agreement. They all had a real soft spot for Henrietta after meeting her for the first time at the Christmas Extravaganza.

'Well, I think she's a brave woman,' Polly said.

On hearing about the intended visit, they had all concurred that it would not be inconceivable for Mrs Evans to take her anger out on Henrietta. Even if it was just verbal, they'd said, it would still be awful.

'Let's just hope that Mrs Evans doesn't blame Henrietta for what happened to her daughter,' said Hannah.

'Not that she should,' Martha chipped in.

Again, the women voiced their wholehearted agreement.

'Let me get a round in,' Helen said, looking down at the table and seeing that most of their glasses were almost empty.

Before anyone had time to object, Helen turned and

started to make her way over to the bar. She made slow progress as the pub was already almost full.

Seeing Joe at the far corner of the bar, she waved over to him. He looked every inch the brave soldier in his army uniform – and Bel, who was by his side, was looking every inch the proud wife. The pair were chatting to Major Black. Lucille was by his side, gripping the armrest of his wheelchair, her head gently resting on his shoulder as she listened to the grown-ups chatting.

Arriving at the bar, Bill greeted her. 'Hello, Helen, grand to see you.' Bill always liked to make Helen feel welcome as she was not exactly a typical regular with her stunning good looks and expensive clothes. Some of the locals stared at her as though she were a sideshow at the circus.

Feeling himself being nudged out of the way by Pearl, Bill stepped aside.

'Let me guess, another round for yer mates 'n a drink for my son-in-law – the war hero?'

Helen smiled and nodded. It was probably the first time she'd heard Pearl refer to Joe as her son-in-law. She guessed she wanted to remind everyone that she was related to the man of the moment.

As Pearl started pulling a pint of Vaux for Joe, she raised her eyes up to Helen's.

'Everything gan all reet at Mrs Evans's?' She was still surprised that Henrietta wanted to chat to Mrs Evans, never mind that Mrs Evans wanted to speak to Henrietta.

'Well, she's there now. I've just dropped her off – and Mrs Evans let her in. But who knows how it'll go when they start chatting? I said if there were any problems to ring the pub.' Helen looked over at the phone behind the bar.

'I'll get yer if she calls,' Pearl said, before waving over at Joe and pointing at the pint and then at Helen.

Joe grabbed his walking stick and made his way round a group of old workmates from Bartram's shipyard with whom he still kept in contact.

'Thank you, Helen,' Joe said. 'You shouldn't have.'

'There's plenty'll have it if yer dinnit want it,' Pearl butted in, before ordering Bill to help her get the rest of the women's round sorted.

*

'I'm sorry I wasn't able to see you sooner,' Mrs Evans said as she showed her daughter's former employer into the living room. 'I've recently started a new job and I've been busier than usual.'

Henrietta waved a hand to dismiss Mrs Evans's apology. 'Not at all. I'm just thankful you've agreed to see me.'

Mrs Evans went to fetch the pot of tea that was brewing in the kitchen. When she returned, she found Henrietta standing by the mantelpiece, holding the silver-framed black-and-white photograph of Gracie. It was the only picture Mrs Evans had of her daughter and had been taken by Mr Clement, the east end photographer whose fees were just about affordable to working folk.

Putting the brown ceramic teapot down on the coffee table, Mrs Evans straightened up and joined Henrietta in looking at the photograph of her daughter, who was, of course, the reason why they were both here in this room.

Henrietta put the photograph back. Her vision had become blurred, but she was determined not to allow any tears to fall whilst she was with Mrs Evans over the course of the next hour. It would feel wrong. Very wrong. Her own deep sorrow and grief for little Gracie were incomparable to Mrs Evans's suffering.

'She looked like an angel, didn't she?' Mrs Evans said as she sat down.

'She did,' Henrietta agreed. 'I used to tell her just that.'

'I know,' said Mrs Evans, stirring the tea in the pot, then gesturing for Henrietta to sit down too. 'She used to come back home and tell me everything you said.'

'Did she really?' Henrietta asked, again feeling the tears smart. 'I used to say all my maids were my favourites, but Gracie really was.'

'And she thought the world of you too,' Mrs Evans said, pouring their tea and handing Henrietta her cup. 'Her father and I were so happy when she got a job at "the big house" – that's what we all used to call your home, "the big house".' There was bitterness in Mrs Evans's tone as she said the words, recalling that time – a time of naïvety, when working at 'the big house', for such rich, important people, was something to feel thankful for. Even to boast about.

Mrs Evans picked up her own cup and saucer, but didn't take a sip. 'I said to Gibson, "That's it – Gracie's sorted. She's got a job she loves. A mistress she adores. A job for life. Or at least until she meets someone and wants to marry and start a family."' As she spoke, Mrs Evans thought of Ethan. *Poor Ethan.* Another victim.

What she was going to do, she would do for him too.

'A job for life which ended in her death,' Henrietta said, her eyes fixed on Mrs Evans. She could see – almost feel – her pain, her bitterness, her heartbreak.

Mrs Evans put her tea back on the coffee table. Suddenly she didn't feel like she could keep anything down.

'Did you not know? Did you really have no idea, Henrietta?' Mrs Evans beseeched her.

Did you not know your own husband was violating my daughter in your 'big house'? Under your roof? Under your nose?

The words were unspoken but hung heavy in the air.

Henrietta shook her head. 'I didn't.' She fixed her eyes on Mrs Evans. 'But I want you to know that I don't expect that to be viewed as any kind of defence. That not knowing somehow equates to not being to blame.' A pause. 'Quite the reverse.' Henrietta clasped her hands, her eyes still on Mrs Evans. 'I blame myself for *not* knowing. For *not* realising.' Henrietta's face had become flushed. 'For being so stupid. So completely stupid. *Stupid. Stupid. Stupid.*'

Mrs Evans looked at Henrietta. She was dressed more conservatively than when she had seen her all those years ago, but just now she'd seen a glimpse of a slight instability of mind. She had guessed from what Gracie had told her about her employer that she was a little off-kilter. She leant forward and put her hand on top of the knot of Henrietta's cold, clasped hands.

'You see,' Henrietta continued, 'I'm not a stupid person. I'm quite intelligent, educated, well read. There was no excuse for me not knowing what was going on back then.' She felt a chill go down her spine just thinking about her husband's atrocities.

Mrs Evans sat back. She knew that Henrietta was speaking the truth.

'The mind is a strange thing,' Mrs Evans said. 'Perhaps it

was fooling you, blinding you to reality because it was too awful for you to contemplate.'

Mrs Evans had often wondered if this had been the case with herself. That somewhere in her mind she had known what was happening to Gracie but would not allow herself to acknowledge it. When she had finally learnt the horrible truth, she had looked back and realised that there had been a change in her daughter. A subtle change – but a marked one, all the same. Gracie had become more withdrawn. She should have asked her if something was wrong. But she hadn't. She had been working full-time at the launderette, and Gibson had been working all hours at the glass factory. They had mentioned it once when Gracie had gone to bed early, but had simply put it down to her age. She was growing up, becoming a woman. Which was why Mrs Evans hadn't thought too much about the initial changes in her daughter's body. She was simply filling out.

Mrs Evans forced herself to breathe normally. She realised she had been holding her breath, something she found herself doing when thinking of the circumstances surrounding her daughter's death.

'Did you ever think,' Mrs Evans asked Henrietta, 'that your husband might have done the same to your daughters?'

'It has gone through my mind many times. Many times,' Henrietta said. 'And during those times I have had a glimpse of what you as a mother would have gone through on realising that such an abomination had been inflicted on your daughter.' She paused. 'But no, in answer to your question, no, I don't think Charles touched either of my daughters. But that's not to say I don't believe he didn't want to.'

141

Again, Henrietta felt the tears and fought them back. 'The irony, the terrible irony, is that I missed my daughters so terribly because, as I'm sure you know through Gracie, both Miriam and Margaret spent very little time at home. First boarding school and then finishing school. And because I missed them so, I employed young girls who looked very much like them – blonde hair and blue eyes.'

Henrietta looked at Mrs Evans with eyes that spoke of her lifelong torment.

'I ended up being an unwitting procurer for my husband,' she said. 'I might not have done it on purpose, but I enabled him. And for that I will always carry the burden of guilt.' She paused. 'An apology seems an almost pitiful offering, but it is all I have to give you – my deepest, most heartfelt apology that I was a part of what happened to your daughter.'

Mrs Evans heard the deep sincerity in Henrietta's voice – saw the grief in the darkness of her eyes.

'So, this is the reason you have come today – to ask me for my forgiveness?' she asked.

Henrietta gave a sad smile. 'Your forgiveness would be welcome – more than welcome – but I don't expect it. Most of all, I just needed you to hear how sorry I am – and also, how much I cared for your daughter.'

Mrs Evans looked at Henrietta and knew that the guilt had eaten away at her for all these years.

'I will forgive you if that helps to ease the burden I can see you carry – and which has clearly weighed on you so heavily.' Mrs Evans sighed. 'But you are not the one who needs to be forgiven – or is in any way to blame. I, too, have blamed myself and also had to forgive myself, having realised that I've been looking at the wrong culprit. There really is only one person to blame – and that is Charles Havelock. His guilt is made greater still by his refusal in any way to acknowledge that what he did to Gracie, and Pearl, and to the others whose names I don't know, was not only unlawful, but unholy and evil.'

Henrietta had heard similar words before from Helen and also from her lovely seamstress Kate, but it was only now, at this very moment, hearing the words spoken with such power and conviction by Gracie's mother, that she finally – *finally* – began to believe that she was not to blame.

After all these years, she could take off the heavy cloak of guilt and lay it at the feet of the man who should have been wearing it all along.

'After Gibson died,' Mrs Evans continued, 'I had a kind of epiphany. I realised that it was easier to blame myself for what happened to Gracie, because then I wouldn't have to do what I knew deep down *had* to be done.'

Henrietta looked puzzled.

'Sometimes it's easier to punish yourself than someone else,' Mrs Evans explained.

'Are you saying,' Henrietta asked, 'that the time has now come to punish the person who really is to blame for what happened to your daughter?'

Mrs Evans nodded and poured them each another cup of tea.

Chapter Fifteen

As soon as Helen left to get the drinks in, Dorothy scanned the women's faces. 'Do you think our plan will work?'

'I think Marie-Anne will sort out what she's got to do without too much of a bother,' Polly said.

'She can be a reet bossyboots, can't she?' Angie eyed her best mate. 'Worse than Dor here.'

Everyone chuckled.

'I think you're right there,' Polly said. 'Even with Dahlia, who likes to think she's the Queen Bee.'

On hearing Dahlia's name, Dorothy pulled an expression as though she'd just tasted something thoroughly unpalatable.

The women laughed.

'What's Dahlia got to do with all of this anyway?' Dorothy asked. 'I hope Marie-Anne's not told her anything.'

Hannah shook her head. 'She hasn't. I think the plan was to get Dahlia to concoct some last-minute job that needed to be done ahead of *Moraybank* being launched on Monday, especially as Short Brothers are launching *Empire Dominica* on Monday as well.'

'Good idea,' Rosie said. There was always a little friendly rivalry when there were two launches on the same day to see which yard attracted the biggest crowds.

'Something that would either make him late,' Martha added, 'or force him to cancel altogether.'

'I'm sure Dahlia will manage that no problem,' Dorothy added bitchily.

'Yeah, especially as I reckon she's got the hots for Matthew,' Angie said.

'What makes you say that?' Gloria asked.

'Dahlia's got the hots for anyone who's either good-looking or rich, and Matthew Royce ticks both those boxes,' Dorothy said with conviction.

Gloria looked at Rosie, whose expression showed she did not disagree with Dorothy and Angie.

'Shh,' Polly said, just as Helen reached them.

'Here we go.' Helen put the tray of drinks on the table.

'Yer one short,' Angie declared.

'You've forgotten your own drink,' Hannah pointed out.

'Honestly,' Helen laughed. 'I'd forget my head if it was loose. I'll be back in a minute.'

'I'll get it for yer,' offered Gloria.

'No, no, I won't be a minute,' Helen said. 'Just save me a seat. It's getting busier in here by the minute.'

Gloria smiled and watched as Helen made her way through the growing throng to the bar. There was a time when she would have been nervous as hell being in a pub like the Tatham and sitting with them all en masse, but not any more. It was good to see.

'So,' Hannah asked the women when Helen was out of earshot, 'do you think Georgina seemed confident that *her* plan would work?'

'Of course, when Georgie says she's gonna dee summat, she does it,' Angie said, her voice full of admiration.

'Talk of the devil,' said Martha, looking over to the lounge door.

They all followed her line of vision and watched as Georgina quickly made her way over to them.

'Did you do it?' Dorothy asked, eyes wide, as soon as Georgina reached their table.

Martha pulled out a stool and Georgina sat down.

'I did,' she said, a little breathless.

'Do you think it'll work?' Polly asked.

'Of course,' Georgina said. 'She has no option. She has to fill in if someone calls in sick, or –' she looked at the women conspiratorially '– there has been a mistake in the weekly rota.'

'I can't help but feel this is all a bit underhand,' Rosie said.

'You might think differently when you hear what I found out,' said Georgina.

The women leant forward.

'It would appear that when it comes to love, Dr Claire Eris has no qualms about playing dirty.'

'No surprise there,' said Dorothy.

Georgina looked round the table as she took a sip of the orange juice that Angie had just handed her.

'Go on,' Gloria encouraged.

'Well, it would seem that the old receptionist at the Ryhope – a woman called Denise – was actually tipping off Dr Eris whenever Helen called Dr Parker. They had an agreement that if the receptionist "forgot" to pass on messages to Dr Parker from Helen, then Dr Eris would endeavour to set her up with an eligible doctor.'

'Never!' Polly was shocked.

'Cor, that *is* really underhand,' Angie said, glancing at Rosie.

'How did yer get to know that?' Gloria asked, aghast that someone could be so devious.

'I'm afraid I can't reveal a contact,' said Georgina.

'But it's definitely true?' Rosie asked.

'Definitely,' said Georgina. She would have liked to tell them that it was one hundred per cent true, as she had heard it directly from the horse's mouth. That she had decided to accidentally run into the former receptionist simply in order to find out any kind of gossip from the hospital, only to end up hearing a rather guilt-ridden confession. Denise, who was now married to the father of one of the doctors Dr Eris had set her up with, had felt terribly guilty about what she had done on behalf of Dr Eris, but she'd also been terribly desperate not to be left on the shelf.

'So, if she wasn't calling him, or returning his calls,' Martha said, 'that would have made Dr Parker think Helen wasn't bothered about him.'

'And vice versa,' Dorothy added.

'Exactly,' said Georgina.

They were quiet for a moment.

'Do yer think we're doing the right thing?' Gloria asked.

'Definitely,' said Dorothy.

Just then the lounge door opened and Maisie appeared, along with Vivian, Lily, Charlotte and George.

Rosie waved over to them.

'George's got his uniform on,' observed Hannah, surprised.

'And his medals,' said Martha. Everyone knew of George's reticence about broadcasting the fact that he had won medals for bravery in the First War.

'He didn't want to,' Polly said, 'but Joe asked if everyone who had served their country would wear their uniform – and medals.'

'To deflect the attention away from himself, I'm guessing,' Rosie said.

Polly nodded. Her brother had not seen the need for a medal. Despite losing much of the mobility in his right leg, Joe said his reward was simply surviving. Unlike his twin brother, Teddy.

'Oh. My. God.' Dorothy grabbed Angie's arm and squeezed it.

'What's wrong?' asked Gloria.

'Dr Parker,' Hannah said.

'He's here,' Martha added.

'Without that cow,' Angie said, prising Dorothy's talon-like grip from her arm.

Rosie and Gloria looked at each other and raised their eyebrows. They had been in two minds as to whether they should be meddling in Helen's love life.

The women watched transfixed as Dr Parker entered the lounge bar. He stood for a moment, his eyes scanning the smoky room before he found who he was looking for.

They continued watching as his face lit up – as did Helen's, when she saw him heading towards her.

'No Claire today?' Helen asked as soon as Dr Parker reached her. She looked over his shoulder, hoping Dr Eris wasn't behind him.

'No,' Dr Parker said, 'she got called away at the last moment. She sends her apologies.'

Helen felt her heart lift. Dr Parker kissed her on her cheek, and she returned the gesture, forcing herself to pull away when all she wanted to do was kiss him back – his neck, his lips, breathing in the smell of his skin.

'Oh, never mind,' Helen said, trying her hardest to keep her feelings under wraps. *God, if she'd known, she wouldn't have invited Matthew. The only reason she had was because she thought Claire would be here, lording it over her.*

'Let me get you a drink,' she said. 'And then you can tell me all your news.'

A few minutes later, they had managed to find a quiet spot at the end of the bar where they could chat. Helen listened intently as Dr Parker told her about his 'new recruits', and how the majority of the hospital's intake were now released prisoners of war, most of whom had been captured during the evacuation of Dunkirk or the war in Libya.

Helen confided in Dr Parker about how her superiors had warned her that the seven hundred or so women working in the shipyards on the Wear would be expected to step aside when the men came back from war. 'Which might be sooner than expected,' she said.

Dr Parker nodded his understanding. Last weekend, there'd been a major push into German territory and all resistance in the Ruhr had ended, with hundreds of thousands of prisoners taken.

'How do you think the women will react to being told to go?' Dr Parker asked, glancing over at the table in the far corner where they were all sitting.

Helen sighed. 'Well, I've chatted to Rosie about it, and she's gutted, obviously. She's had a really hard-working, all-woman squad under her these past five years and she's going to miss them dreadfully.'

Dr Parker looked over at Rosie, who was chatting to Gloria.

'Do you think Rosie will stay working at Thompson's?'

'Oh, yes, the yard's Rosie's life. Well, a part of it . . .' Neither of them needed to say that Lily's was the other part.

'But she's married – and Peter's back?' Dr Parker raised his eyebrows, not needing to say the obvious.

'That might well be,' Helen mused, 'but I just don't see Rosie suddenly packing in work to start a family.'

'No?'

'No,' Helen said, 'I think she's happy the way she is – with the life she has.'

'Well, that's an enviable position to be in,' Dr Parker said.

Helen looked at him. 'A position I'd have thought you're in – as a soon-to-be-married man?'

Dr Parker forced a smile. 'Of course, and I am.' *God, why did he sound totally unconvincing?* 'And the rest of her squad?' he asked, wanting to change the subject. 'Do you think they might be a little miffed that they're being booted out to make way for the men coming back?'

'Yes and no,' Helen said. 'Yes, because it seems to belittle all the hard work they've done – and the skills they've acquired – but, at the same time, deep down, I don't think they'll be too upset.'

Dr Parker looked surprised.

'I think they've all got things they want to go off and do,' Helen said.

'Is Hannah still determined to find her parents?' Dr Parker asked.

'Yep, ever since the news of the Red Army's liberation of the Auschwitz concentration camp – but her aunt Rina is still determined that it's too dangerous for her to go.' Helen glanced across to Hannah before looking back at John, a grim expression on her face.

Dr Parker looked at Helen. 'Do you still feel guilty? About the way you treated Hannah when she first started?'

'I do,' Helen said. 'I keep wanting to apologise to her properly about being so awful. I can't believe I did it, to be honest.' Helen had tried to get shot of Hannah by giving her jobs she knew would be too much for her. 'The only reason Hannah wanted to work in the yard was to help the war effort.' Helen sighed. 'And there was I, trying to stop her. All because I wanted to split up the squad to get back at Polly for courting Tommy.' She shook her head in disbelief at her former self. 'I was a different person back then.'

'But it all worked out for the best,' Dr Parker countered. 'Hannah ended up being much happier in the drawing office. And far more useful.'

'I know, but that's not the point,' said Helen. 'I need to tell her how sorry I am. It's just about finding the right moment.'

'Well, I for one look forward to that time. Even though you have more than made up for your past transgressions.'

'You will be the first to know when I do,' Helen said. *If you're still here.*

'And what about Dorothy?' Dr Parker asked, bringing the subject back to the women and what they would do once the war was over. 'Is Dorothy still determined to become a female version of Phileas Fogg?'

Helen laughed. 'Yes, only on a ship rather than a balloon, and with Bobby rather than some French manservant – oh, and I think she intends to be away for much longer than eighty days.

'And Angie's going to be a married woman soon,' Helen continued.

'Of course,' Dr Parker smiled.

151

'And as for Polly, I really don't think Tommy will want her staying on at the yard even if she's allowed to – not with Artie at home.'

'And I'm guessing they'll also want more children?' Dr Parker asked.

'Exactly,' Helen agreed. 'Polly's said that Tommy has always wanted a big family. I'm guessing to make up for the fact he never had much of a one himself.'

Dr Parker knew Tommy's father had died in the First War and his mother had killed herself shortly afterwards. He had no other siblings and had been brought up by his grandparents.

Helen desperately wanted to ask John if he and Claire had talked about having a family. It hurt her just thinking about it, but it was something she had found herself wondering about more and more of late. Claire was at the age when most women of her class were having their first child – and it would explain the short engagement.

'And Gloria?' Dr Parker asked.

'She's done her bit,' said Helen. 'She wants to be at home with Hope and to be what she calls a "proper wife" to Jack.'

'Which leaves Martha?' said Dr Parker.

'It does.' Helen sighed heavily. 'Anyone in their right mind can see that Martha was born to work in the shipyards. It's just convincing the powers that be what an asset she is. And could continue to be.'

Dr Parker laughed loudly. 'Well, if anyone's going to convince them, Helen, you will.'

'What do you think?' Dorothy asked the women, her eyes darting surreptitiously to where Helen and Dr Parker were chatting.

'They look like they're very involved in what they're talking about,' Hannah said.

'And they're stood quite close together, aren't they?' Polly pointed out.

'Yer can see they fancy each other,' said Angie, feeling guilty that Helen's true love had hit a brick wall, in part because her own mam was having it off with some bloke.

'They've definitely only got eyes for each other,' Rosie said. Seeing them together, she was more convinced that they had done the right thing.

'Let's just hope we've bought them enough time,' said Georgina.

'Yeah, at least given them a few hours together,' Martha said, still angry that her family secret was being used to keep the pair apart.

'But is it going to be enough time to make Dr Parker realise that Helen's the woman for him – not Miss Manipulative?' Dorothy queried.

'It's a long shot,' said Gloria.

'But we can hope,' said Hannah.

Rosie looked at the group's 'little bird'. She was always so optimistic.

'And if he does,' Polly said, 'Dr Eris can't blame Helen, as it'll just be a natural end to their relationship.'

Rosie looked at her friends. They had all found love: Polly had met and married Tommy, Dorothy had found her Mr Right in Bobby, Angie had found her soulmate in Quentin, as had Hannah with Olly, and Gloria had finally been reunited with Jack and was now his wife. Even Martha had started to see Adam, the Salvation Army tuba player she'd met at the extravaganza, although she was at pains to stress that he was *just a friend*.

It was clear that what they all now wanted, more than anything, was for Helen to find love too.

*

It was a release for both Mrs Evans and Henrietta to talk so candidly, for they had held so much inside for so long.

Mrs Evans took comfort in recounting to Henrietta how when Gracie had given up the baby for adoption, something had changed within her. 'It was as if a part of her died. The life seemed to just leave her. Or rather, the will to live did. Now I look back, I think the same could be said of Gibson. He never recovered from Gracie's death, and perhaps never wanted to. I think he only stayed alive all these years for me.' Mrs Evans's eyes flicked to their wedding photograph, when life had seemed so simple – so untarnished.

'And what happened to Gracie's son after he was adopted?' Henrietta asked. She wondered if Mr and Mrs Evans would have wanted their grandchild in their lives. After all, the boy was as much his mother's child as he was his father's.

Mrs Evans simply shook her head. 'Gracie gave up all rights to the baby when she handed him over for adoption.' She fell silent. 'So,' she asked eventually, 'what happened after I left you that Christmas Day all those years ago – after I told you about Gracie?'

'Oh,' Henrietta sighed. 'A long story. And not a particularly pleasant one.'

'Tell me,' Mrs Evans asked. 'I want to hear.'

And so Henrietta told her the story of how Charles had paid an unscrupulous doctor to have her sectioned and carted off to the asylum. She spoke of how desperately she had wanted to do what she could to help other maids who might find themselves prey to Charles's deprived perversions in the future, and of how powerless she'd felt.

Mrs Evans listened with growing consternation. She remembered well her own last words to Henrietta. She had told her the lives of those who entered the Havelock residence rested on her shoulders – and that it would be on her conscience if any other young girls should suffer like Gracie had.

She had added to Henrietta's guilt.

'I tried to tell every doctor who I spoke to after I'd been admitted to the hospital that Charles was violating innocent young girls in his employ, but, of course, no one listened . . . Charles was very clever – he'd told them I would be making such claims and that I had become delusional, that I'd always been "a little touched" and hooked on Gothic fiction, and as a result, my mind had become "diseased" . . . The more I talked, and the more accusations I made, the more drugs they gave me, and the more disorientated I became. I even started to believe that I really was delusional.'

This was the first time Henrietta had spoken of her life at the asylum and it was a relief.

She had just finished telling her story when the doorbell rang. It was Helen. Feeling they had more to talk about, Mrs Evans asked if Henrietta would like to stay longer and continue their chat.

'Most definitely. I feel as though I have been waiting

a lifetime for this moment,' Henrietta said, as she went to reassure Helen that everything was fine and that she would ring for a taxi when she was ready to leave.

*

Driving back to the Tatham, Helen was glad that her grandmother seemed all right. More than all right. Happy would be too strong a word to describe her demeanour – more 'at peace', perhaps.

She thought of her grandfather and of all the suffering he had caused, and was still causing. She had just left two of his victims trying to find solace in each other from the hardship and heartache he had caused them and their families.

At least, for now, she had managed to put him in a hold whereby he was unable to do any more harm – a precarious one, but a hold all the same.

As she drove along the Suffolk Road, her mind wandered to John. She felt a buzz at being able to return to the celebration earlier than anticipated – or rather, at being able to return to John.

Reaching Tatham Street, Helen parked up and gave a few of the children who had come to admire her sports car some coins in return for looking after it. She laughed when they offered to wash it for a shilling. She bent over to shake their little hands.

'A gentlewoman's agreement,' she told them.

They looked at the very posh and very glamorous woman and nodded mutely. As soon as she had turned to go into the pub, they rushed off to get a bucket of soapy water. The car, they were determined, would be so clean by the time they'd finished with it that 'yer'd be able to eat yer dinner off it', as their mams often said.

Walking back into the pub, Helen quickly scanned the room and felt a stab of guilt at feeling happy that Matthew still hadn't turned up. He'd probably got held back at work. She automatically looked to where she and John had been talking by the end of the bar. He was still there, chatting to Bobby and Olly. It would seem the gods were looking favourably upon her.

She sighed heavily as she made her way over to him.

Who was she fooling?

She might well have a hold over her grandfather, but the one Dr Eris had over Helen was so tight, it almost choked.

*

When Henrietta came back from waving Helen off, Mrs Evans topped up their cups of tea.

'Now,' she said, taking a sip and sitting back, 'I want to hear how you ended up at the Royal?' Pearl had told her snippets of what had happened, but she was keen to know more.

She listened carefully as Henrietta explained that she had only got to know the cause of her illness relatively recently. Helen had told her one evening not long after she had been discharged from hospital. She'd been shocked, but also not surprised. Nothing surprised her when it came to Charles.

Henrietta explained to Mrs Evans that she had been poisoned by a plant that in the last century used to cause a fatal illness in adults called 'milk sickness'. It had not only killed off livestock, but all those who drank the milk and ate the meat of the cattle that had fed on the poisonous plant.

Mrs Evans listened intently on hearing that both Henrietta and Helen were of the opinion that although the plant could be found in the town's Winter Gardens, it was highly likely that Charles had cultivated his own 'white snakeroot' plant in the huge greenhouse in the grounds of her former home.

Henrietta gave a sad smile.

'When I was drifting in and out of consciousness,' she said, 'I kept thinking of Gracie . . . I could feel her near . . . I'd have been happy to go, if I'm honest. But then I kept hearing Helen's voice, demanding I live, saying she needed me and I wasn't to give up . . . And here am I, although what benefit I am to Helen is still beyond me.'

'It sounds as though she *does* need you,' Mrs Evans demurred. 'I hope you don't mind me speaking out of turn, but from the bits and pieces I've picked up, your daughter Miriam does not seem to be the best mother in the world.'

'I'm beginning to see that,' Henrietta admitted.

Henrietta then confided in Mrs Evans about all the women welders' secrets and how Charles had threatened to expose those secrets if his own crimes were made public, and if Henrietta's real identity were ever to be revealed. Hearing this made Mrs Evans feel even more determined to do what she had planned to do. For this was no longer just about Gracie, but about all those others whose lives he was threatening to ruin.

'As we're both being so open and honest,' Mrs Evans said, 'and I feel as though I can trust you?'

Henrietta nodded.

'Well, then,' Mrs Evans said, 'I'd like to tell you about my new job. And the reason for it.'

*

After everyone had enjoyed a few drinks and caught up with those they hadn't seen for a while, Joe nodded to Pearl, who crushed out her cigarette and marched over to the brass bell at the end of the optics. She gave it a good clang, but not as aggressively as if it was for last orders.

'Dinnit worry,' she shouted out from behind the bar. 'Yer've still got a few hours left. Our Joe here wants to say a few words. So, if yer can all shut yer gobs for a few moments – I knar that's hard for some of yer here – and give my son-in-law a chance to speak.'

Joe was standing by the bar, holding a small blue box, inside which was his military campaign medal – the Africa Star. He looked uncomfortable with everyone's eyes on him and the quietness that had descended.

'Sorry to disturb,' he said. 'I just wanted to say a quick word.'

He cleared his throat nervously and shifted his weight onto his good leg.

'I'm chuffed to pieces that I've been given this medal.'

He opened the box and held it up for people to see.

'Just as I am that our Teddy has also been awarded the same medal.'

The pub seemed to go even quieter at the mention of Teddy Elliot, whom many had known growing up on this very street, and others from his years working as a riveter.

Joe looked over at Bel and saw her eyes were already shining with tears. Agnes looked like she, too, was finding it hard to keep her emotions in check.

'Teddy was the best brother to me and our Pol and husband to Bel – and if he had lived longer, I know without a doubt that he would have been the best da in the world to his daughter, Lucille.'

Joe put his hand out to Lucille, who was standing a few yards away, between Bel and Maisie.

'Come here, LuLu,' he coaxed. 'This medal is yours to look after,' he said, pulling out an identical blue box from inside his khaki uniform and handing it to the little girl whom he loved as though she were his own daughter. 'You can show it to everyone today, if you want?'

Lucille nodded vigorously. She took the box and opened it, staring at the shiny medal, then back up at the man who was her 'other daddy'. She turned and proudly walked back to her mam and aunty.

'There's a part of me doesn't feel deserving of being singled out and given a medal for my service to King and country –' there were a few rumbles of disagreement '– for I believe wholeheartedly that every man, and every woman . . .' Joe looked over at his sister and her workmates '. . . who has been working hard in the shipyards, and in the factories, and down the mines, and all those in the Home Guard, and all those doctors and nurses who have been saving lives –' he looked across at Dr Parker '– and all those who have been fighting behind enemy lines and whose work has had to be kept a secret . . .' He glanced over at Peter.

He raised his voice.

'They *all* deserve a medal.'

There was a gentle ripple of agreement across the room.

'So, the toast I'd like to make is to everyone who is on the side of goodness and what is right – may victory come soon, as soon as possible, before any more lives are lost.'

Joe looked across the crowded pub and knew that just about everyone here had lost someone they loved or cared for.

'To victory!' Joe declared, raising his glass.

'To victory!' everyone chorused.

As Bel took a sip of her port, she knew she should be happy – thankful for what she had been blessed with. Like so many other women here in her home town, she'd lost a husband to this war, but, unlike many, she had been lucky to find love again. A real, deep and true love with Joe.

She looked at Lucille, holding the blue box with the medal in it close to her chest, and felt blessed to have such a lovely daughter. Watching Maisie as she fussed over Lucille, Bel knew she was also incredibly fortunate to have been united with a sister that, growing up, she hadn't realised she had. Despite their differences, and the rather fractious start to their relationship, they had grown so close. Hearing Pearl's gravelly voice ordering Bill to go and change a barrel, she smiled to herself. Her ma mightn't be able to show it, but Bel knew she cared for her and loved her in her own way.

But still, despite all of this, the joy of adopting the twins and the love and care of all her family and friends – *still* she craved another child.

Polly took a sip of her port, fighting back the tears that often came unexpectedly when she thought of her brother Teddy. She glanced across at Bel and her ma and knew they too would be feeling exactly the same. Just as she also knew they would not let their sadness show as they wanted to be happy for Joe, who, of course, had made this day as much about Teddy as about himself. Polly knew Joe had lost a part of himself when Teddy had died. As twins, her two older brothers had shared a special bond. They'd been identical in looks,

161

but not in personality, which had only seemed to make them closer still.

Polly glanced across at the Major, who was presently puffing away on his cigar, listening intently to the wounded soldier he had taken under his wing four years ago when Joe had returned from the front line, mentally and physically wounded. Thank goodness he had made Joe a part of his Home Guard unit. It had given him purpose – just like the new role the Major had given him as an army recruiter. Joe's injured leg meant that not only would he have to walk with the aid of a stick his entire life, but it would be so much more difficult to find work.

Looking over at her ma, who was sitting next to Dr Billingham under the pub's stained-glass window, Polly thought how at ease they seemed with each other. If a stranger saw them now, they could be forgiven for thinking they were a couple. They had grown close this past year. Polly had wanted to ask her mother if she saw Dr Billingham as more than a friend and companion, but so far had not summoned up the courage.

Dr Billingham looked at Agnes, whose eyes were shining with a mix of pride and love, but there was also a great sadness there. A sadness he understood only too well. He, too, had lost a child – his daughter, Mary – and like Agnes, he knew that as a parent you never got over the death of your child. You just had to learn to live with it. Which in itself was no easy task.

'You must be incredibly proud of Joe *and* Teddy?' Dr Billingham asked gently.

'I am,' Agnes said, blinking hard. 'Very proud. Of them

both.' That was about all she trusted herself to say. She did not want to cry.

'But I think Joe is right. Everyone who has done their bit to help this war is a hero – or heroine.' She looked at Dr Billingham. Seeing the change in his face, she knew he was thinking of Mary, who was never far from his thoughts. He had told Agnes that since she'd been killed in the Blitz, he always carried her picture in the top left-hand pocket of whichever jacket he was wearing, so it would be as near to his heart as possible.

Dr Billingham took hold of Agnes's hand and held it for a short moment.

Then he looked at her, wanting to gauge her reaction to what he said next.

'Do you still miss your husband?'

Whenever Harry, a casualty of the First War, cropped up in conversation, Dr Billingham thought he could detect a little guilt in Agnes. He hoped it was a sign that she saw him as more than just a friend, but he also worried that she might feel she had to stay faithful to her late husband. Many widows Dr Billingham knew had done just that.

'Honestly?' Agnes said.

Dr Billingham nodded.

'I don't miss him,' she admitted. 'Which is an awful thing to say, but I'd be lying if I said otherwise.'

She looked at Dr Billingham and seeing no judgement in his face, she added, 'I loved Harry to pieces. But he was taken from me over twenty-five years ago.'

Dr Billingham cleared his throat.

'I was wondering how Polly or Joe might feel if you were to start courting someone?'

Agnes looked at Dr Billingham.

'Well,' she said, 'I suppose I would have to start courting someone to find out.'

Dr Billingham digested Agnes's words.

Then he smiled.

Helen and John stood next to each other, their eyes on Joe but their minds on each other.

Helen kept thinking of their conversation and how they had talked about everyone else's futures apart from their own. Not that she hadn't *thought* about John's future. Ever since Dr Eris had dropped the bombshell that she and John planned to move to London, Helen had thought about little else.

She had to accept that John might well have had feelings for her, but he was now with Dr Eris. *She* was his future. He had proposed to *her*. You didn't get more serious than that. She really had to get John out of her head and move on.

Suddenly, she took a mental step backwards and looked at herself. If she was a psychologist like Dr Eris, she might determine that she was becoming fixated. It was time to stop this. Stop these thoughts and replace them with sane ones.

John was with Dr Eris. He was due to marry her in *six weeks*. He would move to London, where no doubt they would start a family.

She was with Matthew. One of the town's most eligible men – certainly the most eligible widower in the area. She should be cock-a-hoop. He was handsome, from a good family, was rising through the ranks at Doxford's, and they got on well.

Not as well as with John, a little voice butted into her thoughts.

She felt like screaming at herself: *Stop it!* Stop thinking about what you don't have – or rather, *who* you don't have. And start concentrating on who you've got.

Perhaps it would not be such a tragedy for John to move to London.

Perhaps then she could finally stop obsessing about him and move on with her life.

Dr Parker could feel their bodies almost touching as he stood at the bar with Helen, listening to Joe's speech. Helen was standing with her back turned slightly to him and it took all his strength to stop himself sliding his hands around her waist and pulling her close. For a brief moment he imagined nuzzling his face into the crook of her neck, breathing in her scent and kissing her.

Standing up straight, he forced himself to take a drink of his beer and banish the sexual thoughts and desires that rose dangerously close to the surface whenever he was near Helen. Perhaps those feelings had rushed more readily to the fore as this was one of the first times in quite a while that the two of them had been on their own together. Well, not exactly alone – he scanned the packed pub – but without Claire or Matthew close by.

Concentrate on Joe's speech! he chastised himself.

But it was no good, his mind kept wandering off.

He replayed the conversation he and Helen had just had.

Helen was always so kind about Claire. Always so interested in hearing about them as a couple. He should really have asked more about Matthew. But he hadn't. Only the basics. Just enough to scrape through being polite. Try as he might, whenever Matthew was mentioned – or even if he simply thought of Matthew and Helen together – he couldn't stop the green-eyed monster taking centre stage.

Since the pair had officially started courting, he dreaded asking about him more than usual because he was sure it wouldn't be long before Matthew proposed to Helen. Any man in his right mind who had been courting Helen for even the shortest period of time could not be blamed for dropping down on one knee and asking her to be his wife.

But would he feel the same about Matthew if he wasn't seeing Helen?

John thought he probably would. There was something untrustworthy about the bloke. He couldn't quite put his finger on it, but his gut told him the man was a bit of a charlatan. Which actually didn't make sense as Matthew's life and background were transparent. His family was well known, respected and, by all accounts, very wealthy. He came from good stock and had a good job, even though he'd clearly only got the manager's job at Doxford's through nepotism after his father had suffered a stroke.

God, listen to yourself! John berated himself. *You sound like some catty fishwife!*

*

When Henrietta left, Mrs Evans allowed herself to cry. Something she hadn't done for a long time. The first few years after her daughter had killed herself, there had been no end to her tears. But they had eventually dried up and been replaced by an anger that had become impossible to dislodge.

As she sat in her armchair and cried, she did nothing to stop the flow of tears. They were soothing and it felt good

166

to feel something. Henrietta's honesty – the candour of her thoughts and emotions – had paved the way for them.

When the tears finally stopped, she stood up, smoothed down her skirt and went to the kitchen to make herself a fresh cup of tea.

The crying had been cathartic, but there was still only one thing that would uproot the anger buried so deeply in her being.

And that was retribution.

Chapter Sixteen

Two days later

Monday 26 March

'To *Moraybank*!' Matthew said, raising his glass of wine to Helen.

'To *Moraybank*!' Helen chinked her glass against Matthew's.

It had gone six o'clock and they had just sat down at a table for two at the Palatine Hotel, which housed the most exclusive and expensive restaurant in town.

'Will you be able to come to the launch of *Ambassador* on Thursday?' Matthew asked.

Helen laughed. 'If only I had the time! I'm amazed I got away today to come and see *Moraybank* take her first dip.'

'Harold?' Matthew asked. He knew that Helen was doing almost twice the workload at Thompson's due to Harold, the manager, refusing to give up his position, even though he did next to nothing at the yard, save sitting in his office, chatting about the old days and drinking whisky.

Helen nodded. 'It's so frustrating. I can't understand why they can't force him to retire.'

'Because he's connected,' Matthew said simply. 'And he's a stubborn old mule who wants to stay on his throne until his dying day.'

'Meanwhile, everyone else has to run around and do his work for him – and not get the title or the wage for doing so,' Helen said, not hiding her resentment.

'Your time will come,' Matthew said. 'Unless you decide to marry and start a family.'

'And I can't do both?' Helen retorted.

'Could you?' asked Matthew.

'Of course I could,' Helen laughed. 'There's plenty of women who work full-time and have families to look after. I don't see any reason why I couldn't.'

'But would you want to?' Matthew was listening intently.

'Of course I'd *want to*,' Helen said. 'I've not worked my way up the ladder – a climb, I hasten to add, made so much harder because I'm a woman – to chuck it all away simply because I want a family.'

Matthew laughed. 'That's what I like about you, Helen. You are determined to have your cake and eat it.'

'Of course I am,' Helen said, taking up the menu. 'Anyway, talking of eating, I'm starving. Let's order.'

After they had chosen their meal, the conversation turned to family, with Helen asking about Matthew's father, Royce senior.

'The old man's doing well – he's got some of his movement back on his left side. He's not doing too badly, all things considered.'

'I'll bet you he misses the cut and thrust of the yard,' Helen said. Matthew's father had been well liked by his staff – it was something Matthew also strove to be. Sometimes a bit too hard. Seeing him today with Dahlia and some of his other staff, she thought he could be a tad overfamiliar.

'And how's the old man?' Matthew asked.

'Dad's good,' Helen said. 'Loves it at Crown's.'

'Sorry, I actually meant your grandfather,' Matthew said. 'I thought he might be at the launch today.'

'So did I,' Helen said. Which was why she had enjoyed the afternoon so much. And why she would most definitely not be going to Thursday's launch, as her grandfather would not miss another.

'Tell him my father was asking after him the other day,' Matthew said.

Helen smiled. She had no intention of passing on any messages to her grandfather. Especially as he had never had much time for Royce senior in the past and had only started being pally with him since she had become friendly with Matthew.

Not wanting to tarnish her evening with any more chatter about family, or rather, about *her* family – the Havelock side, anyway, which was the only side Matthew ever seemed interested in asking about – Helen changed the subject.

'So, it was a good launch this afternoon, wasn't it? A really good turnout,' she said.

'Made all the better because you were there,' Matthew said with a twinkle in his eyes.

'Honestly, Matthew, flattery *won't* get you everywhere,' Helen batted back.

'I swear there were more people at the launch so they could see the famous Helen Crawford.' He laughed. 'I've even heard you called "Helen of Thompson's".'

Helen looked puzzled.

'You know, instead of Helen of Troy.'

Helen smiled.

'The most beautiful woman in Greece,' Matthew added.

'And also the indirect cause of the Trojan War,' Helen hit back.

Matthew chuckled. He enjoyed Helen's company. Her verbal jousting. She was unlike most women he had dated, and very unlike his first wife, God rest her soul. They had all been too eager to please. But not Helen. Quite the reverse. She seemed almost determined not to be liked.

'Talking about war,' Matthew said, taking a sip of his drink, 'you can almost feel the anticipation of victory, can't you? I can at Doxford's, anyway. I'm sure it's the same at Thompson's?'

Helen nodded. 'Yes, there's certainly a change in the air.'

'And there's reason to be,' Matthew said. 'With the Soviets advancing from the east and the Americans from the west, they've effectively cut Germany in two.'

They were both quiet while the maître d' came with their soup starters.

'And today,' Matthew continued, picking up his spoon, 'the *Mirror* had a fantastic photograph on its front page of soldiers from the Scottish Division being the first to cross the Reine – along with all the latest news about the capture of Darmstadt.'

Helen smiled at Matthew's enthusiasm and positivity. 'I know. I read the papers too – although I take *The Times*.'

'Honestly, Helen, you are such a snob sometimes,' Matthew chuckled, pushing back his mop of thick black hair.

Helen had overheard one of the women at work compare Matthew to Rhett Butler in *Gone with the Wind* and at this moment in time, she had to agree. There was no denying that Matthew was a very handsome man.

When they reached Helen's car, which she had parked nearby on Toward Road, Matthew pulled Helen close. He kissed her and felt encouraged by her response. He'd noticed a slight change in Helen this evening. He couldn't put his finger on it, but whatever it was, it boded well for him – and his intentions.

After they stopped kissing, Matthew kept his hand on the back of her neck and caressed her skin softly.

'I love you, Helen Crawford,' he said, his tone soft and gentle.

Helen pulled away. This was the first time he had told her he loved her.

Matthew looked at Helen's serious face.

'I'm not going to apologise,' he said earnestly. 'Because I *do* love you.'

He paused, trying to read her reaction.

'I am *in love* with you.'

Another beat.

'Which I think you've known from the off.'

Helen looked at Matthew. But did *she* love *him*? Was she *in love* with him? *Or were her feelings for John stopping her from loving another man?*

'Thank you, Matthew. That's a lovely thing to be told.'

Matthew roared with laughter.

'Oh, Helen, I think I love you even more now. I must be the only man to have been given a polite "Thank you" after declaring my undying love. You really are one in a million.'

He opened the car door for her and watched her climb in.

'I'll see you on Sunday – unless you can squeeze me in before then?' Matthew said.

Helen gave him an enigmatic smile and turned the ignition.

'See you Sunday,' she said, as she shut the driver's door and drove off.

Chapter Seventeen

Six days later

Easter Sunday, 1 April

Making good on their promise to be there for Angie and Quentin when they went to tell Angie's mam and dad that they were getting married in just over a month's time, the women had arranged to meet them afterwards in the Seaburn café where Polly used to waitress, before she began working at the yard.

An hour before, Rosie, Gloria, Polly, Dorothy, Martha and Hannah met at the Cat and Dog Steps and walked along the clifftops to the seafront. Rosie felt particularly sentimental as it reminded her of her first date with Peter. She smiled when Hannah asked why they were called the Cat and Dog Steps, as Rosie had asked Peter the same question that day four years ago. Omitting to tell Hannah one of the theories that it was where people had disposed of unwanted litters, Rosie instead relayed the more palatable reason that it was because the waves were often so huge when the tide was up that the spray made it feel as though it were 'raining cats and dogs'.

As they walked and talked and enjoyed the feel of the sun on their faces, they indulged in ice cream – something that had not been available for most of the war because of rationing. The ice cream might have been made with powdered milk and margarine rather than fresh milk, but everyone agreed it was still delicious.

The beach was filled with families enjoying a day out and the sea air was infused with the smell of fish and chips and the screams and shouts of children enjoying the sand and sea and the nearby funfair. Bathers had been warned they entered the water at their own risk as there was no guarantee that all the barbed wire, which had lain submerged for almost six years, had been cleared. There was also the danger of explosives being brought in by the tide.

Still, there was a good smattering of people swimming and splashing about in the water, although mostly in the shallows. Nothing was going to spoil this bank holiday weekend when even the shipyards were closed for the whole three days – the first time since the start of war. Especially as the headlines in all the Sunday papers told of American troops invading Okinawa, the last island held by the Japanese, giving hope that victory over Japan would follow soon after the impending victory in Europe.

When they reached the café on the promenade, Polly's old employer, Mrs Hoggart, was overjoyed to see her former waitress, whispering to her that none of the girls who had followed in her footsteps had been a patch on her. She gave the women the best table by the window, which once again gifted a view of the shimmering blue sea in the distance, now that the obstructions afforded by the coastal defence had been removed.

The women ordered sandwiches and tea, and Mrs Hoggart fussed over them, telling them how proud she was that her former employee had been building the ships that were helping to win the war. She confessed, though, that when Polly had first told her of her new job, she'd thought she was 'as mad as a hatter' and that shipyards were no place for a woman. Everyone chuckled.

'I'm sure that's not the first time you've all heard that said,' Mrs Hoggart smiled.

Not long after their arrival, and sooner than expected, Angie and Quentin pushed open the glass-panelled door of the cafeteria. Hearing the bell above the entrance tinkle, the women all stopped talking and looked over.

'They don't look full of the joys, do they?' Gloria said to Rosie out of the corner of her mouth.

'They don't,' Rosie agreed. 'Although I'd be more surprised if they did.'

Dorothy waved them over and patted the two spare seats they had kept for them.

'How did it go?' she asked as soon as they reached the table.

Angie looked at Quentin as they sat down.

'Well, let's just say it's done,' Angie said. There was no cheer in her voice.

Quentin took her hand and squeezed it.

'It is,' he agreed. 'No more worrying.'

He looked round the table at the women's anxious faces and thought how wonderful it was that Angie had such good friends.

Polly poured them each a cup of tea.

'Thank you,' Quentin said, taking a quick sip. Angie smiled and did the same.

'So, what happened?' Dorothy demanded impatiently. 'We want details.'

'Well, I think they were rather surprised that Angie was getting married – and so quickly,' Quentin admitted.

'Yeah, first words out of Mam's mouth were, "Are yer up the duff?"' Angie said, outraged.

'Which, obviously, Angie's not,' Quentin added, in case anyone else was wondering. He and Angie had agreed to wait until they were married. Although he wasn't so sure if either of them would have been quite so agreeable had it been a long engagement.

'So,' Rosie asked, 'when they were reassured that this isn't a shotgun wedding, then what did they say?'

'The first thing Dad said was that we'd have to pay for it ourselves – that they had nowt to give us,' Angie said, rolling her eyes.

Gloria threw Rosie a look. They'd both agreed Angie's mam and dad were a right pair.

'At which juncture,' Quentin jumped in, 'I reassured them that there was absolutely no need whatsoever for them to contribute to the wedding in any way – that we would just be happy to see them there and for them to partake in the celebrations.'

Dorothy looked at Angie and thought she looked a little tired and weary. She felt annoyed at Angie's mam and dad. *Couldn't they simply have been happy for her? This should be a joyful occasion – one to be celebrated.*

'And then what did they say?' Martha asked.

'They seemed a bit stuck for words,' Angie said. 'Which is not so unusual for my dad, but not for Mam, who can talk the hind legs off a donkey.'

'Were they *pleased*?' Hannah asked. She had never come across parents like Angie's.

'I think so,' Angie said, twiddling her diamond engagement ring.

'They are going to *go* to the wedding, aren't they?' Dorothy asked.

'They are, but they both made a point of saying they'd have to ask for the day off – and Mam pointed out that they'd both be sacrificing a day's pay.'

Angie looked at Quentin.

'I was going to offer to make it up to them,' Quentin said.

'But I knew what he was gonna say 'n stopped him,' Angie said, looking at Dorothy. 'You can just imagine what that'd lead to, can't you?'

Dorothy nodded. 'Quentin becomes their cash cow.'

'Exactly,' Angie said. 'And one they'd definitely keep on milking.'

Everyone was quiet. They knew Angie's dad was quick to temper and didn't think twice about giving Angie or the rest of his children a slap, and that her mam believed in tough love, but they hadn't realised her parents were also quite so mercenary.

'So, is yer dad gonna give yer away?' Gloria asked.

Angie nodded. 'I asked him 'n he said, "Who else is gonna dee it?"'

Hannah offered Angie and Quentin the sandwiches, but they shook their heads. Their visit had clearly scuppered their appetites.

'So, you've just got to meet with Mr and Mrs Foxton-Clarke now?' Polly said.

'Ah, we have dodged that bullet,' Quentin said. 'My mother

and father weren't able to arrange their diaries around the leave I've been given.'

'So, you're just going to meet them on the day?' Martha asked. Like Hannah, she found both Angie's and Quentin's parents very peculiar.

Angie and Quentin nodded. Neither seemed particularly upset. If anything, they seemed relieved.

Wanting to lift the mood, Rosie turned the conversation to the day itself, asking them about the vicar who was going to marry them, which led to excited chatter about the church. Angie and Quentin were to be married in St Peter's in Monkwearmouth. It was a small but very beautiful church, located just a stone's throw from the Wear, and was famous for being one of the oldest churches in the country, with part of it dating back to Anglo-Saxon times. It also had amazing stained-glass windows, which they had been told would be freed of anti-blast tape on the day.

'And how's the dress coming along?' Rosie asked.

They all knew that Quentin had told Kate not to spare any expense when it came to his bride's wedding dress, which was his attitude to the whole wedding.

'It's going to be amazing!' declared Dorothy, who had been appointed maid of honour and was therefore heavily involved in organising every aspect of her best friend's wedding. 'Especially as Quentin has managed to acquire a load of parachute silk for Kate to use.'

As soon as the words were out, she looked guilty and shamefaced.

'Really?' Polly asked, surprised. Silk was like gold dust these days.

'How did you manage to get hold of that?' Hannah asked, genuinely curious.

'A little subterfuge and a bribe of whisky,' Quentin chuckled.

'But yer can't tell anyone,' Angie said, throwing Dorothy a look of exasperation. 'It wasn't exactly all above board.'

Dorothy had the decency to look apologetic and mouth 'Sorry' to Quentin.

Angie let out a sigh. 'Honestly, Dor, yer my best mate 'n all that, but yer really are the worst person ever for keeping a secret.'

'Sorry.' This time Dorothy articulated her apology.

'Don't worry, Quentin, your secret's safe with us, isn't it?' Gloria said, looking round the table.

The women all nodded.

'I'll bet Kate was over the moon?' asked Hannah.

'She was,' said Angie. 'As soon as she saw it and felt the material, she said she knew exactly what she was going to do.'

'So, you're just going to give Kate free rein with the design?' Polly asked.

'Of course,' Angie laughed. 'I wouldn't have any idea where to start. Kate's the expert.'

They all murmured their agreement.

'Well, she certainly did an amazing job on my dress,' Polly said, remembering Tommy's face when he'd seen her walking down the aisle in her beautiful ivory chiffon dress.

Suddenly Dorothy looked at her watch and jumped up.

'Right, time to go!'

'What's the rush?' Angie asked, finishing off her tea but following her friend's lead and standing up.

'Oh, sorry, I forgot to tell you – Helen asked if we'd pop in to hers. She really wanted to come here, but there was some kind of plumbing emergency . . . Is that all right?' She looked at Angie and Quentin, who both nodded.

'And we thought it'd be nice to see Henrietta too,' Gloria added, standing up and looking over to Mrs Hoggart for the bill.

'Especially as she's still not quite up to going out in public yet,' Hannah chipped in.

Quentin went to the counter to pay the bill after telling everyone that it was the least he could do.

'Knowing you were all here for Angie meant the world to her – *to us both*,' he said, his tone showing he meant every word.

Chapter Eighteen

As they all left the cafeteria, Dorothy pulled Angie away from Quentin.

'So,' she whispered, 'how did they take to him?' She looked at Quentin, who was walking ahead, chatting to Rosie.

Angie rolled her eyes.

'As soon as Quentin was out the door, Mam grabbed me 'n asked how I'd managed to bag myself "some rich toff".'

Dorothy shook her head. 'Sounds like your mam.'

'I told her that Quentin was a neighbour and I hadn't "bagged" him – that we'd fallen in love.'

'God, I can imagine her reaction when you said that,' Dorothy sympathised.

'Yeah, she laughed loudly 'n said yer'd been taking me to see too many daft films at the flicks. She said falling in love only happened on the big screen – not in real life.'

'What did you say?' Dorothy asked. She had only met Angie's mam a few times, but could well imagine her standing with her arms folded, her lip curled upwards and a mocking look in her eyes.

'I asked her, if there was no such thing as falling in love, then what was she doing running around behind Dad's back with a man half her age?'

Dorothy's eyes widened. 'You didn't, did you?'

'I did,' Angie said.

'I bet that shut her up,' Dorothy said, impressed by her friend daring to give any backchat to her mam, who was also not averse to giving her children a good clip round the ear.

'It did,' Angie said.

Dorothy linked arms with her best mate. 'Brave woman.'

As they all trekked up Seaburn Terrace and along Sea Lane to Park Avenue, Polly asked about Angie's brothers and sisters.

'They seemed excited about being bridesmaids and page-boys, although I had to warn them that they had to behave – or else,' Angie related.

'Or else what?' Martha asked with a chuckle. 'I can't see you giving them a smack.'

Angie smiled. 'Yer right there, Martha. I think they've all probably had enough smacks to last a lifetime. I've promised them all a new pair of shoes if they behave,' she admitted.

'Ah, bribery,' Gloria laughed. 'Works every time.'

As they approached Helen's home, Angie turned to Rosie.

'That cow Miriam won't be in, will she? I dinnit think I've got the stomach for two mad mams in one day.'

Rosie smiled. 'No, no more *mad mams* today.'

'Besides,' Dorothy added, 'Helen said Miriam's practically living at the Grand now.'

'Actually,' Gloria informed, 'she's just taken a suite there.'

Everyone looked at Gloria, who was always privy to news about the Havelocks before anyone else due to her closeness to Helen.

'So, a person can actually live in a hotel?' Hannah asked.

'A lot of the Admiralty are billeted there,' Polly explained. When she and Tommy had had their wedding reception and honeymoon at the Grand, an entire floor had been given over to the navy.

'Which explains why Miriam is so keen to be there,' Dorothy said, raising her eyebrows.

As they opened the side gate, they saw that the main door was open.

'Welcome!' called Henrietta, her focus on Angie and Quentin, whom she had only met once before. Her face was a picture of excitement and curiosity.

The women smiled. Henrietta might now dress as though she lived in the present day as opposed to the turn of the century, but her whole being exuded eccentricity. Conservative clothes and a modern haircut could only go so far.

'The soon-to-be Mr and Mrs Foxton-Clarke – welcome!' Henrietta declared, stepping aside and waving in the couple, who might look very similar, with their strawberry blond hair and fair complexions, but were, from what Helen had told her, complete opposites in every other way.

'Let me show you the front reception room,' Henrietta said, turning the ornate brass doorknob.

As soon as the door opened, there was a huge cheer from inside.

'Congratulations!'

Angie and Quentin stood rooted to the spot in shocked surprise. The room had been decorated with balloons and streamers and there was a huge 'Happy Engagement' banner hanging across the large mirror above the mantelpiece. Everyone they knew was in the room – Helen and Matthew, Peter and Charlotte, Agnes and Dr Billingham, Bel and Joe with Lucille and the twins, Olly, Jack, and Bobby, who had Hope on his shoulders. Kate was standing next to Lily, George,

Maisie and Vivian. And Dr Bernard was by the drinks cabinet, holding two glasses of champagne ready to give to the happy couple.

Angie automatically looked behind her at Dorothy and the women.

'I can't believe you've done this!'

'Go on in!' Dorothy gave them both a gentle push forward and they all crowded into the packed living room.

Dr Bernard handed Angie and Quentin their champagne, before tilting his head at the rest of the women to follow him so that he could give them each a glass for the toast.

Helen hurried over to Dorothy. 'Are you sure you want me to do this?' she asked.

'Absolutely,' Dorothy said. 'You're the host.' The idea for the engagement party might have been Dorothy's, but Helen, Henrietta and Mrs Westley had done all the hard work.

Helen looked around the room, coughed loudly and raised her glass in the air.

'A toast!' Helen declared. 'To the happy couple, Angie and Quentin!'

'*Angie and Quentin!*' everyone repeated.

'May you both have the most wonderful wedding and a very happy marriage!'

'*Hear! Hear!*' everyone chorused.

Angie had gone bright red and was beaming from ear to ear, as was Quentin, who was raising his glass and saying 'Thank you!' to the room full of revellers.

Henrietta went to put on a record and soon the room was filled with the wondrous vocals of Judy Garland singing 'The Trolley Song', as well as the sounds of lively chatter and laughter. A trail of cigar smoke followed Dr Bernard, who was now at Henrietta's side as they both worked their way round the room, introducing themselves to those they didn't know and every now and again pulling Quentin over to meet someone he had yet to be acquainted with.

Henrietta was in high spirits and had been ever since Helen had asked if she would be up to helping to organise the party. The look of elation on Henrietta's face had answered her question and she had immediately told Helen to leave everything to her and Mrs Westley, with whom she had become good friends. The pair had plotted and planned and worked hard to make the engagement party quite fabulous. Helen had been forbidden from helping as both women had agreed that she 'had far more important work to be doing at the yard, and a courtship to attend to'. Matthew had, of course, won over both Helen's 'great-aunty' and the house-keeper with his good looks and charm. Mrs Westley had been particularly enamoured by him as he had treated her as an equal and not as a servant, unlike Miriam, who Mrs Westley was glad had decided to up sticks and move to the Grand.

Chatting to Kate about Angie's wedding dress, Helen ten-tatively asked her if she'd decided whether to move to the capital.

Kate shook her head, indicating that she was still undecided.

'Well, if I had your talent, I'd be there in a shot, especially now the war's almost at an end.'

Kate smiled at the compliment.

'Although,' Helen added, 'I will be bereft – as I'm pretty sure all your regular clients will be too.'

When the doorbell went, Helen went to answer, knowing it would be Mr Emery and Mrs Evans. Helen had been right in her supposition that the two were somehow connected by Gracie. Henrietta had told her after her visit to Mrs Evans's house the previous week that Ethan had been Gracie's childhood sweetheart and that he, too, had been heartbroken by her suicide; so much so, that he had never married.

Ushering them both in, Helen showed them into the front room, where the party was now in full swing, with Guy Lombardo singing 'It's Love-Love-Love'. Henrietta immediately bustled over and gave them a warm welcome. Helen smiled. Her grandmother was a natural hostess. Watching as she took them over to introduce them to the soon-to-be-weds, Helen heard Henrietta ask Mrs Evans, a tad conspiratorially, how the 'new job' was going. She was just wondering why Mrs Evans would want a new job, since she already worked for Mr Emery, when she felt Matthew kiss her on the back of the neck.

'So,' he whispered into her ear, as he wrapped his arm around her waist, 'if you were to get married, where would it be, church or chapel, or council office?'

Helen tutted and ignored his question. As she glanced around the room, she saw Agnes and Dr Billingham chatting in the corner. Watching how they were with each other gave credence to Polly's growing belief that they were more than friends. There was an undeniable chemistry between them.

Seeing Hope trip over the edge of the rug and fall with a thud on the floor, Helen hurried to pick her up.

'There, there,' she consoled, just as Hope was about to start crying. 'It didn't hurt that much, did it?'

Matthew ruffled Hope's mop of black hair.

'Oh,' Helen pulled a surprised face, 'look over there.' She nodded over to where Dr Bernard was starting to perform a magic trick for Lucille, who was sitting on Charlotte's knee on a chair by the window. Hope immediately started to struggle out of her big sister's hold and as soon as her feet hit the ground, she was hurrying across to watch the man with the handlebar moustache perform his wizardry.

'You'd make a terrific mother, you know?' Matthew said, his eyes twinkling.

Again, Helen didn't say anything, but this time Matthew thought he caught a sadness in her emerald eyes.

'Come on,' she said, touching his arm, 'I need to talk to Dorothy about the wedding reception.'

As all the guests had arrived, Mrs Westley brought a large silver tray of canapés, which she set down on the sideboard. She returned a few moments later with some ham sandwiches for the children.

Watching Lucille and Hope tuck in, Angie thought of her four younger brothers and sisters. Her heart suddenly felt heavy, despite the upbeat music and happy atmosphere. They'd all looked in need of a good feed. It made her realise how much she and her older sister Liz had taken care of their younger siblings when they'd been living at home. If Liz had seen them today, she'd have said, 'There's not a pickin' on any of them.' And Angie would have had to agree with her. The bairns were definitely skinnier than when she'd seen them last. And dirty. She felt angry at her mam for spending time with her fancy piece when she should have been at home looking after her children.

Thinking of Liz, Angie wondered how her sister was doing. She'd written to Angie and told her she'd had to get married and that the baby was due the first week in May, which meant she couldn't come to Angie's wedding. She didn't want to risk going into labour in the middle of the church. Angie didn't mind. Her sister sounded happy. They would see each other in a few months, when both their lives had settled down.

When the doorbell went again, Mrs Westley hurried to answer, knowing it would be Vera and Rina with the engagement cake – a carrot cake, which was Angie's favourite. Seeing Rina's 'friend' Harvey sitting in the car, having brought them to the house, she waved him in, partly out of politeness and partly out of curiosity, as she had heard that Rina had an admirer.

Walking into the lounge with the cake, Vera and Rina found themselves the centre of attention – with everyone taking it in turns to shake hands with Harvey.

After Quentin had thanked the two older women profusely, he went over to talk to Dorothy.

'It was incredibly thoughtful of you all to meet us after the visit to Angie's parents,' he said, 'but then to organise such a wonderful party . . . well, really, I'm bowled over. I can't thank you enough.'

'It was a team effort,' Dorothy said. She gave Quentin a questioning look. 'So, the meeting of the parents hasn't managed to dampen your fervour for your future wife?' She chuckled. 'We thought you might go running to the hills – or back to London – as soon as the deed was done.'

Quentin laughed. He'd got used to Dorothy's sense of humour. He took a sip of his drink.

'You know,' he said, his tone now serious, 'I didn't think it possible to admire Angie more than I already do, but after meeting her mam and dad . . .' He sighed. 'Well, it's amazing she's turned out the way she has.'

'I know,' Dorothy agreed, now equally serious.

For a moment, they watched everyone in the room chatting.

'I have to say, though, Quentin, I did feel for you today. Every time I've had to go there, I have to brace myself.'

'It's her brothers and sisters I feel sorry for,' Quentin said. 'What hope have they for a decent life?'

Dorothy looked at her friend's future husband. 'I know.'

Quentin shook his head sadly.

'Anyway, enough sad talk,' Dorothy said, seeing Angie heading over to them. 'This is a happy occasion and I wanted to say to you that I think you're both really lucky to have found each other.'

She paused.

'Which I have to add is totally down to me.'

'Ahem,' Angie said, hearing the last part of their conversation. 'I don't know how you work that one out?'

'Sometimes,' Dorothy explained, 'love needs a little help. And I was there to offer that help.'

Angie pulled a puzzled expression.

'If I hadn't forced you to invite Quentin to Polly and Tommy's wedding,' Dorothy explained, as Hannah and Martha came over to join them, 'you'd not be stood here now with a great big diamond ring on your finger.'

Angie immediately looked down at her engagement ring. She looked back up to see that Polly, Rosie and Gloria had joined them too.

'I don't think your forcing Angie was purely for altruistic reasons,' Hannah smiled.

Angie pulled another puzzled expression.

'Unselfish,' Rosie explained.

'Yes,' Polly agreed. 'If my memory serves me correctly, you needed a last-minute plus-one for Angie as you had decided to invite Toby.'

Dorothy's face dropped. 'Don't mention the T-word. I still feel awful about what happened.'

' "What happened" being the part where yer copped off with Bobby when yer were still with Toby – or when yer said no to marrying him?' Angie asked, deadpan.

'Or when Toby and Bobby ended up scrapping in the street over you?' Gloria said, equally poker-faced.

Dorothy put her fingers in her ears and started humming.

By seven o'clock, Angie and Dor saw that their neighbour, Mrs Kwiatkowski, was looking tired and had started to chat in Polish, seemingly unaware that the person listening to her had no idea what she was saying.

By half past, everyone had said their goodbyes and Angie and Quentin had thanked everyone for the umpteenth time for the 'the best engagement party anyone could ever want', made all the more special for being such a surprise. They'd really had no idea what was in store for them when Henrietta had waved them in.

Later on, when Angie and Quentin were alone in the basement flat, they chatted about those at the party Quentin had not met before, and about Angie's workmates and how lucky she was to have them. As they snuggled up on the sofa with the wireless playing in the background, they were quiet for a short while before they said what had been in the back of their minds since their visit to Angie's mam and dad.

'I keep thinking about your brothers and sisters,' Quentin admitted. He had been unsure whether to say anything for fear of upsetting Angie or poking his nose in where it wasn't wanted. He needn't have worried.

'Really?' Angie said, clearly relieved.

Quentin nodded. 'Really.'

'What yer thinking?' Angie needed to know if he'd been plagued by the same thoughts as she had.

'Can I be totally honest?' he asked.

'Always,' Angie said in earnest.

'Well, they all looked like they needed a good bath and a decent meal,' he said, looking at Angie, still unsure if he was overstepping the mark.

'They did, didn't they,' Angie agreed.

Quentin wanted to add that not only did they seem physically neglected, but also lacking in any kind of love or care. Angie's mam and dad hadn't shown their offspring any attention – none at all. Even towards Jemima, the youngest, who was only three.

But he didn't.

Instead, he suggested that perhaps once they were married, they should visit often and keep an eye on them.

Angie agreed wholeheartedly and felt a little less worried.

But only a little.

Chapter Nineteen

'Really, Matthew, it's time for you to go home,' Helen said.

They, too, were sitting cuddled up together on the sofa. The fire had been lit a few hours ago, not so much because it was cold, but to make the room cosy. It was now past ten and the fire was starting to dwindle. The house was quiet. Mrs Westley had gone after clearing up after the party. Dr Bernard had also said his goodbyes, after which Henrietta had retired to bed, very tired, but also very happy.

'OK, I'll go,' Matthew said, kissing Helen gently on the lips.

Helen watched as Matthew made to get up from the sofa, but instead of standing up straight, he bobbed back down on one knee. He took Helen's hand. As she was still curled up on the low sofa, Matthew was able to look straight at Helen, a smile playing on his lips.

'Helen Crawford,' he said, squeezing her hand, 'forgive me for my impatience, but I really can't wait any more.'

He took a deep breath.

'I'm sure this will come as no surprise to you – I've told you that I love you, am very much in love with you – it's something I think you have known for quite some time.'

He looked into Helen's eyes but could not read them.

'I desperately want you to be my wife.'

He paused.

'Will you marry me?'

Matthew waited a beat.

'Will you make me the happiest man alive?'

Another beat.

'Would you have me as your husband?'

Again, he tried to read Helen's expression. If he'd had to guess the odds, it would have been fifty-fifty as to whether Helen would say yes – or no.

She shuffled on the sofa, unfurling her legs from underneath her and sitting up straight. She tugged Matthew's hand, showing him she wanted him to get up and sit next to her. He did her bidding, all the time keeping his eyes on her, waiting, watching, wishing.

Finally, Helen spoke.

'Matthew . . . oh, Matthew. What a wonderful compliment.' She put her hand to his face and gently touched his cheek and then his lips. She gave him a kiss.

'You do make me feel very special,' she began. 'Very loved.' She paused.

'*Adored* . . . I could certainly see us together. I think we'd make a good match.'

Matthew could feel his hopes start to grow. *Sixty-forty.*

'We have so much in common. Our work. Our backgrounds. And I love how you accept me for who I am – for what I do. I know I intimidate a lot of men, but not you.' She smiled a little sadly, as she had often thought that Matthew's maturity and liberal thinking were because he had already been married – and widowed. He had loved and lost. It was something else they had in common. Only, her lost love was still very much alive.

Matthew suddenly leant forward and kissed her. This time sensuously. Passionately.

Helen responded.

When she pulled away, she looked at him.

'And there's no denying that there is an attraction there,' she said.

Matthew felt his hopes rise. *Seventy-thirty*.

'But,' Helen said, 'I need more time. More time to think.'

Seeing the disappointment on Matthew's face, she leant forward and kissed him again.

'Is it because I am a widower?' he asked, knowing that this would be an issue for some women.

Helen laughed lightly. 'No, of course not.'

'Why, then?' Matthew asked.

Helen exhaled. 'I've made some rash decisions before – in the past,' she explained. 'And I don't want to make that mistake again. I want to be one hundred per cent sure.'

Seeing the disappointment on his face, she added, 'And we *have* only just started to court each other.'

'But we have known each other for much longer,' he protested good-naturedly.

Helen nodded. 'You're right. We have.'

She stood up and straightened her skirt.

'If I do say yes, I need you to know that I will want to do everything properly.'

Matthew looked puzzled.

'I'll want to wait until our wedding night,' Helen said.

Matthew blew out air. 'Of course, I wouldn't expect anything else.'

Taking Matthew's hand, she led him out of the lounge and to the front door.

'Just give me some time to think.'

She kissed him goodnight and he kissed her back.

'I'll give you as long as you want.'

He walked down the steps and turned.

'As long as the answer's "Yes",' he added with his trade-mark roguish smile.

While Helen was getting undressed for bed, her mind churned over the events of the day, and how the party had been a great success, mainly thanks to Henrietta and Mrs Westley. As she got into bed, though, and turned out the light, she knew she couldn't avoid thinking about Matthew's proposal any more. It hadn't come as a surprise. Matthew was not one to hide his feelings and it had been clear from the moment they'd gone on their first date that his aim was to get her down the aisle. Matthew, she knew, was an impatient man. He had clearly waited long enough and, in hindsight, tonight had been the perfect occasion, following a day that had been all about love and marriage and weddings.

Unfortunately, all the chatter about Angie and Quentin's wedding had not made Helen think of her own future – and of the time when *she* would be a bride – but rather of John's forthcoming marriage to Claire.

John had rung her the other day, confirming they'd be tying the knot at Claire's local church in her home town of Northallerton on the second Saturday in May. He'd added, though, that he still intended to go to Angie and Quentin's wedding on the Tuesday of that week.

Helen had tried to sound excited for them both and had asked about the church and where they were going to have the reception.

She couldn't, however, bring herself to ask him anything about the honeymoon.

Chapter Twenty

Over the next fortnight the news seemed to be full of reports that further cemented the belief that it was now just a matter of weeks before victory was declared. Russian forces captured Vienna, and the Japanese were now in full retreat.

And with the good news came the good weather. Having suffered one of the harshest winters in years – below-zero temperatures had led to milk bottles freezing solid on doorsteps, and part of the river resembling a glacier – the town was now melting in temperatures that by the middle of the month had reached 72 degrees.

After proposing to Helen and being told she needed time to think, Matthew knew he should take his foot off the accelerator and give Helen some breathing space. If he pushed too hard, he would risk losing her – and he couldn't have that.

Helen had, of course, told Henrietta about her proposal, and she had told Mrs Westley. They both agreed they made a perfect pair. Helen had not told her mother, though – partly because she rarely saw her these days, and also because she knew she'd manage to put a dampener on it, or come out with some catty remark.

Gloria and Jack had made all the right sounds when Helen told them, saying how happy they were for her, but in private they aired their true feelings that Matthew seemed to be rushing things, and that Helen was still holding a light for Dr Parker.

It was a view echoed by the rest of the women when they were told the news by Gloria over lunch in the canteen. The consensus was that it was too soon. And that Helen was still in love with Dr Parker.

'To meddle or not to meddle?' Dorothy asked.

No one seemed sure either way.

*

Pearl, too, had been wondering whether or not to meddle in her daughter's affairs, and had managed to see Agnes on her own one afternoon. Getting straight to the point, she had asked if there was anything Agnes's fella could do for Bel.

Agnes had told Pearl that she had already asked Dr Billingham if he could help in any way and that he had seen Bel and 'checked her over', but could not find anything obvious that might be the cause.

'But Isabelle had Lucille without any problem,' Pearl argued. 'Something must be up. Unless the problem's with Joe.'

Agnes had glowered at Pearl. She'd wanted to tell her that it was not her son's fault, but how did she know? Besides which, Pearl was just saying something she had thought herself, and which she was sure both Bel and Joe had also thought about, if not discussed.

Marching back to the pub, puffing on a cigarette, Pearl felt angry.

Angry that her daughter had only ever wanted to be married and have lots of children.

Was that really too much to ask?

*

And in the Havelock residence, much to Eddy's annoyance, the new cleaner was becoming quite chummy with Agatha. The pair were spending all their breaks together, chatting and drinking tea – their growing friendship hindering any chance of him regaining the closeness he had once shared with Agatha before their involvement with the master's attempts to poison Henrietta.

And if Agatha wasn't spending her free time with Mrs Bevan, then she was out in the back garden chatting to Sinclair the gardener, helping him cultivate a little herb garden next to the greenhouse.

When Eddy had commented on her new love of horticulture, she'd told him he could do with getting outdoors a bit more himself as he looked very 'pasty-faced', which had dented his ego, even though he knew it to be the truth.

Chapter Twenty-One

Thursday 19 April

Hannah, Olly, Rina and Vera were sitting in the cafeteria, which had closed half an hour beforehand so that they could enjoy their tea in peace before switching on the wireless to listen to a report from a journalist called Richard Dimbleby, who had been at the Bergen-Belsen concentration camp when it had been liberated by British and Canadian troops four days previously.

A few minutes before the broadcast, Vera brought in a fresh pot of tea and topped up their cups, while Rina placed the radio in the middle of the table and switched it on.

There was the usual crackling of static as she tuned it, before the plummy vowels of the BBC presenter announced that the next programme was an eyewitness account of the liberation of the concentration camp.

'I have just returned from the Belsen concentration camp,' the voice of Richard Dimbleby began, *'where I drove slowly about the place in a jeep with the chief doctor of the Second Army. I find it hard to describe adequately the horrible things that I've seen and heard, but here unadorned are the facts.'*

Rina looked at Hannah and wished more than anything she could protect her from what she was about to hear, but she knew she couldn't. This war had not just robbed people of their lives, but also of their innocence.

'In the last few months alone, thirty thousand prisoners have been killed off or allowed to die. Those are the simple, horrible facts of Belsen.'

Vera looked up at her friend. Her dark brown eyes were pooled with such deep sadness as the reporter continued to relay how he had found himself in 'the world of a nightmare', where there were over 13,000 unburied bodies, some of them decaying, lying strewn about the road.

'And along the rutted tracks on each side of the road were brown wooden huts. There were faces at the windows. The bony, emaciated faces of starving women too weak to come outside.'

Hannah leant forward, her hands clasping her head. How could she not imagine the face of her mother as one of those emaciated, starving women? She knew that the men and women were separated in all the SS camps, but this image of the women on their own, without the men they loved by their sides, hit home hard. The thought of her mother, her softly spoken, loving mother, on her own, without her father, caused her chest to constrict in pain.

Knowing what Hannah would be thinking, Olly put his hand on her back, showing her that he was there. That she was not alone. That he would be there for her. Always.

The narrative continued, describing a hell on earth where 'ghosts wandered aimlessly about', where men, women and children were 'dead and dying', their bodies 'crawling with lice and smeared with filth.'

Vera shuffled in her chair and grasped her friend's hand. She held it tightly while they forced themselves to continue

201

listening as the reporter detailed his visit to the crematorium where the Germans had burned alive thousands of men and women in a single fire.

'Every fact I've so far given you has been verified, but there is one more awful than all the others that I've kept to the end.'

Hannah, Olly, Rina and Vera sat up straight as though to brace themselves. How could there be horror *'more awful'* than what they had already heard?

'Far away in a corner of Belsen camp,' the reporter said, trying to keep the emotion out of his voice, but clearly finding it hard, *'there is a pit the size of a tennis court. It's fifteen feet deep and at one end it's piled to the very top with naked bodies that have been tumbled in one on top of the other.'*

He paused before ending his report:

'May I add to this story only the assurance that everything that an army can do to save these men and women and children is being done and that those officers and men who've seen these things have gone back to the Second Army moved to an anger such as I have never seen in them before.'

And with those words, the ten-minute broadcast ended.

Vera switched off the wireless, but no one spoke.

No one had touched their tea, which was now cold.

They all had tears running unashamedly down their faces.

Finally, Vera pushed herself to her feet and went off to make a fresh pot.

Rina looked at Hannah. She saw heartbreak, horror, outrage and anger. A reflection of what they were all feeling – what anyone would surely feel having listened to the words of the BBC reporter.

She also realised at that moment that there would be no stopping Hannah. If Rina had imagined before that she had a sliver of a chance of stopping her niece going over to Europe to track down her parents, what they had just endured had obliterated that remaining hope.

Hannah and Olly didn't stay for a fresh brew and instead walked all the way back home. Olly put his arm around Hannah and held her close every step of the way. As he walked down the cobbled streets of his home town, he resolved to be strong and brave for the woman he loved.

Meanwhile, Rina and Vera sat chatting in the quietness of the cafeteria. Vera had agreed with her friend that there would be no changing Hannah's mind.

'Yer job now is to help her prepare the best she can for what she's about to dee. To help them both, 'cos where Hannah gans, that lad's gannin too. Make no mistake. If she walks into a blazing inferno, the lad'll be right there next to her.'

It was then that Rina knew what she could do to help, and after the two women hugged each other, Rina left and went to see the rabbi.

Chapter Twenty-Two

The next day, Hannah and Olly both went to the British Red Cross offices in the town centre. They sat and listened as the middle-aged woman who introduced herself as Mrs King, the regional coordinator, told them that the charity was putting together teams to go to Belsen, as well as any other camps that were liberated as the war in Europe drew to a close. Hannah had asked what skills they were looking for and been told that they needed doctors and nurses for the hospitals, welfare officers to take care of children, and cooks to establish canteens to feed the inmates. Others were needed to set up first-aid posts, handle stores of fuel and clothing supplies, and to drive patients from the camps to hospital.

'Will you be in need of translators?' Hannah asked.

Mrs King nodded and listened as Hannah explained that she was fluent in English, Czech and German, and was able to speak a little Polish. Olly added that he was also able to speak Czech, which was an exaggeration, but as he and Hannah had both agreed last night, who would know any different? It was unlikely the person interviewing them would know a word of Czech, never mind enough to test him.

'And I take it you're married?' Mrs King asked, looking down at Hannah's left hand.

They nodded as Hannah raised her hand, showing a gold band that had been given to her last night when they had sat and told Rina of their plans. Knowing that those in charge at the Red Cross would keep Hannah and Olly together if they believed them to be man and wife, Rina had taken off her wedding ring and put it on Hannah's finger. She'd been relieved it fitted.

This morning, before they had gone into town, Rina had produced a marriage certificate. She had smiled on seeing the looks of shock on their faces. Before her niece had a chance to ask her how she'd managed to get hold of what looked like a very credible forgery, Rina told them, 'In the words of Oliver Goldsmith, "Ask me no questions, and I'll tell you no fibs."' Rina had then handed Olly a well-worn kippah, a navy blue skullcap embroidered with the Star of David, as well as a thick piece of parchment signed by the rabbi, which, she told him, meant that he was also now officially a Jew. 'You've studied well,' she told Olly, 'so you know everything you need to know.' She'd looked at them both with tears starting to show in her eyes. 'And when you come back, we'll do it all properly – the conversion and the marriage – all right?' Hannah had flung her arms around her aunty and thanked her, choking back the tears. Rina had done what she could to make sure they would be together – not just as man and wife, but as two Jews. There would be no reason whatsoever for them to be separated.

'So,' Mrs King asked as she uncapped her fountain pen, 'what war work have you been doing?'

When they told her that they both worked in the drawing office at Thompson's as draughtsmen, Mrs King's face lit up. 'Oh, that's interesting. I've known a few draughtsmen in my time, and they were also quite talented at drawing. Would you say that you are too?'

Knowing this was no time for modesty, Hannah chirped up, 'We are. Aren't we, Olly?'

Olly nudged his spectacles up the bridge of his nose and smiled. 'Yes, without wanting to seem like we are blowing our own trumpets, I'd say we are.'

Mrs King smiled. 'Excellent. We've decided to send an official war artist to record and reflect the work we are doing over there – when you have any free time, you can help him.'

Mrs King glanced down at her hands before looking back at Hannah and Olly.

'I have to know that you are both aware of what has been happening over there in the camps?'

They nodded.

'We heard the broadcast last night,' Hannah said.

'And the rabbi has been keeping us informed,' Olly added.

'Good,' she said. 'You will need to be prepared – or as prepared as can be.'

When she asked about their parents and heard that Hannah's mother and father had been taken to Auschwitz, she nodded her understanding. The young woman sitting in front of her would not be the first or the last to volunteer to work for the Red Cross in the hope of finding loved ones. She hoped the young woman looking at her now with her soulful brown eyes had realistic expectations. The sadness she saw in her suggested she did.

The next couple of days were a flurry of activity.

Mrs King had told Hannah and Olly that there were two places left in the fifth group that was due to fly out to Belsen, and asked if they'd want to fill those seats. They had agreed without hesitation. After leaving the Red Cross office, they had gone straight to Thompson's. First of all, they'd seen Basil, their boss, who had become quite emotional, and told them to take care and come back and see him when they returned.

They promised they would. Then they had headed over to see the women welders, who were all shocked, not so much that they were going over to Europe, but that they were going so soon. They were even more shocked when Angie spotted Hannah's ring and they learnt of Rina's subterfuge. Determined to give them a send-off, it was immediately agreed they would all gather at Vera's café to wave them off.

The 'newly-marrieds' had then gone and told Olly's aunty and uncle, who were also taken aback at how quickly it was all happening, but had asked them what they could do to help with their preparations.

Saving the worst until last, they had gone to see Rina and Vera at the café. Vera had become uncharacteristically emotional and had disappeared into the kitchen under the pretext of getting them some tea. She had not been able to stop thinking about the broadcast and thought Hannah and Olly the most courageous people she had ever met for willingly going to such a godforsaken place. Rina, surprisingly calm, had sat them down at one of the tables to the side of the cafeteria and got her niece and Hannah's new 'husband' to take her through everything that had been said during their meeting with the Red Cross recruiter. On hearing that they were to leave within forty-eight hours, she managed to remain strong, something she had promised herself she would be – at least until after they had gone. Only then would she allow herself to weaken.

The following day went in a blur against the backdrop of the news that on Friday, Hitler's fifty-sixth birthday, Soviet artillery had begun shelling Berlin, and the Americans had taken Nuremberg. Clothes were laundered, bags were packed, documents real and fake were put safely into money belts. They had another meeting with Mrs King, who gave them their official accreditation, as well as stamped visas and travel cards. More than once Hannah was reminded of the days before she had left Prague, the slight panic, the hastily drawn-up papers, her parents' worried faces, their smiles betrayed by tears as they had waved her off at the train station with the other children, all bound for the safety of foreign lands.

On Sunday, they said their farewells to Olly's aunty and uncles and cousins, promising them they would write as regularly as they could. They then nipped into the synagogue on Ryhope Road and said their thanks and their farewells to the rabbi, who gave the Priestly Blessing, known in rabbinic literature as 'raising of the hands', which was often given before a long journey.

After picking up their stuffed haversacks and leather satchels – and with their money belts already tied securely around their waists – they set off for Vera's café, having arranged to be collected from there by the Red Cross truck that would be taking them to RAF Usworth, just a few miles outside the town.

When they walked into the café, Martha was the first up to give Hannah a big bear hug. Out of them all, Martha was probably the closest to Hannah, and would miss her the most.

'Mam and Dad said "Good luck and take care",' Martha said, taking their bags and dumping them by the door. 'And Mam insisted I give you some of her home-made flapjacks for the journey.' Martha presented a cardboard box tied with string and put it next to their luggage.

'Come on, sit down, *Mr and Mrs Bell*!' Dorothy commanded, forcing herself to sound full of cheer.

As they sat, Hannah looked around at everyone and very nearly burst out crying. It had suddenly hit her just how much she was going to miss her friends. Friends who had become like family to her in her adopted homeland.

'How are you feeling?' Rosie asked.

'Honestly?' Hannah looked round at her friends' expectant faces.

They all nodded.

'Frightened,' she admitted, glancing at Olly, who took her hand, sensing her fight to keep the tears at bay.

'Afraid of what we're going to see over there,' Olly explained.

'But also glad,' Hannah added. 'Glad we can do something to help. Glad that we've got a chance of not only trying to find my mother and father, but helping other people like them.'

'That makes sense,' Gloria said.

Hannah and Olly nodded as Vera came bustling out of the kitchen, carrying a tea tray.

She was followed by Rina carrying a tray with a mound of sandwiches.

'Make sure yer both eat plenty,' Vera commanded Hannah and Olly as the tea and sandwiches were put in the middle of the table. 'Yer'll need to keep your strength up.'

Rina didn't say anything, just gently touched her niece's head and then turned back to the kitchen, followed by Vera.

'How's your aunty been?' Polly asked.

Hannah gave a sad smile. 'She's putting on a brave face.'

'It's only normal that she's gonna be worried,' said Gloria.

'She wouldn't be human if she wasn't,' Rosie agreed.

'Come on, tuck in, everyone,' Martha said, putting two sandwiches each on Hannah's and Olly's plates.

As the women drank their tea and ate their sandwiches, the talk turned to the day they had all started at the yard. Dorothy hooted with laughter. 'Eee, I'll bet Rosie's heart sank when she saw us lot tip up.'

'Yeah,' Angie chuckled, 'I bet yer thought yer'd got yourself a right lot.'

Rosie smiled at the memory of Dorothy, Gloria, Polly, Hannah and Martha on their first day at Thompson's. 'I knew I had my hands full, that's for sure.' She smiled. 'But I have to admit that you all surprised me. You were quick learners.'

They reminisced a while longer before their chatter was stopped by the doorbell tinkling, and the women looked up to see Helen arriving. Everyone welcomed her and made room around the table.

'Thanks,' said Helen. 'I'm not staying long, though.' She looked at Hannah and Olly. 'I just wanted to wish you both all the best and a safe journey – and, Hannah, I really hope you manage to find your mother and father.'

'Thank you,' said Hannah. 'I'm going to send updates to Martha so she can tell you all how we're getting on.'

'Well, fingers crossed. And you know, when you do come back, there'll still be jobs for you both,' Helen relayed.

Hannah's face lit up. 'That's great to know. Thanks, Helen.'

Olly looked equally pleased.

'Well, it's the least I can do,' Helen said. 'Especially after the way I treated you when you first came to the yard.' She felt herself blush with embarrassment, thinking of the old Helen. The one who had tried to break up Rosie's squad of welders. 'I want you to know how much I regret the way I behaved. And that I really am so sorry.'

'You don't have to apologise,' Hannah said.

'I do.' Helen smiled.

'Well, your apology is accepted,' Hannah said, knowing it was important for Helen to hear her say so. 'And I think everyone would agree with me when I say that what you have done since then has more than made up for it.'

The women murmured their agreement.

'On top of which,' Hannah continued, 'it all worked in my favour, because I ended up working in the drawing office, where I was a lot more useful . . . and I met Olly – my "husband".'

They all chuckled.

'I heard the good news,' Helen said, arching her eyebrows. 'Congratulations!'

The mention of Hannah and Olly's speedy nuptials got the women chatting about how they would celebrate in style when the newly-weds returned from their very unusual 'honeymoon', everyone wanting to keep the atmosphere light-hearted and focused on Hannah's return rather than her departure.

'Talking about weddings,' Hannah said, looking apologetically at Angie and Quentin, 'we're so sorry we won't be at yours.'

'Dinnit be daft. I'll get my wedding organiser to write 'n tell yer all about it,' Angie said.

'Definitely,' Dorothy agreed, tapping the top pocket of her overalls, where she had put the address for Red Cross correspondence.

Helen suddenly started scrabbling around in her bag. 'I almost forgot – I need to give you the wages you're owed. Here we are . . .' She produced a brown envelope. 'I hope you don't mind me taking the liberty, but I got the money changed into dollars. Apparently, that's the best currency to trade with over there.'

'Oh, thanks, Helen,' Hannah and Olly said at the same time.

'You're welcome,' Helen smiled and took a sip of her tea. She was glad Hannah hadn't checked it and seen that the notes amounted to much more than a week's wages.

Seeing it was nearly time for Hannah and Olly to leave, Helen got up.

'Good luck!' she said. Hannah stood up and gave Helen a hug.

'Thank you,' Hannah said, raising the brown envelope, which she knew by its thickness contained more than a week's wage – much more.

'And good luck to you too,' she said, as Helen turned to go.

Helen pulled a puzzled expression.

'With your decision,' said Hannah.

Everyone looked at Helen, trying to read her reaction. *Would she say yes or no to Matthew's proposal?*

Helen laughed. 'I'll probably still be dithering by the time you come back.'

Everyone chuckled, although none of them thought that patience was top of Matthew's virtues. He would want an answer sooner rather than later.

Hearing the door close as Helen left, Rina came to sit at the table. She had tried to convince herself that she wanted her niece to enjoy the company of her friends before she went, but the truth was she'd kept busy in the kitchen because she didn't know how long she could last without giving in to the tears.

'Well,' she said, looking up at the canteen clock, 'looks like it's almost time.'

Everyone looked at Hannah and Olly, and then at Rina. Vera came out of the kitchen and stood in the doorway, arms folded, knowing that her friend had something she wanted to say to Hannah before she left.

'I remember when you started work at Thompson's,' Rina began, looking at her niece and then around at her work-mates. 'I remember thinking you were crazy – even more so when I saw how exhausted you were and how every night you fell into bed.' Rina put her hand to her chest. 'I felt such relief, hearing that you'd been offered an apprenticeship in the drawing office, knowing that this was something you were more suited to doing – and knowing that you would be happy, too, as it would fulfil your need to do something to help win the war.' Rina swallowed hard. 'And now that this war is almost won, you want – you *need* – to help those suffering in the aftermath. People like your dear mama and papa who have been brutalised in the Nazi death camps.'

She took Hannah's hand and squeezed it. 'I know how very proud your mother and father would be of you. For everything you have done. For the person you have become since leaving them.'

She swallowed hard, glancing at Olly, then back to her niece.

'But I need to know that you understand that it is unlikely they are still alive?'

'I do,' Hannah said. 'Although I still have hope. For what is life without hope?'

Rina smiled as the tears started to blur her vision.

*

When the Red Cross truck arrived, Rina took her niece in her arms and squeezed her tight.

'You take care out there,' she told her. 'Write as often as you can, and if it all gets too much, you come straight back home. What you are doing is honourable and brave, but you must not sacrifice your own health or sanity, do you understand?'

Hannah nodded. 'I understand, Aunty.'

All the women took it in turns to give Hannah and Olly a hug before the pair climbed into the front passenger seats of the truck. The driver was a young woman who smiled at the overall-clad women and the two older women in pinnies who had come to send them off.

As the truck slowly pulled away, they all stood and waved their arms in the air, shouting 'Good luck!' and 'Keep safe!' and 'We love you!' as the truck trundled off down High Street East. They didn't stop waving until the truck disappeared from view. Only then did they all turn to one another to see that their cheeks were wet with tears, and their smiles upended.

'Right,' Rosie said, taking charge. 'I think we are all going to go to the Tatham.'

'Good idea,' Gloria said, turning to Rina. 'All of us. No excuses.'

'Yer'll have nee argument from me,' Vera said. 'Nor from this one.' She looked at her friend. 'Will we, Rina?'

Rina hesitated. All she really wanted to do was to go home, go to bed and cry her eyes out, but it was clear Vera and Hannah's friends were not going to let her.

'No argument,' she acquiesced.

Chapter Twenty-Three

When Helen left the café, she felt unburdened. She had wanted to apologise properly to Hannah for a long, long time and now she had done it – and in front of everyone.

She looked at her watch. It was nearly five o'clock.

She could nip to the yard and do an hour's overtime. She certainly had plenty of paperwork to catch up on. And there wouldn't be any distractions as it was a Sunday.

She reached her car, which she had parked round the corner in Church Street East.

Or she could go and tell John? She'd said he'd be the first to know.

She jumped in her little sports car and turned the ignition.

Why not? It wasn't as if Dr Eris would do anything now. She'd got her man, after all. They were due to be married in three weeks.

Checking her rear-view mirror and pulling out, Helen felt strangely liberated.

Driving along the coastal road, there was a light April shower, but by the time she reached Ryhope village, the sun had appeared. Turning into the main driveway of the red-brick, purpose-built Emergency Hospital, Helen smiled at seeing a faint rainbow in the sky. It felt like a good omen.

She was proved right. After parking up and going to see the young receptionist, who had replaced Denise some months previously, she asked her to find out if Dr Parker was free, and to pass on the message that Miss Crawford was here to see him. Her heart almost burst with glee when a few minutes later he came striding into the main foyer. He wasn't wearing his usual white overcoat, but a short-sleeved blue cotton shirt and a pair of tailored grey trousers.

'Is everything all right?' he asked, worry etched across his handsome face.

'Yes, yes, everything's fine,' she reassured.

Seeing the relief on his face as he brushed back his mop of blond hair, Helen immediately apologised. 'Oh, sorry, John, I didn't mean to cause alarm. I just thought I'd pop in on the off chance you were free.'

Dr Parker's smile was as bright as it was wide. 'I am. In fact, you couldn't have timed it better. I've just this minute finished my shift.'

Helen said a quick prayer of thanks. 'Let's have a walk round the grounds. It's a beautiful day.'

Without thinking, she put the crook of her arm out for John to link.

Without hesitation he obliged.

They walked through the main door, which had been latched back due to the warm weather, neither of them speaking as they walked down the steps. Both simply enjoying the feeling of closeness.

As they turned right and walked past the wooden bench where Dr Parker had proposed to Dr Eris, neither said anything. Helen had never admitted that she had stood stock-still in shock at the top of the steps after stumbling upon the proposal, and John had never asked if the person he'd caught out of the corner of his eye walking back into the hospital was Helen.

'So, tell me,' Dr Parker asked, 'something's happened – something good?'

'Well,' Helen began, feeling the goosebumps on her arms, which had nothing to do with the slight chill in the breeze and everything to do with the feel of John's bare skin on hers, 'I've just been to say goodbye to Hannah and Olly.'

'They're going?' he asked, surprised. 'So soon?'

Helen nodded and proceeded to tell Dr Parker all about Hannah and Olly volunteering their services to the Red Cross, their 'marriage', and Olly's overnight 'conversion' to Judaism.

'Well I never!' Dr Parker couldn't hold back his surprise.

'Everyone met at the café this afternoon to say their farewells,' Helen explained.

They continued walking along the gravelled pathway, still arm in arm.

'And I did what I've wanted to do for such a long time,' Helen said.

Dr Parker looked at her. 'You apologised?'

A wide smile spread across Helen's face. 'I did.'

Dr Parker squeezed her arm with his free hand. 'That's wonderful to hear.' Now he knew why she'd come to see him. Just like he knew the guilt she had felt over her behaviour towards Hannah had been compounded every time she heard some news about what was happening to Jews abroad.

'And what did she say?' Dr Parker asked.

'She said she accepted my apology, but she claimed it had all worked to her advantage.'

'By allowing her to work in the drawing office?'

'Exactly,' Helen said.

They walked on, their arms still linked.

Helen knew she should ask how the preparations for the wedding were going, now that it was just three weeks away, and so she forced herself. From what she could gather, Dr Eris was doing most of the organising. All John had to do was hire a morning suit.

Dr Parker knew he should ask after Matthew, even though he had no desire to bring him into the conversation. But it would seem odd if he didn't.

'So,' Dr Parker said, forcing a lightness into his tone, 'how's Matthew doing?'

Helen smiled. 'Matthew's doing fine. As always.' She paused. 'Actually, he's asked for my hand in marriage.'

Dr Parker stopped in his tracks, his arm dropping as he stood back and looked at Helen.

'Well, that is a bit of a shocker!' He couldn't contain his surprise.

Helen laughed. 'Shocking that someone proposed to me?'

'No, no, of course not,' Dr Parker said. 'It just seems all of a sudden. You haven't been courting for that long, have you?'

'That's true,' Helen said, starting to walk again, aware that their arms were no longer touching.

'Well, I guess congratulations are in order,' Dr Parker said, trying to sound upbeat.

'That might be a little premature,' Helen said.

Dr Parker looked askance.

'Because I haven't said yes,' Helen said.

'You turned him down?' said Dr Parker, feeling his heart lift.

'No.' Helen threw Dr Parker a sidelong glance. 'I've just told him that I need time to think.'

Dr Parker didn't say anything.

'The thing is,' Helen said, dropping her voice, even though there was no one around to hear, 'it's not just about me being unsure.'

Again, Dr Parker raised his eyebrows.

'It's about him not really knowing me.'

'Really?' Dr Parker said. 'The impression I got was that you both seem very at ease with each other.'

Helen shook her head. 'No, I mean he doesn't know anything about *my past*.'

'Ah,' Dr Parker said, his tone immediately softening. 'Your miscarriage?'

'That and the circumstances around it. Theodore. Him being a married man . . .' Helen let her voice trail off.

'Well, that shouldn't matter – not one bit!' Dr Parker said, immediately feeling defensive of Helen should anyone dare to judge her.

Helen stopped walking, turned to Dr Parker and put her arms out.

'Do you mind?'

'Of course not,' Dr Parker said, allowing Helen to step forward and give him a hug.

'I wish everyone thought the same as you,' she said, squeezing him and holding him for a few seconds, enjoying the feel of her arms around him and his around her.

'I do love you, John.' The words just slipped out as she pulled away.

'I love you too, Helen.'

If only you knew how much.

As Dr Parker waved Helen off in her car, he thought that if he needed any more assurances that Helen saw him as a friend and nothing more, then he'd just had proof. Why did he keep tormenting himself with thoughts that perhaps she did have feelings for him – feelings that were not just those of a friend? When it was obvious that all she had ever wanted from him had been the love and care of a good friend.

The hug had said it all.

As well as the fact that she was clearly going to marry Matthew.

Later on that evening, when Helen was sitting at her dressing table, brushing her hair, her mind kept going over and over her conversation with John.

He'd been surprised by Matthew's proposal, but he hadn't seemed in any way upset. But why would he be? He was with Claire now. He might have thought he loved Helen last year when they had chatted in the canteen and he had confessed his feelings for her. But that was ten months ago. Time had passed. Feelings change. John had proposed to Claire. What more evidence did she need? He would never have asked Claire to be his wife if his love wasn't one hundred per cent. Or if he still harboured feelings for her? *Would he?*

And the hug they had shared had been purely platonic. She had not picked up a hint of passion or any kind of physical attraction. It had been purely a loving embrace between two friends.

*

After Dr Parker told Dr Eris about Helen's impromptu visit, Claire had quietly seethed – until John told her about Matthew's proposal.

Then the only feeling she had was one of relief.

Helen had clearly conceded defeat and moved on, as Claire had hoped she would.

Now Dr Eris could really enjoy the run-up to her wedding.

She just wished she could see the face of her ex-fiancé when the invitation dropped on his doormat.

It was a thought made all the more pleasurable as she had heard from her best friend that his marriage to the woman he'd jilted her for was far from being one 'made in heaven'.

Quite the opposite, by the sounds of it. Or rather, by the sounds of them arguing, which had been heard by their next-door neighbours.

Dr Eris smiled.

Everything had worked out just perfectly.

Chapter Twenty-Four

Monday 23 April

'Who's that I just saw coming out of the servants' entrance?'

Miriam walked into her father's study.

'Some matronly-looking, older woman?'

'Ah,' Mr Havelock said, pausing to puff on his cigar, 'that's the new cleaner ... Mrs ... What's her name?' He tapped his head with a bony finger. 'Mind's going as well as the old body,' he complained.

He thought hard for a moment.

'*Bevan!* That's it. Mrs Bevan!' he declared triumphantly.

Miriam walked over to the large gilt-framed mirror above the mantelpiece and checked out her reflection.

'See – you got there in the end, Father.' Miriam tried not to sound condescending, but failed.

She turned to see her father take a sip of his brandy.

'Although I have to say, Papa, drinking brandy all day long probably doesn't help the old memory.'

'Pfah! You're a fine one to talk.' Mr Havelock spat out the words.

Miriam put her hands on her hips, challenging him. 'I rarely have a drink before five o'clock – unless there's some sort of function on.'

'Which is most days,' Mr Havelock remonstrated.

Miriam tutted and turned to see Agatha appear with a small tray with a single cup of tea on it. Looking across at her father as he took another sip of his Rémy, it took all her restraint not to proclaim him a hypocrite.

'Thank you, Agatha,' Miriam said, inspecting her father's housekeeper as she left the room. She thought she seemed more sour-faced than usual.

'So, how come you've got a new cleaner? What happened to your old one?' she asked, walking over to the large sash window, now no longer marred by crosses of brown anti-blast tape. She was not at all interested in her father's new employee, but she needed a distraction. It was actually quite difficult to see her father drink and not partake herself. But she couldn't. She didn't want him thinking her a lush. Not now he'd made her the main beneficiary of his will.

'According to Agatha, she got another job with some *east end* solicitor,' Mr Havelock said, raising his eyebrows. 'Now, come and sit down, drink your tea and tell me all the latest.'

Miriam did as she was told and sat down.

Taking a sip of tea, she put her cup back on the saucer and widened her eyes.

'Well, it would seem that your granddaughter might finally have bagged herself a husband,' she said, enjoying watching her father's reaction. *And they say women are gossips.*

'Really?' Mr Havelock said. 'Do tell me more.'

Miriam happily relayed to her father how Matthew Junior had proposed to Helen on Easter Sunday, but she had yet to give him an answer. She did not tell him the only reason she knew of her daughter's offer of marriage was because she had come back to the house one afternoon and overheard Henrietta and Mrs Westley chatting about it.

'So, why hasn't your daughter given the Royce boy an answer?' Mr Havelock asked, taking another sip of his brandy. 'I'd have thought she'd be jumping at the chance – *especially with her history.*'

'History?' Miriam asked. Her mind had started to wander to her afternoon drinks with Amelia and two captains from the Admiralty.

'Now look whose memory is going?' Mr Havelock mocked. 'You know, your daughter's dalliance with that married surgeon. The baby?'

'Of course I remember,' Miriam said. 'But it's not as if the Royce boy, as you call him, is ever going to know about that, is he?'

'I suppose he isn't, is he?'

Unless someone tells him.

As soon as Miriam had given her father an update on Henrietta and reassured him that she was pretty much housebound and didn't appear to have any desire to leave her new home or, more importantly, disclose her true identity, Mr Havelock sent his daughter packing on the pretext that he was sure she had better things to be doing than sitting with 'her aging relic of a father'. Miriam responded accordingly, rejecting her father's description, and plumping up his ego by telling him he was as fit as a fiddle and far from being a 'relic'. She uttered her words whilst walking out of the study. She didn't needed telling twice.

As soon as he heard the front door close and the engine of the Jaguar turn over, ready to take his daughter wherever she wanted, which was probably straight back to the Grand, Mr Havelock picked up the receiver and dialled the operator.

After giving the young telephonist the relevant name and the address, he heard a couple of clicks before being connected.

The phone rang several times before it was finally answered.

'Good afternoon, Royce senior speaking.' The old man's voice was out of puff and slightly slurred due to the stroke he'd suffered.

'Royce, old boy,' Mr Havelock said, full of gusto, 'how are you? Up for a visitor?'

Mr Havelock listened and smiled. He was glad he'd got chummy with the old man when it was clear his son was sniffing about Helen. He knew it would pay dividends.

'Good. Good. Shall we say tomorrow?'

Having agreed a time, Mr Havelock hung up.

Pouring himself another brandy, he took a sip.

Sometimes the minor victories were as enjoyable as the major ones.

And this one he would at least be around to see for himself.

Chapter Twenty-Five

'I'll see you all tomorrow,' Polly shouted to the squad as they picked up their haversacks and made to leave. She turned to head off in the opposite direction.

'Where are you going?' Rosie asked, putting her hand to her forehead to shield her eyes from the sun.

Polly pointed to the wooden shed near the quayside, where the dock divers could be found when they weren't carrying out underwater repairs that would otherwise require the ship to be hauled into one of the dry docks.

Rosie nodded her understanding.

Throwing her haversack across her shoulder, Polly headed over to see the 'monster men', a name the women had given the deep-sea divers after seeing them in their twelve-bolt helmets, huge metal boots and oversized canvas suits shortly after starting work at the yard – a moment etched in Polly's mind as it was when she had first clapped eyes on Tommy. When she had realised that love at first sight was not a myth, but a very real phenomenon.

As she hurried to the quayside, her haste was aided by the sudden gust of a sea breeze. As soon as she reached the wooden cabin, she flung open the door and was relieved to see her trip had not been wasted, for Ralph, the head of the diving team, was there, sitting chatting to one of his lines-men. The pair were smoking rollies and sipping from tin cups of hot tea. Seeing a half-bottle of rum on the small wooden table, Polly knew this meant they were finished for the day.

'Polly!' Ralph's weather-beaten face lit up on seeing Tommy's wife.

The linesman tipped his hat and gave her a gummy smile.

'Hi, Ralph,' Polly said. She smiled at the linesman, whose name she didn't know.

She swung her haversack onto the table, rummaged inside and pulled out a letter.

'From Tommy,' she said, handing over the envelope.

Ralph smiled and gestured to an upturned wooden crate. 'Make yerself comfortable, pet.'

Polly shook her head. 'No, thanks anyway, Ralph. If I sit down, I mightn't get up again.'

Ralph looked at the tired, sooty-faced, pretty young woman with whom his best diver Tommy had fallen head over heels in love. They'd had a tricky start to their court-ship, which had nearly ended before it had got going, but thankfully, Cupid had triumphed. Ralph and his team had helped them celebrate their wedding, and after Tommy had gone back to the naval base in Gibraltar, they had prayed for his safe return. Anyone working as a mine-clearance diver needed all the prayers he could get.

'Let me guess,' Ralph said, looking at the envelope and relighting his cigarette. 'He wants to make sure there'll be a job for him when he gets back?'

Polly smiled, pushing a thick strand of her long chestnut-coloured hair back into her headscarf.

'That's about the nub of it,' she said. 'Although between

you and me, I think it's just as much about being able to get back into his diving suit and into the Wear as it is about earning a wage.'

They all chuckled. Tommy, like his grandfather before him, was born to be a diver. He was never happier than when he was submerged in water. He was also an invaluable asset at the yard as he could find his way around the bottom of a ship with his eyes closed.

'You write him back, pet – tell him not to worry.' He took another deep drag on his thin, hand-rolled cigarette. 'He'll be back in that river before he can say Bob's yer uncle 'n Fanny's yer aunt.' He let out a bark of laughter. 'Tell him we hope he's not gone soft working out there – what with all that sun, clear skies 'n crystal blue sea.'

Polly smiled. Relieved. She had hoped there'd be a job for Tommy on his return, but the war had taught them all that nothing was a certainty.

After leaving Ralph and the linesman, Polly hurried back home. Reaching the ferry, she jumped aboard just as it was about to leave.

'Polly!'

She turned to see Bobby.

'No Dorothy?' she asked, making her way over to him. The ferry lurched forward, and she grabbed the rail.

'I had to work a little later. I told her to get herself home. Besides, I think I've been put on the back burner until after Angie's wedding.'

Polly chuckled. 'She's certainly taking her duties as wedding organiser very seriously.'

'And doing so with military precision,' Bobby added.

'At least it's only temporary – you'll have her back as soon as the wedding's over.'

'Twelve days to go – I'm counting down the days.'

There was a lovely cooling breeze as they crossed the breadth of the river.

'You get held up?' Bobby asked, knowing if Polly had left on time, she'd have been home by now, cuddling Artie before getting out of her dirty, sweaty work clothes.

'I went to see Ralph,' Polly said, knowing she didn't need to explain why. She had already chatted to Bobby regarding Tommy's concerns about getting a job when the war ended. 'You were right,' she added.

Bobby nodded. From what he'd learnt about Tommy since he'd moved in with the Elliots in March last year, he'd be welcomed back with open arms. Not just because he was the best diver the Wear Commissioner had employed, apart from his grandfather, Arthur, in whose footsteps he was clearly following, but because the man was a war hero. If not officially, he certainly was in the eyes of those who knew he'd spent a good part of the war pulling limpet mines off the hulls of Allied ships. The man must have nerves of steel.

Reaching the south docks, they piled off the old steamer with the rest of the shipyard workers and started the ten-minute walk back to Tatham Street in the east end.

'Do you think they'll let him come back early?' Bobby asked. He knew that Tommy had returned to Gibraltar against doctor's orders. He'd nearly died after being caught in an underwater explosion and had been brought back home, where they'd had to operate on him to remove his spleen. Dorothy had told him Tommy had persuaded Dr Parker to sanction his return.

Polly let out a slightly frustrated laugh. 'Even if they did, Tommy wouldn't take it. He's determined to see this war through to the bitter end.'

Bobby nodded. He understood. It was something he had been deprived of when he'd suffered a head injury during the Battle of North Cape more than a year ago. A head injury that had caused him to lose the hearing in his left ear and be medically discharged from the navy.

'Dorothy's still not speaking to her mam, by the sounds of it?' Polly knew it had been nearly five months since Dorothy had taken Bobby to meet her mother and stepfather – an occasion that had been a total disaster and which had ended with Dorothy spilling the beans about her mother's bigamy. Something Dorothy's stepfather, Frank, had known nothing about.

'No, I've tried to encourage her,' Bobby said. 'Told her that she doesn't have to fall out with them because of the way they were towards me.'

Dorothy had told them all how demeaning and outright snobby both her mother and Frank had been towards Bobby. Her stepfather had said that if Bobby had come to ask for Dorothy's hand in marriage, then he should think again. Dorothy's mother had nodded her agreement as Frank had carried on insulting Dorothy's beau by telling his stepdaughter that they would not allow her to marry below herself. And that they had allowed her to play around being a welder at the shipyard, but that didn't mean she could marry 'some shipyard worker'. It was this that had provoked Dorothy into enlightening her stepfather that he was not legally married to the woman with whom he had four daughters.

Bobby sighed. 'Dorothy is adamant that it's her mother and stepfather who need to make the first move and apologise.'

'Well, I must say, I think she's right,' Polly said.

'I know, but I just don't like to be the person who has divided a family,' he said.

'Oh, I don't think their relationship was particularly brilliant before then. If it wasn't you, it would have been something else,' Polly reassured him.

They reached the front door of the Elliot household, where they knew they would be met with Agnes wanting to know why they were both late, Lucille's demands for attention and Bel's need for 'adult conversation'. There was also a good chance that Beryl would be there, and possibly Audrey and Iris, if they were back from work, though they'd only stay long enough to say hello to Bobby, on whom they both had huge crushes.

Polly took a deep breath and looked at Bobby. 'Ready for the madness and mayhem?'

Bobby laughed. 'Into the fray.'

Chapter Twenty-Six

Friday 27 April

As Helen drove into work, the sun was shining and it seemed like a sign that what she was going to do today was the right decision. She'd taken an entire month to make up her mind. She'd kept herself awake at night thinking about it, chatted about it to her grandmother, and to Gloria, and they had both given her the same advice. *Follow your heart.*

Her heart was torn between a love that could never be requited and one that most definitely would. It would be madness to sacrifice a love that could be real for one that could not.

And so, she had made up her mind.

She was going to say yes to Matthew.

And she was also going to tell him the truth about her past.

Pulling up outside the main gates at Thompson's and parking in her usual place just up from the quayside, she wondered what Matthew's reaction would be. Instinct told her that he would still want her. He'd been married himself and widowed. He was a man of the world.

Climbing out of the car, she felt a rush of nerves.

She would be making herself vulnerable. There was a possibility that he would reject her. She wondered if she would be able to handle it if he did spurn her because of her past.

Well, she told herself as she smiled up at Davey, the time-keeper, *it didn't matter. She had to tell him. It was the only way.* She could not start married life with secrets. And while she knew that Matthew had his faults, she believed he was an open and honest man, which was part of the reason she had come to feel love for him.

It was a busy day. Thompson's launched *Empire Arrow*, which, it was expected, would be the last launch before the end of the war in Europe. The papers were full of the ending of the battle of Berlin and the Americans linking up with the Russians along the central German front . The Allies rejected Himmler's offer to surrender all German forces in the west, refusing to let this split their alliance with the Soviets. It was obvious that it would not be long before Hitler and his army raised the white flag.

After the launch, the women came to see Helen to tell her they'd just received a letter from Hannah, and that she and Olly were doing well. They hadn't located Hannah's parents, but were still glad they had made the decision to become Red Cross volunteers.

The day's events further buoyed Helen, making her feel positive and hopeful about the war and her own life – particularly, her love life.

She refused to think about John today. Telling herself instead to live in the real world – with a real love.

At five o'clock, Helen rang Matthew at Doxford's.

'Mr Matthew Royce's office, how can I help you?' Dahlia's slightly breathy voice sounded down the phone.

Helen fought back the wave of irritation she felt whenever

she had any dealings with Matthew's secretary. Or rather, his *personal assistant*.

'Hi, Dahlia, it's Miss Crawford here, can you put me through to Matthew.' It wasn't a request, rather a demand. There was something about the woman that brought out the bitch in Helen.

'Sorry, Helen . . . I mean, *Miss Crawford*,' Dahlia said, sounding anything but sorry, 'but Matthew's unavailable at the moment. Can I get him to call you back? Or perhaps you'd like to leave a message?'

Helen watched as her staff started to leave for the day. She guessed Dahlia, too, would be wanting to get off.

'Just tell him – or leave a message – saying I'll be over in about half an hour.' She paused.

'Anything else?' Dahlia asked, sensing Helen's hesitancy.

'Actually, yes, there is,' Helen said. 'Tell him I've got the answer to that question he asked me a little while ago.'

'Oh,' Dahlia said. 'That sounds very cryptic?'

Again, Helen felt piqued by Dahlia's overfamiliarity.

'If you can just pass the message on, Dahlia,' Helen said before hanging up.

Opening her handbag, she got out her compact and lipstick.

As she applied her favourite Victory Red, she felt a shiver of anticipation.

Excitement.

The war was coming to an end. Everyone's lives were on the precipice of change.

And that included her own.

*

234

Carefully placing the receiver in its hold, Dahlia sat back in her chair.

Tell him I've got the answer to that question he asked me a little while ago.

She picked up a pencil and pressed it so hard into the piece of paper, the pointed lead broke.

Matthew had certainly kept that one quiet.

But then again, he wouldn't have told her, would he? He'd have known her reaction.

Dahlia thought for a moment before standing up and straightening her clinging, low-cut dress.

She was glad she had worn this dress today.

'Who was that on the phone?' Matthew shouted through from his office.

Dahlia sashayed her way into her boss's domain.

'Only Marie-Anne asking if I'm up for a night out,' she said, reaching his desk and splaying her hands out on the embossed leather top, giving Matthew just a hint of cleavage.

'And are you?' Matthew asked, unable to keep his eyes from the dip of Dahlia's dress.

'Well, that depends,' Dahlia purred, pushing aside the paperwork that was sprawled across Matthew's desk and leaning across towards the man she loved.

The man she was determined to have.

Even if she had to play dirty to get him.

*

Helen hurried out of the office, across the yard, which was now quiet, or as quiet as the yard ever got, and out to her car. She checked her watch. It was twenty-past five. It would take her ten minutes maximum to get over to the other side to Doxford's. Hopefully, Dahlia would have left, as well as the rest of his staff, and she could give him the answer she knew he desperately wanted.

She'd decided not to spoil the moment, but would tell him that yes, she wanted to be his wife, and then later, over a drink, she would tell him more about her past.

The traffic wasn't too bad and the trip through South-wick and across the Queen Alexandra Bridge was quicker than she'd anticipated. Arriving outside the arched red-brick entrance with the large ornate metal gates, Helen parked up.

The gates were closed, but not locked, and Helen slipped through and walked over to the admin building.

Hurrying up the stairs, she felt a spring in her step, sud-denly in a rush to see Matthew.

Finally, she had let down her barriers and it felt good. Very good.

Once she was in the main office, which, like Thompson's, was open-plan and light, thanks to the large windows over-looking the yard, Helen slowed her pace.

Her heart was racing.

Seeing the door to Matthew's office was closed, she thought she'd surprise him.

Tiptoeing across the linoleum, she reached for the door handle.

But as she did so, she heard a noise.

It sounded as though Matthew was in pain.

Had he hurt himself?

She turned the door handle.

Was that a woman's voice she could hear?

Opening the door, Helen stopped dead in her tracks.

She stared in disbelief at the scene that greeted her.

Matthew and Dahlia were kissing. *More than kissing.*

Dahlia was sitting on the edge of the desk – her dress was hitched up, showing the tops of her stockings, and the straps had dropped down her arms, revealing a lacy black bra.

Hearing the door open and Helen's gasp of shock, Matthew looked up.

His hair was dishevelled and his shirt had been unbuttoned and pulled out so that it was hanging over his trousers, which, Helen noted thankfully, were still on.

Thank God she hadn't come any later.

'Oh my God! Helen!' Matthew pulled away from Dahlia, who turned her head to see Helen standing in the doorway, her green eyes blazing.

He hurriedly pushed his shirt back into his trousers and buttoned it up.

'I'm so sorry—' he began.

'*Sorry?*' Helen gasped, watching as Dahlia straightened her dress and pushed her straps back up onto her shoulders.

Glancing at Matthew, who ignored her, Dahlia walked, a little unsteadily in her high heels, over to the doorway.

She looked at Helen, who was barring her way, half expecting a slap.

'Sorry,' she muttered, hoping that might prevent any kind of violence. If the shoe had been on the other foot, she would be administering more than a slap – that was for sure.

Helen glowered at Dahlia.

'I'll bet you are,' she said, stepping aside and letting Matthew's lover sidle past.

As soon as she was out of the office, Dahlia allowed herself a self-satisfied smile.

That had gone better than she could ever have expected. Timed to perfection.

She hadn't been named the Swedish seductress for nothing!

'Well, that's a turn-up for the books,' Helen said, trying to keep her voice steady when inwardly she was shaking with shock and anger.

'I can explain,' Matthew said, brushing back his hair and walking over to her.

Helen put her hands out to halt him in his steps.

'Don't come near me,' she hissed.

Matthew looked at Helen, saw the look of coldness in her green eyes and knew he'd mucked up. Big time. He knew Helen and there was no way she'd have him back. Not after what she'd just seen. He walked to his desk and flopped down into his chair. The adrenaline of being so turned on by Dahlia, coupled with the shock of Helen walking in on them, had suddenly left him feeling light-headed.

'I came to tell you that yes, I'd marry you,' Helen said in disbelief. 'Looks like I've had a close shave.'

She walked forward and looked down at Matthew, suddenly seeing him for exactly the man he was.

Why hadn't she realised it before? Why was she such a poor judge of character when it came to men?

'Is there anything I can do or say to change your mind?' Matthew implored. He had to at least try, hopeless though he knew it was.

Helen gave him a look that left Matthew in no doubt as to what her answer was.

Seeing Helen standing there, making him feel small and the villain of the piece, he sat up.

'I think you need to get off your high horse, Helen,' he said. 'None of us are perfect, are we?'

'What do you mean by that?' Helen asked, feeling herself panic.

Did he know? Now that there was no way in a million years she was going to marry him, she did not want him knowing about her past.

'I think you know exactly what I mean,' Matthew accused, narrowing his eyes. 'All that "I want to wait until I'm married" spiel. What a load of rubbish all that was!'

Helen suddenly felt awash with shame. She tried to counter it, but it clung to her. She felt herself flush.

'For want of sounding like a broken record,' Helen said, *'what do you mean by that?'*

'I *mean* that behind the squeaky-clean façade lies quite a tale of sordid secrets and lies.'

Helen felt sick.

He knew.

'You,' Matthew said, 'were having it off with some married bloke – and not only that, but you were stupid enough to end up pregnant. *Ha!* And there was me thinking you had brains!'

He stared at Helen, feeling slightly victorious that he had turned the tables so swiftly.

'You were lucky, by all accounts, that you lost the baby.' He shook his head in disbelief, letting out a gasp of incredulity. 'Can you imagine the scandal?'

Helen had to restrain herself from stomping over to him and clawing the sickening grin off his face. *How could she ever have entertained marrying someone so revolting?*

'It's *you* who should be begging *me* to get married,'

Matthew continued, 'because, let's face it, no one wants to have soiled, second-hand goods, do they?'

Helen stared at him. *He sounded exactly like her mother! Had actually used the same words.* Helen swallowed back her fury. She would not lose control.

'Talk about the pot calling the kettle black.' She spoke her words through gritted teeth.

Matthew laughed.

'What world are you living in, Helen? Men get to play the field – women stay virgins until they're married. That's just the way it is.'

'Times are a-changing, Matthew, or haven't you noticed?' She paused, before fabricating a look of surprise.

'But *of course* you haven't noticed. You've been too busy screwing your *secretary*.'

'*Personal assistant*, don't forget,' Matthew smirked.

Helen knew then that what she had just witnessed between Matthew and Dahlia was not simply a one-off, and that they had obviously been having an affair for some time.

She'd heard enough.

She wanted to get away from this two-faced, two-timing, despicable louse.

'So,' Matthew said, sensing Helen was about to leave, 'let's call it quits, eh? You would have married me if you hadn't found out about Dahlia, and I would have married you if I hadn't found out your dirty little secret.'

Helen felt her head throbbing.

She needed to leave.

How could she have been so foolish not to have seen through this godawful man?

She gave Matthew the most hate-filled, derisory look she could muster, then turned on her heels and left.

Matthew listened to her high heels clomp down the stairs. He got up, looked out of the window and watched as she slipped through the iron gates. A few moments later, he heard the rev of an engine and the sound of Helen's little green sports car pulling away at speed.

He sighed and walked back to his desk, opening his top drawer and taking out a half-bottle of whisky.

Pouring himself a drink, he took a large gulp, grimacing as he felt the burn in his throat.

He was annoyed that Helen had found him out.

He couldn't have cared less how many married men she'd slept with – his reason for wanting her was not love, although he would certainly not have minded free access to her bed whenever the urge took him.

No, he would never have spurned her because of her past indiscretions – not with the money her family had. Money his family needed. Needed desperately. His father had told him that Charles Havelock had written Helen out of his will, but Matthew was sure he would have been able to get Helen to make it up with her grandfather. Families were always falling out and making up.

Helen wasn't the only one with a dirty little secret.

The highly respected Royce family was bankrupt.

Matthew took another gulp of whisky.

And as for Dahlia – well, she had certainly got what she wanted.

He knew he'd been taking a gamble when he'd started carrying on with her.

A gamble that had just lost him everything.

Chapter Twenty-Seven

Ten minutes later, Helen pulled up into the driveway of the Havelock residence. She was angry, very angry. Getting out of her car, she slammed the door shut, and took a deep breath.

Walking up the steps to the glossy black front door, she pulled the brass lever and waited impatiently.

When Eddy answered the door, she practically pushed past him. Glancing into the living room, she saw the back of the cleaner, who was on her knees, polishing the hearth surround. Looking right, she saw the study door was ajar. Before Eddy had time to speak or run ahead to announce her arrival, she had already barged into her grandfather's wood-panelled sanctuary.

As expected, he was sitting at his desk. He had a cigar in one hand and in the other he had the handset of his black Bakelite phone. He was, of course, the one talking, loudly and arrogantly.

Just looking at him made her bristle and feel the return of her disgust that they shared the same blood.

Marching over to his desk, she leant over and pressed the two buttons, ending the call.

Mr Havelock looked at his granddaughter in complete astonishment that she had dared to do what she had just done.

'What the hell?' he exclaimed.

'What the hell indeed!' Helen repeated, her voice raised.

The two looked at each other. Helen's emerald green eyes were blazing. Her grandfather's rheumy blue eyes were staring back – first of all with anger, then amusement.

'Oh, dearie me,' he said, a thin smile slowly inching across his sinewy old face. 'Let me guess.' He put his finger to his temple and tapped it. 'Might this have something to do with a certain Matthew Royce? A certain proposal of marriage?'

Helen continued to glower at her grandfather.

'How dare you divulge my personal life to those outside the family!'

Mr Havelock forced out mock laughter.

'What hypocrisy,' he chortled, 'when you are prepared to tell the world all of my secrets. Family secrets. At least I didn't air your dirty laundry to all and sundry – I only told my dear friend Royce senior. What he then did with that information was clearly his decision.'

Helen stepped forward so that she was looking down at her grandfather. 'The two don't compare. What you did to those young girls destroyed their lives – my own misdemeanours only hurt one person, and that was myself.'

'I'd say you're splitting hairs, Helen, dear,' Mr Havelock said, taking a puff on his cigar, causing Helen to stand back.

'And a word of wisdom from your dear old grandpapa.' He smiled and Helen felt herself shiver involuntarily. 'We've all got to pay for our actions. One way or another. There are always consequences.'

'No, Grandfather, this is about you getting what little satisfaction you can from hurting me. This is part of my punishment for being disloyal to you – for not doing what you want.' Helen spat out the words. 'You are a sick and perverted man.'

She turned to leave.

'Oh, Helen, you are still so very naïve, aren't you?' Mr Havelock was pleased to see his words had stopped Helen in her tracks. 'You don't think that was the reason the Royce boy retracted his proposal, do you?'

Helen wanted to correct him – to tell her grandfather that it was *she* who had rejected Matthew. But there was no way she wanted him to have the added satisfaction of knowing why – that the man she'd just been about to agree to marry had been seeing another woman behind her back. Sleeping with another woman – *and very nearly right in front of her*.

Mr Havelock smiled, seeing the mix of confusion and curiosity on Helen's face.

'The boy would have married you if you'd laid on your back for half the male population of the town. He wouldn't have given two tosses, especially as he's probably had more women than hot dinners himself, and that includes the years he was married to his dearly departed wife.'

Helen felt revulsion on imagining the man she had actually considered marrying being a compulsive skirt-chaser, someone who couldn't keep it in his pants if he tried. Not even when he was married.

'So why then?' Helen demanded. She saw the sadistic pleasure it was bringing him to toy with her, to play with her like a cat might a mouse.

'He didn't want to marry you because I told his dear father that unfortunately there would be no dowry as such – that your father was now penniless, having divorced your mother. But what really sealed the deal – or should I say, *undid the deal* – was when I told him that you would not be in my will, that I had effectively cut you out of any inheritance.'

244

Helen's mind was whirring.

'You look confused, my dear. So let me explain.' He took a leisurely pull on his cigar, enjoying the moment. Knowing that much as Helen wanted to leave, she couldn't until she knew the whole truth.

'You see, the Royces are broke.' He paused, waiting for the information to sink in. 'The family are what you might call "on their uppers".' Another pause. 'And the only way they can save themselves – keep themselves afloat financially – is by marrying money.'

Another puff on his cigar. Another plume of smoke.

'And you, my dear, were the perfect choice – and a very attractive one too, although it has to be said, you could have been last in the queue when it came to looks and he would still have pursued you.'

Helen stood and stared.

Then she inhaled deeply and slowly exhaled.

'Well,' she said calmly, 'if that's the case, Grandfather, I have to thank you.'

It gave Helen the tiniest taste of satisfaction to see it was now her grandfather who appeared confused.

'Because,' she explained, 'by doing what you did, you've just saved me from making one of the biggest mistakes of my life.'

And with that, she turned and walked out of the study.

As soon as he heard the front door slam, Mr Havelock went to pour himself another brandy. Seeing that the glass decanter was empty, he shouted out for Eddy.

Almost immediately he heard a short sharp rap on the door, before the rounded form of his new cleaner appeared.

'I believe Eddy's been sent out on an errand, Mr Havelock. Is there anything I can help with?'

'Yes.' He waved at the empty decanter. 'Fill it up. And make it sharp!'

'The Rémy?' Mrs Bevan asked as she picked it up.

'Of course,' Mr Havelock snapped. 'What else!'

As Mrs Bevan hurried out of the room, she smiled to herself.

For she now knew exactly what it was she was going to do.

She was actually surprised the idea had not come to her before. It was so obvious. *Such poetic justice.*

Sometimes, she mused, the answer to a problem was right there in front of you.

Chapter Twenty-Eight

When Helen pulled out of the driveway, she turned right and started driving along the main stretch of Glen Path. Turning left into The Cedars, she felt tears trickling down her face. She had been such a fool. So stupid. So very stupid. *Why was she so blind when it came to men?*

Turning left onto the Ryhope Road, she knew she didn't want to go back home. Henrietta and Dr Bernard were having their weekly book review. They would know something was wrong and try to wheedle it out of her.

Turning right and then left, she found herself driving down Burdon Road. On reaching the crossroads, she turned right into Borough Road and two hundred yards later, she was parking up.

Knocking on the basement-flat front door, she was surprised when Bobby answered.

'Helen, this is a surprise!' As he spoke, he saw that she had been crying.

'Are you OK? Come in.' He ushered her into the flat.

'Helen!' said Jack.

Hope squealed with excitement at seeing her big sister and toddled towards her.

Picking her up, Helen forced herself to smile. 'How's my little sweetie pie?' she asked.

Hope nodded.

'What's wrong?' Jack asked, seeing that his daughter was clearly not in a good way.

He walked over and took Hope from her.

'Go and get your book for your bedtime reading,' Jack said. Hope pulled a face.

'Now,' Jack said, firmly.

Hope looked at her father, then at her brother and sister, and seeing their serious faces, did as she was told.

'I take it Gloria isn't in?' Helen asked, trying to keep her voice steady and not succeeding.

'She's at the Tatham with the rest of the women,' Jack said. 'What's happened? And don't say nothing, because I can see something's up.'

Helen looked at her father and then at Bobby.

'You're right. Something has happened . . . It's about Matthew—'

'Ah, say no more,' Jack said.

'Come on,' said Bobby, pulling on his coat. 'I'll walk you there.'

Helen hesitated. Gloria knew all about Theodore and her miscarriage, but none of the other women did. No one did. Apart from her grandfather, her mother – and, of course, *John*.

Thinking of him made her heart ache.

'Come on,' Bobby said. 'A problem shared is a problem halved.'

Helen followed him out of the front door.

Walking into the Tatham, Helen was relieved to see it wasn't busy. Gloria and the rest of the women were sitting round a table near the window. They all had drinks. Dorothy had a reporter's pad in front of her and a pencil in her hand and was, as usual, taking centre stage.

On seeing Helen and Bobby enter the lounge bar, they looked surprised.

'Helen!' Dorothy called out. Everyone in the pub turned to look.

Gloria nudged Dorothy to keep quiet and waved Helen across.

'Vodka and lemonade?' Bobby asked.

'Thanks,' Helen said, sitting down on a stool Gloria had just pulled up for her.

'What's happened?' asked Rosie.

They all looked at Helen. They had never seen her look so pale, so despondent. She barely had any make-up on. No trademark red lipstick and her mascara was smudged. She'd clearly been crying.

'Sorry to interrupt . . .' she said, looking at Rosie, Gloria, Polly, Dorothy, Angie and Martha.

'Dinnit be,' Angie said, 'yer've done us all a favour. If *I'm* sick of talking about my own wedding, I'm sure everyone else is.' She glanced at her maid of honour. 'Apart from Dor, of course.'

'There are only *ten days* to go!' Dorothy defended herself.

Helen let out a light chuckle. She was glad she'd come. Just sitting here with them all had somehow lightened the darkness she felt had engulfed her.

'Here you are.' Bobby appeared and handed Helen her drink.

'Thanks, Bobby,' she said, taking a big swig.

'Anybody else in need of a refill?' he asked.

Everyone shook their heads.

'I have a feeling this is a women's-only discussion,' he said, 'but if you need me, I'll be just across the road.' He walked round and kissed Dorothy quickly on the lips, then left.

'What's happened?' Polly asked as soon as Bobby had gone.

'It has to be about a bloke,' Angie presumed.

'Dr Parker or Matthew?' Martha asked.

Helen gave a sad smile. 'Matthew.'

She took another sip of her drink and then told them how she had decided to say yes to Matthew's proposal and had gone to tell him, only to find him in a compromising position with Dahlia.

'Oh. My. God!' Dorothy's voice went uncannily low, over-compensating for trying her hardest not to shriek.

'Really?' Polly said, aghast. She imagined how she would feel if she walked in on Tommy and another woman. She felt a flash of fury just thinking about it.

'What a bitch,' hissed Angie.

'What a bastard,' Gloria said, leaning over and squeezing Helen's hand.

'Did anyone know?' Helen asked, scanning their faces.

They all shook their heads.

'If we had, we'd have told you,' Martha said.

'I thought Dahlia had her eye on Matthew,' Rosie confessed, 'but not that there was anything actually going on between them.'

'I suppose with hindsight, it's obvious now,' Helen said.

'But it does seem a bit of a coincidence that you walked in on them together?' Rosie queried.

Helen arched her eyebrow and took another sip of her drink.

'Yer not saying it was planned, are yer?' Angie asked, shocked.

Helen nodded solemnly. 'I rang Matthew's office and told Dahlia I was coming to see him.'

'What a sneaky cow,' Dorothy said. 'God, I hate that woman.'

'Whether it gets her what she wants,' Helen said, 'is a different matter.'

'Yeah, I can't imagine Matthew being too chuffed knowing Dahlia set him up,' said Martha.

'Well,' said Gloria. 'This might sound harsh, but I'm glad this has happened. I'd say you've had a close shave. Very close.'

'Exactly what I told Matthew.'

Helen looked at her friends.

'Actually, there was more to it than just me finding out about Matthew and Dahlia,' Helen began with a heavy sigh.

There was no guarantee that Matthew wouldn't tell others about her past. And if he told Dahlia, *everyone* would know.

The women looked at her with puzzled faces.

'Matthew also found out something about me,' Helen confessed, before telling them all about Theodore, the lying, philandering father-of-two, how naïve she had been, how he had ended their relationship and scurried back down south to his wife, who was just about to have their third child, only for Helen to find that she herself was pregnant.

Helen's voice softened as she told them how Dr Parker had helped her after bumping into her when she had gone looking for Theodore at the hospital. He had supported her in her decision to have the baby regardless of the scandal it would bring in its wake. She related how he had been there when she had started haemorrhaging, and how she'd almost died, but

Dr Parker had managed to call an ambulance and get her to the hospital in time. Thankfully, Dr Billingham had been on call and the two had saved her life – but not the life of her baby.

'A baby girl,' Helen added, forcing back the tears.

The women listened in silence, their own hearts breaking at the tragedy Helen had been through and the loss of her unborn baby daughter.

'Everyone was told your appendix had ruptured,' Rosie recalled.

'And that was why you had a week off – to recover,' Martha remembered.

'That's right. That was John's idea. He thought that would be the most believable cover story.'

'Did you know?' Polly looked at Gloria.

She nodded.

'No wonder you were always taking Helen's side,' Martha said.

'I asked Gloria not to tell anyone. Not even my dad,' Helen explained.

'So Jack still doesn't know?' Rosie was surprised.

Helen shook her head. 'Although I'm going to have to tell him.' She glanced over at Gloria. 'Unless you want to?'

'Of course I will,' Gloria said, thinking it would be good coming from her first.

'I suspected something awful had happened to you,' Polly admitted. She had heard Dr Billingham ask Dr Parker about Helen when Polly was being prepped for theatre after her waters had broken prematurely. She had overheard Dr Billingham asking how Helen was 'doing', and as the sedative had started to kick in, she was sure she'd heard him saying something about 'losing the baby'.

'It was why you were so determined nothing would happen to my baby, wasn't it?' Polly said.

Helen struggled to choke back the tears and nodded.

'It was why you got Dr Billingham to keep a close eye on me after I had my scare,' Polly surmised.

The women looked from Polly to Helen. They had wondered why Helen had been so involved in Polly's pregnancy and so kind in paying for Dr Billingham's services, which were not cheap.

Now they knew.

'But how did Matthew find out?' Dorothy asked.

'Well, apart from Dr Parker, Dr Billingham and Gloria, there were only two other people who knew,' Helen said.

'Yer mam,' Angie volunteered.

'And Mr Havelock,' Martha guessed.

Helen took another sip of her drink.

'I'm guessing it was your grandfather who spilled the beans,' said Rosie.

Helen nodded.

The women listened with growing fury to how Mr Havelock had told Matthew's father all about Helen and the surgeon, and how he had cut her out of the will – knowing it would be the lack of an inheritance that more than anything would have Matthew dumping Helen and moving on to greener, more profitable pastures.

What made it worse, though, was that Charles Havelock had nothing to gain from telling Mr Royce all this, other than knowing the hurt it would cause Helen. It would ruin her love life. And, worst of all, it would humiliate her.

*

When Helen left, the women started chatting quietly about Helen's past and her present predicament. They all agreed that she had been 'through the wringer', but that this latest heartbreak was for the best. Matthew, they agreed, was a 'liar and a cheat, and Dahlia had actually done Helen a favour.

They had heard in Helen's voice and seen in her face the deep sadness she still carried after having lost her baby, but they had also seen and heard the love she still held in her heart for Dr Parker.

'Is there any way we could get Dr Parker and Helen together?' Dorothy asked, looking around at the women's faces for inspiration.

She was met by blank looks.

'Well, we need to get our thinking caps on,' Dorothy implored.

They all nodded.

Although they had no idea what they could do. Especially in the little time they had.

It was now just two weeks until Dr Parker and Dr Eris became man and wife.

Later on that night, when Helen fell into bed, exhausted by the events of the day and having told a shocked and sympathetic Henrietta what had happened, she realised that she had to be honest with herself and admit that she hadn't really wanted Matthew. Deep down, she'd known she was making do with second best, and that she had only ever really wanted two people in her life.

Her baby – and John.

Neither of whom she could have.

Chapter Twenty-Nine

The following day

Saturday 28 April

'You still up for tea and cake at Lily's?' Peter asked when Charlotte came clattering through the front door with her hockey stick and gym bag.

Charlotte let out a short bark of laughter. 'Do I even need to answer that?'

Peter forced a smile. 'Well, hurry up then and get yourself cleaned up and changed. I've said we'll meet Rosie up there.'

Charlotte didn't need telling twice and hurried off to the bathroom. Peter felt a knot of dread in his stomach. When Rosie had come back from the Tatham last night, she'd told him what had happened to Helen, that it was proof no good ever came of keeping secrets, and that the time had come to tell Charlotte the whole truth. It was why they were going to Lily's this afternoon.

Half an hour later, Peter and Charlotte were leaving the house, both breathing sighs of relief that their neighbour, Mrs Jenkins, was obviously not in as otherwise she'd have come out to chat as she always did whenever she heard their front door go.

'So, did your schoolmates enjoy yesterday's launch?' Peter asked Charlotte.

'Yes, they loved it.' Charlotte said. 'We had a really good time.'

'It must make you feel very proud of your sister?' Peter probed, as they started the steady climb up the long stretch of Tunstall Vale.

'Helping to build ships?' Charlotte asked, glancing at Peter. She thought he seemed a little uneasy.

'Yes, building ships,' Peter repeated.

'I am,' Charlotte said. 'Very proud.' She had just recently given a talk at school on the women doing war work in the town's yards. She had thought some of the girls might have used the fact that her sister was a welder as an excuse to bully her, but the opposite had happened. She had become quite popular because of it, even more so after a group of them had got the afternoon off to watch the launch.

A few minutes later, they turned into West Lawn.

'Ah, there she is!' Peter said, spotting Rosie waiting at the gate of Lily's. She was in her overalls, having just come straight from work.

'Come on!' Rosie said, opening the gate. 'I don't know about you two, but I'm parched.'

Charlotte thought her sister seemed a little on edge, but perhaps she was just in need of a sit-down and a nice cup of tea.

After the usual fanfare of a welcome from Lily, who managed to give them all a hug whilst still fanning herself and complaining about her hot flushes, they were ushered into the bordello's large kitchen, where they were greeted by George, Kate, Maisie and Vivian.

Kate was overjoyed to see Charlotte in her new summer dress, and they all agreed she looked quite the stunner.

'You'll have all the boys chasing you,' Vivian, who fashioned herself on Mae West, drawled in a convincing American accent.

Lily shot her a look. 'She's too young for boys!'

Rosie suppressed a smile. She pitied any boy Charlotte did start to see. Lily was like a mother bear with her cub when it came to Rosie's little sister.

'Anyway, Charlotte has no time for boys, have you, *ma chérie*?'

Charlotte blushed a little and shook her head.

'Too busy with your studies!' Lily drove the message home as Maisie poured the tea. 'Talking of which, have you decided where you're going to go?'

'I have to decide what I want to study first,' Charlotte said, as Vivian handed out cake. 'From what I can gather, though, there's not a lot of choice. There's only a few universities that take women.'

Lily tutted, but was heartened to hear that Durham University was one of them. Oxford and Cambridge, she felt, were a little too far. For her, never mind for Charlotte.

Lily waved away the offer of cake. 'I just need to look at food at the moment and I've put on another pound.' She got out her Gauloises and lit a cigarette.

'And talking about the future,' she said, eyeing Kate, who was sitting, legs crossed, sipping on her tea. 'Our Kate is still considering a move to the Big Smoke to progress her career, aren't you, *ma chère*?'

Kate looked around the table. They were the only people in the world she loved and cared about and who she knew loved and cared about her. *How could she even think of leaving them all?*

'I'm still "considering",' Kate said.

'How will you feel about being in such a big city on your own?' Peter asked. He could see that Kate was very reluctant to leave the place that had become her home, and he understood why. He had known Kate many years ago when he'd been with the Sunderland Borough Police and Kate was a down-and-out. She had come a long way since then.

'She won't be on her own!' Lily butted in. 'She'll have a flat above La Lumière Bleue – and a studio next door.'

La Lumière Bleue was a bordello Lily owned in Soho, which had been modelled on the Parisian houses that catered to the upper classes and aristocracy and were known to have a blue rather than a red light outside their establishment.

'And I'll be visiting lots, as will Maisie and Vivian. Plus, she'll be so busy with everyone begging for her designs, she won't have time to turn around, never mind feel *alone*.'

Kate raised her eyebrows. 'There you are, Peter. Lily's got it all worked out.'

Sensing an atmosphere, George changed the subject to the news that the Red Army had captured both of Berlin's airports, preventing the capital from receiving any further supplies by air. The end of the war, they all agreed, was imminent, which, in turn, led to a discussion on how they would celebrate – it seemed like every street in the town was planning its own party.

When the cake had been eaten, Lily flashed Maisie and Vivian a look and they made their excuses and left.

Once they had gone, Lily focused her attention on Charlotte.

'I can't believe it's now been over two years since you decided you wanted to live back at home. Or should I say, ran away from that horrid, stuck-up boarding school – and refused to go back.' She fluttered her fan. 'Their loss being our gain, *n'est-ce pas*?' Another wave of the fan. 'I'll never forget seeing you that day in the boutique. Such a wonderful ray of sunshine.'

Rosie looked at Lily, whose love and adoration for Charlotte was plain to see – just as Charlotte's was for Lily.

'But your return has also meant that you've had a lot to digest these past two years, haven't you?' Lily said, her mood sobering.

Charlotte nodded, her face becoming serious.

George stood up. 'I think I shall retire to the back parlour and put on one of my records.'

'And I'm going to head back to the Maison Nouvelle,' Kate said. 'I've almost finished Angie's wedding dress, which is just as well as Dorothy's organised the trial fitting for Monday.'

Charlotte smiled her goodbyes to George and Kate, before turning her attention to Rosie, Peter and Lily and narrowing her eyes.

'Why do you all look so serious?' she asked.

Rosie sighed, moving away from the range and sitting down next to Charlotte. 'Because we need to tell you something – something serious. I've been putting it off and putting it off, but I've been reprimanded by Lily and Peter for – what's that word you love to use? That's it – I've been reprimanded for *procrastinating*.' Rosie tried to keep her voice light. 'But now, with all this talk about universities and you flying the nest, well, I cannot procrastinate any more.'

'It's something we all feel you're old enough – and mature enough – to take on board,' Lily added.

'Is it something about our uncle Raymond?' Charlotte asked, her face clouding over at the mere mention of his name.

'It is, *ma chérie*,' Lily said, lighting a cigarette. 'It's not nice and it's going to make you feel incredibly angry.'

'But you need to know,' Rosie said. 'I made a promise to you that I wouldn't keep any more secrets from you, and it's bothered me that I've not kept that promise.'

Charlotte's eyes were going back and forth between Lily and Rosie.

'The car accident your mother and father were involved in,' Lily said. 'Well, *ma chère*, I'm sorry to tell you that it wasn't an accident.'

'It was Uncle Raymond,' Rosie said. 'He was driving the car. He was the hit-and-run driver. He knocked them over.'

'What? On purpose?' Charlotte asked, shocked.

'On purpose,' Lily confirmed. 'Because he wanted to get his hands on your mother's inheritance.'

Charlotte could feel the anger bubbling up inside her.

'So, we lost Mam and Dad because of him?'

'We did,' Rosie said sadly.

'He *killed* our mam and dad?' Charlotte's face was like thunder. '*Murdered* them?'

'He did, *ma chère*.' Lily rested her cigarette in the ashtray, then got up and went to sit on the chair next to Charlotte. 'He was a sick man. A very sick man. It's hard to believe that there are people like him on this earth, but, unfortunately, there are.'

'He took our mam and dad off us –' Charlotte said in

disbelief '– just so he could get his inheritance. He *killed* our parents for *money*?'

Charlotte looked at Rosie, who nodded. Her eyes were pooled with so much sadness. Sadness that their mam's and dad's deaths had been so unnecessary; that she and her little sister had been deprived of a loving mother and father.

'I wish he was still alive so we could make him suffer – really suffer.' Charlotte spat out her words, her desire for vengeance clear.

Rosie wished she had been able to shield her sister from all of this, but she couldn't. She realised now how foolish she had been ever to think that she could.

Rosie and Lily looked at Peter as he cleared his throat.

'And I'm afraid it wasn't just your sister he hurt. He hurt other women in the town too. Had been hurting other women before he killed your parents.'

'What do you mean, "hurt"?' Charlotte asked, pale-faced.

'He was raping women,' Peter said, trying to keep the anger out of his voice.

'Oh God, that's awful,' Charlotte said, her shoulders sagging, as though exhausted by her uncle's capacity for evil.

'Thank goodness,' Peter continued, 'the police caught him not long after your parents' funeral and he was put in jail.'

'Is that why you didn't hear anything from him for years?' Charlotte asked.

Rosie nodded.

'He was given a five-year sentence, but was let out early due to the war.'

'So, they let him out so he could carry on doing exactly what he'd been doing beforehand?' Charlotte was incredulous.

'I know,' Peter said, 'it's wrong. But ultimately it's the law.'

'Well, the law needs changing,' Charlotte declared.

They were quiet for a while.

The contemplative quietness was broken by the sound of Rosie taking a deep breath.

'Uncle Raymond's actions also had other consequences,' Rosie said. 'You see, after Raymond did what he did that night – the night of Mam and Dad's funeral – I had some problems down there and had to go to the doctor, who helped me, but later he told me that unfortunately I wouldn't be able to have any children.'

'That's awful,' Charlotte said, staring at her sister's face, trying to gauge how much this had affected her.

'It's OK, though,' Rosie said. 'I'm OK about it. I've known for years that this was the case.'

She attempted a reassuring smile as she saw a solitary tear start to snake its way down her little sister's rosy cheek.

'And if I'm honest,' Rosie added, 'even if I was able to have children, I really don't know if I would want to.'

She glanced at Peter.

'I've got my family right here,' Rosie said, looking at Charlotte and Peter and then Lily. 'You are all I've ever wanted. I feel lucky – incredibly lucky.'

Rosie smiled at Charlotte as she allowed Lily to put her arm around her. She was surprised that her sister let herself be cuddled. It was a sight that brought tears to her eyes. Rosie might have felt as though she had, in many ways, been more like a mother to Charlotte, but seeing the two of them together, she realised that now Lily had taken over that role.

Chapter Thirty

'Do you think Charlotte will be all right?' Kate asked George as they left the kitchen.

'Yes, I do,' George said as they walked down the hallway, his walking stick gently striking the polished parquet flooring. 'She mightn't have a mother and father, but she has people around her who love and care for her. If she struggles with this latest revelation, they'll all be there to help her through it.' George took his trilby off the stand and opened the front door.

'Where are you going?' Kate asked, picking up the keys for the Maison Nouvelle and grabbing her handbag.

'I'm taking you to the boutique,' George said.

'I can walk,' said Kate. 'There's no need, honestly.'

'I want to,' said George. 'It'll do me good to get out of the house.'

Kate knew when not to argue with George. Shutting the heavy oak door behind them, Kate stayed by George's side as he carefully made his way down the stone steps, ready to give him a hand if needed.

When they got to the bottom, he raised his walking stick in the air. 'Best thing Lily bought me,' he smiled. 'Hated the thought of it at first, but it makes my life so much easier.'

Kate looked at the ornate ivory walking stick.

'Lily bought it for me in a shop in Kensington High

Street – must have been about four years ago.' He paused. 'You know, she'll be going to London a lot soon. Now we're just about done with this wretched war.' They walked down the garden path. 'So, if you did decide to move down there, you'd still be seeing a lot of her.'

He chuckled as he opened the gate and allowed Kate to walk through first.

'Whether that's a good thing or not, I'm not so sure.'

Kate smiled.

'Same goes for Maisie and Vivian, especially now Lily is slowly winding down the business.'

He opened the passenger door and Kate got in.

'I wouldn't be surprised if Maisie decides to move back to London – and if she goes, Vivian will go too. Once they've got the Gentlemen's Club running smoothly, they'll be getting itchy feet.'

George walked to the other side and opened the door.

'Maisie's a Londoner born and bred,' George puffed as he lowered himself into the driver's seat. 'But Vivian's not got any family here, and I know for a fact she doesn't want to go back to the Wirral, so there'll be nothing keeping her up north.'

He turned the ignition and revved the engine.

'And then there's Charlotte. She'll be going off to university.'

'But Rosie will still be here,' Kate countered.

'She will,' George conceded as he pulled away. 'But from what Peter's told me, he'll be making regular trips down to the capital. The Special Operations Executive will still carry on, although they'll probably change the name.'

Kate looked at George.

264

'I know what you're doing,' she said.

'What's that?' George feigned innocence.

He waited until a mother and her small child had hurried across the road before turning right into Mowbray Road.

'You're trying to show me that if I do decide to move to London, then I won't be alone,' Kate said. 'That everyone I know and love now will either be living there themselves or at least visiting regularly.'

'I'm just saying how it is – or will be,' George said sagely.

He slowed down as he approached the junction to Ryhope Road.

'I think I'm also trying to tell you that everything is changing,' he mused. 'The end of the war is going to change everyone's lives. The people you love will be making changes to their lives – will *have* to make changes to their lives.'

Indicating left, he pulled out and drove slowly down the Ryhope Road, towards town.

'I'm not suggesting that you *have* to make any changes . . .' George hesitated, wanting to get his words right. 'I suppose what I'm trying to say is, you have no reason to be afraid of change.' He exhaled. 'Look at everything you have overcome.' Although George also knew that the trauma Kate had endured at the hands of the nuns who had taken her in after her mother died still echoed in her adult life.

'Change can be frightening,' he added, 'but there really is nothing to be afraid of. And knowing you, my dear Kate, you will overcome any fear you have. Because that's what you do. You work, you sew, you design – you create.'

Kate was quiet for a moment.

They turned right into Vine Place.

'I've never looked at it like that,' Kate mused. 'But I guess

265

you're right. If I ever feel a little down and I start sewing or thinking up a design, after a while, my mood lifts.'

They spent the rest of the journey to Holmeside in comfortable silence.

When George pulled up outside the boutique, Kate gave him a quick kiss on his cheek.

'Thanks, George.' She got out and closed the door.

George leaned over and wound the window down. 'I'll be picking you up in two hours. No arguing.'

Kate smiled.

'No arguing,' she said.

Later on that evening, when Kate was lying in bed in the attic room on the third floor, waiting for sleep to come, her mind went over George's words. He was right. Life *was* about moving on and changing.

At the start of this war, George had simply been Lily's friend, now he was her fiancé and business partner; Rosie had gone from being a call girl to part-owning the bordello, and from being resolutely single to a happily married woman; Charlotte had moved from her boarding school in North Yorkshire to living back home with her sister, something neither of them could ever have foreseen; and probably most shocking of all, Lily was gradually turning the bordello back into a proper home.

Kate realised how much she herself had changed. Five years ago she would never have dared to dream about the life she now led. Living on the streets after leaving Nazareth House, she could never have foreseen that an old school friend would see her in a shop doorway and practically frogmarch her to Lily's, where she'd been taken in like a pitiful stray, given a roof over her head and food to eat. Lily had dried her out, sat through days of sweats and tremors and sickness. She'd been so ill she thought she'd die, but she hadn't. And when she was better, she'd started earning her keep by cleaning until Lily had given her an old Singer. She'd started making clothes for Lily and her 'girls', and then Lily had encouraged her to open the Maison Nouvelle.

As she drifted off to sleep, she thought again of George's words, and also about what Helen had said to her at the engagement party.

And, of course, the many words Lily had spoken on the subject of moving to London were pretty much imprinted on her mind.

Chapter Thirty-One

The following day

Sunday 29 April

When Kate woke in the early hours of the morning – a habit from her days on the street that she'd not been able to break – she drew open the curtains of the small, east-facing window. As she did so, she let out a gasp. The sky was the most amazing mix of fiery amber and fuchsia pink with a swirl of pale blue. It was so beautiful it took her breath away – more beautiful than any painting by any of the great masters she had seen.

Standing and looking at Nature's beauty for many minutes, Kate realised, as though for the first time, just how vast the world was. She thought that if she had to give this scene a title, it would be 'Infinity'.

She knew at that moment it was time for her to go – to spread her wings and fly. It was time to leave her past behind and go out into the world, no matter how terrifying it might seem. George was right, nothing could be more frightening than what she had endured at the hands of the nuns during those years she had been under their care. Nothing.

And so, she argued with herself, if she had already endured terrors that could not be surpassed, why would she feel afraid of leaving her home town and going to London?

It might actually be fun. Exciting.

She might even be happy.

She might even establish her own label.

Kate laughed at herself. *As if.*

But who knew?

Looking at the beauty of the dawning of a new day had given her the belief that the world had endless possibilities that stretched way, way beyond her attic, the bordello and this town.

Having made up her mind, Kate hurried to get ready and go downstairs to see Lily, who she knew would be in the kitchen, making a cup of tea and smoking her first Gauloise of the day.

'*Bonjour, ma petite,*' Lily said as Kate came into the kitchen. 'You're looking very bright-eyed and bushy-tailed this morning,' she added, squinting through a plume of grey cigarette smoke.

'I feel it,' Kate said, pouring herself a cup of tea. She sat down at the long wooden table, glad that just the two of them were up.

'I've made up my mind,' she said, taking a sip of her tea.

'Made up your mind?' Lily asked, still a little hazy from a few too many brandies last night. 'About Angie's wedding dress?' Lily knew that Kate had been debating whether or not to add a gold embroidered border to the bottom of the delicate silk dress.

Kate shook her head. 'No, I mean about moving to London.'

Lily sat up straight and fixed her attention on the young woman she loved as if she were her own blood.

'And?' she asked impatiently. 'Don't keep me in suspense!'

'I'm going to do it,' Kate said decisively. 'I'm going to move to London. I want to create my own label!'

Lily stood up with such excitement she nearly knocked over her chair. 'Come here, *ma chérie*!' She flung her arms wide for an embrace. Kate stood up a little self-consciously and allowed herself to be squashed in a big hug.

'Congratulations!' Lily put her hands on Kate's shoulders.

Kate smiled at Lily's exuberance. 'I'm not sure I have done anything to be congratulated for.'

'Oh, but you have, my dear, you really have,' Lily said in earnest.

For the next hour, Lily and Kate chatted excitedly. Lily chain-smoked and fanned away excited hot flushes. Kate made them a fresh pot of tea and started to make a list of what she would take with her.

Lily made her write another list for herself.

'Gone,' she said, 'are the days when I could retain a thought or idea in my head for longer than a few seconds.'

Kate gave Lily a cheeky smile. 'If I'm making the leap, then I think you should too.'

Lily pretended not to understand, although she knew exactly what Kate meant. Since Lily and George had gifted their Christmas wedding to Polly and Tommy, Lily had promised George she would set another date, but, as yet, had not done so.

'George won't wait for ever,' Kate joked, knowing full well George would indeed wait for ever for Lily.

Lily laughed. 'OK, I promise to set a date. You have inspired me.'

She waved her fan. 'But now, back to the matter at hand.'

She sighed contentedly.

'This is going to be fabulous!' she enthused. 'I'll get the

girls at La Lumière to make up your bedsit – make sure it's spick and span and cosy. And with an electric heater, of course.'

Lily knew that the only luxury Kate had ever wanted after she'd moved in was a heater. The dormitories at the children's home had been freezing cold, and life on the streets colder still.

'And Soho is *the* place to be now – *très* avant-garde. It's next to all the theatres . . . The studio might need a bit of work doing to it,' Lily said, puffing on a cigarette and tapping it in the ashtray. 'Nothing too bad, though. It was a clothes shop before the war, but you can make it your own.'

'It sounds perfect,' Kate said, already starting to imagine how she might like her new workplace to be.

'And we'll have to think of a name for your label!' Lily was overjoyed to hear Kate was aiming high. 'Any ideas?'

Kate smiled. 'I was thinking about calling it "Lily Rose".'

She didn't have to say the name was in honour of the two people who had saved her.

'I thought the logo could be an L intertwined with an R,' she added.

Lily felt as though she were going to burst with pure joy.

'I think that's a wonderful name! This is so exciting!' she gushed. 'Do you think it's too early for champagne?'

Chapter Thirty-Two

1 Park Avenue, Roker, Sunderland

'So, tell me, Mrs *Bevan*, how are you?' Henrietta asked as her guest sat down on the sofa in the front reception room.

'I'm very well, thank you,' Mrs Evans replied. 'And how are you today, *Miss Girling*?'

The women exchanged the slightest of smiles.

'How strange that we are both known by false identities,' Henrietta said, shaking her head.

'It is strange indeed,' Mrs Evans said, plumping the cushion on the sofa and leaning back.

'Although yours is only temporary,' Henrietta said. 'And only used in a certain household.'

'True,' Mrs Evans said, 'but I wonder, even if you had the chance, would you want to go back to being called Mrs Havelock?'

'Not ever!' Henrietta said, quick as a flash. 'If the time ever came when my true identity was to become known, I would refer to myself by my maiden name.'

'Good idea,' said Mrs Evans.

The two women turned as Mrs Westley came into the room with a tea tray. Seeing it was only set for two, Henrietta asked, 'You're not going to join us today?'

Mrs Westley carefully put the tray down on the small rectangular coffee table.

'I've already drunk enough to sink a ship today,' she said. 'And I'm keen to try out Marguerite Patten's latest recipe.'

Both women nodded, knowing Mrs Westley's love of the radio chef who had become quite famous during the war for her BBC radio programme, *Kitchen Front*.

As Mrs Westley started to put the teapot and the cups and saucers on the coffee table, Henrietta asked, 'How do you think Helen is holding up?'

Mrs Westley stood up, a scowl immediately forming on her florid face. 'I could box the ears of that good-for-nothing Royce boy.' As though to demonstrate the point, she raised her clenched fists and shook them.

Mrs Evans looked askance at Mrs Westley and Henrietta.

'Well, let's just say Helen found out the truth about her beau the hard way,' Henrietta said.

'Walked in on him and his secretary,' Mrs Westley said. 'And the floozy was not taking shorthand.'

Mrs Evans's hand went to her mouth.

'Obviously,' Mrs Westley continued, 'Helen told him what to do with his marriage proposal.'

'I'm not surprised,' Mrs Evans said. 'Poor Helen. Is she all right?'

'Well, that's just the thing,' Henrietta said. 'She's not really been upset. And we're a little worried she might be bottling it all up, aren't we, Mrs Westley?'

'We are. Helen keeps saying that she's actually very lucky. That she might well have married him, only to find out then he was a lying, cheating cad.'

'And one that was just after her money,' Mrs Westley added.

'Dear me, this just gets worse,' said Mrs Evans.

'We're keeping a close eye on her, aren't we?' Henrietta said.

'We are,' Mrs Westley agreed.

After Mrs Westley left to make her stuffed meat loaf, Henrietta poured their tea and continued to tell Mrs Evans that during the awful scene in Matthew's office, it had also come out that he had discovered something very private and very personal about Helen.

Mrs Evans tentatively asked what that was and, trusting her friend, Henrietta told her about Theodore and Helen's miscarriage.

'According to Mrs Westley, Helen was in a real state at the time,' Henrietta explained. 'She was extremely low. She wasn't sleeping or eating.'

'But she got over it?' Mrs Evans worried, thinking of her own daughter.

'She did, although I think she still bears the scars. But what makes this all the more terrible,' Henrietta said, 'is that it was Charles who told Matthew's father about Helen's past.'

'Oh, my goodness.' Mrs Evans's voice hardened. 'What a vile thing to do. What a hateful, horrible, inhumane man he is. There's nothing he isn't capable of.'

'I agree. Vile and spiteful,' Henrietta said. 'And made worse still by him telling Royce senior that he had disinherited Helen. That she wouldn't get a penny of the Havelock estate.'

'Really?' Mrs Evans asked, surprised.

'I'm afraid so. By helping me, Helen has forfeited a fortune. She's become the Judas of the Havelock family,' Henrietta explained.

'I think Helen probably forfeited her fortune the moment she didn't dance to Charles's tune,' Mrs Evans said.

They were both quiet for a moment, looking out of the huge bay window at the passers-by. The seagulls could be heard squawking and the park across the road was busy, as it always was when the sun was out.

'I don't know how you manage to work there,' Henrietta said, turning her attention back to Mrs Evans. 'How long's it been now?' She did a quick calculation in her head. 'Two months – or thereabouts?'

Mrs Evans took a sip of her tea. 'Just over two months.'

'How's everything in the household?' Henrietta asked.

'It's seems busy of late. The old man has had a few meetings. Agatha said one of them – a rather rotund chap – was the family solicitor. And there's been some other bloke come, but he had to use the back entrance.'

'Sounds like Charles is up to something,' Henrietta mused.

'Perhaps,' Mrs Evans said.

'And how is it working out with Eddy and Agatha?' Henrietta asked. When Mrs Evans had first told her about her new place of work, she had wondered how she would cope being in such close proximity to the people who'd had a good idea what Charles was up to all those years ago. Henrietta was sure Mrs Evans would deem them both culpable because of their inaction.

'It's difficult,' Mrs Evans said. 'Eddy's a pathetic, spineless man. I try to avoid him as much as possible. The way he bows and scrapes to "the master" turns my stomach. If

Charles told him to go and jump off the pier, I'm sure he would.'

Henrietta put down her empty teacup and sighed. 'The man's not known any different – not that that's an excuse. Charles took him on when he was barely out of short pants. He's done a good job of manipulating Eddy, making him believe that the house is his world and that he'd be nothing and no one were he ever to leave his employ.'

Mrs Evans nodded. 'Like you say, that's not an excuse.'

'And Agatha?' Henrietta asked.

'She's not so easy to work out,' Mrs Evans said.

'Do you think she could be the one behind the note?' Henrietta asked. Helen had told her that someone had got a young lad to pass a scrawled message to Dorothy and Bobby when Henrietta had been rushed to the hospital. The note had directed them to the Winters Gardens, where they had found the plant used to poison her.

'I'm not sure,' Mrs Evans said. 'I feel she's hiding something. And something's not right between her and Eddy.'

'And neither of them recognises you?'

'Eddy said he thought I reminded him of someone when I first started, but he's too busy running after Charles to give it much thought. Agatha hasn't said anything, but sometimes I catch her looking at me in an odd way.'

'Well, just be careful,' Henrietta warned. 'They're both faithful to Charles and they'll be watching their own backs. They always have and always will.'

Henrietta took a long look at Mrs Evans.

'And are you still set on doing what you want to do?' she asked, her tone grave.

Mrs Evans pursed her lips.

'Oh, yes,' she said. 'And I've also decided *how* I'm going to do it.'

As Mrs Evans sat in the tram on her way home, she thought about Charles Havelock and what he had done to his own granddaughter. The man really did not have a trace of humanity in him. No love, compassion or any kind of empathy for anyone – not even his family.

By the sounds of it, he'd used Miriam for information, and he didn't bother much with his other daughter, Margaret. He'd got Henrietta, his wife and the mother of his two children, put away, and had kept her drugged up to keep her quiet for fear she would hang him out to dry.

Mrs Evans mentally listed all the dreadful wrongs he had done. The man had an incredible capacity for gliding through life without having to make any kind of reparation for what he'd done. And he'd done plenty. He had raped Gracie, and then Pearl, and had got them both pregnant. Gracie had not survived the abuse and the legacy he had left her with. Pearl had, but they had left their mark.

She wondered how many other young girls Charles had cast aside when he'd had his fill of them. And the repercussions it had had on their lives.

She thought about him sitting high and mighty in his leather swivel chair in his plush study, continuing to be fawned over by the people of this town.

He'd escaped having his name dragged through the mud in a high-profile court case, which, Mrs Evans had learnt from Pearl, might have happened if Bel had not decided to use what she had in order to bring Jack back home.

If Bel had taken the legal route, it might well have led him to being jailed. And, even if it didn't, at the very least, people would have seen him for the man he was.

Getting off the tram at the top of Villette Road, Mrs Evans thought of the threats Charles had made if his sick secrets were exposed. Threats that would destroy the lives of those who certainly did not deserve it.

As Mrs Evans walked through her front door, she stood for a moment, as she always did, and looked up to the spot where she had last seen her daughter. A picture that had been indelibly imprinted on her mind's eye.

It was time.

Chapter Thirty-Three

Monday 30 April

Rising early the next day, Mrs Evans forced down a piece of toast with her morning cup of tea. The last thing she felt like doing was eating, but she knew she had to put something in her stomach for what lay ahead.

Pouring herself another cup and adding a good splash of milk, she looked at the front page of the *Daily Mirror*. The main headline read: GERMANY – AND THE WORLD – MARKS TIME. There were also rumours circulating that Hitler was missing – and that he was either ill or dead.

Turning the page, Mrs Evans saw that her hand was shaking slightly. She forced herself to read another report, headlined: MUSSO IS SHOT WITH CLARA. German forces in Italy had surrendered and Mussolini had been given a short trial before a people's court, then taken out and shot. His body had been exhibited near Lake Como, and then in Milan. Milan's partisans' radio had broadcast the list of six others who had also faced the firing squad with him, which had included his latest mistress, Clara Petacci.

Reading the reports, Mrs Evans thought of how – finally – the world was being rid of its evil.

Which made what she planned to do today both fitting and timely.

Taking a sip of her tea, Mrs Evans looked up at the photograph of her daughter on the mantelpiece.

'I'm doing this for you, Gracie. My only regret is that I didn't do it sooner.' She spoke as though her daughter were there with her. In the room. Which in a way she was.

Mrs Evans's vision shifted to her wedding photograph. She still hadn't cried over Gibson's death. And she knew why. She would have done this sooner had it not been for her husband. And because of that she felt angry with him. If she had done what she had wanted all those years ago, Charles Havelock would not have been able to enjoy the years he'd had on this earth. He'd already enjoyed five times the length of her daughter's life. Retribution was coming late – too late.

But still, better than never at all.

Seeing the time, Mrs Evans got up and took her cup and saucer into the kitchen. Opening the cupboard drawer, she picked up a glass vial that had been placed carefully under her best tablecloth. She held it in her hand and stared at it. It amazed her how such a small amount of liquid could bring so much devastation. Putting the vial in her handbag, she picked up the bag and headed out to work.

Crossing the busy Ryhope Road and then starting along The Cedars, a much quieter residential street, Mrs Evans thought about Mussolini's execution.

And, again, she justified the actions she was about to take.

When Mrs Evans arrived at the Havelock residence, she felt a mix of nerves and relief. Nerves because of what she was about to do, and relief that time had finally come. Time for justice – justice for her daughter, for Gibson, for herself, for Pearl, and for all those other young girls who'd had their bodies and their lives blighted by this vile, evil man.

'Morning, Tan!' Agatha welcomed Mrs Evans as she hung up her coat and her handbag on the coat rack in the kitchen.

'Cuppa before you start?' she asked.

Mrs Evans shook her head. 'No, I think I'll just get cracking today. I was hoping I might finish a little earlier if I get everything done in time.'

'Good idea,' Agatha said, watching as Mrs Evans put on her pinny. 'It's a lovely day. I don't blame you.' She watched as Mrs Evans grabbed her duster and the cleaning polish.

'You feeling all right? You look a million miles away.'

Mrs Evans turned and forced a smile. 'I'm fine. I was just thinking about something I've been planning for someone I know. A surprise.'

'Sounds intriguing,' said Agatha, and Mrs Evans left the kitchen before she could ask more.

While Mrs Evans spent the morning giving the living room and then the dining room a thorough clean, Agatha divided her time between tending her little herb garden and cooking one of her special hotpots.

At half-past twelve, she ladled out a good helping of hot stew into a bowl, put it on a tray and took it to Mr Havelock, who always ate his lunch in his study and his evening meal in the dining room.

When the grandfather clock struck one, Agatha headed back to the study. Enough time had passed for him to have finished his meal, or for it to have gone cold if he hadn't. She hoped it hadn't. She'd spent a lot of time making this hotpot extra special, adding some of the herbs and other garden produce she'd been cultivating.

She raised her hand and knocked on the door of the study.

'Come in!' Mr Havelock boomed.

'Sorry to bother you, sir.' Agatha appeared round the door. 'I've just come to take out your tray,'

'Yes, yes!' Mr Havelock blustered, barely looking at his trusty housekeeper.

'Was everything to your liking?' Agatha asked.

Mr Havelock grunted.

Agatha looked down at the plate as she picked it up, then smiled. She could see the pattern on it. He'd mopped up every last bit with a freshly baked bread roll she'd given him to go with it.

'Good,' Agatha said, more to herself than to her master. 'Glad you enjoyed it.'

She took one last look at Mr Havelock as she carried out the tray.

Mrs Evans tried to keep calm and stop her hands from trembling. It was difficult, though. Now that the time had come, she felt a little light-headed. Walking into the pantry, she got out the glass vial she had transferred from her bag into her apron pocket. Taking a scoop of air into her lungs and slowly releasing her breath, she told herself to be calm and confident. She removed the stopper from the decanter and carefully put it to the side, then uncapped the vial.

She hesitated for a moment. Could she really do this?

Yes – she could.

Then just do it! she told herself.

She tipped the clear liquid into the brandy.

Putting the stopper back in the decanter, she gave it a quick swirl to make sure the poison had mixed with the Rémy.

Then she put the empty vial back in her pocket and walked out of the pantry.

As she stepped back into the kitchen, Agatha came bustling in with the master's lunch tray.

Judging by the clean plate, Mr Havelock had enjoyed his hotpot. She hoped he'd made the most of it as it would be his last supper.

Seeing that Mrs Evans had refilled the master's decanter, Agatha widened her eyes.

'Dear me, I just refilled that the other day,' she said, banging the tray down on the side and transferring the plate and dirty cutlery into the white stoneware sink.

'Honestly, Mr Havelock is drinking far too much lately,' she declared as she turned on the hot-water tap. 'But still, I suppose when you get to his age, you might as well indulge yourself.'

'Well, there's no denying he's had a good innings,' Mrs Evans said, hearing the hardness in her own voice.

Turning off the tap, Agatha left the washing-up, went over to the Aga and put the kettle on. 'I suppose he has, especially when you think of all those young lads that won't be coming back from the war.'

Picking up the brown ceramic teapot from the wooden table, she looked at Mrs Evans. 'Fancy a cuppa?'

Mrs Evans glanced up at the wall clock. 'I best get off once I've taken this to the study.'

'Yes, of course, the sun's out, you don't want to be at work longer than needs be.' Agatha looked at Mrs Evans as she made to leave. 'Is everything all right with you, Tan? You really don't seem quite yourself today?'

Mrs Evans forced a smile that she hoped hid her growing nerves. 'No, I'm fine. Really. But thanks for asking.'

Taking another deep breath, Mrs Evans knocked on the door to the master's study.

'Come in!' Mr Havelock bellowed, not hiding his irritation at being disturbed yet again.

Mrs Evans walked into the room. Her heart was pounding so heavily she could hear it – feel its rapid thumping against her chest. She hoped what was happening on the inside was not evident on the outside. She looked down at her hands as she walked towards Mr Havelock's desk and saw they were gripping the neck of the decanter as though her life depended on it. After she placed it carefully on the desk and released her hold, her hands immediately started shaking. She clasped them together to try and stop them. She looked at Mr Havelock and realised she needn't have worried. He had the *Daily Telegraph* spread across his desk and was staring down at it. He did not look in a good mood.

Mrs Evans coughed loudly.

'This will be my last day today,' she said, glad her voice did not betray her nerves.

Mr Havelock glanced up at the cleaner with whom he had exchanged barely any words since she had started work at the house two months ago.

'I beg your pardon?' he said, showing his disbelief that she – a lowly cleaner – had dared to speak to him – the master of the house.

'This will be my last day today,' Mrs Evans repeated.

'Really? You've only been here five minutes. What's the matter? Too much like hard work?' Mr Havelock gave her a condescending smile before taking a gulp of the brandy he was drinking from a large, bulbous glass.

He turned his attention back to his newspaper.

Mrs Evans felt herself stiffen.

'Not that you would know,' she sniped back.

Mr Havelock slowly raised his eyes from the newspaper.

Mrs Evans met his gaze. *Now she had his attention.*

'I'm sorry?' he demanded. 'Did I just hear you right?' His voice was raised.

'You did,' Mrs Evans said, her own hackles going up, her nerves now replaced by anger. 'I doubt very much you've ever done a decent day's work in your entire life.'

Mr Havelock's jaw dropped and his cheeks flushed, his astonishment evident. A member of his staff – one of his *servants* – was daring to speak to him in such a way. He took another swig of his brandy and finished it off.

'I've not come to see you to discuss the pampered and easy life you have had the good fortune to lead – nor all the luxuries you have taken for granted, having been born into money.' Mrs Evans spoke clearly and with ease. Her heart had stopped thumping and her hands were no longer shaking.

Mr Havelock looked at his cleaner, stunned. Never before had anyone ever spoken to him in such an insolent manner. No one apart from Henrietta and Helen – and they had paid the price.

'So, what have you come here to discuss, Mrs . . . ?' Mr Havelock frowned, trying to recall her name.

'My name is Mrs Evans.'

Now it was Mr Havelock who could feel his heart beating faster, preparing for the fight, as it was clear this lowly peasant – this plump, old woman – was not just here to hand in her notice.

'What do you want, Mrs Evans? You've got exactly one minute before I call Eddy and get you thrown back out onto the street where you obviously belong,' he said, looking down at his pocket watch.

'You might not remember my name,' Mrs Evans began, 'probably because I am an elderly, unattractive woman, but I'm sure you remember the names of some of your other employees who you paid particular attention to – young maids, blonde, blue-eyed maids – innocent young girls who you defiled.'

Mrs Evans looked into Mr Havelock's dark eyes and saw they were dancing. *He was enjoying this.*

'I'm Gracie's mother,' she said and waited for his reaction.

'Ah.' Mr Havelock's face lit up, his eyes were sparkling with pure evil and his mouth widened into a cruel smile.

'*Little Gracie* – that was what my wife used to call her, wasn't it? *Little Gracie.* Of course I remember. How could I forget.'

Mrs Evans looked at the decanter. She had the sudden urge to grab it, swing it and whack him in the head with all her might.

Wipe that supercilious smile right off his face.

'So, it was *you* who told Henrietta about my – what would you call it? – my predilections?'

Mrs Evans felt the bile rise in the back of her throat.

'Your sick and perverted predilections.' Mrs Evans spat out the words.

'I often wondered who it was who came to Henrietta and

286

told her,' Mr Havelock said, ignoring her words. 'I asked her, of course, before I had her carted off to the asylum, but she's nothing but loyal, that wife of mine.'

As he spoke, Mr Havelock started to rub his chest. 'Now I know.'

Mrs Evans watched as his cheeks reddened while he continued to talk at her.

'It is your fault that Henrietta was sectioned,' he said, 'your fault she's spent the best years of her life in the town's lunatic asylum. I hope you have that on your conscience, Mrs Evans.'

Mr Havelock was starting to enjoy himself. His breathing quickened, as did his heart.

'Now I'm thinking about it,' he continued, 'it is actually *your* fault that I'm in the position I'm in now.'

Mrs Evans spluttered her disbelief. 'And how do you work that one out?'

'Because,' Mr Havelock said, speaking slowly, as though to a child, 'Henrietta's incarceration is being used to blackmail me.'

Mrs Evans looked at Mr Havelock.

'I believe it is *you* doing the blackmailing – threatening others to keep their mouths shut about the crimes *you* have committed,' Mrs Evans said, thinking of all the women's secrets he had threatened to expose.

'*My, my,* you've been doing your research,' Mr Havelock said as he started to loosen his tie. The afternoon's unexpected excitement was making him feel hot.

'Which means I shall have to add you to my list,' he said, pulling out a handkerchief from his top pocket and dabbing his forehead.

Now it was Mrs Evans's time to laugh.

'Do you really think you could do anything else to hurt me after what you did to my daughter? *Really? Do you?'*

She looked down at the decanter again. There was a paperknife lying next to it. Suddenly she didn't care about anything. About any kind of consequences. She went to grab the knife, but Mr Havelock was too quick. He'd seen the look, read her intention, and slammed his hand on top of it.

Mr Havelock started to laugh. A nasty, vindictive laugh.

'Not quick enough,' he taunted. *'Just like your daughter.'*

Mrs Evans had both hands on the side of his desk and was leaning towards him.

'You bastard!' she hissed at him.

Their faces were now just inches apart.

She saw the dark eyes glistening with the thrill of the battle, the leathery skin, the thin-lipped smirk.

And she knew then what it was like to breathe the same air as the Devil himself.

Then something changed.

Suddenly, Charles's eyes looked panicked, the thin lips turned into a grimace.

The hand that had been covering the letter opener went to grab his chest.

His mouth started to open and shut, but no noise came out.

His face crumpled into a show of agony.

He tried to stand up, but instead staggered a little to his right. He made a grab behind him to steady himself on his swivel chair, but he missed, staggering again. His hand was now clutching the left side of his chest, his other hand desperately trying to loosen his tie. He was sweating profusely.

Mrs Evans watched. Entranced. She looked at him and saw in his eyes fear. Pure fear.

Death was coming for him, and he knew it.

White spittle had formed in the corner of his mouth, which was still moving, like a fish out of water, desperately gulping for air.

He reached out for Mrs Evans, who stepped back. He grabbed air, before crumpling on the floor.

It was surprisingly undramatic. Just a very slight thud as his head hit the carpet. His body didn't move, but stayed in the exact position in which it had landed. Mrs Evans stood and waited a few minutes to ensure there was no more show of life. No more movement. No sudden gasp of air that would bring him back to life. Slowly, she crouched down onto her knees and bent over him. She put her ear to his chest and listened to his heartbeat – or lack of one. Then she turned her head to look at his face – his eyes were still open, but the life behind them had gone.

'I hope you rot in hell,' she whispered to his corpse.

Rising, she stood for a moment, forcing herself to think about what she had to do.

This had not gone the way she had expected.

Grabbing the decanter, she took two steps back.

Taking a deep breath, she held it out in front of her and then dropped it on the carpet, at the same time emitting a loud scream.

Chapter Thirty-Four

Eddy was the first to come rushing in.

'Bloody hell!' He stopped dead in his tracks on seeing Mr Havelock's prostrate body lying motionless on the Turkey-red carpet.

'What's happened?' He turned and looked at Mrs Evans.

'I just walked in and there he was – dead!'

Eddy stepped over the decanter, which had rolled onto its side, and crouched down next to Mr Havelock.

Just then Agatha appeared.

On seeing Mr Havelock, her hand went to her mouth.

'Oh, my goodness! What happened?' She looked at Mrs Evans.

'I just walked in,' she said, her voice a hoarse whisper, 'and there he was . . .'

Agatha walked over to where Eddy was hunched over the body. 'Have you checked his pulse?'

Eddy shook his head.

'Oh, for God's sake,' she sniped. 'Get up!'

Eddy moved aside and Agatha checked for a pulse. She then repeated what Mrs Evans had done a few minutes earlier and put her head to his chest.

'No, he's definitely gone,' she said.

'What'll we do?' Eddy asked.

Agatha stood up and straightened her back.

'Well, it's pointless calling an ambulance.' She looked around the study as though for an answer. 'Just dial the operator and tell them we think Mr Charles Havelock has just had a heart attack and that he's dead.'

Agatha looked at Mrs Evans still standing rooted to the spot. 'Are you all right?'

Mrs Evans nodded. 'Just shocked,' she said, bending down to pick up the decanter. The room now stank of brandy as most of the contents had spilled onto the carpet.

'Why don't you make us a pot of tea, Tan?'

'I think I'm gonna need something stronger than a cup of bloody tea!' Eddy said. His face was ashen.

Mrs Evans didn't need telling twice. She had to get the decanter back down to the kitchen and give it a good rinse-out. The last thing she wanted was to get the blame for something she hadn't actually succeeded in doing.

By the time Agatha returned to the kitchen, Mrs Evans had made the tea.

'Are you sure you're all right?' Agatha asked Mrs Evans as she poured them each a cup.

'Yes, honestly, I'm fine,' Mrs Evans said. 'I should be asking you if you're all right – after all, you're the one who's known Mr Havelock for such a long time.'

'Yes, I suppose I have,' Agatha agreed. *Too long a time. Practically a lifetime.*

Agatha added sugar to her tea and stirred. As she did so, she pulled a puzzled expression. 'I thought you were taking the decanter straight to the study?'

'I did,' Mrs Evans said, taking a sip of the sugary tea. Her hands had just started to shake a little as the reality of what had happened started to hit home.

'But it must have been at least five minutes from the time you left the kitchen to when we heard you scream?'

'Ah,' Mrs Evans said, 'I forgot I hadn't finished a little job I was doing in the sitting room.'

Eddy barged into the kitchen before Agatha had a chance to ask about the 'little job'.

'Anyone for a nip of Scotch?' he asked.

Agatha and Mrs Evans nodded and pushed their cups forward. Eddy got the bottle of whisky from the cupboard and tipped a good measure into their tea.

'I'm just going to have a bit of fresh air. I'll be out back if I'm needed,' he said, taking his glass with him.

The women nodded and sipped their tea, both grimacing at the burn of the whisky.

'Bit strong for me,' Mrs Evans said.

'Me too,' admitted Agatha.

'I best be getting home,' said Mrs Evans, pushing her chair back. As she did so, she felt a trickle from her nose.

'Oh dear me!' Agatha jumped up and grabbed a tea towel. 'You're having a nosebleed!'

Mrs Evans managed to catch the dribble of blood before it dropped onto her blouse. She pinched her nose and took the tea towel off Agatha.

'Must be the shock,' Agatha said, going over and fetching a large white handkerchief that was monogrammed with *C.H.*

'Here, have one of these.' Agatha took the tea towel and exchanged it for one of Charles Havelock's clean white handkerchiefs. 'It's not as if he needs it any more, is it?'

'Thank you,' Mrs Evans said, dabbing her nose. The bleeding had stopped.

'Funny that,' Agatha mused. 'Years ago, we used to have a young girl working here – she used to have nosebleeds just like that. Came out of nowhere, they did.'

Agatha tapped the side of her head.

'What was her name?'

She gave Mrs Evans a penetrating stare.

'Gracie. That was it. She was the mistress's favourite maid – she used to call her "my little Gracie".'

'What a strange coincidence,' Mrs Evans said.

'Yes, very strange,' Agatha agreed.

Chapter Thirty-Five

Helen's heart was beating ninety to the dozen as she pulled into the gravelled driveway of the Havelock residence.

Seeing the black van belonging to the coroner, she felt a wave of nausea. She might not feel any sadness on learning of her grandfather's death, but she was still shocked.

Parking behind it, she got out and hurried up the stone steps and through the front door, which was wide open.

As soon as she walked into the hallway, she saw a huddle of people in her grandfather's study.

Walking into the room, she was immediately hit by the smell of brandy.

'Miss Crawford!' The on-call doctor stuck out his hand in greeting. 'I'm so terribly sorry.'

'Thank you, Doctor,' Helen said, looking down at her grandfather, who had been laid out on a stretcher.

She suddenly felt a little dizzy. What was happening seemed so surreal.

The doctor took hold of her arm. 'Do you want to sit down?'

'No, no, I'm fine,' Helen said, standing up straight. 'I suppose I shouldn't be shocked. He *was* old.'

'These things are always a shock,' the doctor said. 'Death might be the only certainty in this life, yet we never fail to be stunned and surprised when it happens – even with someone as old as your grandfather.'

'Do you know what he died of?' Helen asked.

'My guess would be a heart attack.' He looked down at Mr Havelock's body. 'Are you all right for us to take his body to the morgue?'

'Of course,' Helen said. 'Please do.'

Helen watched as her grandfather's body was carried out and put into the back of the van.

'I'll call you once I've spoken to the coroner, but I'm pretty sure it'll be straightforward, and the death will be certified as due to natural causes.'

'Of course,' Helen said, surprised that it could be considered anything else.

She stood at the top of the steps and watched the van drive off.

She stayed there for a few moments, feeling the sun on her face, her mind adjusting to the fact that her grandfather was no longer amongst the living.

As she turned to go back into the house, she felt lighter, as though a weight had been lifted from her shoulders. She waited for the feeling to be followed by guilt, but there was nothing, just a continuing sense of buoyancy.

Seeing Agatha coming out of the staff quarters, she stopped.

'Why don't you and Eddy take the rest of the day off?' she said. 'I'm going to be here a while longer. I need to sort out a few things – make some phone calls.'

'Are you sure?' Agatha asked.

'Yes,' said Helen.

She was just about to go back into the study when she saw another figure behind Agatha. She looked and to her astonishment saw that it was none other than Mrs Evans.

Helen's immediate reaction was to ask what on earth she was doing there. The look on Mrs Evans's face stopped her just in time.

'Ah, this is Mrs Bevan,' Agatha said. 'She was the unfortunate soul to find Mr Havelock.'

'Oh, really?' Helen said. 'Well, that was indeed unfortunate.'

'It was,' Agatha said. 'She dropped a whole decanter of brandy, she got such a start.'

'Ah, that explains the smell,' Helen said, rapidly regaining her composure. 'Well, I'd say Mrs Bevan will probably need to get herself home and have a strong brandy herself,' she said, before turning to go back into the study.

As she did so, the doctor's words came to her mind.

I'm pretty sure the death will be certified due to natural causes.

Hearing the front door close, Helen sat back in her grandfather's swivel chair. It seemed odd to be on this side of the desk and see the room from this different perspective.

She looked at the empty tub chair opposite and thought of all the times she had either sat in it or stood behind it, her hands clenching the curved back as she locked horns with her grandfather.

Now that everyone had gone, she was glad of the quietness, although she'd had to open the sash window to disperse the overwhelming smell of brandy.

Her grandfather's death had been totally unexpected.

What to do now?

Her mind was all over the place.

She thought of John.

Why was it when she had any news – either good or bad – her first instinct was to tell John?

She looked at the glossy black Bakelite phone.

Sod it! It wasn't every day your grandfather dropped down dead. A grandfather you hated. And whose death had a number of repercussions.

She thought of Mrs Evans.

A death that might *not* have been due to 'natural causes'.

She picked up the receiver and dialled a number she knew by heart. After speaking to the receptionist, Helen was amazed to be put through more or less straight away.

'John!' Her voice showed her surprise.

'Helen!' As did Dr Parker's. 'Is everything all right?'

'Oh God,' she said, suddenly at a loss for words. 'No, not really . . . Grandfather's dead!'

'Where are you?' Dr Parker asked immediately.

'I'm here – at the house,' Helen said. Her voice sounded shaky.

'In Glen Path?'

'Yes.'

'Are you on your own?'

'Yes.'

'OK, stay put, I'm coming straight over.'

Knowing that John was on his way gave Helen a focus. She immediately picked up the phone again and rang the Grand, asking to be put through to Mrs Miriam Crawford, who, she told the receptionist, would either be in her suite or down in the bar.

Luckily, Miriam was in her suite.

'Darling, this is a surprise!'

Helen could hear voices in the background and was pleased.

'Have you got company, Mother?' Helen said, her tone grave.

'Yes, darling, Amelia's here, and a friend of mine,' Miriam said.

Good they could deal with her.

Helen heard the sound of ice cubes against glass.

'I'm glad,' Helen said, glancing at the little clock on the desk and seeing it was only two o'clock.

'Honestly, Helen, you're always so serious. You sound like someone's died.'

'That's because someone *has* died,' Helen said, fighting back her irritation.

'Really?' Miriam said, her interest clearly piqued. 'Who?'

'Grandfather,' Helen said. 'They think he had a heart attack.'

There was a moment's silence.

'He's dead?' Miriam asked.

'Yes, the doctor's just been and certified the death. They've taken his body off to the morgue.'

'Oh my goodness,' Miriam said. 'I can't believe it . . . What should I do? Where are you?'

Helen could hear the slur in her mother's voice.

'I'm at the house, but I won't be here for long. There's nothing you can do, Mother. Just stay put. I'll call you tomorrow and we can sort out what's got to be done.'

Helen heard her mother take a drink.

'All right,' she said. 'Ring me tomorrow . . . A heart attack, you say?'

'Yes, that's what they think,' Helen said. *Fingers crossed.*

Helen waited a beat.

'Ring Rupert,' Miriam said. 'He'll need to know.'

'Yes, Mother, he was on my list,' Helen said through clenched teeth.

She hung up.

Typical. It had taken her mother all of a few minutes to start thinking of the legal ramifications of her grandfather's death. Or rather, of her promised inheritance. She wondered if her mother would be grieving or celebrating this evening with Amelia and her 'friend'.

Taking another deep breath, Helen again picked up the receiver. This time she dialled home.

'Mrs Westley,' Helen said on hearing the housekeeper's voice, which always sounded wary whenever she answered the phone, 'is Henrietta about?' *Of course she was. Henrietta was still living like a recluse.*

'Yes,' said Mrs Westley, sensing the urgency. 'I'll get her for yer.'

A few moments later she heard footsteps, then Henrietta's voice.

'Is everything all right?' Henrietta asked, concerned.

'Yes, I'm fine,' Helen said. 'I'm just ringing to tell you that Grandfather's died.'

'Really?' asked Henrietta.

'Yes,' Helen said, thinking her grandmother didn't sound terribly surprised. 'He had a heart attack.'

'Really?' Henrietta repeated.

'You all right, Grandmama?'

'Oh, yes, I'm fine, sweetheart. I won't pretend to be upset,' she said.

'No, of course not,' said Helen.

'Still, always a bit of shock, isn't it?' said Henrietta. 'Even if it's expected.'

299

'Expected?' Helen queried. 'I'm guessing you mean because of his age?'

'Of course,' said Henrietta. 'Because of his age.'

When Helen hung up, an image of Mrs Evans leaving the house again flashed through her mind.

She pushed it aside and called her grandfather's solicitor.

Rupert offered his condolences and told her that Mr Havelock had left him 'clear and detailed instructions' in the event of his death, which didn't surprise Helen.

'I'm sure he has,' she said.

Her grandfather, she knew, would want to be in control in any way he could, even after his death.

Well, he might be able to have the funeral he wanted and leave all his money to whoever he wanted, but he no longer had any control over her and any of her friends.

They were free.

Finally.

Helen sat for a quiet moment, her mind racing through the many after-effects of her grandfather's death. Hearing a car pull up outside, she looked out of the window and saw it was John being dropped off by one of the hospital transport cars. She hurried to open the front door to greet him. She had to stop herself from running down the steps and flinging herself into his arms.

'John!'

'Helen!' Dr Parker took the steps two at a time and put his arms around her.

'How are you?' he asked, holding her tight, not wanting to let go.

'I'm fine,' Helen said, melting into him.

Dr Parker forced himself to step back and look at her.

'Are you really all right?' he asked again.

Helen smiled. 'Yes, really.' She took his arm.

'Is that brandy I can smell?' Dr Parker asked.

'It is,' Helen said. 'Come in and I'll explain.'

Five minutes later, they were sitting in the living room with cups of tea.

Dr Parker listened as Helen told him that her grandfather had collapsed and died in his study – and had been found by the cleaner.

'She got such a shock she dropped a decanter of brandy – hence the smell,' Helen said.

'Ah,' Dr Parker nodded, listening intently.

'But this is where it gets a little strange,' she said. 'I didn't know who the cleaner was until I saw her as she left.'

She paused.

'Guess who it was?'

'No idea,' Dr Parker said, looking at Helen and chastising himself for feeling the usual pull of attraction whenever he was in her company.

'It was *Mrs Evans.*'

'Mrs Evans being?'

'*Gracie's mother,*' Helen said, wide-eyed.

'Really? Well, that is a little odd, isn't it? Why would she want to work for the man she holds responsible for her daughter's death?'

'Exactly,' Helen said.

Another pause for thought.

'The thing is, the doctor said he was sure that death would be deemed to be due to "natural causes". But what if it isn't?'

301

Dr Parker took a sip of his tea and thought for a moment.

'Let me make a phone call,' he said, putting his cup and saucer down on the coffee table.

Five minutes later, he returned from the study.

'Good news,' he declared. 'It's going to be ruled a natural death.'

'No post-mortem?'

'No, apparently the doctor you saw – a Dr Hardy – said there were no suspicious circumstances. He said taking his age into consideration and the amount he was drinking and smoking, he was surprised the old man's heart had lasted this long.'

'Oh, that's a relief,' Helen said. 'Dear me, I think my imagination ran riot for a while there.'

'Understandable,' Dr Parker said. 'The fact that Gracie's mother has been working here as a cleaner *is* odd.'

He looked at Helen, who still appeared shaken by the sudden turn of events.

'Come on, let's get out of here,' he said. The house had the feeling of a mausoleum, and he was sure it was not just because someone had died under its roof.

Helen's face brightened up considerably. 'Where to?'

'Wherever you want,' Dr Parker said.

Helen was so glad her first call had been to John.

*

As soon as she'd heard the news about her estranged husband, Henrietta ordered a taxi and went to see Mrs Evans.

On seeing her friend's face, she was relieved. Whatever had happened had been for the best.

Henrietta had been worried about Mrs Evans's plans – not

because of what she intended to do to Charles, but for any adverse reaction it might have on her friend.

She had suffered enough.

Once they were both settled in the front room with cups of tea, Mrs Evans gave Henrietta a first-hand account of the events leading to Charles's sudden death. How she had taken the decanter of Rémy to his study and confronted him – but that he had collapsed and died before he had taken even a sip.

'Well, that *is* a turn-up for the books,' Henrietta said. 'How do you feel? Glad of the divine intervention? Or do you perhaps feel as though you were deprived of your opportunity for vengeance?'

Mrs Evans thought for a moment.

'A bit of both, I suppose.'

'And if our good Lord hadn't intervened,' Henrietta asked, 'what would you have done? Just left him there with his brandy?'

'Yes,' Mrs Evans agreed. 'After I'd said my piece, I was simply going to leave and let things take their natural course. I would have only had to wait until he'd had a few mouthfuls before he took bad. Then I would have somehow got rid of the brandy while everyone was running around trying to help him.'

'But what if anyone else had had any brandy?'

'That was never a worry as the old man never shared the best brandy with anyone else. They always got the cheap stuff.'

'You really did have it all worked out,' Henrietta reflected.

'Yes,' Mrs Evans said, 'but the best laid plans . . .'

They drank their tea.

'I wonder if he knew he had a bad heart. And that his days were numbered?' Henrietta pondered.

*

Within minutes of learning of her father's demise, Miriam was ordering champagne to be brought up to her suite, knowing that it would not look proper were she to be seen sipping such a celebratory drink in public on the day her father – one of the town's most important dignitaries – had popped his clogs.

'A toast to my dear father.' Miriam raised her glass. 'To a life well lived. A long life, well lived . . . So, rather than mourn, I do believe we should celebrate his life. I'm sure he would prefer that.'

As Miriam sipped her chilled glass of Monopole, she felt a shiver of excitement and anticipation.

She was about to inherit an absolute fortune.

*

'Where to?' Dr Parker said as they walked down the steps. 'My treat – wherever it is – and no argument.'

'I know exactly where I want to go – and it won't cost the earth,' Helen said, fishing out her car keys.

'Let me guess.' Dr Parker smiled across at Helen. 'The Tatham. You want to tell Pearl.'

'A mind reader as well as a skilled surgeon,' Helen said as she opened the car door.

'No,' John laughed, 'I just know you.'

Helen looked at John with undisguised love. *The only man who has ever really known me – and everything about me.*

As they drove to the Tatham, they chatted away. John had

to admit to himself that he was enjoying every minute of it. It occurred to him that he probably shouldn't be feeling so happy as the reason he was there was because someone had died. But considering who that someone was, any guilty feelings were soon batted away.

As soon as they walked into the Tatham, Dr Parker went straight over to Bill and ordered their drinks, while Helen made a beeline for Pearl, who, she was glad to see, was sitting on the other side of the bar, having a fag break. As it had just gone half-five, the pub was relatively empty, with just a few shipyard workers having a quick drink before they headed home.

Seeing Helen approaching, Pearl eyed her suspiciously.

'What's happened? What's wrong?' she demanded, worried that someone she knew had been hurt. Helen would not normally have chosen the Tatham for a quiet drink with her doctor friend.

'Nothing's wrong,' Helen reassured, sitting down on the bar stool next to her. 'I just came to tell you some news.'

She looked at Pearl through a cloud of cigarette smoke.

'Charles Havelock is dead.'

Pearl looked at Helen, letting the words sink in.

Then she turned to her husband.

'Get the good stuff out, Bill!'

She turned back to Helen.

''Bout bloody time. I thought he'd outlast the lot of us.' She took a deep drag on her cigarette and blew out a long plume of smoke.

'Good riddance to bad rubbish, that's what I say, eh?'

Helen smiled her agreement.

*

Over the next hour, word of Mr Havelock's death spread. Pearl went over to the Elliots and told Bel, who told Polly, who went round to see Gloria. They walked round to Foyle Street to tell Dorothy and Angie, who used Mrs Kwiatkowski's phone to call Rosie and Martha.

By seven o'clock they had all gathered round a table at the Tatham, which was just starting to get busy.

'So,' Angie said, 'he just snuffed it there 'n then?'

Helen nodded.

'And they think it was a heart attack?' Dorothy asked, looking at Dr Parker for confirmation.

'That's what the doctor said.'

Rosie, Gloria, Polly, Dorothy, Angie and Martha took a sip of their drinks.

Helen and Dr Parker exchanged smiles.

'So, we're all free of his threats,' Martha said.

'What a relief,' Dorothy agreed, looking at Angie. Their mothers were now off the hook.

'I rang Lily as soon as I heard. She sounded relieved too,' Rosie relayed.

'So,' Gloria said, giving Helen a meaningful look, 'I guess everyone's free to do what they want.'

The women looked at Helen and then at Dr Parker, who was looking down at his watch.

'I'm afraid I'm going to have to leave you all,' he said. 'The night shift calls.'

'Well, I'm taking you home. No argument,' Helen said. 'It's the least I can do. I don't know what I would have done without you.'

Dr Parker smiled. 'You'd have managed. You always do.'

The women all looked at Helen and Dr Parker as they left the pub.

'Do you think she will tell him?' Dorothy asked.

'About what?' said Martha.

'About how she feels!' Dorothy said, exasperated.

'Now that our secrets have died with Mr Havelock,' Polly explained, 'Helen can tell Dr Eris to go and take a long jump off a short pier.'

'I know that,' Martha argued, 'but if Dr Eris does tell the truth about Mr Havelock, everyone's attention's going to be on Henrietta, isn't it? And she mightn't want that.'

'Martha has a point,' Rosie said.

'Well, I think Henrietta would deal with it, if it meant Helen was happy – and was able to be with the man she loves,' said Dorothy.

'I think so too,' Angie agreed.

'Still, knowing Helen,' Gloria surmised, 'she'd need to have Henrietta's blessing before she said anything.'

Dorothy allowed a few minutes' contemplation before she perked up.

'OK, so she mightn't tell him tonight – but tomorrow, after she's spoken to her grandma . . .'

Everyone agreed.

Their optimism that Helen looked likely to get her Happy Ever After ending was evident on all their faces.

As Helen drove along the coastal road to Ryhope village, she felt aware of Dr Parker's proximity. The car was small, and every time she changed gear her hand brushed against his leg.

'So, I keep meaning to ask you,' Dr Parker said, glancing at Helen's profile, 'have you made up your mind yet?'

Helen furrowed her brow.

Dr Parker forced a laugh. 'About whether or not you're going to accept Matthew's proposal?' Even just saying the words hurt.

'Oh, God.' Helen's voice dropped in despair.

'That doesn't sound promising.' Dr Parker tried to keep his own voice from sounding the antithesis of despairing.

'I was going to call and tell you,' Helen said, taking her eyes off the road for a second and giving Dr Parker a dejected look.

'Something happened?' he guessed. 'And whatever it was, it was not good.'

'You're right. Something *did* happen,' Helen said. 'Something *not good*.'

And as they drove slowly through Ryhope village towards the Emergency Hospital, Helen told Dr Parker about what she referred to as 'the most recent episode of the debacle of my love life'.

As Dr Parker stood on the steps to the hospital and waved Helen off as she drove away, he could still smell her perfume on him. He had given her a hug. He hadn't wanted to let go of her – and he felt that she, too, could have stayed in his arms a while longer, although she was probably simply enjoying the comfort of a friend, whereas he had had to force himself to refrain from kissing her neck and making his way up to her lips.

He felt guilty for feeling so elated that Matthew had turned out to be exactly what he'd suspected him to be. A womanising chancer.

Dr Parker knew it wasn't normal to feel such cheer about

Helen's misfortune. And the fact that she was once again a single woman. It wasn't right, he knew that, but he didn't seem to be able to change the way he felt.

He knew he had to move to London.

Out of sight – out of mind.

He hoped.

Helen put her hand out of the window and waved as she pulled away. Glancing in her rear-view mirror at Dr Parker as he stood on the steps, she could still feel his arms around her. She wanted to keep that feeling for as long as possible.

He hadn't seemed too surprised about Matthew. He'd obviously had the take on him from the off but hadn't wanted to meddle.

With hindsight, she should have seen it herself.

Perhaps, she mused, she hadn't seen it because she needed Matthew as a buffer against her feelings for John.

But now that her grandfather was dead, she didn't need a buffer, did she?

She was now free to tell John that she loved him – *had always loved him*.

She just had to speak to her grandmother.

If Henrietta felt she could deal with the repercussions should Dr Eris carry out her threat and tell the world that the recently deceased Mr Havelock had lied about his wife's death and locked her away in the town's lunatic asylum, then she'd do it.

She felt a nervous tingle in her chest as she imagined telling John how she felt.

Finally.

After all this time.

Chapter Thirty-Six

Tuesday 1 May

When Helen woke early the next morning, she felt happy, excited and nervous. She had butterflies in her stomach thinking about what the day, hopefully, had in store for her.

After she'd forced down some tea and toast, Henrietta came down to see her off to work – and to wish her luck. They had chatted when she had returned home last night after driving back from Ryhope and Henrietta had insisted that she tell Dr Parker exactly how she felt, and not to worry 'one little bit' about her if Dr Eris did follow through with her threat of telling the world that Charles Havelock had lied about his wife's death, and that Mrs Catherine Henrietta Havelock was very much alive.

Grabbing her handbag and checking herself in the mirror, Helen turned and gave her grandmother a gentle hug.

'Good luck.' Henrietta clasped her hands as though in prayer. 'I'll be thinking of you all day.'

Driving to the shipyard, Helen thought how lucky she was to have her grandmother in her life. How strange that the mad wife in the attic – or the asylum, in her grandmother's case – had turned out to be the wisest and most level-headed and loving person she knew.

Helen had decided to get to work early as she knew there would be a lot to do before she went to see John later in the day.

Saving the best till last.

As arranged, Rupert rang shortly after 9 a.m. and told her that her grandfather had stipulated that he be buried within six days of his death.

'He did not like the thought of his body lying around in some mortuary or funeral parlour for longer than absolutely necessary,' Rupert informed her.

'Which,' he added, 'is probably just as well because everyone's going to be taken up with celebrating victory in Europe.'

Rupert told Helen how Mr Havelock wanted a service at Christ Church and then a burial in the town's main cemetery. And he was very clear on his instructions that he wanted the reading of the will to take place on the same day.

Mr Havelock had left Rupert a list of those who were to be invited to the service and the wake afterwards, which he wanted to be held at the house. He had organised everything down to the finest details – what kind of hearse he wanted, the exact order of service, even which caterers to use. Helen was relieved. She didn't have the time or inclination to organise it – and her mother would not be capable. From what she could gather, since she had taken a suite at the Grand, Miriam had made quite a name for herself as the resident souse.

Helen was also thankful that neither she nor her mother would be called upon to give any kind of speech about the revered Charles Havelock. She didn't feel as if she could utter one good word about her grandfather without choking on it – and she doubted her mother would be able to get through any kind of speech without the aid of a drink in her hand.

Her grandfather, she was told, had written his own eulogy,

311

which was to be read out by one of the town's bigwigs. Probably, Helen mused, someone high up in the Masons.

Rupert told Helen he would ring Miriam and Margaret and tell them what he had just told her. Helen was grateful. She had a lot to do today, and she was determined to make it over to Ryhope a couple of hours before John started his night shift.

She just hoped she managed to catch him on his own – and that Dr Eris wasn't anywhere to be seen.

At lunchtime, the women dumped their masks and welding rods and pulled off the top part of their overalls. It was hot and they were sweating. But no one was complaining – life was good, the war was coming to an end, Angie was getting married and Gloria had just told them the news that Helen was going to tell Dr Parker that she loved him.

Dorothy had almost burst with excitement, emitting a very loud 'Hallelujah!'

The women rolled their eyes, but they all had smiles on their faces.

They, too, were over the moon for Helen.

'It's certainly about time,' Polly said.

*

Seeing Dr Parker sitting at their usual table in the canteen, Dr Eris hurried over and gave him a quick kiss on the cheek. Everyone at the hospital knew they were engaged, but public displays of affection were still frowned upon and deemed unprofessional.

'I missed you last night,' she leant forward and whispered in his ear.

'I missed you too,' Dr Parker said, which was a little bit of a white lie. It had been an unusually busy night shift and when he hadn't been dealing with patients, his mind had been going over the events of his time with Helen.

'You look tired,' Dr Eris said. 'And a little preoccupied?'

'I am a bit,' Dr Parker admitted.

He took a sip of his tea and then proceeded to tell Dr Eris that he had been with Helen yesterday afternoon after she'd called him about a family emergency.

Dr Eris immediately felt a flash of anger. *Bloody damsel in distress*. And it was clear that John had dropped everything and rushed over to see her.

'And what was the emergency?' Dr Eris asked.

'Her grandfather died,' said Dr Parker.

Dr Eris felt her stomach turn. 'Mr Havelock?'

'The one and only,' Dr Parker said, knowing that Dr Eris would not be at all sad to hear of his passing.

'Gosh, that's a turn-up for the books,' Dr Eris said, trying to sound calm when in reality her mind was whirring. Now that Charles Havelock was dead, Helen could come clean about her feelings for John. Threats to bring shame on Helen's grandfather and the Havelock family in general might well stand – but they did not carry half as much weight now that the old man had dropped off his perch.

'The thing is,' John said, topping up both their cups, 'Mr Havelock's death has actually been a cause for celebration for quite a few people.'

'Really?' Dr Eris said, only half listening, her mind trying to work out a new strategy for keeping Helen away from her fiancé.

'Mmm,' John said, taking a sip of his tea. 'You see, Helen's grandfather has had her in rather a straitjacket for quite some time.'

Dr Eris widened her eyes. 'How so?'

Dr Parker took another sip of tea. He hesitated for a moment, wondering whether or not to tell Claire, but then reprimanded himself. There should be no secrets between a man and his wife – which they would be in twelve days' time.

'Well, you see,' he began, 'Mr Havelock was holding the women welders to ransom.'

'Really? How come?' Dr Eris asked.

'He knew some of their closely guarded secrets and had threatened to expose them if they ever disclosed what he had done in the past – or if it ever came out that Henrietta was not just some distant relative, but actually his wife, a wife he claimed had died. A wife, as you know only too well, who had been confined against her will and given a false identity.'

Dr Eris's ears pricked up.

'Dear me, those closely guarded secrets must have been serious?' she asked, her tone full of concern.

At first, Dr Parker was simply going to agree that, yes, they were indeed serious, but Claire sounded so interested and empathetic that against his better judgement he disclosed exactly what those closely guarded secrets were.

When he'd finished, Dr Eris sat back.

'Well, it's sounds awful to say this, but it looks as though there's been a lot of good to come out of Mr Havelock's death,' she said, lightening her tone and smiling.

Dr Parker looked at the woman he was to marry and thought how lovely it was that she was so happy for others – and for Helen in particular.

*

314

Pretending she had forgotten about an appointment, Dr Eris left Dr Parker on his own in the canteen to finish his tea and sandwiches. Within twenty minutes she had hurried back to the asylum, cancelled all her appointments for the afternoon and ordered a taxi to take her into town.

As she jumped into the black cab, Dr Eris prayed she wasn't too late and that Helen wasn't driving over to see John now. She looked at her watch. It was not beyond the realms of possibility, as Helen might use her lunch hour to race over and claim John as her own.

She could not be jilted at the altar for a second time.

She had made sure that her ex-fiancé had got to know she had bagged herself a very eligible bachelor – a surgeon, no less, and one with money. Feeling sick to the very pit of her stomach, she imagined the embarrassment should she be dumped less than two weeks before her wedding day.

Dr Eris demanded the driver put his foot down, telling him that this was an emergency.

At least Helen had not confessed her feelings to John yesterday. Thank God!

Fifteen minutes later, the taxi was pulling up outside the main gates of Thompson's shipyard. Dr Eris told the driver to wait and that she would not be long.

Stepping out of the car, she was immediately hit by the overwhelming din of the shipyard, along with a wave of acrid heat. The sun had been hot in Ryhope, but here it was a different kind of heat. Dr Eris glanced up at the boy she knew to be the timekeeper, pointed up at the admin building and mouthed 'Miss Crawford'. The freckle-faced lad tipped his cap at the smartly dressed woman. He was not going to ask her for a visitor's token as she was clearly a Very Important Person.

Two minutes later, Dr Eris was at the main doors. She took a quick look around, wondering if perhaps she might see Rosie and her group of women welders – *women with secrets* – but she couldn't. The grey yard was a jumble of metal, machinery and men in flat caps.

Taking a deep breath, she hurried into the building, up the stairs and, ignoring Marie-Anne asking if she could help her, she walked straight into Helen's office and shut the door.

So far, so good.

Helen was here.

And she was on her own.

Ten minutes later, Dr Eris was hurrying back out of the admin building and walking at a brisk pace towards her waiting taxi.

Her eyes sparkling with victory.

*

As soon as the klaxon sounded out the end of the day's shift, Rosie headed up to see Helen, having told the rest of her squad to go to the Admiral.

'We all saw Dr Eris turn up just after lunch,' Rosie said as soon as she walked into the office.

Helen looked up. She was smoking and looked as miserable as sin.

'Something tells me you won't be going to see Dr Parker after work?'

Helen nodded forlornly.

'Well, if that's the case, you're coming to the Admiral for a drink,' Rosie commanded.

A wan smile spread across Helen's face.

'Your commanding tone tells me that I don't have a choice.'

'What a total cow,' Dorothy exclaimed on hearing how Dr Eris had informed Helen that her grandfather might well be dead, and that might well make her believe she could now tell Dr Parker how she felt, but she was very much wrong in thinking so.

'So, basically, *she's* now wielding the axe over our heads instead of Mr Havelock,' Martha said angrily.

'What a horrible woman,' Polly said.

'I wish Dr Parker knew what he was letting himself in for,' Gloria chipped in. 'He'd run a mile.'

'I wish my mam would just bugger off with her fancy man, then my dad will just have to take it out on someone else,' Angie moaned.

'And I wish my mother would hand herself in and admit she's got two husbands,' Dorothy added.

'No, this was all my mother's fault,' said Helen. 'If she hadn't found out your secrets in the first place, no one would know, and then no one could keep using them for their own needs and wants.'

They chatted for a little while longer about the ruthless Dr Eris and poor Dr Parker before Helen changed the subject to Angie's wedding.

'That's my job!' Dorothy said, trying to lighten the mood.

Everyone forced a laugh.

'So, come on, then,' Helen cajoled, wanting a break from thinking about John. 'You must be getting excited, Angie? Only a week to go! Take me through the plans. And I want to hear all about the dress. Rosie said that Kate's finished it . . .'

Chapter Thirty-Seven

Over the next few days, the whole country celebrated a plethora of good news. First of all, reports hit the wires that Hitler, who had been said to be unwell, was in fact dead, having committed suicide with his lover, Eva Braun, whom he had only recently married. They had killed themselves in the air-raid shelter near the Chancellery in Berlin when Soviet troops were less than 500 metres from the Führer's bunker. Hitler had shot himself with his own pistol; his new wife had died after taking a cyanide capsule, which had already proved lethal after being tested on Hitler's dog, Blondi. Their bodies, it was reported, had been burnt. Helen thought it was timely that her grandfather had actually died on the same day as Hitler. The world was rid of two evil men. Then came the headline news declaring that German forces in Berlin had surrendered to the Red Army.

When Field Marshal Sir Bernard Law Montgomery accepted the unconditional surrender of the German forces in the Netherlands, northwest Germany and Denmark, as well as naval ships in those areas, it meant, for all intents and purposes, that the war in Europe was over. The nation started making arrangements for VE Day, which, it was speculated, would likely take place the following Tuesday – the eighth – *the day of Angie and Quentin's wedding*.

When Quentin heard, his heart sank. He was going to get

married on the worst day possible – when the entire country would be out celebrating and whooping it up. But when he rang Angie and she seemed not the least bit concerned, he knew all would be well.

During it all, the women's main topic of conversation tended to swing from Angie's wedding – with Dorothy going over her long list of what had been organised and what still needed to be organised, making sure that everyone knew exactly what they had to do and when – to then discussing in more muted tones how they could possibly get Helen and Dr Parker together.

Georgina, who saw the women whenever she could, told them that she'd done a little digging and found out that Dr Eris had been going to marry someone she had met at university, but had been jilted at the altar. She'd also heard that Dr Eris had made no secret of the fact that she was glad of it now that she was due to marry someone who was far more highly esteemed and far richer.

It begged the question: Was this really a marriage of love – or simply one she had contrived to save face and to prove she'd done better – much better?

The women decided it was not just Helen who needed saving – but Dr Parker too.

Although they hated to admit it, with just nine days before the wedding, saving them in the time they had left seemed like an impossible mission.

Helen, meanwhile, was trying to keep her heartbreak hidden and was working all hours to keep busy and to stop herself from thinking about John and Claire.

She was glad her grandfather had stipulated that the funeral was to be held so soon after his death, as she just wanted it over and done with. Every day, the *Sunderland Echo* had written some kind of article or feature on 'the town's great philanthropist'. It made Helen sick to read all the fawning words and the way the editor of the paper heaped praise upon praise on the 'great' Charles Havelock, who had done so much for 'our town'. If only they knew.

*

The funeral took place on Sunday 6 May. Helen had not wanted to travel in the funeral cortège, but her aunty Margaret had persuaded her to 'do the right thing', regardless of how she felt about her grandfather, so Helen drove over to Glen Path and left her car parked near the house. She found the Havelock residence buzzing with activity. The caterers had taken over the kitchen, and there was a team of maids making the place spick and span. Sinclair the gardener was even in the back garden with a couple of young lads, ensuring, as dictated by the master in his instructions, that the grounds looked their very best.

Mr Havelock had also stipulated that two dray horses from the Vaux Brewery should pull the hearse. It was a company he had shares in, and it was more than happy to oblige.

After a painfully slow drive in the funeral cortège along Glen Path and The Cedars, and then along the Ryhope Road, the chief mourners reached the very large, very traditional Christ Church on the corner of Mowbray Road, where the vicar was at the entrance to greet them. He was perspiring, which Helen thought was as much to do with nerves as the hot weather, as this was the biggest high-society funeral the town had seen in a long time.

Before long, the church was packed with the usual show

of leading businessmen, shipyard owners and members of the town council. There were also representatives from the Municipal Museum and Winter Gardens, whom Helen overheard singing Mr Havelock's praises and conveying how indebted to him they were for all the wonderful flora and exotic artifacts he had gifted them after his travels abroad. Helen wondered what they would say if they knew that the holier-than-thou Mr Havelock had also used one of those plants to poison his wife. A wife he had made everyone believe was already dead.

Seeing a group of elderly gentlemen who had earlier introduced themselves to her as the board of trustees for the Sunderland Borough Asylum, Helen speculated whether any of them knew the truth about the man who had donated so much money to the hospital, and why he had singled out the asylum for such generosity. She had a feeling they knew exactly why. Her grandfather's regular donations had bought their silence.

Helen, who was seated between her mother and her aunty Margaret, felt as if she was going to suffocate on the mixture of her aunty's overzealous application of Chanel N°5 and her mother's gin fumes. Her aunty had given Miriam some mints to suck on, but it was no good. The smell of booze seemed to be emanating from her pores, not just her breath.

The service seemed to drag on, and although it was a hot, sunny day outside, inside the nineteenth-century Gothic church it felt dark and cold. The words of the vicar seemed to drift over Helen's head as her mind kept wandering to John and his impending nuptials, and she argued with herself that perhaps this was the way it was meant to be. Perhaps she wasn't meant to be with John. Perhaps Dr Eris's actions were proof that Claire did in fact love John desperately, and this was why she had taken such extreme actions to bag him.

After the singing of the final hymn, 'The Lord is my Shepherd', the service at last came to an end, and everyone shuffled their way out. Helen couldn't help but sense that people were trying hard to keep the mood sombre, as would be expected at any funeral, but it was difficult. Victory in Europe was just days away. It was clear people didn't want to mourn, but to celebrate.

Walking out into the sunlight, Helen took a deep breath and smiled at seeing that some of the local children had crowded around the hearse and were stroking the two dray horses. The scruffy faces of the young boys and girls were full of delight at being able to get so near the horses that normally they were only able to watch as they clip-clopped past on their daily deliveries.

Opening her handbag, Helen pulled out her purse and went to give the children some coins. It was common practice at a wedding, so why not a funeral? Besides, she knew it was something that would have irritated her grandfather.

'Come on, Helen!' Miriam's voice hissed behind her. 'Let's get this done!'

Helen glowered at her mother and bit back a reply for her to have a little patience. There was only one part of the day Miriam was interested in, and that was the reading of the will. That and her knees-up with Amelia at the Grand later.

Driving at a snail's pace along the Ryhope Road, passing the outskirts of Hendon and travelling to the area known as Grangetown, they finally reached the cemetery.

As she watched the coffin being lowered into the grave, Helen gave a sigh of relief. The heartache and hurt, upset and misery her grandfather had caused could now, hopefully, be put to rest.

After throwing a handful of soil on top of the coffin, she made her way back to the car, imagining as she walked that John was next to her, both of them chatting away about the day so far and some of the characters at the funeral. That fantasy was immediately followed by the realisation that it would not be long before John was gone for good. They might promise to keep in touch when he moved to London, but that would soon fizzle out – especially if Dr Eris had anything to do with it.

*

Agatha and Eddy, dressed in their Sunday best, had walked to the church for the service and then caught a bus to the cemetery. As mere 'servants', they were not allowed to sit in one of the funeral cars, even though they had probably been closer to the dead man than anyone else there.

They were also last in the line of the mourners to throw soil onto the coffin.

'You go on ahead, Eddy,' Agatha said. 'I won't be long. I'm just going to see my brother's grave.'

Eddy nodded. 'So that's why you've brought that mankylooking bunch of weeds,' he chuckled unkindly. There was no denying that Agatha's little hand-tied bouquet seemed rather scabby compared to the number of beautiful wreaths and arrangements waiting to be laid once the grave had been filled in.

'That's right, Eddy,' said Agatha, looking down at her gloved hands holding the small posy of purple flowers, which were already wilting in the heat. 'That's why I've brought my manky-looking weeds.' She made to turn. 'See you back at the house.'

'Well, don't be too long,' Eddy said, slightly put out he was having to make his way back on his lonesome. 'You don't want to miss out on all that lovely grub.' He paused, still a little reluctant to leave. 'Or the reading of the will.'

Agatha smiled and started to walk off towards the area of the cemetery where her brother had been buried many years previously.

After walking very slowly and stopping to pretend to look at the intricately carved headstones of those long gone, Agatha turned to look back. She relaxed on seeing that all the mourners had now left, probably, like Eddy, eager to get back to the spread that was guaranteed to make them forget there was rationing.

Doing an about-turn, she carefully made her way back across the uneven grass to Mr Havelock's grave. She was glad the gravediggers had not turned up early. She knew from experience that they usually waited an hour or so before returning the soil to the place it had come from. Taking a deep breath, she stood quietly by the side of the grave, raising her head slightly towards the sun and enjoying the feel of its rays on her face and the sound of the birds' melodic chirping.

After a short while standing there and thinking, she suddenly became aware of the sound of a car engine. Distant, at first, but then louder. Getting nearer. She felt annoyed. She had just wanted a few more minutes to enjoy this moment of solitude.

A few minutes to mull over what she had done.

Turning her head, she saw that the small, old-fashioned

car was driving slowly along the wide gravel pathway towards the grave.

The glint of the sun on the shiny black metal obscured her vision for a moment.

Putting her hand up to shield her eyes, she watched as the car stopped and a chauffeur got out. He walked around the vehicle and opened the passenger door.

Agatha watched and was surprised to see that it was Mrs Bevan – the cleaner.

Or rather, Mrs Evans – Gracie's mother.

The driver hurried round to the other side and helped out another elderly woman, who was most definitely not dressed for a funeral in her colourful summer dress and wide-brimmed summer hat.

It was only when they both started to walk towards her that she recognised who it was.

Henrietta Havelock.

Her former mistress.

Agatha suddenly felt drenched in guilt.

She had much in her life to be punished for – she had stood back rather than stand up for those who needed help. Not just those poor maids who had fallen foul of the master, but Henrietta too. The guilt had grown over the years and, of late, it had begun to overwhelm her. She had gained some solace from knowing that if it had not been for her interference – had she not got the young lad to give the woman welder and her bloke the note telling them where to go to find out what had poisoned Henrietta – her former mistress would not be here now.

She looked down at her 'weeds'. The greatest risk she had

taken, though, had been rewarded with the greatest feeling of reprieve from her guilt.

'*Agatha, my dear.*'

Agatha was glad to hear there was no hint of animosity in Henrietta's lilting voice.

'This is a surprise!' Henrietta put her arms out and embraced her former housekeeper.

'We presumed everyone would have gone back to the house by now.' Henrietta turned to Mrs Evans, who looked warily at Agatha. She knew Agatha must have worked out her identity, but was uncertain about her reaction to that knowledge – especially if she had realised why Mrs Evans had got a job working for the man she hated with every fibre of her being.

'It is indeed a surprise,' agreed Agatha. 'For I certainly didn't expect to see you here, Mrs Havelock.'

'*Please*, call me Henrietta. I stopped being Mrs Havelock a long time ago, as I'm sure you are aware.'

Agatha looked from Henrietta to Mr Havelock's former cleaner. 'And Mrs Bevan – or is it *Mrs Evans*? I would not have expected you here either.'

'Life is full of the unexpected,' Mrs Evans replied.

They were all standing by the edge of the grave, looking down at the coffin.

Mrs Evans's gaze went down to the posy Agatha was gripping. She was surprised to see that she was wearing black leather gloves as it was such a warm day.

'That's an unusual bunch of flowers,' she said. 'Might I ask what they are?'

Agatha looked at Henrietta and then at Mrs Evans. 'It's a rather unusual plant – not really indigenous to this country.'

'Really?' Henrietta said, her interest piqued. She looked at Mrs Evans, who also looked intrigued.

'It's from a plant Mr Havelock brought back from one of his many trips abroad,' Agatha explained. 'Not the white snakeroot plant that I believe you know all about, Henrietta – but another poisonous plant, which goes by the name of monkshood.'

Mrs Evans's mouth dropped open and she looked in disbelief at Agatha. Her mind was suddenly in overdrive. She had a flash of Mr Havelock's face as he'd clutched his chest. As he'd gasped for air. The look of alarm that his life was coming to an abrupt end. Knowing he had not drunk a drop of the poisoned brandy she had taken to him, she had presumed he'd had a heart attack. But it hadn't been that. Had it?

'The monkshood plant has the most unusual qualities,' Agatha continued. 'You see, if ingested it causes symptoms akin to a heart attack – it's a little bit more complicated than that, but, basically, it can kill a person, fairly immediately. As I do believe you saw for yourself, Tan.'

Henrietta and Mrs Evans stared in pure astonishment at Mr Havelock's housekeeper.

'So, you poisoned him?' Mrs Evans gasped, still trying to take on board what Agatha, of all people, had done.

'I did,' Agatha admitted.

'Well I never!' was all Mrs Evans could muster.

'I guess it was a case of great minds think alike,' Agatha said.

'A case of the master of the house getting a taste of his own medicine!' Henrietta declared, wide-eyed.

The three women looked at each other and then down at the soil-splattered coffin.

They were quiet for a moment.

'So, how did you do it?' Henrietta asked, curiosity getting the better of her.

'Well,' Agatha said, taking a breath. 'I got Sinclair the gardener to help me create a herb garden, and whilst doing so, I also got him to educate me on all the flowers and plants growing in the greenhouse. I said it was my new hobby – something I might pursue when I retired.'

She looked down at her hands, still clutching the poisonous plant.

'Mr Havelock had, of course, got rid of the white snakeroot plant, but there were other poisonous plants which he had brought back from abroad – rather a lot. He was quite the collector.'

'Why doesn't that surprise me,' Mrs Evans interjected.

'So, I took the monkshood, being careful that Sinclair wouldn't notice any missing . . .' Agatha paused, gauging Henrietta and Mrs Evans's reactions. It actually felt a relief to be able to chat about what she had done, and the preparation that had gone into it. 'Conveniently, the leaves of the plant look like parsley . . . Anyway, I added the amount needed to one of my special hotpots—'

'Charles always did like his hotpots,' Henrietta said, with a smile.

'And, well,' Agatha concluded, 'let's just say the master enjoyed his last supper – very much so. His plate was practically licked clean.'

Agatha took a long breath and exhaled slowly.

'You see, your arrival at the house, Tan, gave me the push I needed.'

'So, you knew who Mrs Evans was from the start?' Henrietta asked.

'Not at first,' said Agatha, looking from her former mistress to Mrs Evans. 'It came to me gradually. Like Eddy, I knew I recognised you, but I couldn't put my finger on it. Then, one day, you were helping me bring the laundry in off the line and the sun caught you at an angle and I saw Gracie in you. And then I knew. Knew what you were going to do.'

'But how did you know I was going to do it that day?' Mrs Evans asked.

Agatha looked a little guilty.

'I'd thought about how you'd do it and knew you couldn't do it with your bare hands. I'd thought about what I'd do if I was in your shoes, and poisoning seemed like the only option. I knew you'd never be able to kill him in cold blood – if for no other reason than you'd probably not be strong enough. Poisoning seemed the only option . . . So, anyway, I started checking your bag every day when you came into work . . . Seeing that you were going to do it that day forced me into action.'

'But what if she'd done it before you'd given him the hotpot?' Henrietta asked.

'I'm afraid I chucked the poison down the sink and filled the vial with water.'

'So, all I did was water down the brandy,' Mrs Evans said, recalling how her hands had been shaking as she tipped what she had believed to be poison into the decanter.

'Why didn't you just let Mrs Evans poison Charles?' Henrietta asked, genuinely puzzled.

Agatha looked at Mrs Evans.

'If anyone was going to get caught and done for murder, I wanted it to be me. It wouldn't have been fair on you. Especially if you'd been caught. You've been through enough.'

Mrs Evans looked at Agatha and knew it had been her way of making amends, although she wished Charles Havelock had died at her hands. Still, at least he was gone – and with any luck he was now stuck in a purgatory of his own making.

'I just wish—'Agatha started to say.

'—that you'd done it sooner,' Mrs Evans finished her sentence for her.

The two women looked at each other and exchanged melancholy smiles.

'Well, this day is not about regrets,' Henrietta said, 'but rather about moving forward with our lives.' She nodded to the posy. 'Do you want to do the honours, Agatha?'

Agatha smiled and tossed her pretty posy of poison down into the grave, where it landed with a soft thud.

They were silent for a moment. All saying their individual prayers of thanks.

'Right,' Henrietta said, looking at her watch. 'It's time for our next little venture, isn't it, Mrs Evans?'

'It is.'

Agatha gave them a quizzical look.

'We'll give you a lift, Agatha. I do believe we are all heading to the same destination.'

Chapter Thirty-Eight

Rupert Gourley from Gourley and Sons had a quick sip of water before he addressed the three women sitting round the oval cherrywood table in the dining room of the Havelock residence. He had resisted having a stiff whisky as he knew he would need all his wits about him for the official reading of the will. It had been hard to resist, though, as Mr Havelock had ensured that his wake was a no-expense-spared feast of fine food and wine – with an array of single malts. It had cost a pretty penny. Rupert knew exactly how much as he had been the one to organise just about every detail of Charles's funeral. He couldn't complain, however, as he was being well paid – very well paid. Which was just as well, as this was not going to be a pleasant experience.

Looking round the table at Charles's granddaughter, Helen, and two daughters, Miriam and Margaret, Rupert forced a smile. Legally, there didn't have to be a reading of the will. Copies could have simply been sent to the beneficiaries, but Mr Havelock had wanted to make it an occasion. One that he had certainly not foreseen happening so soon. Charles's doctor had claimed there was nothing wrong with his heart, which just went to show that the quacks didn't always get it right.

Rupert self-consciously patted his own pot belly, which

his personal physician had told him to get rid of if he desired a good innings.

'First of all,' Rupert began with a suitably grave expression, 'I'd like to offer my condolences. Charles Havelock was not only a client but a friend. He will be sorely missed.' He glanced at the three women looking back at him. None of them were making any kind of show that they felt the same. Still, he shouldn't be surprised. They certainly wouldn't be feeling that way after they heard what he was about to tell them.

He looked a little nervously at Miriam. She already looked half-cut.

'Without further ado,' he continued, 'I shall commence the reading of the Last Will and Testament of Mr Charles Havelock.'

'About time,' Miriam mumbled under her breath.

Helen and Margaret both glared at her.

'As you know, Charles asked me to carry out his wishes in relation to his funeral and his wake—'

'Which,' Margaret interrupted, 'you have done a tremendous job with. I'm sure Miriam and Helen will agree too.' She glanced at her niece and sister, who forced smiles of gratitude.

'Thank you,' Rupert said, flushing slightly. He had always had a slight crush on Margaret, whom he had known since their youth. Unfortunately, she'd been snapped up before he'd worked up the confidence to make his feelings for her known.

'Your father,' he looked at Margaret and Miriam, 'and your grandfather,' he glanced at Helen, who looked a little distracted, 'asked me to dispense with the formalities and simply tell you in layman's terms exactly who will be benefiting from his not insubstantial estate.'

Miriam shuffled in her chair, a look of impatience on her face.

'So, without further ado,' Rupert looked down at the typed document he was holding, 'I shall begin.' He cleared his throat.

Miriam took a drink of her gin and tonic.

'Mr Havelock has instructed me to leave the entirety of his estate to a selection of chosen charities and institutions. The main beneficiaries being the town's Museum and Winter Gardens and the Sunderland Borough Asylum in Ryhope.' Rupert did not add that there was a proviso that the truth about the admittance of a patient called 'Miss Girling' should never be disclosed.

'Mr Havelock felt it was in keeping with his desire to be remembered as one of the town's greatest patrons – if not *the* greatest.'

'I'm sorry!' Miriam exclaimed loudly. 'I think that there has been a mistake!'

Rupert took a deep breath. This was exactly why he was glad he'd not had a drink, although he was going to have a large glass as soon as this was over.

'Mr Havelock informed me that he had promised to leave his estate to you, Mrs Crawford, but that he decided against the matter.' He looked down at his document. 'To quote: "I've realised that it would not be to my daughter's benefit to leave her such a large amount of money. I hope she realises that what I have done, I have done for her own well-being."'

Rupert looked up on hearing Miriam gasp. He'd prepared for every outcome, knowing that he was dropping a bombshell. He nervously touched his pocket, where he had put a small bottle of smelling salts should Miriam faint.

Mr Havelock's daughter did not, however, look like she was about to faint – more like about to go to war. Not wanting to give Miriam a chance to say anything more, he looked at Mr Havelock's granddaughter.

'Helen, I'm afraid it will probably come as no shock to you that your grandfather has left you out of his will. He said you would understand his reasons. He has, however, left you a letter.' Rupert pulled a sealed envelope out of his file and pushed it across the table to Helen.

'Margaret,' Rupert's tone softened and again a slight flush crept across his face, 'your father decided that there was no reason to leave you any money as, in his words, you had "more than enough" – that you would probably "struggle to know what to do with any more".'

Margaret smiled kindly at her old childhood friend. 'Of course, Rupert, that makes sense.'

They looked at Helen, who was holding the white envelope and staring at it, and then at Miriam, who had just taken a swig of her gin and emptied her glass.

'I'm actually at a loss for words!' Miriam said, beginning to slur. 'The old man was clearly not in his right mind when he made his will!'

Rupert had expected Miriam's comeback – as had Mr Havelock, who had made sure he had covered all the bases.

'I'm afraid, Mrs Crawford, on the day your father made out his will he had a full and thorough mental-capacity test carried out by one of the town's top doctors, which I have here.' Rupert pulled out a signed document proving that Mr Havelock had been of sound mind.

Miriam looked at her sister and then at her daughter. 'Can you believe this! This is outrageous!'

334

Margaret put her hand on Miriam's to try and calm her, but she snatched it away.

'It's all right for you, Margaret, you've got Angus – and money coming out of your ears! I have nothing! Nothing!'

'Mr Havelock did add,' Rupert said, 'that you still have your trust fund, Mrs Crawford, which, to paraphrase Mr Havelock's words, might not be enough to maintain the kind of life you are enjoying at the moment, but will certainly ensure that you are never destitute.'

'Pennies!' Miriam spat out the words. 'Let me examine the will! I must see it for myself. This feels like some kind of wind-up!'

While Rupert handed Miriam the page of the will that confirmed what he had just relayed, Helen took the opportunity to open her grandfather's letter and quickly read it.

Dear Helen,

I know it hurts you to hear this, but you are a chip off the old block. You might look like a Crawford, but really you are a pure-bred Havelock. We are more alike than you think.

Helen felt her stomach turn and her mind scream: *We are nothing alike!*

You will learn imminently that I have put a plan in place in the event of my death to make you pay for the injustices that you – my own granddaughter – have done to me, your dear grandpapa.

Helen wanted to laugh with disbelief. The only person in this sorry saga who had committed an injustice – and not just the one, but many – was her grandfather. The man really did not have any understanding of his own wrongdoings.

I hope you enjoy watching the shame and ridicule – which, I hasten to add, are long overdue – that will be meted out to those you seem so desperate to want to like you. I hope they come to realise that their lives have been ruined in part because of you.

I won – you lost, my dear Helen.

I know you won't tell the world what I did to my wife, because I can't see you putting Henrietta through all that trauma, so my secrets will remain intact.

I will live on after my death as an honourable do-gooder.

I hope what you are about to learn will teach you an invaluable lesson in life, which is 'Never underestimate someone', my dear. You might well have won a few battles, but in the end it was I who won the war. I only wish I were there to witness the payback. Perhaps I will be able to from wherever I am now.

I really do hope so.

Your Grandfather

Folding up the letter, Helen felt a sense of panic as her grandfather's carefully penned words started to sink in.

'You can come in now, Thomas!' Rupert shouted over in the direction of the door, which he had noticed was ajar.

Dressed in a hired black suit and black tie, Mr Havelock's chauffeur stepped into the room.

Rupert waved him over.

'I am pleased to tell you, my dear man, that Mr Havelock has very kindly left you his Jaguar in thanks for your years of service.'

Miriam gasped in disbelief.

Thomas's face showed his own disbelief.

'His only requirement is that you do one last job for him.'

Thomas nodded. There wasn't a lot he wouldn't do in exchange for a car – never mind a Jaguar, which would sell for enough money to enable him to make his dream of opening his own garage come true.

'Mr Havelock has asked you to take this letter straight to the editor of the *Sunderland Echo* – and this one here to the chief constable at the Sunderland Borough Police headquarters in town.'

'Of course, consider it done,' Thomas said, reaching out and taking the two white envelopes.

As he turned to leave, Rupert called out for Eddy.

'Yes, Mr Gourley!' Eddy hurried into the dining room.

'Mr Havelock has left you a cheque to show his gratitude for all your loyal service over the years.' He showed Eddy the cheque and saw Charles's trusted valet's eyes almost come out on stalks. 'But before I hand it over, Mr Havelock has also asked that you do him one last chore.' Rupert handed him a sealed letter. 'Your instructions are in here. Again, his request was that you do it straight away. The cheque will be waiting for you on your return.'

Eddy couldn't leave quickly enough. He ignored Miriam waving her empty glass at him. She could get her own drink.

'Well, I do believe that concludes matters,' Rupert said, thinking that now at least he could have a well-earned whisky.

'*I'm afraid that's not quite the case, Rupert dear.*'

Everyone turned round in their seats. All three women recognised the soft, well-spoken, slightly lilting voice.

Rupert did not.

'I'm sorry. Can I help you?'

337

He watched as an attractive older woman, dressed in the most colourful summer dress he had ever seen, entered the room. She was holding a large cream-coloured sunhat in one hand, and an embossed leather folder in the other, not unlike one he himself possessed, which he used to transport important documents to clients.

'Forgive the intrusion,' Henrietta said, glancing at her two daughters and granddaughter and smiling. 'I should have come in a little earlier and saved you the bother of going through all that spiel about who got what and who didn't.'

She looked at Miriam and her face softened. *How had she gone so wrong with her younger child?*

Rupert watched as Henrietta pulled out a chair and sat down, crossing her legs and putting her hat and folder on the dining-room table. There was something about her that was familiar. *Was it her looks, her voice or her mannerisms?*

'This might well come as a shock to you, Rupert,' she smiled. 'You don't mind me calling you by your Christian name, do you? I remember you well as a boy.' She glanced at her eldest daughter. 'I do believe you had a little crush on Margaret here.'

Rupert blushed and looked at Margaret, who smiled at him. *So, she knew.* His adoration of the Havelock girl had not been the secret he'd imagined.

Rupert looked again at this woman, and then the penny dropped.

'It can't be?' he stuttered slightly, now more than ever in need of a drink. *'You can't be?'*

Henrietta let out a tinkle of laughter. 'Yes, it can be. It is me. Not exactly back from the dead. But back from a supposed death.'

She opened up her leather folder and pulled out a small square certificate that had yellowed with age. 'And just in case there is any doubt, I've brought my birth certificate. Not that I think you really need it – but just for legal purposes.'

'But I thought you died during some trip abroad – years ago?' Rupert asked. He had gone quite pale.

Henrietta leant forward and put her hand on top of Rupert's. 'I do apologise. I know this must be a big shock for you.'

She looked up at the doorway. 'Agatha, my dear?'

She waited a beat before Agatha appeared.

'Would you be so kind as to get Rupert here a drink?'

Henrietta looked at Rupert. 'Scotch?'

Rupert nodded.

'A good measure of single malt, please,' Henrietta requested. 'Thank you.'

Agatha slipped away.

'As a lawyer, and a very good one at that, I believe, you must know what I'm about to say, don't you, Rupert?'

'I do, Mrs Havelock.' Rupert sighed. 'I'm afraid I do.'

He looked at the Havelock women – Henrietta, Miriam, Margaret and Helen. It had always irked Charles that he had never had a male heir – not even a male grandchild.

'You are going to tell me,' Rupert said, somewhat resignedly, 'that legally, as Mr Havelock's spouse, you will inherit the entirety of the Havelock estate.'

'That's right,' Henrietta said. 'It is legally but also morally right, as the dowry my parents handed over when I married Charles far surpassed the financial worth at the time of my soon-to-be husband. But really, that is by the by.'

She pulled out another dog-eared certificate from her folder.

'If my claim is contested, I also have some documentation

to prove that I was incarcerated in the Sunderland Borough Asylum under a false name – and that my death was faked. I'm guessing this would not go in the defence's favour if you did intend to contest my claim in a court of law?'

Henrietta looked at Helen and smiled. The day Dr Eris had told Helen to keep her hands off John, otherwise the women's secrets would be revealed to the world, Helen had agreed to do so on the condition that she be given Henrietta's admissions forms – both of them – one stating her real name and the other with her fake identity. Dr Eris, having no need for them any more, had happily agreed to hand them over. Helen had then given them to her grandmother, although she'd had no idea that Henrietta was planning to use them for today's purpose.

Agatha returned with a small silver tray on which sat a large tumbler of single malt.

Rupert took it gratefully, downing half of it in one go.

'I'd say you have me – or rather, the deceased – in somewhat of a legal checkmate,' Rupert said, enjoying the taste and afterburn of Mr Havelock's finest Scotch.

'Good,' Henrietta said, placing the documents back in her folder. 'I shall introduce you to my solicitor. You might have heard of him – Mr Ethan Emery.'

Rupert nodded. He had indeed. Mr Emery had been the one to handle Jack Crawford's divorce. Something he knew most of the town's other solicitors had refused to touch with a bargepole.

'Right!' Henrietta stood up. 'I think it's time to join the party, don't you?'

She chuckled.

'Sorry, I mean, the wake.'

Chapter Thirty-Nine

As soon as they were all out of the dining room, Helen grabbed hold of her grandmother's arm. 'You were brilliant in there, Grandmama! Absolutely brilliant!'

'Why, thank you, my dear. There's life left in the old gal yet.'

'There certainly is – lots,' Helen agreed.

She then took a deep breath and her face hardened.

'The thing is, I think Grandfather has put something in motion which might end up being catastrophic –' she lowered her voice '– for certain people.'

Helen handed Henrietta the letter. She quickly read it.

'*That man!*' Henrietta hissed. 'Go and do what you can. Can I help in any way?'

Helen hugged Henrietta. 'Oh, Grandmama, you've helped enough already – in so many ways.'

And with that, Helen turned and hurried out of the house.

Jumping into her car, which she had parked a little way from the house so as not to get blocked in by those attending the wake, she fired up the engine and sped back to the yard, her mind skipping from one thought to another.

By the time she reached Thompson's, she was sweating. The day was hot and it had taken her an age to get back over to the north side as it seemed as though the whole town was out and about, getting prepared for the big VE celebrations.

Thankful that the Sunday shift had ended and the place was relatively quiet, she hurried through the main gates.

As soon as she made it to her office, she picked up the phone and dialled the Ryhope Emergency Hospital and asked to be put through to Dr Parker.

She waited a while before he picked up.

'Oh, John! You're there,' she said in a flurry.

'What's wrong?' he asked.

'Oh God, where do I start?' Helen said, starting to scrabble around in her handbag for her cigarettes.

'I thought your grandfather's funeral was today?' Dr Parker asked.

'It was,' Helen said, pausing to spark up her cigarette. 'I've just left the wake. We had the reading of the will.' She blew out a plume of smoke. 'He left me a letter which basically said he'd won and I'd lost.'

'I don't understand,' Dr Parker said. 'How's he won? He's dead.'

'I know,' Helen said, 'but . . . hang on, let me read you the letter.' Again, she dug into her handbag, pulled out the letter and read it aloud.

'That sounds ominous,' Dr Parker said. 'I think you need to warn the women that he's up to something.'

'Yes, but there's something else – Eddy was given some sort of instruction in a sealed envelope, and Thomas was given a letter to the *Sunderland Echo* and another to the chief constable . . .'

There was silence for a moment before they both spoke at once.

'Lily's!'

'And Dorothy's mother,' Dr Parker added.

'Oh my God!' Helen felt her hand shaking as she tapped ash into the steel ashtray.

'OK, I've got an idea. Ring Peter – see if there's any way he can find out what's in that letter. I know he's now with the SOE, but he'll still have plenty of contacts in the police. He might be able to find out more.'

'Good idea,' Helen said, pulling out her top drawer and pushing pens and elastic bands around. 'When Henrietta was ill in hospital, Rosie wrote down Lily's number as well as her own home number on a piece of paper, which I put in here for safe keeping . . . Got it!'

'Good!' Dr Parker said. 'You ring them, and I'll call the *Sunderland Echo* and ask to speak to Georgina – see if she can find out what's in the other letter.'

'Brilliant idea!' Helen said. 'But what about Eddy's last "chore"? How can we find out what that is?'

'Let's leave that for now. Hang up and ring me when you've spoken to someone – I'll do likewise.'

'OK – oh, and John.'

'Yes?'

'Thank you – you're always there for me.'

'And always will be.'

Helen wanted to say no, he wouldn't be. Not when he was married and living at the other end of the country.

They both hung up.

Helen immediately dialled first Rosie's home number and then Lily's, but both times there was no answer.

A quarter of an hour later, she rang Dr Parker back.

'I can't get through to anyone!' she said frantically. 'Both numbers are just ringing out.'

'Don't panic,' Dr Parker said. 'I've left a message

with the editorial assistant asking Georgina to call you as a matter of urgency as soon as she gets back from a job she's on. The woman I spoke to said she didn't know how long she'd be, but she reassured me that the message would be given to her as soon as she stepped back into the newsroom.'

'I've got to warn everyone else,' Helen said. 'I can't just sit here and twiddle my thumbs.'

Dr Parker was quiet for a moment as he thought.

'Right, this is what we're going to do,' he said, taking charge. 'I'm going to get Mr Sullivan, the caretaker, to bring me across to you – if I leave now, I can be with you in twenty minutes, half an hour max. If you've still not spoken to anyone, we can go and find them.'

'Are you sure?' Helen asked. 'Haven't you got patients?'

'Let me worry about that – I'll see you soon.'

When Dr Parker walked into Helen's office, he could almost feel the desperation in the air.

'I don't believe it!' Helen said as soon as she clapped eyes on him. 'No one's answering their phones!'

'OK, if that's the case, where to first?' Dr Parker asked.

'Lily's,' Helen said. 'They've got the most to lose.'

As they drove over to Ashbrooke, Helen told Dr Parker exactly what had happened at the reading of the will, how her grandfather had not left anything to his two daughters or his granddaughter.

'Then Grandmama came in and stole the show,' Helen said, smiling for the first time. 'She sacrificed her own need for anonymity and a quiet life to stop her husband from

344

maliciously throwing away the family fortune. She did what she did for her family.'

Dr Parker suspected that Henrietta had done what she'd done for the sake of her granddaughter and her future security.

'But, just going back to the will,' Dr Parker said, puzzled, 'I thought your grandfather said he was leaving everything to Miriam?'

'So did she,' Helen said. 'You should have seen her face. To be honest, I almost felt sorry for her.'

'Really?' Dr Parker was surprised. Helen's mother had been consistently awful to her daughter for as long as he had known the Crawfords.

'I know, the irony – me feeling sorry for my mother – but she's never done anything bad to Grandfather, you know. She's only ever sucked up to him and done his bidding.'

'And how did she take it?' Dr Parker asked.

'Not well,' Helen said. 'She was already half-cut before Rupert dropped the bombshell. I'm guessing by now she will not be in a good way.'

'Oh dear,' Dr Parker empathised.

As they drove up Toward Road, Helen glanced to her right at Mowbray Park. There were corporation workers setting up a marquee, which she guessed was for the anticipated victory in Europe celebrations.

'I can't believe he's done this.' Helen suddenly let out a burst of resentment. 'This should be the happiest time and here we are running around like headless chickens, desperately wondering who to try and save first. We've already made a judgement call and put Lily's welfare over everyone else's. What happens if the police go round and arrest

345

Dorothy's mum while we're at Lily's? And poor Angie – the only thing on her mind should be her wedding on Tuesday. Now she's going to be worried sick about her mam.'

Dr Parker gently put his hand on Helen's, which was gripping the gearstick.

'I think going to Lily's first is probably the wisest decision as there are more lives at stake – there's George, Maisie and Vivian as well as Lily, and all the working girls.'

'And Kate – they might try and put something on her as she lives there,' Helen added, feeling reassured she had made the right decision.

'And as soon as we've been to Lily's, we can go and see Mrs Williams.'

'We can't. I don't know her address,' Helen said, the worry in her voice returning.

'Well, we'll just have to find Dorothy,' Dr Parker said, trying to keep the growing concern out of his own voice.

Knocking on the door of Lily's, Helen suddenly felt nervous. She had only found out that Lily was a madam and her home a bordello at Christmas.

Looking at Dr Parker as they stood at the top of the steps, she could see that he also looked apprehensive, which was not surprising as she was pretty sure he too had never been inside a bordello.

When Lily answered the door and saw who it was, her face dropped.

'Sorry, Lily,' Helen began apologetically, 'but I need to talk to you about something urgent.'

Lily snapped open the fan she was holding and started fanning herself before opening the door to allow them in.

'I tried to ring, but there was no answer . . .' Helen's voice trailed off.

'Oh, I keep meaning to get the ringer sorted,' Lily explained, 'but the moment I remember it needs fixing, I promptly forget.'

Lily sighed.

'Never get old, my dear!'

As Helen and Dr Parker stepped into the hallway, they both stood and stared at the amazing decor. It was like stepping into some kind of French palace. The walls were lined with gilt-framed oil paintings, there was a beautifully carved grandfather clock at the end of the hallway and an amazing twelve-armed chandelier hung from the ceiling. The air smelled of perfume and cigar smoke, and classical music was drifting out of the back reception room, along with the muffled sound of women's voices and the odd burst of manly laughter.

'Come into the kitchen.' Lily ushered them down the hallway.

Walking into the large room, Lily pointed her fan at the wooden table. 'Please sit yourselves down. Would either of you like anything to drink?'

Helen and Dr Parker shook their heads.

'One moment,' Lily said, disappearing through the kitchen door. She returned seconds later with George.

'Sorry to just turn up like this out of the blue,' Helen said, smiling a welcome at George as he lowered himself into a chair with the aid of his stick, 'but we've got a problem. A huge problem.'

'Oh, *mon Dieu*!' Lily said, fanning herself and sitting down next to George.

'We have reason to suspect that the Sunderland Borough Police have been tipped off about . . .' Helen hesitated '. . . about this place.'

She raised her hands and looked around to demonstrate her point.

'How so?' George asked, looking at Dr Parker.

'Charles Havelock has had a letter hand-delivered to the chief constable,' Dr Parker explained. 'And he wrote a letter to Helen saying he was going to exact his revenge.'

'We might be putting two and two together and getting five, but we didn't want to take the risk,' Helen added.

'You did right, my dear,' Lily said. 'That sounds exactly the kind of thing that man would do. *Exactly the kind of thing*.'

Just then, Maisie popped her head round the door. 'Everything all right?' she asked. Vivian had told her that she was sure she'd just caught a glimpse of Helen and her doctor friend walking down the hallway.

'No, not really, *ma chère*,' Lily said, continuing to fan herself rather frenetically. 'We need to shut up shop.'

'Now?' Maisie looked at Helen and then back at Lily.

'Yes, *tout de suite*,' she said. 'The boys in blue could be knocking on our door any minute.'

Panic spread across Maisie's face before she turned quickly and left. Her footsteps could be heard on the tiles, then lighter footsteps as she ran up the stairs.

George stood up. 'I'll get shot of everyone in the parlour.' He doffed an imaginary cap at Helen and Dr Parker and hurried out of the kitchen.

'If we're at risk,' Lily said, as Helen and Dr Parker scraped back their chairs and stood up, 'I'm guessing there's others at risk too?'

'Yes,' Helen said, grimly.

'Dorothy's mother,' Dr Parker said.

'And Angie's mam,' Helen added.

'Oh, the poor girl! Not what she needs just before her wedding . . . You best get a move on,' Lily said, getting up.

As they made their way to the front door, Helen saw two middle-aged gentlemen making their way hurriedly down the stairs, tucking in their shirts. She tried not to stare, but curiosity got the better of her. Behind the two men, she could see the flash of two partially clad young women running from one room to the next.

'Thank you, *ma chère*,' Lily said, opening the door and seeing them out. 'You might have just saved our bacon.'

As soon as Lily had wished them good luck, she shut the front door and hurried into the front reception room, which had been converted into an office. She started gathering up ledgers, pulling out files and grabbing anything else that she most definitely did not want the Old Bill to get their hands on. The time to close the bordello for good had come – albeit sooner than expected. She just had to hope that it was *she* who brought the curtain down on her business – and not the local constabulary.

Catching sight of her engagement ring, she looked at the clock on the mantelpiece. She had an idea, but they'd have to get a move on.

So much to do. So little time.

'Dorothy next?' Dr Parker said to Helen as he opened the gate and they stepped out onto West Lawn.

'Definitely.'

'And with any luck she'll be with Angie.'

349

'Fingers crossed.'

'For the sake of both their mothers, but especially Angie's mam,' Helen said, pulling a pained face as she imagined the consequences of Angie's father finding out about his wife's indiscretions.

*

Eddy was sitting in the Alexandra public house on Dundas Street in an area of town called Monkwearmouth, or the Barbary Coast, as it was known by locals. He had a perfect view of the colliery worker's house. Normally, he would have been in a foul mood, not only at having to trudge all the way over to the north side, but because he was missing out on the wake to surpass all wakes.

Supping on a beer, he kept his eyes trained on the mid-terraced cottage; his mind, though, was on the amount he'd seen written on the cheque. His cheque.

Just the thought of it had made him happier than he had ever been in his life.

The master had seen him all right. All those years of servitude – and, in particular, turning a blind eye to his master's leanings – had all been worth it.

He was going to retire a rich man.

So what if he had to sit here, waiting for the miner to come home?

He'd wait.

It was worth it.

*

Helen and Dr Parker didn't stop talking during the drive to Dorothy and Angie's flat, both admitting that they had been bowled over by the sheer opulence of the bordello, and that it was nothing like they'd expected.

They were also fired up as they knew that they had managed to buy Lily some valuable time, not just to clear the place of girls and clients, but for getting rid of any evidence that the outwardly respectable house was actually a high-class bordello.

Their spirits took a dip, though, when they arrived at Dorothy and Angie's flat and Mrs Kwiatkowski informed that them that the pair had gone away for the day with Bobby and Quentin. When asked if she knew where Dorothy's or Angie's parents lived, Mrs Kwiatkowski shook her head.

'Can you pass on a message when they return?' Helen asked.

Mrs Kwiatkowski nodded.

'Tell them the cat is out of the bag,' Helen said, unsure how much Dorothy and Angie's neighbour knew about their personal lives. 'And they are to ring me as soon as they get this message.'

Helen wrote her home number on a piece of paper and handed it to Mrs Kwiatkowski, who assured them that she would do exactly as she'd been told.

Chapter Forty

While the mourners enjoyed a sumptuous buffet and drank a little more than they probably should have, Henrietta, Agatha and Mrs Evans did a tour of the Havelock residence.

It was the first time Henrietta had been in the house since she had been judged as being of unsound mind and a danger to herself and others by some out-of-town doctor who had been quick to ditch his morals and forget his code of ethics in exchange for a large bundle of cash from Charles. That had been a quarter of a century ago, and Henrietta was surprised now at how little the house had changed.

As the three women walked around the large, twelve-bedroomed mansion, with its sumptuous, high-ceilinged reception rooms, huge kitchen and scullery and beautiful grounds, an idea started to form in Henrietta's mind.

It was an idea she shared with Agatha and Mrs Evans as they sat at the kitchen table, drinking perfectly brewed cups of tea and nibbling on some salmon and cucumber sandwiches.

Rupert, meanwhile, was discussing the rather shocking turn of events with Mr Emery, who had gone through the legal ins and outs of challenging the will with a fine-toothed comb and knew there was no way Henrietta's claim could be opposed. It was ironclad, thanks to the admission forms for the asylum.

Mr Emery's sense of satisfaction was not just because he was helping Henrietta right some of the wrongs her husband had committed against her, but also because it made him feel as though he personally was able to make Charles Havelock pay a little for taking the young woman he had loved so fervently away from him.

Following the reading of the will, Miriam spent her time slowly drinking herself into oblivion. Margaret stayed by her side, trying to keep her calm and prevent her from showing herself up too much. It was difficult, though, as the more Miriam drank, the louder she became, her mood swinging like a pendulum – one minute moribund and deeply depressed, the next outraged and angry.

Margaret had to listen to Miriam repeatedly telling her how she had been lied to by their father, that she should have realised something was afoot when she'd seen Rupert at the house, that *she* should have inherited the lot, having been the only one to be there for her father – the only one to *jump to his bloody tune.*

Margaret's own mood fluctuated between annoyance at her sister's drunken narcissistic behaviour and pity, as she really was a complete mess – and had clearly been used and deceived by their father.

Since Helen had first told her, Margaret had always been a little suspicious that their father would leave everything to Miriam. She knew her father didn't hold either of his daughters in particularly great esteem. In their father's eyes, Margaret had been too bolshy and Miriam too much of a work-shy lush – but most of all, their chief sin had been their gender.

353

When Miriam went to get herself a refill, she tripped and would have gone flying across the room had Margaret not grabbed her arm just in time and saved her from making a spectacle of herself.

It was at this point that Margaret asked Thomas, who had returned from delivering the two letters, if he would take them both back to the Grand. Margaret was glad she and Angus had taken a suite there as it meant she could keep an eye on her sister.

Leaving her husband to play host and see the wake through to its bitter end, Margaret carefully guided Miriam out of the house, gripping her arm as she walked in an ungainly fashion down the stone steps, before finally helping her into the back of the Jaguar.

By the time they had pulled out of the driveway, Miriam's head was bobbing down onto her chest. By the time they were at the end of the road, she had started to snore softly.

Margaret took the opportunity to tell Thomas that Henrietta would honour Mr Havelock's wish that Thomas be gifted the Jaguar. Margaret added, however, that it would be very much appreciated if, in return, he would not repeat anything he might have heard about the reading of the will and the events of the day.

Thomas was more than happy to reassure her that he would have done so whether or not he'd been asked.

It was the answer Margaret wanted to hear.

*

Georgina didn't get back from the job she'd been on until later – much later than anticipated. By which time the editorial assistant had long since gone. And the message she had left Georgina about an urgent call was now buried under a heap of other correspondence and readers' letters.

Slumping down at her desk, Georgina took one look at the pile and groaned. There was no way she was even going to try and make a dent in it. It would have to wait until tomorrow.

Pushing herself back up and going to make herself a cup of tea, Georgina looked around the newsroom. It was calmer now that everyone had filed their copy and tomorrow's edition was just about to be put to bed.

Heading back over to her desk, she saw the editor pop his head out of his office.

'Do you want a peek at the proofs?' he asked.

Georgina nodded enthusiastically, abandoning her mug of tea on the nearest desk and hurrying over. That was the other benefit of working late – she got to see the paper before it went off to the printers.

'We had some top stories come in today,' the editor said, lighting a new cigarette with the one he'd just smoked down to a butt. *One in particular meant he could retire sooner than anticipated.* He glanced automatically at his top drawer, where there was an envelope that had been hand-delivered by a well-dressed man in a suit and black tie. Inside the envelope there was a cheque. A very large cheque. A cheque that had his name on it. A cheque that came with a condition, however. The attached note spelled out clearly that the cheque would only be honoured once a certain story had been published in the following day's paper. Normally, he would never have let anyone dictate to him what to print in his paper, but this was a lot of money.

Georgina took the proofs and started reading.

The front page declared:

LAST-HOUR SURRENDER RUSH BY
WEHRMACHT
THE WAR IN EUROPE IS FIZZLING
RAPIDLY TO A CLOSE

The article told how three more Nazi armies had surrendered and that the Czechoslovakia flag flies again over Prague. Georgina thought of Hannah and knew she would be overjoyed. Turning over the page, the editorial comment was on how the town had been the seventh most badly bombed town in the country due to the shipbuilding yards, which had escaped more or less unscathed, thanks to inaccurate bombing and the protection offered by barrage balloons. The downside, though, was that the bombs had instead fallen on nearby homes.

The piece went on to give details of how many had been killed (267), seriously injured (362), less seriously injured (638), the number of HE bombs dropped (384), parachute mines (39), firepots (36), phosphorous (23), small incendiaries (1000s). And how ninety per cent of the houses in the town had been damaged.

Seeing an article celebrating the contribution of the shipyards to the war, Georgina smiled. The women welders would be chuffed to pieces.

But when she turned to the double-page spread in the middle of the paper, her smile disappeared and she let out a loud gasp.

OFFSPRING OF EVIL LIVING IN OUR MIDST!

Georgina had her hand over her mouth as she read how the townsfolk were being told to lock up their children for fear of what the surviving daughter of the infamous child murderer might do. The name 'Martha Perkins' had been set in bold type. The report ended by asking the question: *Like mother, like daughter?*

Georgina knew if the article made it into the following day's edition, it would more than likely work the townsfolk up to such an extent that Martha would become a walking target. She and her mother and father would be forced to leave town if they wanted to avoid the risk of potentially harmful repercussions. If they chose to stay, at the very least they would be ostracised. The heinous murders committed by Martha's mother were known by young and old alike.

The editor looked at Georgina – she was the only female journalist he had ever employed. She'd been a quick learner, and was now considered his best 'newshound'.

She was also one of his least emotional hacks, and none of them were exactly known for their soft centres.

'What's up, Georgie?' he asked through a fog of smoke.

*

After leaving Mrs Kwiatkowski, Helen decided that all she could do now was go home and sit by the phone – and hope to God it rang. She and John discussed what to do about Martha's secret, but had no idea how they could stop that coming out. They didn't think going to see Martha and her parents and worrying them would help matters – not until they knew more, anyway.

Helen asked John back for a cup of tea and something to eat, saying it was the least she could do after he had dropped everything and come to help her. Her heart lifted when he took her up on the offer as she had thought he might have to go back to work – or worse still, go back to see Dr Eris. Her mood was further bolstered on realising it was Mrs Westley's day off, as it meant that she would have John all to herself, even if this might be one of the last times she saw him before he tied the knot.

But her heart plummeted when the conversation turned to John's wedding on Saturday. Helen felt obliged to ask how the preparations were going.

'Ah,' Dr Parker said, a little nervously, 'they're going well – from what I'm told.'

'It sounds like Claire's been happy to take charge and do it all?' Helen asked. *Now why didn't that surprise her?*

'Yes, she has,' Dr Parker admitted. 'Although I have volunteered my services, Claire seems to know exactly what she wants . . . and, well, that's the bride's prerogative, isn't it – to have the wedding of her dreams?'

Helen forced a smile.

Dr Parker took a sip of his tea and looked at her.

'Actually, there's been a slight change of plan, which has only really just come about.'

For a glorious second, Helen thought he was going to say that it had been postponed. *Perhaps he was finally seeing the light?*

'Oh yes, and what's that?' she asked, her heart racing in anticipation.

'Claire wants us to leave for Northallerton earlier than planned.'

Helen felt as though she'd just been punched in the stomach.

'Really?' was all she could manage.

'Yes, she's desperate for us to celebrate Victory in Europe

Day in her home town. She says it'll give her the chance to "show me off" to all her family and friends before the wedding at the weekend.'

I'll bet you it does, Helen thought bitterly. *Like you're a bloody trophy.*

'And the hospital's all right with you leaving earlier than expected?'

Dr Parker laughed. 'Yes, Claire's got the director twisted round her little finger.'

'Does this mean you won't be coming to Angie and Quentin's wedding on Tuesday?'

Dr Parker shook his head. 'You don't think they'll mind, do you?'

'No, of course not,' Helen said. *They might not – but I do.*

'So, this will be the last time I see you as a single, unmarried man,' Helen said, trying to hide how utterly gutted she felt.

'I guess so,' Dr Parker conceded. 'Although you will be coming to the wedding – won't you?'

'Of course,' Helen lied. She had no intention of going and would be ringing the night before to explain that she had been struck down with the most awful stomach bug and would not be able to make it. It had already been agreed with Claire – had been demanded by Claire. Although even if she hadn't, wild horses wouldn't have been able to drag Helen there.

'And is the plan still to honeymoon in London and combine sightseeing with looking for a new job?' Helen forced the words out.

'Ah, that's the other news I wanted to tell you – I've just been offered at job at St Bartholomew's Hospital.'

'Oh, so you might not even be coming back?' Helen asked.

'Well, I'll be coming back to visit,' John said. 'And I'm hoping you'll come to visit us in London?'

Helen manufactured a smile.

'Of course,' she said. 'And congratulations.' She had to swallow hard to stop the tears. She was losing John for good. She couldn't kid herself any more that something might happen to prevent the wedding. Dr Eris had done a sterling job of packaging up her prize and keeping it well away from anyone who might try to take it off her.

Leaning forward, Helen touched the teapot, which was now cold.

'Another cuppa?' she asked. 'Before you leave me for good?' She tried to make her tone jocular, but failed.

As she got up, Dr Parker reached for her hand. 'I'll always be your friend. You know that, don't you?'

Helen looked into his soulful brown eyes and then down to his mouth. She smiled and pulled her hand away.

'Yes, I do. I know that,' she said, but in her heart she knew those words would become a distant memory when he had his new life – his new *married* life and his new job down south.

'*I'm home!*' Henrietta's voice trilled out as she stepped into the hallway.

'Grandmama!' Helen exclaimed. 'You're back from the wake.'

'I am indeed,' she said, walking into the lounge. 'And I've had quite a wonderful time with Mrs Evans and Agatha – we've been throwing around a few ideas . . . Oh, Dr Parker! How lovely to see you here.'

'John's been helping me today, trying to untangle the knot grandfather's got us in,' Helen explained, giving her grandmother a big hug.

'Oh, I'm so glad.' Henrietta's eyes sparkled as she looked from Dr Parker to Helen. 'I'm hoping you had success?'

'Not exactly,' Helen said. 'There's still a way to go. It's why we're here now. Waiting for the phone to ring.'

'Well, I shall leave you to it,' Henrietta said, faking a yawn. 'I'm jiggered.'

'Oh, and Grandmama . . .'

Henrietta turned. 'Yes, my dear?'

'You were fabulous today – quite an inspiration.'

'No, my dear, *you* are the inspiring one.'

As Henrietta made her way upstairs, she couldn't help but think that one positive had come of Charles's last-ditch attempt to avenge perceived wrongs – it had brought Helen and her doctor together. There was still hope.

When it was time to say goodbye, Helen saw Dr Parker to the front door.

'Well, I suppose it's goodbye,' she said, no longer attempting to keep the sorrow out of her voice.

'Until the wedding,' Dr Parker said.

'Yes, of course, until the wedding.' Helen forced herself to sound upbeat. *Six days and she would have lost him for good.*

Dr Parker opened his arms.

'One last hug as a "single, unmarried man",' he said, a smile playing on his lips.

Helen smiled back and put her arms around the man she loved.

They stood still, arms around each other, enjoying the feel of their bodies being so close, the familiar smell of one another, before they both reluctantly parted.

'See you,' Helen said, waving one last time.

361

Dr Parker turned and waved back.

It was an image Helen was determined to remember, for she knew it was unlikely she would see John again.

*

Travelling back to Ryhope in a taxi, Dr Parker felt terribly deflated.

A feeling he tried to shake off, unsuccessfully.

He looked out of the window at the darkness. He had purposely sat in the back so as to avoid conversation with the driver, who also looked relieved that he didn't have to converse with his late-night customer.

Thinking about their farewells, Dr Parker thought he had seen a real sadness in Helen's emerald eyes.

The sadness of losing a friend?

But she wasn't losing him, was she?

Who was he trying to kid? They would be living hundreds of miles apart. He would be married. And married men didn't really have female friends, did they? Especially ones who looked like Helen.

*

When Dorothy and Angie tiptoed back into the flat at midnight, Mrs Kwiatkowski was fast asleep.

She had planned to push a note under their door if they had not returned by the time she was ready to go to bed, but she had become distracted and had completely forgotten that this had been her intention.

In fact, within an hour of Helen and her handsome chap leaving, she had completely forgotten about their visit and the message – and the phone number on the piece of paper she had left folded up by the phone.

The old woman's short-term memory was fading – not that she minded too much. Remembering the past and her halcyon days growing up in Poland brought her untold joy.

It was like rereading her favourite book over and over again.

Chapter Forty-One

Monday 7 May

When Dorothy and Angie woke up the next day, their chatter was full of excitement about Angie and Quentin's wedding.

'Eee, I can't believe it's tomorrow!' Angie said, forcing down some toast. The pre-wedding nerves had started to kick in. 'Yer sure everything's sorted?'

'Do you even need to ask?' Dorothy said. 'The church, the flowers, the order of service, the reception, the catering, the cake, the music – all sorted. Oh, and the dress, of course.'

'Eee, it's really happening, isn't it, Dor?'

'It really is.'

'Yer knar how much I appreciate all yer've done, don't yer?' Angie said.

'I do – but do *you* know how much I appreciate you letting me do it? And giving me free rein?' Dorothy laughed. 'I've had a ball.'

Having finished their breakfasts, Angie put on her overalls for one last time. She knew that today was about them all marking her last day at work. She felt a tinge of sadness, but brushed it away. Like Dorothy had said yesterday when

Angie had admitted she was going to miss working at the yard, *when one door closes, another one opens.*

Clomping downstairs to check on Mrs Kwiatkowski before they left for work, Dorothy and Angie found their elderly neighbour looking a little dishevelled and confused.

'Yer alreet, Mrs Kwiatkowski?' Angie asked.

'No – I can't remember why I have this note . . .'

Dorothy and Angie exchanged worried looks.

'Here!' Mrs Kwiatkowski stretched out her hand and gave the note to Dorothy. 'It's got a number on it, and I can't remember for the life of me who gave it to me or why.'

Seeing how distressed Mrs Kwiatkowski was becoming, Angie guided her to her chair and sat her down.

'Let's get you a nice strong cuppa, eh?' she said.

'Yes, a nice cup of tea will bring it all back to you, Mrs Kwiatkowski,' agreed Dorothy. She looked down at the small piece of paper, which had a telephone number scrawled on it.

'Why don't I ring it?' she suggested. 'See who answers?'

'Good idea,' Mrs Kwiatkowski said, her face brightening.

Dorothy dialled the number, casting more worried looks at Angie, who was pointing to the gas stove, where one of the rings was burning. *Heaven only knew how long that had been on.*

The phone had only just started ringing when it was snatched up.

'Hello, Georgina?'

'No, it's Dorothy – *is that Helen?*'

*

Chief Constable Duncan Metcalf had been surprised to receive the post-mortem correspondence from Charles Havelock yesterday afternoon. He had been due to attend the funeral in person, but he had been so busy there'd been no way he could leave his office for five minutes, let alone take the entire afternoon off. He had, of course, sent his deputy as his representative from the Sunderland Borough Police. It would be unseemly not to. Mr Havelock had, after all, been one of the town's richest and most admired businessmen.

The chief constable would have likely carried through the old man's requests as soon as he'd received them yesterday afternoon – the sooner he'd done Charles's bidding, the sooner he could cash his very substantial cheque. As it was, however, he'd barely been able to turn around. The imminent surrender of Germany had caused a wave of euphoria the length and breadth of the country and a surge of frantic activity. He'd done well to get his men briefed and out the station this morning, especially after the news of Germany's official unconditional surrender had come down the wires in the early hours.

As a rule of thumb, Chief Constable Metcalf favoured early-morning arrests as it added to the element of surprise. Those who ran the upmarket knocking shop would definitely still be in bed. And it was highly unlikely that the woman who had committed bigamy would be up and out early – not with four children to tend to.

*

'Oh my God. Oh my God. Oh my God.' Dorothy kept up her mantra as she and Angie ran like the clappers out of the flat and down Foyle Street. Flying round the corner, they nearly collided with a couple of shipwrights chatting and smoking as they made their way to work. The pair managed to dodge out of the way as Dorothy and Angie tore past.

'Watch yerselves!' one of the men shouted, shaking his fist at their backs.

They sprinted across Borough Road, drivers blaring their horns at the two frantic-looking, overall-clad women clattering across the cobbles in their hobnailed boots.

'There's a tram!' Dorothy shouted. 'Run!'

Angie thought that was exactly what they were doing, but tried to increase the pace, although it was hard. She could feel the tea and toast she'd had for breakfast jostling around in her stomach, ready to make a reappearance at any moment. And it wasn't just the movement that was making her feel sick, but the thought of what might happen to both their mothers.

'Ger it, Dor!' she shouted, seeing her friend sprint to the front of the tram just as it reached the bus stop.

Angie kept running as she saw Dorothy put one foot on the tram's platform – leaving the other firmly planted on the pavement. She was waving frantically at Angie to hurry up.

Dorothy pulled her on and the tram moved off. They both collapsed on the first seats they came to. They were breathing so heavily they were barely able to tell the conductor where they wanted to go.

Dorothy gasped for air as she said, 'The Cedars!'

*

'Doesn't feel right, somehow. Arresting someone for not getting a divorce,' PC Potts said to his partner as he indicated right and overtook a tram on the Burdon Road.

'Well, it's against the law and it's as simple as that,' PC

Stubbs said, turning his head as he heard the angry blare of car horns.

'I know,' PC Potts argued, keeping his eyes on the road. 'But what if the poor woman *thought* she had a divorce and married her new fella in good faith?'

'Well, that's a matter for the courts, isn't it?' PC Stubbs said.

'Suppose so,' PC Potts said, unconvinced. When he'd joined the Sunderland Borough Police, he'd done so under the impression he'd be catching real criminals – not arresting some poor woman for having one too many husbands.

A few minutes later, they were pulling up outside the address they had been given.

'Nice house,' PC Stubbs said as he opened the passenger door and got out.

*

'Please God, let us get to her in time,' Dorothy begged.

'We will,' Angie said. 'Then she can go and sort it all out.'

'Imagine how awful it will be for her if they arrest her – take her away in handcuffs – put her in a cell,' Dorothy worried.

Angie looked at her friend. Mixed in with the anxiety, she could hear the guilt that Dorothy had not had any contact with her mother or her siblings since the day she'd taken Bobby to meet them. Not that Dorothy should feel guilty. It was her mam and her snobby stepdad who should be sorry.

'Just remember that this isn't yer fault,' Angie said. 'Just as it won't be my fault if owt happens to my mam.'

'Oh God.' Dorothy gave Angie another look of extreme anxiety. 'You do think your mam'll be all right?'

'She'll be fine. She doesn't start her shift until nine. We'll have plenty of time to get over there and catch her before Dad gets back . . . Anyway, like I said, none of this is our fault,' Angie stressed.

'I know,' Dorothy said, forcing herself to believe it.

'There's only one person to blame, 'n that's Charles bloody Havelock,' Angie stated solemnly.

Dorothy and Angie had to stop themselves screaming with frustration when the driver of the tram decided to count his takings at the stop halfway up the Ryhope Road.

Asking him why he'd stopped, the driver told them he was ahead of schedule and needed to wait a few minutes.

'Wouldn't want anyone to miss their ride because I was too early,' he said.

'If yer went now, yer'd make up for all the times yer were late,' Angie argued.

The tram driver chuckled and kept on counting his fares.

'Trust us to get some jobsworth!' Dorothy said as she tugged Angie off the tram.

Angie groaned. 'I'm knackered, Dor.'

'One last push,' Dorothy cajoled, keeping hold of her arm and starting to jog.

A few minutes later, even more exhausted, Dorothy and Angie reached the stop adjacent to The Cedars – just as the tram pulled up.

Dorothy scowled at the driver, who seemed to think it was all very amusing.

Hurrying across the Ryhope Road, they speed-walked along the wide, tree-lined road, trying to get their breath back.

'Oh. My. God!' Dorothy stopped in her tracks and put her arm out to stop Angie from taking another step forward.

Parked outside her mother's house was a police car.

'Ah, nar, I dinnit believe it.' Angie could feel tears of frustration building, along with a few dribbles of sweat that had started to trickle down her face.

'Nooo,' Dorothy said, crushed. She was still standing with her arm as a barrier in front of Angie. 'What shall we do?'

'Well, we've not just busted a gut getting here to turn round 'n gan straight back,' Angie huffed, removing Dorothy's outstretched arm.

'True,' Dorothy agreed, looking at Angie and feeling a wave of guilt. She was as red as a beetroot and looked exhausted. Today was meant to be an enjoyable last day at work with all her mates before she became a married woman. Instead, here she was, running around town like a loon.

'OK, let's go in,' Dorothy said, trying to sound positive. 'We might be able to sweet-talk the coppers into just giving her a caution.'

'Like this?' Angie exclaimed, looking down at her dirty overalls and scuffed leather boots, which were now killing her. She was sure she felt a blister starting to form on her heel.

When Dorothy knocked on the door, she was surprised to see the eldest of her four younger sisters answer the door.

'The police are here!' she whispered excitedly, before running back into the front room.

Dorothy and Angie stepped over the threshold.

'She won't be so pleased about it when she realises they're here to arrest her mother,' Dorothy said out of the corner of her mouth to Angie.

Hearing voices, they walked towards the living room.

Dorothy had a sudden flash of when she was last there

with Bobby. She no longer felt angry. If anything, that day had cemented her love for Bobby and his for her. It had been the silver lining to a very dark and cloudy day.

Taking a deep breath, Dorothy pushed open the door, expecting to see the worst – her mother being handcuffed and read her rights, Frank looking broken, and the children in tears.

'Oh, Dorothy!' Mrs Williams exclaimed in surprise on seeing her daughter. 'Come in! And Angela – it is Angela, isn't it?'

Angie nodded, her eyes wide in astonishment. There was Dorothy's mam standing in the middle of the room beaming at two uniformed police officers, her husband Frank positioned next to the drinks cabinet and Dorothy's four siblings sitting squashed up on the sofa – all still in their dressing gowns, having just got up minutes before the loud knock on the front door.

'Don't be shy. Come in and meet these two fine members of our town constabulary. PC Potts and PC Stubbs,' Mrs Williams continued, waving her hands at Dorothy and Angie as though she too were a member of the constabulary, directing traffic.

Dorothy and Angie stepped into the room. The two policemen strode over to them and shook hands.

'There's been a little bit of a mix-up,' Mrs Williams explained. 'But it's all been sorted.' She looked back at the two policemen. 'The council's births, marriages and deaths records clearly haven't been updated, which isn't surprising in the current climate. Bureaucracy has to take a back seat when we're trying to win a war, isn't that right?'

'A war which we've all just had confirmed this morning

we have won – at least in Europe,' Frank interjected. He smiled at the two coppers. 'Are you sure we can't entice you into partaking of a quick toast to King and country in celebration?' he asked.

'Tempting,' PC Potts said. 'Very tempting. But if we go back to the station stinking of booze, we'll be celebrating victory with a trip down the labour exchange.'

Everyone chuckled – apart from Dorothy and Angie, who were still looking stunned.

'Well, we best be getting off,' PC Potts said.

PC Stubbs looked at Dorothy and Angie.

'Shipyard or factory?'

'Shipyard,' Dorothy and Angie answered in unison.

'Thompson's,' Dorothy added.

'You must be very proud of your daughter,' PC Potts said to Mrs Williams. 'Not for the faint-hearted, shipyard work. My sister's over at Doxford's. Hard graft, that's for sure.'

With that, PC Potts tipped his hat and cocked his head to PC Stubbs to follow. He was happy with the outcome of this morning's job. Now, perhaps, they could get on with some proper police work.

After Mrs Williams saw the two policemen out the front door and had waved them off as they drove away, she hurried back to the sitting room.

'Did you come to warn us?' Mrs Williams asked.

Dorothy and Angie nodded.

'How did you know?' Mrs Williams asked, puzzled.

Dorothy briefly explained how some of their secrets had been used against them by a very unpalatable character who had decided to take revenge after his death. She didn't go into detail, or name names, but instead turned her attention back to her mother.

'So, what happened?' Dorothy asked. 'How come they let you off?'

'They didn't let her off,' Frank said, taking the stopper out of the cut-glass decanter and pouring himself a much-needed whisky. 'Your mother is now officially my wife. There was nothing to arrest her for.'

Dorothy turned to her mother for further explanation.

'Well, it's all thanks to you, actually, Dorothy.' She took hold of her daughter's hand and squeezed it.

'After you were here last . . .' She paused, remembering that awful day and the scene she'd had with Frank afterwards. 'Well, to cut a long story short, we sorted it out.'

Frank coughed.

'Or should I say, your stepfather sorted it out,' Mrs Williams added. 'He went to his solicitor, and they sorted it out.'

'How?' Dorothy asked, relieved but intrigued.

'The case was argued that your mother believed her husband to be dead when we were married, but only later discovered he was still alive,' Frank informed, taking a mouthful of Scotch and swallowing hard.

'And she was believed?' Dorothy asked, knowing that her mother was well aware that she was still married when she said her vows to Frank.

'The divorce was pushed through post-haste,' Mrs Williams said, ignoring Dorothy's question. 'And then Frank and I were married. No fuss, of course. Although we did have a little party here afterwards with the children.'

Dorothy looked at her four sisters, still sitting obediently on the sofa. They had been so unusually quiet and well behaved she'd forgotten they were there.

'We had cake!' the youngest perked up.

'Well, it would have been nice to be told,' Dorothy huffed. 'I think Ange and I have just aged a few years trying to get to you in time.'

'We haven't exactly been on speaking terms,' Mrs Williams said. Her tone, though, was more placatory than accusatory.

'Well, I'm glad,' Dorothy said. 'Glad that Ange and I didn't arrive here to find a very different scenario.' She looked at her sisters. She might not be close to them, but she wouldn't have wanted them to be damaged by the image of their mother being dragged off by the police, prosecuted and possibly imprisoned for being a bigamist.

'Won't you stay for some breakfast?' Mrs Williams said, looking at the clock. 'I know you're probably due to start work, but I'm sure you can be late just this once?'

'We've got to go,' Dorothy said. 'Yours wasn't the only secret that's been let out of the bag.' She glanced at her best friend.

'Your mother?' Mrs Williams asked Angie.

She gave the slightest of nods.

'And Angie's getting married tomorrow,' Dorothy said.

'Oh, congratulations, my dear,' Mrs Williams said, genuinely happy for her daughter's friend. 'Well, you'd better get going – you've got a lot on your plates by the sound of it,' she said, walking them to the front door.

As Dorothy and Angie stepped out into the early-morning sun, Mrs Williams caught her daughter's arm.

'Can I just say, Dorothy, that I *am* proud of you, you know?' She took a breath.

374

'Not just because of what PC Potts said about shipyard work, but I'm proud of *you* – as a person. How you've turned out. You're not the person that we wanted you to be, but you're the person *you* want to be – and that's the important thing.'

Dorothy let out a genuine laugh.

'I think there's a compliment in there somewhere, Mum,' she said with a smile.

Dorothy and Angie walked down the front steps.

'And don't be a stranger,' Mrs Williams called out. 'Pop round sometime – and bring Bobby.'

Dorothy's smile widened as she waved goodbye.

Chapter Forty-Two

A loud hammering on the front door made everyone at Lily's jump, even though they were expecting it. They were all like cats on a hot tin roof.

They immediately fell into their agreed roles and activities.

Lily bustled to the door just as there was another loud hammering.

'Police!' a deep, commandeering voice shouted out from the other side.

Lily opened the door.

'Oh, dearie me!' Lily exclaimed, putting her hand on her bosom. 'I did not expect to find the boys in blue on my doorstep so early in the morning.'

The uniformed officer stared at the very English-sounding woman he knew to be some sort of French madam and felt disappointed. First of all, she didn't sound French – if anything, he'd caught a slight London twang. And secondly, she looked so ordinary. She even had an apron on over her Jaeger herringbone Utility suit. He knew the design as his wife had just bought one, and it had cost a pretty penny. Four pounds, if he remembered correctly. Never mind the coupons.

'Can I help you?' Lily asked, looking over the sergeant's shoulder and seeing half a dozen other uniformed coppers.

'I've got a warrant here to search your property, Miss Lily Asher.'

'It's *Mrs Lilian Macalister*,' Lily corrected.

She took the piece of paper the policeman was holding and read it. She widened her eyes dramatically. 'Why on earth would you want to search our home?'

'Who's that at the door, darling?'

On cue, George appeared in the doorway. He was wearing his Durham Light Infantry uniform, complete with medals. Lily stood to the side to show him who their unexpected visitors were.

'Golly me!' he explained. 'Looks like you brought the cavalry!'

'Sorry to bother you, sir,' Sergeant Cooper said, immediately feeling intimidated by the man's rank and class. 'I was just explaining to Mrs Macalister—'

'My wife,' George said. 'I'm *Mr* Macalister.'

The sergeant paused. The information he'd been given did not have them down as a married couple. And there had been nothing mentioned about the man of the house being a war hero, which he clearly was, judging by the medals he was wearing.

'I was just telling your wife, sir, that we have a warrant here to search the house,' Sergeant Cooper repeated.

'For what reason?' George asked. 'Do you think we're harbouring German spies?' He laughed at his own joke.

Sergeant Cooper remained sombre.

'No, I'm afraid we have been informed that this house is . . .' he hesitated '. . . that this house is a house of ill repute.' Even as he said the words, he felt a little ridiculous. He had thought it strange that a knocking shop would be working from somewhere as salubrious as West Lawn. Still, stranger things had been known.

George let out a loud guffaw. 'My dear man! I've never heard the like! But please, do come in!' He opened the door wide and let out another loud burst of laughter.

Lily looked at George and thought he should have been on the stage.

'Unfortunately, you'll find nothing so exciting or salacious here. More's the pity!' George chuckled.

Lily stood aside, taking off her pinny and patting down her hair, which was actually a wig to hide her own vibrant, dyed-orange hair. She had no make-up on or jewellery. Kate, who had dressed, or rather disguised, Lily, had described her as 'the personification of a good housewife'. Lily had taken one look at herself in the mirror and refused to look again.

'I hope you won't take long,' George said. 'I was just off to see my old comrades-in-arms – hence the uniform.'

Sergeant Cooper stood aside as his men entered the house. 'We'll be as quick as we can, sir.'

'Oh, can I just ask you to take your shoes off, please?' Lily glared down at the half-dozen or so pairs of polished black police regulation footwear. 'My cleaner will have my guts for garters. She just did a thorough spring-clean yesterday.'

The men looked at their sergeant, who nodded his acquiescence. They all took off their shoes and put them by the doorway. This must be the most unusual house search they had ever done in all their time with the force.

'Do you need me to show you around?' Lily volunteered, keeping her fingers crossed that nothing had been overlooked or left out. They'd all worked round the clock from the moment Helen had tipped them off to just minutes before the dreaded knock on the door.

'No, no need,' Sergeant Cooper said.

'Well, if that's the case, let me at least make you a cup of tea. I, for one, am parched.'

And with that Lily led the way down the hall.

Showing him into the kitchen, Sergeant Cooper was greeted by two young women sitting at the table having their breakfast.

'Ah,' Lily said. 'This is Rosie and her not-so-little sister, Charlotte.'

Rosie and Charlotte both fashioned suitably surprised faces at seeing a policeman in the house.

'Don't worry, darlings,' Lily said, a hint of Cockney sneaking its way through the almost perfect King's English. 'There's obviously been some sort of a mix-up. The law-keepers of our lovely town are under the misapprehension that this is actually a "house of ill repute".'

Before Rosie and Charlotte had time to express their shock and then mirth as planned, one of the younger policemen came into the kitchen.

'Sorry, ma'am,' he said as he edged past Lily and started to open drawers and look in cupboards. Lily stared daggers. The young man, she thought, would have fitted in well with the Hitler Youth. She watched as he pulled out cookery books and started to flick through them. She wanted to quip that he wouldn't find any 'johns' in there, but held back.

'You'll only find recipes in there, my young man,' she said instead.

'Please, take a seat,' she implored Sergeant Cooper. 'This looks as though it might take some time.'

As she nodded towards the kitchen table, she saw that she had left her 'little black book' next to a small vase of flowers in the centre of the table. It contained the names of all their clients and their payments. The book was partly hidden under a copy of *The Times*.

Charlotte caught Lily's look at the same time as the blond-haired Hitler Youth.

He stepped over and reached for the book.

Charlotte, though, beat him to it.

'There it is!' she exclaimed, making a grab for it. 'I've been looking for that all morning and it's right under my nose!'

She grabbed the book and hugged it to her chest.

'Miss Webster would have loved nothing more than to give me a detention for not bringing in my French homework today,' she declared truculently.

The Hitler Youth looked at his sergeant, who looked at the black book that Charlotte was now shoving into her brown leather satchel.

Suddenly their attention was drawn to the back door as it swung open.

It was Peter.

Bang on time.

'Well! What do we have here?' he asked, shocked.

He looked at the two police officers and then back at Charlotte.

'You've not been up to mischief, have you?' he asked, sounding very fatherly and very strict.

'No, no,' Sergeant Cooper said. 'We have a warrant to search the house.'

'Really?' Peter said, his voice raised in disbelief. 'Whatever for?'

Before Sergeant Cooper had a chance to answer, Peter had walked over to him and stuck out his hand.

'DS Peter Miller, glad to make your acquaintance.'

'Sergeant Cooper, sir. Sorry, sir, I didn't recognise you.'

'That's probably because I haven't been with the police these past few years. I was needed elsewhere. Need I say more?'

'Ah, yes, I understand,' said Sergeant Cooper.

The kitchen door opened.

'All clear, Sarge,' one of the police officers said.

Peter looked quizzically at Sergeant Cooper.

'We had a report that this was a *disorderly house*.' The sergeant raised his eyebrows apologetically. 'But, obviously, there seems to have been some kind of mistake.'

'Obviously,' Peter said, his jaw tightening.

'Well, we'd better get going,' Sergeant Cooper said, suddenly wanting to get out of there pronto.

'As should *you*.' Peter looked down sternly at Charlotte. 'We don't want you being late for school, do we?'

Charlotte shook her head, scraping back her chair and getting ready to leave.

'I'll see you all out.' George appeared in the doorway, where he had been loitering, keeping a check on what was happening upstairs during the search. He walked down the hallway, his ornate walking stick striking the parquet flooring.

When he reached the front door, he opened it wide as the uniformed officers filed out.

He stretched his arm out towards Sergeant Cooper and the two men shook hands.

'You know, old boy,' George said with a half-smile, 'I have a feeling I know what might have happened here.'

'Really?' Sergeant Cooper said. He was glad someone did because he had not a clue.

'I might be amiss in saying this, but I would bet my bottom dollar that this has been a rather elaborate hoax.'

'Really?' Sergeant Cooper said again.

'I have a feeling my old chum Charles Havelock might have just had the last laugh – from beyond the grave, as it were,' George said with a light chuckle.

Sergeant Cooper was starting to understand.

'You see, my good man,' George explained, 'Charlie and I go back years and years. He was such a prankster – and I have to admit that I am a little partial to the odd wind-up every now and again. It became a bit of a competition between the two of us, and, you see, I was one up on him – something old Charlie would not tolerate.' George chuckled as though remembering a dear lost friend. 'One of the last things the old boy said to me was that he would have the last laugh, and I guess with you coming here today – he has!'

'You know,' Sergeant Cooper said, 'what you've just told me makes complete sense.'

'But don't be annoyed,' George said. 'If I know Charles, I'm sure he would have left a nice wad to be shared around to make up for the joke. You ask your boss. I'm sure you'll find there's more than one drink in it for you all.'

Sergeant Cooper smiled. The slight resentment he'd felt at being used to carry out someone's joke suddenly dimmed.

'I will,' he said. 'And you have a good meeting, sir.' Sergeant Cooper took another look at the medals, even more impressed on seeing that one of them was the Distinguished Service Order for bravery. 'Good day to you, sir!'

'Cheerio!' George waved them off and closed the door.

*

Charlotte left via the back entrance to the house. Her heart was hammering. It had been in her mouth when she'd seen Lily's black book still on the table. She was surprised Lily hadn't had a coronary right there and then.

Walking down the garden path, she hooked her satchel over her shoulder and unlatched the wooden gate.

As she swung it open, she came face to face with the Hitler Youth.

She stopped dead in her tracks.

'Sorry,' he said, not sounding the least apologetic. 'But I'm afraid I *do* need to check that the black book you took from the kitchen table does in fact belong to you.'

Charlotte felt her face flush.

She hesitated.

'OK,' she said, her voice shaky.

She took her time opening her satchel and rifling around.

Finally, she pulled out a black book.

She held it for a moment before reluctantly handing it over.

The young copper looked at her suspiciously before opening it.

As he flicked through the pages, the self-satisfied look on his face disappeared.

'Like I said,' Charlotte said, seeing his expression change, 'it's for my French homework.'

The young officer closed the book and handed it back.

'Sorry,' he said. This time he sounded as though he genuinely meant it. 'I get a bit overzealous sometimes.'

'Don't worry,' Charlotte said. 'Overzealous isn't a bad thing.'

She then gave him her most beguiling smile, which she

had learnt from Vivian, and waved him goodbye as she walked off.

As she reached the end of the back lane and turned right up The Grove, she pushed the black book back into her satchel – where it bumped up against another identical black book.

Lily's black book.

Charlotte had bought herself a stack of the lovely hardback notebooks after seeing Lily's one day. She should really have used the school's standard blue notebooks for her homework, but her form teacher had bent the rules for her star pupil; she was, after all, destined for one of the country's top universities.

Chapter Forty-Three

It had taken longer than anticipated for Dorothy and Angie to get over to the other side of the river due to one of the main roads being blocked off in anticipation of the upcoming celebrations.

'Come on,' Dorothy said, looking at Angie as she trailed behind.

They broke into a half walk, half run.

A few minutes later, they reached the home Angie had been brought up in – a small mid-terrace in Dundas Street. They'd made it in plenty of time before Angie's mum had to leave for work. Mrs Boulter worked at the local ropery, and the women employed there were known as 'Craven Angels', named after the owner of the factory. Dorothy had never been sure whether the name had been given ironically – she reckoned it must have been if the other women who worked there were anything like Angie's mam.

As soon as Angie and Dorothy walked through the front door, they were immediately accosted by her brothers and sisters, who were even more excited than usual as their big sister was getting married the next day and they were all going to be a part of it.

Dorothy found herself staring at a shiny new shoe one of the boys was holding up with an outstretched arm. She thought of her own sisters, who had never wanted for any-thing, and for the first time she felt sorry for Angie's siblings. Their little faces were grubby but they were full of excite-ment and chatter. Making them all part of the wedding had been such a good idea. Although Dorothy also wondered if it might give them a taste of a life that could never be theirs – certainly not while they lived here.

'Mam,' Angie said, ruffling the hair of the youngest child, who was tugging on her overalls, 'I need to talk to you. About something serious.'

'Well, it'll have to be quick. I've got to leave in a minute.'

Angie glanced over to Dorothy, who did as planned and cajoled the children into showing her their outfits for the wedding; not that they needed much persuading.

As soon as they were out of earshot, Angie turned to her mam.

'Dad's gonna find out about yer fancy bit,' she said. There was no time for mincing words.

Mrs Boulter looked at her daughter.

'Dinnit deny it, Mam, 'cos I knar – and someone else knars who wants to cause trouble, 'n they're gonna tell Dad.'

'What?!'

'Dinnit shoot the messenger, Mam,' Angie bit back. 'I'm deeing yer a favour. Give yer a chance to spike yer guns 'n decide how yer gonna deal with it. Ger in there before he hears it off someone else.'

Angie's mam stomped into the scullery and returned with a packet of Winston's. She slumped down into the armchair by the range and lit her cigarette. She sat there, staring at the dirty rug on the even dirtier floorboards, not speaking, just smoking.

Angie had never seen her mother like this. She rarely smoked. And she was rarely quiet.

'You all reet, Mam?' Angie asked. She could hear Dorothy in the front room oohing and aahing at the bridesmaids' dresses and the boys' morning suits, which had been hired for the day. Quentin had suggested buying them their outfits, but Angie had said there was no point as they'd never go anywhere they could wear them.

'Mam?' Angie asked again. 'Speak to me! What yer gonna dee?'

Mrs Boulter's head snapped back up to look at her daughter.

'I'll be fine, Angie.'

She looked nervously at the clock on the mantelpiece.

'I'll think of summat.' She got up and stubbed out her cigarette. 'You 'n yer mate best ger off. The least people here the better when he gets in.'

'What about the bairns?' Angie asked.

'Do us a favour, will yer? Take them to school. Then I can just deal with yer dad on my own.'

'Will yer be all reet on yer own?' Angie said, suddenly worried, not liking the idea of her mam being alone with her dad when she told him she'd been shagging another bloke.

'I'll take him to the pub. Tell him somewhere public, so if he does kick off . . .' She let her voice trail off and looked nervously at the clock again. 'So, haddaway. Get yerselves off . . . *Bairns!*' she shouted.

Four happy, excited faces appeared along with a rather frazzled-looking Dorothy.

'Angie 'n her mate are taking yer all to school today.' Her words were met by a burst of excitement, with the little one jumping up and down on the spot.

Mrs Boulter opened her arms and gave them each a quick cuddle.

Angie watched, open-mouthed. She couldn't remember the last time she'd seen her mam show any of them any kind of affection.

Dorothy rounded them up and got them out the front door.

'Oh, 'n Angie,' Mrs Boulter said, 'I'm glad yer've got yerself a decent bloke. He seems like a nice lad.'

Angie stood stock-still as her mam then gave her a quick hug.

'Now, scram!' she said.

Angie went to leave, but stopped.

'I'll see yer tomorra?'

Her mother's face looked blank.

'At the church?' Angie reminded her.

'Course yer will,' she said, making shooing motions with her hands. 'Now bugger off!'

After Angie and Dorothy had taken the children to school and waved them goodbye in the playground, they made their way to work.

'What a day, eh?' Dorothy said.

'What a day,' Angie agreed. 'And it's only just started.'

Dorothy looked at Angie and thought about tomorrow's wedding.

'You'll have to go to bed really early tonight,' Dorothy nagged. 'Can't have the bride walking down the aisle looking exhausted with "git big bags" under her eyes.'

Angie chuckled at her friend's attempt to take her off.

They walked in silence for a little while.

'You worried about your mam?' Dorothy asked. 'Worried about how your dad might react?'

Angie nodded. 'A bit.'

They turned right and started walking along Dame Dorothy Street.

'She said she was gonna tell him in the pub, so there'd be others around.'

'That's a good idea,' Dorothy said.

'And, of course, the bairns won't be caught in the crossfire,' Angie added.

They continued walking.

'What else is bothering you?' Dorothy asked, knowing there was something else playing on her friend's mind.

'I dinnit knar, Dor,' Angie said, puzzled. 'There was just something about Mam which didn't sit right.'

'In what way?'

'Well, she cuddled the kids, for starters – and told me she thought Quentin was "a decent lad".'

Dorothy raised her eyebrows. 'High praise indeed.'

Angie smiled. 'It is for Mam . . . I dunno, I just have a feeling, 'n it's not a particularly good one.'

Dorothy looked at her best friend and suddenly she felt angry at Charles Havelock for setting the timer running on all their secrets, and at Angie's mam for being the cause of the worry she saw on her friend's face when all she should be seeing was a nervous bride the day before she got married.

'Well, you've done all you can do,' Dorothy said, wanting to reassure her friend. 'It's your mam's mess, she's got to sort it out.'

Hearing herself speak, Dorothy realised her words were probably not the most comforting.

'She'll be fine,' she said, taking it down a notch. 'She'll probably have a right old ding-dong in the pub with your dad, and it'll all be out in the open, and that'll be it. And if your dad leaves, that mightn't be such a bad thing, eh?'

Angie smiled and nodded, but the worry on her face remained.

Chapter Forty-Four

As Dorothy and Angie made their way to work, Eddy was making his way back over the river to complete his final chore for Mr Havelock. A chore he had been unable to do yesterday, much to his irritation. One of the workers from the Wearmouth colliery had told him they were all on irregular shifts as the demand for coal was unrelentingly high, and if Mr Boulter had been working that afternoon, he'd only be in the pub this morning. The miner was clearly on the night shift.

Eddy yawned as the tram squealed its way across the Wearmouth Bridge. Looking left, his view partially obscured by the railway bridge that ran parallel, he could see the overhead gantries of Doxford's. Turning his head right, towards the mouth of the Wear, ships and cobles crowded the main thoroughfare to the North Sea, with a couple of wide, flat-bottomed keelboats loading at the two staithes.

It had been a struggle to get up this morning as he had a hangover from hell, having overindulged when he had got back to the house yesterday. With all the mourners gone and Agatha already in bed, he'd had himself a feast with the leftovers and then walked around the house as though *he* were the master, supping single malt from a large cut-crystal tumbler.

He and Agatha had been asked to continue living at the house until it was decided what was to be done with the place, which was just as well as neither of them had anywhere else to go. Although he wouldn't be surprised if Agatha ended up moving in with Mrs Bevan. The pair had seemed very chummy at the wake. Not that it mattered if she did. He and Agatha had grown apart this past year. Besides, once he'd carried out Mr Havelock's last order, he'd be snatching up his cheque from the solicitor's and going straight out to find himself somewhere new to live. With the amount he'd been left he could afford one of the little terraced cottages just off Villette Road. He'd always liked that area of the east end, with its library, park, pubs and assortment of shops.

Arriving back at the pub, which he knew was where the miner would come for at least one pint before heading home, he pulled open the door and walked in.

The place smelled of stale beer and smoke. He wrinkled his nose. Still, he argued with himself, he couldn't complain. It was going to be worth it. *Well worth it.*

'What can I get yer?' the barman asked.

'Whisky,' Eddy said.

Hair of the dog.

And a little Dutch courage.

Chapter Forty-Five

'Dear me.' Dr Eris tried to sound sincere. 'That man's awful. Awful. Awful. Awful.'

Dr Parker had relayed the outcome of Mr Havelock's wake and how he was determined to wreak revenge, despite no longer being in the land of the living.

'But,' Dr Parker said, 'there's still hope the situation can be rectified.'

Dr Eris forced a smile.

'That's true. Where there's hope . . .' Her voice trailed off.

If Charles Havelock triumphed and the women's secrets were exposed, Helen would be over here in a flash. Of that, she was sure.

Dr Eris breathed deeply. *She had not come this far to fall at the final hurdle.*

'I wonder,' Dr Eris said, 'whether we should leave a little earlier and set off later on this evening? I reckon it's going to be pandemonium tomorrow with the VE Day celebrations.'

Dr Parker hesitated. He'd wanted to have time to see his patients before he left – and his work colleagues. After the wedding on Saturday they were going straight to London for a short honeymoon before he started his new job at St Bartholomew's.

'I'll see what I can do,' he said.

'Good,' Dr Eris said, taking his response as a yes. 'I'll come and help you pack as soon as I've sorted out my office,' and she gave him a long kiss before playfully pushing him out of the door.

Chapter Forty-Six

Georgina was back at the *Sunderland Echo* offices, waiting for the first edition of the day to come off the press. It was later than normal, having been delayed by a last-minute change to the front page due to the news that had come down the wires in the early hours telling of Germany's surrender. Admiral Doenitz, Hitler's successor, had ordered the laying down of arms by all German fighting troops. The announcement itself had been made by Count Schwerin von Krosigk, the German foreign minister, who had declared: *'To continue the war would only mean senseless bloodshed and a futile disintegration of all of Germany.'*

The front page was one everyone in the town had hoped and prayed for these past five years and eight months:

END OF THE WAR IN EUROPE
DOENITZ ORDERS THE UNCONDITIONAL SURRENDER OF GERMANY

'Not often we see one of your lot down here!' one of the printers shouted above the noise of the machinery.

Georgina forced a smile.

'Important story!' she shouted back.

As the first batch of newspapers landed with a thud, Georgina grabbed a copy and hurried off.

Chapter Forty-Seven

When Eddy saw the first colliery worker enter the pub, closely followed by his 'marrer', he sat up straight. The whisky had made him a little light-headed and he wished he'd had some breakfast. He scrutinised the dozen or so miners, their overalls shrouded in coal dust, as they trudged into the bar. The men's smiles as they greeted the barman seemed unnaturally white in contrast to their begrimed faces. The barman started pulling pints, not needing to be told who wanted what.

The last man in was the one Eddy had been waiting for. He was exactly as described. He was a tall man, but it was his width and muscular build that caused Eddy to feel the first wave of nerves. The top of his overall was tied around his waist, showing off dirt-smeared arms the size of boulders.

He waited until the muscle-bound miner had got his pint before he went over to deliver his message.

As he approached the bar, the miner seemed even more of a giant.

Even more forbidding.

He would not like to be in the wife's shoes after her husband learnt she'd been playing away from home.

The woman must have a death wish.

Chapter Forty-Eight

By the time Georgina reached Thompson's, her face was paler than normal and she felt sick with nerves.

After speaking with Davey the timekeeper, who gave her the necessary temporary pass, she hurried up to see Helen.

Five minutes later, they were both back in the yard, their faces equally grave. Helen told one of the young apprentices working nearby with a group of caulkers to go and see Rosie's squad and tell them that they were all needed in the canteen. The young lad ran off, eager to please the big boss.

Ten minutes later, they were all sitting at a table away from the main counter so as to lessen the chance of Muriel earwigging in on their conversation.

'Martha,' said Helen, 'I'm afraid this concerns you.'

Rosie, Gloria, Polly, Dorothy and Angie looked at Martha. It didn't take a genius to work out what this was about.

'Is this about my mam?' Martha asked.

'It is,' Helen said. 'Grandfather did what he always threatened to do.'

Martha nodded. After what she'd heard had happened this morning at Lily's and Dorothy's mam's, she was not surprised. Her thoughts went to her mother and father. It was them she worried for the most.

'As you know, Grandfather put something in place for

when he died. A sort of revenge from beyond the grave,' Helen began.

'What's he done?' Martha asked with dread.

Helen looked at Georgina. It had been agreed that she should explain.

'He sent all the information about your mother to my editor yesterday – after the funeral. Looks like he'd put some kind of private eye on it as he had everything he needed to go with the story. He had a copy of your birth certificate and had even provided my editor with back copies of the *Echo* that reported the original trial.'

Georgina pulled out the freshly printed first edition of the *Sunderland Echo*.

'I tried my hardest to get him to ditch the story, but he wouldn't.'

Even graver faces.

'But,' she said, 'he did let me rewrite the article, as I explained to him I know you personally and could add to the story.'

Georgina omitted the fact she had argued with her editor until she was blue in the face, and in doing so had risked her job. She was just a lowly reporter – her editor had worked in the business longer than she had been alive. Of course, she'd had no knowledge of the cheque stashed away in her boss's top drawer. It had only been when she had called him to task on the ethics of printing such an article, however, that he'd finally relented. They both knew that if he went ahead and published the story after hearing what Georgina had told him about her friend and her amazing acts of courage, he would be going against everything he purported to believe in. Georgina had been given the green light to do a rewrite – on the proviso that the article was written within the hour. She'd practically run back to her desk and had immediately started bashing the keys of her typewriter, writing in a frenzy, drawing on all her reserves, for this was the most important story she had ever written.

Now came the moment of reckoning.

Georgina nervously looked at Martha and held her breath as she opened the *Echo* and showed her the article, which was spread across two pages in the middle of the paper.

Everyone strained to look and gasped on seeing the headline.

DAUGHTER OF INFAMOUS MURDERER
PROVES HERSELF A SHIPYARD HEROINE

Martha quietly read the article. The rest of the women craned their necks and were able to get the gist of the article, which told the inspirational story of shipyard welder Martha Perkins, who was doing her bit to help win the war building ships by day, and at night had worked tirelessly as a volunteer ARP warden.

Miss Perkins, the article informed, had not only saved the life of a fellow worker at J.L. Thompson & Sons when he'd been trapped under a metal plate, but she had also risked her own life rescuing a mother and her young child during the Tatham Street bombing.

The fact that Martha's mother was the notorious child killer who had been hanged for her crimes had been dropped down in the copy.

The article had ended with the words: *Brave Martha's story drives home the message that it really does not matter where you come from – it's what you do that counts.*

Martha sat back and looked at Georgina. 'Do my mam and dad know?'

Georgina nodded. 'They do. I went to see them this morning and showed them the story so they could read it before it hit the streets.'

'And are they OK?'

Again, Georgina nodded. It had been quite an emotional meeting. Both Mr and Mrs Perkins had shed a few tears.

'They said to tell you that they were absolutely fine. More than fine. That they were very proud. And they would be buying several copies of the paper to show all their friends and family.'

A big, gap-toothed smile spread across Martha's face.

'Then all's well that ends well,' she said.

'Eee! That's my saying!' Dorothy said, bursting with relief.

Martha ignored Dorothy and looked at Georgina.

'Thank you. It's a wonderful article.' Martha sighed heavily. 'More than anything, though, it feels such a relief to have the truth out in the open. I've hated the fact that it's been used to threaten and blackmail'

Dorothy and Angie nodded their heads vigorously. They felt exactly the same.

The women took turns reading the article properly, reverently quoting the odd word or sentence as they did so.

When Muriel came over to see what the fuss was about, her eyes nearly popped out of her head.

'Can I show the lasses out the back?' she asked.

Martha nodded and Muriel hurried off in quite a tizzy.

'Eee, you'll have people asking for yer autograph next!' Angie said.

Everyone laughed.

'Well,' Helen said, looking at her watch, 'I think you should all knock off early today. I think everyone's already had quite a day of it.' She looked at Angie. 'And you're getting married tomorrow! I'm sure you've got a million and one things to do?'

'Thanks to Sergeant Major Dorothy here –' Angie nodded at her best mate '– everything's in hand . . . Although that's not to say we dinnit wanna knock off early.'

Helen made to move and was surprised to see that everyone remained seated.

'Before we go,' Gloria said, 'we wanted to have a quick word about you and Dr Parker.'

Helen sat back down.

'You're free to tell him how you feel, now that everyone's secrets are out there,' Polly said. 'Dr Eris can no longer gag you.'

'Yes, it's safe now,' Georgina agreed.

'No more threats,' Martha smiled.

'Yes, yer can tell that conniving cow to do one,' Angie drove the point home.

'You can tell Dr Parker that you love him,' stressed Dorothy.

'And just in the nick of time. Their wedding is on Saturday.'

Helen laughed a little sadly.

'I don't know. I'm not so sure any more,' she said.

'Why not?' Dorothy demanded, shocked.

'Well, for starters, John's leaving tomorrow,' Helen said.

'Tomorrow?' Rosie asked, surprised. 'I didn't think he was leaving for Northallerton until just before the wedding on Friday?'

'Neither did I,' Helen said resignedly, 'but apparently Claire's had a last-minute change of heart and wants him

401

to go earlier to meet everyone and get to know them a little beforehand.'

'Nowt to dee with the fact she wants to keep him as far away from yer as possible,' Angie snorted.

'He's probably packing as we speak,' Helen said. 'Besides which, with the wedding so near, it just all feels too late now.'

'It's not too late until he says "I do",' Polly ventured.

'Yeah, until she's gorra ring on her finger,' Angie agreed.

'If only it were that simple,' Helen said.

'Why can't it be that simple?' Georgina asked tentatively.

'Because,' Helen explained, 'John's chosen the woman he wants to marry. He might have wanted to be with me before – but I honestly think he now just sees me as a friend. I've probably done too good a job of convincing him that my feelings are purely platonic, so now his feelings for me as just those of a good friend.'

'Fiddlesticks!' Dorothy exclaimed.

Helen smiled sadly at the women as she stood up, ready to leave.

'This past week, I've been thinking,' Helen said, 'and I'm really not sure me telling John how I feel is the right thing to do. I just think that sometimes in life when obstacles are put in your way, it's for a reason – and perhaps they're there to tell you that's not the right path to go down. I really think John and I are not destined to be together.'

Helen looked at Gloria, Rosie, Dorothy, Angie, Martha and Georgina – none of them appeared as if they agreed with her.

As soon as Helen had left the canteen, the women started chatting animatedly.

'It just doesn't feel right to give up now – after all this time,' Polly said.

'I agree,' Martha said.

'It's like you're just about to win the race and you suddenly stop running and bow out,' Dorothy analogised.

'Perhaps she's frightened that Dr Parker will reject her if she goes to him. Especially after what happened with Matthew,' Polly wondered.

'Do you really think that Dr Parker just sees Helen as a friend?' Georgina asked.

'No way!' Dorothy said. 'Even Bobby says Dr Parker still fancies the pants off her, and he should know – he's a bloke. Blokes can read each other better than women can.'

'You might be right there,' Polly said, thinking how badly she had read Tommy when they'd started dating.

'Helen's not as confident as she looks,' Gloria said. 'I think Polly's right in her being frightened of being rejected. Again.'

'Well, if we all think that Dr Parker loves Helen – and not just as a friend – we have to do something,' said Polly.

'I agree,' said Rosie.

'Definitely,' Dorothy stressed.

'She's done so much for us – now it's our turn to dee summat fer her,' said Angie.

'Yes, and what could be better than getting her back the love of her life,' Dorothy concurred.

'So, what are we going to do?' Martha asked.

They were quiet for a moment, all thinking.

Finally, Georgina perked up.

'I've got an idea.'

Chapter Forty-Nine

Dorothy and Angie waved goodbye to their workmates, wishing them luck with their plan. They would have liked to have been a part of it, but logistically they couldn't, which was probably just as well as Angie really needed to start focusing on her big day. Looking at her best friend now, Dorothy thought that the wedding seemed like the last thing on her mind. Angie might have put on a good show in front of everyone this afternoon, but behind the bravado she was still worried about her mam. Not that Angie's mum deserved such concern, in Dorothy's opinion. She'd made her bed, now she had to lie on it. As long as the children were out of the firing line, that was all that mattered.

'You want to go and check on your mam, don't you?' Dorothy said with a heavy sigh.

Angie's look answered her question. 'Yer dinnit mind, do yer?'

'Course not,' Dorothy said, hooking her friend's arm. 'Can't have the bride-to-be worrying about anything other than her big day . . . Not that there's any need to worry about your big day as you happen to have picked the best maid of honour ever who has got everything sorted down to the last detail.'

Angie linked arms even tighter. 'I dinnit knar what I'd dee without yer, Dor.'

Dorothy smiled. 'Neither do I.'

'Eee, Dor,' Angie chuckled, 'yer might be lots of things, but modest yer not.'

They both laughed as they retraced their steps from earlier on.

When they turned the corner into Dundas Street, they saw Angie's siblings playing on the street with some of the neighbours' children. The girls were playing with a skipping rope and the boys had set up two gas masks as goalposts and were playing football. When they saw their big sister and her friend, they ran towards them. The youngest started to tug at Dorothy's trouser leg, demanding to be picked up. Hauling the little girl onto her hip, Dorothy realised how unkempt she was. Her dirty blonde curls didn't look like they'd had a brush put through them in days.

'Is Mam 'n Dad about?' Angie asked as they walked towards the house.

The children all shook their heads in unison.

'Mam's not in,' Danny, the eldest sibling said, the corners of his mouth turning down.

Angie cast Dorothy a worried look as she opened the front door.

'And your dad?' Dorothy asked, hoping he wasn't in either.

There was a communal shrugging of shoulders.

As soon as Angie and Dorothy stepped over the threshold into the small, terraced house, they knew something was amiss. It seemed too quiet. Walking into the living room, Angie spotted two old wage envelopes propped up on the mantelpiece above the range. One of them had her name scrawled on the front – the other her father's. She picked up the one that was addressed to her and showed it to Dorothy.

They exchanged looks of foreboding. Angie pulled out the note and read it.

Angie,

I'm leaving and I won't be back. I love Carl and he loves me. We're going to make a new life for ourselves away from here. Please make sure the bairns are OK. I know you will. Tell them I'm sorry but this is something I had to do.

Love Mam

Dorothy looked at Angie as she read the short note and saw her turn pale.

Reaching out, she took the scrappy piece of paper from her and read it.

The children were staring at them, suddenly silent. Intuition telling them that something was wrong. Very wrong.

'Where's Mam?' Jemima, the youngest, asked, her big blue eyes showing the beginnings of panic.

Angie looked at Dorothy. She opened her mouth, but nothing came out.

'Well,' Dorothy began, forcing herself to sound convincing, 'it looks as though your mam has had to go away for a couple of days. Unexpectedly.'

The children continued to look from their big sister to her friend.

'Let's go and see what your dad's up to, eh?' Dorothy suggested.

'Good idea, Dor,' Angie agreed, finally finding her voice. 'But you lot stay here. We'll be back in a minute.'

Dorothy put the little one down on the armchair, but she immediately shuffled off it and started following them.

Angie picked her up and gave her to her elder brother.

'Danny, keep an eye on her until we get back,' she commanded. 'We'll only be a jiffy.'

As soon as they were out of the house, Dorothy turned to Angie.

'You all right?' Dorothy asked.

'Oh God, Dor! What am I gonna dee?'

'Let's see your dad first and go from there,' Dorothy said, bracing herself as she took Angie's arm and guided her across the road to the pub.

Everyone stared and fell silent as they walked into the pub. Women weren't allowed in the bar area, only the snug.

Angie quickly scanned the pub, but couldn't see her dad. She felt Dorothy nudging her.

'The barman's waving you over,' she said quietly, still feeling the unwelcome stare of dozens of pairs of tired, bloodshot eyes. By the blackened looks of them, the men were all miners who had just come off shift.

Angie looked up to see Billy the landlord, cocking his head to show them he wanted a word.

'There's been a bit o' trouble here,' he said, wiping down some spilled beer from the bar. 'Yer dad got into it with some bloke 'n gave him a bit of a pasting.'

'What bloke?' Angie asked.

The barman shook his head. 'Nee idea. He wasn't local. That's for sure. Had a suit and black tie on. Looked like he was on his way to a funeral – or had just left one. Nearly ended up being his own, 'cos whatever he told yer dad sent him loopy. I dinnit knar if it was luck or not, but the Old Bill were passing, heard the rumpus and carted yer dad off afore he could finish the poor sod off.'

'Oh God!' Dorothy gasped.

'Yer dad'll be alreet,' the barman said to Angie. 'Plod said they'd just keep him in overnight till he cooled off.'

'And was the other bloke OK?' Angie asked.

'Well,' Billy rubbed his stubbly chin. 'He wasn't in a good way. His face was pretty messed up. Broken nose, black eye, split lip.'

Angie and Dorothy grimaced.

'One of the coppers asked if he wanted to press charges, but he just shook his head. He didn't want us to take him to the hospital. Just mumbled summat about a cheque 'n that he needed to gan into town.'

Angie and Dorothy looked at each other, wide-eyed.

'Anyway, pet, congratulations!' the barman suddenly perked up. 'I hear yer getting hitched tomorra at St Peter's . . . Lovely church.'

Angie forced a smile. *Her wedding.* She'd almost forgotten about it.

'Thanks, Billy. Come along if you want?'

'Thanks for the offer, pet, but it'll be mad here tomorra – VE Day 'n all.'

'Of course,' Angie said.

A few minutes later, Angie and Dorothy were back out on the pavement.

'Sounds like it was that Eddy bloke Helen mentioned,' Dorothy said.

'Yeah, the one who was gonna get a big cheque once he'd done *one last job,*' Angie agreed.

They both sighed.

'What a mess,' said Angie.

'You can say that again,' Dorothy agreed, thankful that not

only were they out of the dark, smoky and rather scary pub, but that they had not been the ones to tell Angie's father that his wife had done a bunk with her fancy man.

'What am I gonna dee?' Angie asked.

Dorothy put her arm around her friend and squeezed her. 'I think you mean "What are *we* gonna dee?"'

They walked back across the road and saw that Angie's brothers and sisters were sitting on the front step of the house awaiting their return.

Seeing their dirty, downcast faces, Dorothy felt a pull in her heart.

'I think I might have a temporary solution,' she said.

Chapter Fifty

'Everyone ready for the off?' Rosie asked nervously as she pushed the gearstick into first. It made a terrible crunching sound.

'Clutch!' George shouted from the front door.

'Oh dear, I do wish they'd have let me drive them,' George said to Lily, who was standing next to him, fanning herself and screwing up her face at the sound of the engine being maltreated.

They both looked at the shiny red MG. Rosie was in the driver's seat, concentration etched into her face.

Martha was in the passenger seat, her shoulders almost touching Rosie's, her man-sized hands gripping the dashboard.

In the back seat they could just about see Georgina's slight frame squashed between Gloria on the left and Polly on the right.

'They car's sagging at it is,' Lily said. 'You couldn't squeeze another person in there if you tried.'

They both watched with identical pained faces as George's cherished sports car bunny-hopped down West Lawn.

They both cringed as there was another crunching sound.

'I hope they're all right,' George said.

Lily laughed as they turned back into the house.

'Let me rephrase that for you, darling husband – *you hope your beloved car is all right.*'

They walked down the hallway.

'Let's hope the roads are relatively empty,' George added.

'A drink to calm your nerves?' Lily asked.

'I don't think I've got any nerves left after today,' George joshed back.

They were just walking into the kitchen when they heard the phone ring.

Lily clutched her chest.

'I wish you hadn't fixed that blummin' ringer. It gives me the shock of my life.'

George started towards the front office to answer the call.

'No, darling,' Lily ordered, 'you get the drinks, I'll get the phone.'

*

The mechanical bunny-hopping only lasted for a short while before Rosie tamed her nerves and the metal beauty she was driving. She had been quite envious when Helen had learnt to drive, so when Peter returned from France, she'd got him to teach her. She'd been a fast learner, but hadn't been able to get much practice.

'The more miles you get under your belt, the better you'll be,' Peter had said.

Driving to Ryhope was giving her just such an opportunity, although she would have preferred to have gone in Peter's car. She'd not been able to get hold of him, though, and as time was of the essence, George had been their next port of call.

As they pulled out smoothly onto the main coastal road, Rosie gave Martha a sidelong glance. 'You can stop gripping the dash now, Martha.'

The group's gentle giant had proved her bravery many times over, but being in the car with Rosie driving was more terrifying than anything she had yet experienced.

Glancing in her rear-view mirror, Rosie checked out the passengers scrunched up in the back seat. Three pairs of eyes were staring anxiously at the road ahead. She wasn't sure if it was her driving that was causing their concern or what they were about to do.

Fifteen minutes later, when Rosie pulled up outside the Sunderland Borough Asylum and turned off the engine, there was a collective sigh of relief.

'I wasn't *that* bad, was I?'

'Of course not,' Polly said unconvincingly.

Martha looked at Gloria.

'Are you sure you want to do this on your own?' she asked.

'Yes, definitely,' she said with certainty. 'It'll be best just one to one. And our own personal private eye has given me the low-down on everything.'

Everyone smiled at Georgina.

'Right,' Gloria said, opening the passenger door and stepping out. 'Wish me luck!'

'Luck!' they all chorused.

Rosie, Polly, Martha and Georgina watched as Gloria strode purposefully towards the entrance of the mental hospital.

Walking up to the reception desk with more confidence than she felt, Gloria asked the receptionist – a wiry, elderly woman with grey hair – if Dr Eris was in. On being told she was, but not for long as this was her last day, Gloria smiled and said she knew, and it was for this reason she was here – and why she wanted to surprise Dr Eris.

She followed the directions to Dr Eris's consulting room and was amazed she got there without getting lost. The place was like a rabbit warren. Standing in the open doorway of Dr Eris's plush office, Gloria took a deep breath, rapped on the door and walked into the room, which had the most amazing floor-to-ceiling windows.

At first she didn't think Dr Eris was there, until her face suddenly appeared above a stack of boxes on her desk.

'Oh gosh! Where did you come from?' Dr Eris asked, not hiding her shock, nor the fact that she was not particularly pleased to see her.

'You look just about all packed up and ready to go?' Gloria asked, nodding towards the boxes and books.

'I am,' Dr Eris said.

'I thought you weren't meant to be leaving until later on in the week, just before the wedding?'

'That's right.' Dr Eris eyed Gloria suspiciously. Although she had known Gloria for a good while, they had not spoken much. Probably because they had little in common, but also because she knew Gloria was close to Helen. 'Then I thought it would be good to leave earlier so that John could get to know everyone a little before the big day.'

Gloria stepped forward and looked Dr Eris in the eye. 'Nothing to do with the fact that yer were worried yer hold over Helen might be slackening? Slackening to such an extent that Helen would be free to tell yer fiancé how she really feels?'

Dr Eris glared at Gloria. 'I'm guessing that if you've made the trip all the way over here, you've got something to say.'

Seeing that Gloria didn't disagree, she continued. 'In which case, why don't you save us both a lot of time and trouble and just spit it out.'

'We want yer to tell Dr Parker what yer've been up to.'

'We?' Dr Eris asked.

'Yes, me 'n the rest of the women.'

'Ah, of course, I forgot Helen's a little bit of a misfit, isn't she? Doesn't have any friends from her own circle . . .' Dr Eris let her voice trail off.

Gloria ignored the put-down.

'We want yer to tell Dr Parker how yer've won him over by deceitful means 'n that Helen's been prohibited from telling him how she really feels because of what yer've threatened to do.'

Dr Eris raised her eyebrows. 'And why on earth would I do that?'

'Because if yer don't,' Gloria spoke clearly and confidently, 'we will tell Dr Parker ourselves.'

'Really?'

'Yes, really.'

'If you do,' Dr Eris said, 'that means all your secrets are spilled. And from what I can gather the consequences would not be good. Not good at all. A beating and a prison sentence at the very least.' Dr Eris knew she was hedging her bets. She kept her fingers crossed that they had all managed to keep their skeletons under lock and key in spite of Mr Havelock's interference.

'Well, that's where there's been some developments,' Gloria said. 'Everyone's dirty laundry has been well and truly aired.'

Dr Eris stared at Gloria. She would have loved to have

believed that she was trying to con her, but experience and her training told her that Gloria was not lying.

'So,' Gloria repeated, 'either yer tell Dr Parker what yer've been up to – or we will.' She paused. 'It will come better from yer. If it comes from us, it might well come out that the real reason for yer going all out to get Dr Parker was 'cos yer suffered the humiliation of being jilted at the altar 'n yer wanted to show everyone yer'd gone one better – got yerself a bigger 'n better bounty.'

Dr Eris looked shocked. *How had they found that out?* She wouldn't humiliate herself, though, by asking.

'So, do we have a deal?' Gloria asked. 'Yer tell him by the end of today. If yer don't 'n yer carry on with yer plans to go to Northallerton 'n carry on with yer wedding this Saturday, make no mistake, we will drive there 'n tell Dr Parker ourselves.'

Dr Eris looked at Gloria and had no doubt she and the rest of her motley crew would do just that.

Chapter Fifty-One

Angie and Dorothy stood for a moment on the top step of the rather magnificent Edwardian town house and turned around to look at their four charges. Their scruffy little faces showed a mix of anxiety, awe and excitement. Angie's siblings had spent their entire lives living within the confines of the Barbary Coast. They had not been over the river, never mind taken to the poshest area of the town.

Angie had told them that as their mam had gone away for a while, they would be staying at a friend's house for the next few days. She had been vague about the time scale – just as she had been about their father, who she'd said had had to work a double shift.

'Best behaviour!' Angie said sternly to the four upturned faces.

She then nodded at Dorothy, who already had her hand on the large brass knocker.

Before she had a chance to use it, though, the glossy black front door swung open.

Four little mouths dropped open on seeing the small, slightly plump older woman with a blaze of orange hair that was piled high on her head in a slightly chaotic bun. Loose wisps framed her ageing but attractive face. Her voluptuous body was wrapped in a meringue-shaped dress consisting of layers of red taffeta, corseted at the waist and with a plunging neckline to show off her ample bosom. Lily was making up for having to play the dreary housewife earlier on in the day. Besides which, having got wed in haste yesterday, this was her first day of being a married woman.

The children all stared, mesmerised.

'*Mes chers!*' Lily exclaimed. 'Come in, come in!'

The little one toddled through the door first, her rosebud mouth still open, her eyes wide. She was followed by the middle two children, with Danny at the rear.

Angie and Dorothy watched as they all looked about in amazement at the interior – the likes of which they had never seen.

'Welcome, my little darlings, to your new, temporary residence,' Lily said, bending down and cupping Jemima's dirt-smeared face in her bejewelled hands.

'Indeed! Welcome!' George appeared from the back reception room. He was now in his civvies, his uniform back in his wardrobe, where he hoped it would stay.

'I'm George – Lily's husband.' He glanced at Lily and gave her a quick smile before reaching out his hand to shake the eldest child's.

Seeing that her siblings had momentarily lost the ability to speak, Angie stepped forward and introduced her brothers and sisters to Lily and George.

'Jemima is the youngest, then there's Bertie, Marlene and Danny, who is the eldest.'

'Pleasure to meet you all,' George said with a cheery smile.

'What wonderful names!' Lily declared. 'Now, I'm guessing,' she said, looking at them all, 'you must be getting a bit peckish – it being well past teatime?'

Four heads nodded. They were starving and hadn't had any breakfast or dinner, never mind tea.

'And I'm also guessing everyone likes fish and chips?' Lily said, snapping open her fan and fanning herself.

Four heads nodded with even more enthusiasm.

Lily looked over them, through the open front door, to see Maisie and Vivian coming up the front steps carrying enough food to feed an army.

'Talk about perfect timing!' she exclaimed. 'Go on into the kitchen, wash your hands and then you can eat your fish and chips off the paper, how about that?'

Four heads nodded once more, although they knew no other way of eating a fish lot.

Angie smiled at Vivian and Maisie as they hurried past and immediately took charge of the children, guiding them into the kitchen.

'Thank you, Lily!' Angie said.

'No, *ma chère*, thank you! I was just feeling a little down in the mouth – having had to close my business with such immediacy.'

She fanned herself again at the thought of the franticness of the past twenty-four hours.

'This is the perfect antidote.' She glanced back to the kitchen, where she could see the children were standing in line to wash their hands at the sink.

'I shall have them fed, watered, washed and ready to go for your big day tomorrow. And like I said over the phone, they can stay with me for as long as you want. It will be an absolute joy to have them – and to make use of all these free bedrooms we have suddenly found ourselves with.' She gave them a mischievous smile.

'They will be well cared for.' She took Angie's hand and patted it. 'Rest assured. And if there are any problems, which there won't be, I have your neighbour's phone number.'

Angie suddenly felt as though she was going to burst out crying – might have done, had she not needed to keep a brave face on for her siblings, who were waving goodbye to her at the same time as shoving chips and battered fish into their mouths.

'Now go!' Lily said, shooing Angie and Dorothy down the hallway. 'You've a wedding to get ready for!'

'I would offer to take you home,' George said, 'but I'm afraid the old gal has been taken out for an urgent mission.' He winked at Dorothy and Angie.

'The walk will dee us good,' Angie lied. She actually felt as though she'd already run a marathon today.

As Lily waved them off at the front door, George came up behind her and slipped his arm around her waist. He could hear the excited voices of the children. Maisie and Vivian were clearly doing a good job of bringing them out of their shells.

George kissed Lily's cheek.

His new wife, he knew, was never happier than when she had a waif or stray to look after.

Now that she had four, she would be in her element.

Chapter Fifty-Two

Miriam was sitting at the bar on her own, nursing her ump-teenth gin and tonic of the day. Since yesterday's funeral and reading of the will she had lost track of time – and now, it seemed, of reality too, for she was looking down at a photo-graph of the woman she'd always referred to as 'Big Bertha'. Miriam thought she'd been quite the comic when she'd first thought up the moniker, as not only did it sound like Martha, but 'Big Bertha' was the nickname given to the town's mas-sive anti-aircraft gun.

Spreading out the *Sunderland Echo* on top of the polished mahogany bar, she leant in closer to read the words of the art-icle, which was easier said than done as they seemed very blurry. Either she needed spectacles or the print had smudged.

Taking another sip of her drink, Miriam focused hard on the words of the article.

After a few moments she let out a gasp of disbelief.

Big Bertha was actually being hailed as some sort of heroine.

She read on.

Ha! If only her father were alive to see it! Instead, he would be turning in his grave! The woman he was going to expose as the daughter of a child murderer had turned the tables on him. What a scoop!

As soon as she thought of her father, she felt the return of her anger.

Why had he done what he'd done? Why had he written her out of the will? His own flesh and blood? How could he be so cold and callous?

Of course, it didn't occur to Miriam that he had also left nothing to her daughter – not a single penny. And unlike Miriam, Helen did not have the luxury of a trust fund to fall back on.

'Oh, Amelia . . .' Miriam moaned. She turned on her stool to speak to her friend and found herself looking at an empty seat. She tutted. She'd forgotten. Amelia had been summoned home by her demanding husband, who was now permanently back from the war. Miriam felt her mood drop even further, if that were at all possible. Now that he was back for good, she wouldn't even have her friend on tap.

And, worse still, as of tomorrow, the Admiralty billeted at the hotel would all be leaving.

She raised her glass to the barman.

'Another,' she demanded morosely. She heard the slur in her voice and didn't care.

Not one jot.

*

Seeing Rosie arrive back at Lily's to drop off the MG, George hurried out. Rosie wasn't sure who looked most relieved. George that his car had been returned in one piece, or Martha, Gloria, Polly and Georgina, who, she noted, couldn't get out of the car quick enough.

'So, that's it,' Rosie said. 'We're agreed we won't say anything to Helen.'

They all nodded.

'Just in case,' Gloria added, 'Dr Eris persuades Dr Parker to forgive her and marry her.'

'Although I'd think that's unlikely,' Georgina said.

'I agree.' Martha and Polly spoke at once.

'Well, stranger things have happened,' Gloria said, 'and it would break Helen's heart all over again if she got to hear that Dr Parker knew the truth about Dr Eris and still chose to be with her.'

Just then, they all looked up to see four young children charging out the front door to come and look at George's fancy car.

Lily was standing in the doorway, looking as happy as Larry, a Gauloise in one hand, her fan in the other.

They all looked at George for an explanation.

'Well . . .' he began.

*

'John, I've got something to tell you,' Dr Eris said as soon as Dr Parker stepped into her room.

Dr Eris had just spent an hour sitting there, thinking hard, before ringing the Ryhope and asking the receptionist to get a message to Dr Parker, requesting him to come straight over as a matter of urgency.

'You look dreadful, Claire. Are you all right?' Dr Parker asked, concerned.

'No, not really,' she admitted. 'Sit down, please.'

'What is it?' Dr Parker sat down and leant forward, taking her hand in his and holding it gently.

'Tell me,' he coaxed. He had never seen his fiancée look so grave.

Dr Eris took a deep, juddering breath.

And then she told Dr Parker how she had blackmailed Helen into keeping her feelings for him a secret. How, initially, she had told her that she would reveal Henrietta's true identity if Helen were to tell him that she loved him. And then, when Charles Havelock had suddenly died and she lost her bartering chip, she had threatened Helen with revealing the secrets of her friends.

Dr Parker listened aghast. It was as if Claire was describing the actions of a totally different person.

'I can't believe it,' he said. 'I really can't believe it.'

He got up and walked around the room.

'I need a moment.'

Dr Eris gave him a moment before continuing. She might have promised Gloria that she would tell John the truth, but she hadn't agreed not to try her hardest to keep him.

'I know it sounds awful – it even sounds awful to my own ears,' Dr Eris said, her eyes doe-like and imploring. 'I'm totally ashamed of myself. But, you see, it wasn't as cold-hearted as it seems.'

And then she told Dr Parker how, before she had started work at the asylum, she had been engaged to a young man she'd met at university, but that she had been tossed aside just before she was due to walk down the aisle. She admitted that she had seen Dr Parker as a way of thumbing her nose at her ex-fiancé and all those who had snickered behind her back.

'But,' she said, genuine tears forming in her eyes, 'I really did start to fall in love with you. The more I got to know you, the more I liked you, and then, around the time of Henrietta's poisoning at Christmas, I realised that I had fallen for you – *really* fallen for you – and that I loved you – deeply.'

Dr Parker looked at Dr Eris and knew she was speaking

the truth. Part of him felt angry at her for being so devious, the other part felt terribly sorry for her that she had been so desperate and had gone to such extremes.

'I loved you too,' Dr Parker said.

Dr Eris felt hope. *Perhaps there was a chance?* A chance he might still choose her over Helen.

'Oh, John, we could be so happy together. The wedding's all arranged . . . Then there's your job at Barts – so perfect for you . . . And, well, it has to be said, we are *so* well suited . . .'

She wanted to say *much more than you are to Helen*, but she left the words unsaid.

'And most of all we love each other – we are *in love*. And there's no doubt we find each other attractive.'

She put her hand on his leg and was relieved to see he did not remove it.

'You and Helen would never last.'

She paused.

'Whereas we could be so happy together – we really could.'

Dr Parker sighed.

Dr Eris waited a beat

'What do you think?' she asked with bated breath.

Dr Parker exhaled deeply.

*

When Dr Parker hurried back into the Ryhope Emergency Hospital, he was greeted by the new receptionist, who was looking frantic.

'Oh, thank goodness, Dr Parker,' she said. 'I've been trying to contact you. There's been an emergency. One of the POWs has taken a turn for the worse. You're needed in theatre now.'

424

Seeing his slight hesitation, she added, 'I've tried all the other doctors. No one else is available.'

'Call and tell them I'm on my way,' he said, striding towards the main corridor.

*

When the phone rang later on that evening, Helen hurried to answer it. A call this late could only mean an emergency.

She picked up the receiver.

'Miss Crawford speaking.'

'Helen, darling, it's your aunty Margaret.'

'Oh, Aunty, I thought something had happened. How are you? You still enjoying your stay at the Grand?' Helen knew her aunty was not exactly mourning her father's death and she and her husband were using the trip as a short holiday, which they were combining with some sightseeing and catching up with old friends.

'I'm afraid something has happened,' Margaret said, trying to get the tone right. She didn't want to panic her niece, but nor did she want to underplay the situation.

'What is it?' Helen asked, her mind whirring. 'Is it Uncle Angus?'

'No, no, darling,' Margaret said, a smile in her voice. Her niece adored them both – as they did her. She had developed into such a lovely person these past few years. Rather unexpectedly, it had to be said.

'No, my dear, I'm afraid it's your mother.'

'Oh God, what has she done now?' Helen said, sounding as though she were the mother and Miriam the child.

'I'm afraid she's in a bit of a bad way with the drink,' Margaret began.

'No surprises there,' Helen said wearily.

'I know, but I think she's taken quite a dive since the reading of the will,' Margaret explained. 'From what I gather, she's been on a bender ever since and only stops drinking when she's passed out. And this evening she passed out at the bar. Angus and the manager had to carry her like a rag doll back up to her suite. She didn't move a muscle. Completely blotto. Out for the count. Angus is in there now, making sure she doesn't choke on her own vomit, or tries to get up and has an accident.'

Helen sighed. 'I'm not surprised. I can't remember the last time I saw her when she wasn't at least a few sheets to the wind.'

'I've had a chat with Angus, and we have agreed on a plan of action, but obviously we wanted to make sure it's all right with you.'

'Go on . . .' said Helen.

Chapter Fifty-Three

VE Day

Tuesday 8 May 1945

When Helen woke the next morning, her first thought was of John.

She looked at her bedside clock. It had just gone seven.

Knowing Claire, she'd have all their bags packed and ready so they could leave as early as possible. She would be worried the women's secrets might have been exposed and her threats now superfluous.

Ever since talking to the women welders in the canteen yesterday, Helen had argued relentlessly with herself.

Did she really believe what she had told them? That there had been so many obstacles thrown across the path she'd wanted to walk with John that it was clearly fate's way of showing her that their love for one another was not to be?

Even as she thought about it now, a part of her was rebelling against that way of thinking. It sounded terribly defeatist. And she had always been a person who fought for what she believed in. Now that the women's secrets were out in the open – and Lily's was no longer a bordello – her hands were no longer tied. She was free to declare her love to John.

So why didn't she?

Because somewhere in her being it didn't sit right with her to go and bad-mouth Claire in order to nab John for herself.

Helen flung herself out of bed, just as she forced herself to fling thoughts of John to one side.

Tomorrow. She'd think about it tomorrow.

Today, she had enough on her plate. What with her mother to sort out – and the wedding.

And, of course, it was an historic day. She should at least attempt to enjoy it.

She waited to feel her spirits lift.

They didn't.

Henrietta saw Helen to the front door.

'Good luck, my dear,' she said, taking Helen's hand and squeezing it gently. 'You're doing the right thing, so don't feel in any way bad. From what Margaret told me last night, this really is the only way forward.'

She looked at Helen's anxious face.

'And it in no way compares to what happened to me,' she reassured her.

'Thanks, Grandmama,' Helen said. 'I'll let you know how it all goes. In the meantime, you get yourself ready for the wedding. Have you chosen an outfit?'

'I have indeed,' Henrietta said with a smile.

'And you're not having any second thoughts?'

Henrietta chuckled. 'Honestly, my dear, you make it sound as if I'm the bride, having pre-wedding jitters.'

Helen smiled. This was her grandmother's first proper social event away from the house since being discharged from the asylum. She was hiding it well, but Helen knew she was nervous.

428

'And Dr Bernard is still picking you up?'

'He is. And Mrs Evans and Ethan are meeting me there. They haven't said as much, but their reason for going is as much about supporting me as it is to see dear Angela married . . . Now go! Get what you have to do over and done with, and then you can relax and enjoy yourself.'

Helen forced a smile as she left.

How could she enjoy herself knowing that John would be leaving town today and most likely would never be back?

Certainly not if Claire had it her way.

*

Dorothy woke up just minutes before her alarm clock was due to go off. She switched it off so as not to wake Angie. She wanted to let her sleep for as long as possible. Yesterday had been as traumatic as it was exhausting for her best friend. The worst day-before-the-wedding any bride could imagine. Not only was Angie physically exhausted from all the running around they'd done yesterday, but it had drained her emotionally too. The dark eyes and gaunt look were evidence of that. Angie being Angie, she had put a brave face on it, but Dorothy could read her friend well, and she knew that inside Angie was feeling shocked and upset by the turn of events.

As she padded into the kitchen to make herself a cup of tea, Dorothy mentally went through her to-do list.

Thank goodness Angie and Quentin had decided on an afternoon wedding.

Dorothy smiled to herself as she thought about the wedding reception. Her idea had been pure genius, and what's more, both Angie and Quentin had thought so too.

First on her list, though, was to get herself ready and look-ing fantastic. She wanted to remind Bobby what she looked like in a dress. Lately, she had been so busy, with every spare minute spent organising the 'best wedding ever', he'd rarely seen her in anything other than her overalls.

*

When Helen reached the Grand, she saw that the staff were outside hanging up bunting, with one of the workers posi-tioning a huge Union Jack on a pole at the front entrance. They all stopped what they were doing and allowed Helen free passage as she hurried up the stone steps and into the main foyer, where she was greeted by her uncle Angus, who was looking, unsurprisingly, very sombre.

'She's in her suite with Margaret – and the doctor, of course,' he informed her.

Angus looked at Helen as they made their way slowly up the wide, carpeted stairs that led to the first floor.

'I have to warn you, though, she is not in a good state,' Angus confessed as they reached the door to what had been Miriam's home these past five weeks

*

Dr Parker rolled over and slammed his hand on the alarm clock. For a few seconds he wondered where he was. At Claire's? At home? He fought the pull back to sleep and opened his eyes. *Of course*, he was in the hospital room. Or rather, cupboard – the 8 foot by 8 foot room put aside for doctors who wanted to crash between shifts or were simply exhausted and needed to catch forty winks before they went back into surgery.

He'd gone there straight after he'd come out of theatre at two in the morning. It had been a gruelling five-hour operation that had left him exhausted, but it was worth it. He and his team had saved a young man's life. He'd slumped on top of the hard single bed and as soon as his head hit the pillow he'd been out for the count.

As he sat up and swung his legs out of bed, yesterday's revelations started to filter back into his consciousness.

Combing back his hair with his fingers, he stood up and brushed down his crumpled clothes, before bending down to put on his shoes.

He knew exactly what he was going to do.

He had decided after leaving Claire at the asylum, as he'd walked back to the hospital.

He looked at his watch.

The train was due in an hour.

He'd better get a move on.

*

Arriving at the Sunderland Borough Asylum in Ryhope, Miriam was helped out of the back of the car by Angus and one of the male orderlies, who looked more like a weightlifter than a hospital attendant

Margaret got out of the passenger side and anxiously chewed her lip as the orderly explained to her and Angus that it was his job to escort new patients into the hospital and get them settled in their rooms. He didn't have to say the reason he'd been chosen for this particular task as it was clear that if there was any reticence, or the new arrival kicked off, he would be more than able to handle the situation.

Margaret clutched Angus's hand as the burly orderly draped Miriam's arm across his Herculean shoulders and wrapped his other bulging arm around her waist.

Miriam was barely conscious. The doctor who had sectioned her at the Grand had given her a sedative to calm her down. When Margaret had explained what was happening, Miriam had been hysterical. Margaret had seen it all before when Miriam was staying with them in Scotland and had spiralled so deeply into alcohol addiction, they'd had to put her in a sanitorium to dry out.

Helen, Margaret mused, had looked shocked and very sad. Margaret knew she and her mother didn't see eye to eye. They had certainly drifted apart these past five years, but Miriam was still her mother. Helen had been upset, though she had done a good job of hiding it.

Margaret just hoped her sister would sort herself out and that, without the drink, she would be a better person – and a better mother.

'If you can just fill out the paperwork,' the weightlifter-orderly said when they reached reception, 'I'll take it from here.'

Margaret and Angus nodded. 'We'll come and visit when she's settled in.'

Five minutes later, the orderly was met by a doctor and a nurse at the room that had been put aside for the new admission. Margaret had requested the best room – it was the least she could do for her sister. And the hospital manager, knowing their new patient was a Havelock, had been more than happy to accommodate. The pay-off would be a generous donation.

'Here we are, Mrs Crawford,' the orderly said, helping Miriam sit down on the side of the bed.

'We'll take it from here,' the male doctor said with a practised smile. The young nurse was standing next to him with a stainless-steel trolley containing various medications and a hospital nightgown.

Suddenly, Miriam looked up at the doctor and the pretty nurse.

Then she slowly surveyed the room.

Her eyes widened as it slowly dawned on her where she was.

'What am I doing here?' she demanded.

'This is my mother's room!' she hissed.

The doctor and nurse exchanged looks.

Seeing the look of alarm and panic in Miriam's bloodshot eyes, the doctor nodded to the nurse, who immediately handed him a sedative-filled syringe she'd prepared beforehand.

'She's worse than expected,' the doctor said out of the corner of his mouth as he injected Miriam in the arm.

'Delusional,' the nurse opined.

'Yep,' the doctor said, watching as Miriam's eyes started to flutter shut. 'Alcohol-induced psychosis, otherwise known as alcohol hallucinosis. It's a rare complication of chronic alcohol abuse, occurring during or after a period of heavy drinking.'

'I'm guessing this one's here for quite some time?' the nurse queried.

The doctor nodded solemnly.

'Without a doubt.'

*

When Chief Constable Metcalf walked into the crowded room, which was filled with all the police officers and detectives on duty today, he puffed his chest out and inhaled deeply.

After speaking about the importance of the day and the pride and joy he was sure they all felt having heard the Allies had achieved victory in Europe, he took a sip of the water that had been left on the wooden trestle from where he was addressing his men.

'I also have some news which I'm sure will give you cause to feel even more celebratory.'

With great aplomb, he pulled out a cheque from the inside pocket of his uniform.

'As I'm sure you all know, last week the town lost one of its most eminent and generous dignitaries – Mr Charles Havelock. He was primarily known for his many large donations to our hospitals, as well as to the town's Museum and Winter Gardens. He did, however, also think highly of this town's police force, and as a show of his appreciation he has left a substantial amount to be donated to the Sunderland Borough Police.'

There was a general hum of surprise and delight.

'As a result, you will all be getting a bonus this month. And I have personally organised our own VE Day celebration with food and drink. So, spread the word. And for those on duty today, fear not, we'll make sure there's plenty held back for when you finish your shift.'

The room erupted into a round of applause.

The chief constable made the most of the show of gratitude. It compensated in some way for not being able to deposit the cheque into his own account.

He was still a little perplexed, though.

Had Charles really wanted to pay through the nose to get the last laugh on his army veteran pal?

And what about Mrs Williams? That had clearly not been a prank. What had that been all about?

He left the room with the applause still ringing in his ears.

It was a mystery, which he knew would remain just that.

Charles could be a bit of a dark horse.

Instinct told him to let sleeping dogs lie.

*

It had been decided that the bride should get ready at Lily's and go to the church from there. Angie had been worried that the children would panic at waking up in a strange environment and had suggested bringing them over to the flat while she got ready. It was a suggestion that had immediately been dismissed by Lily as both 'ridiculous' and, knowing the size of their flat, 'a physical impossibility'. The bride, she'd ordered, would come to her 'modest abode' to get ready.

Dorothy had worked hard to contain her excitement. Not only because she had been fascinated by the bordello, or, rather, the *former* bordello, from first hearing about it, but more than anything because it would make Angie's wedding day even more special and extravagant. If anyone deserved it, her friend did. Yesterday had brought it home to Dorothy just how tough Angie had had it growing up.

Angie's brothers and sisters were bursting with excitement when the pair arrived at the house shortly after ten o'clock. Dorothy thought Angie had worried too much, as her siblings looked very much at home at Lily's.

After a cup of tea, Angie was ushered up the sweeping staircase and into the front bedroom, which had a large balcony with the most fantastic view of the cricket ground.

Kate had brought the wedding dress from Maison Nouvelle last night and it was now hanging up, ready for the bride to step into.

Today might well be Angie's big day, but it was also Kate's, for she had decided to leave for London this afternoon, after the church service. She knew if she held off any longer, she might well chicken out.

Never one to be demure about her talents, Vivian had declared that she would work her magic on Angie's hair, and had a table set up in the room with all the necessary styling brushes, curlers, hairgrips, slides and combs.

Maisie, likewise, had brought her make-up box and set up a variety of lipsticks, eyeshadows, rouge and foundation on the dresser, which Dorothy and Angie viewed with wide eyes, although they knew better than to ask how Maisie had managed to obtain such rationed rarities.

From the balcony, George could be viewed outside by the side of the road, giving the bridal carriage one last polish. His red MG had been cleaned and buffed and the 'old gal' taken out for a quick spin to double-check she was still in good working order after her impromptu trip to Ryhope.

Lily, meanwhile, was rallying the children and getting them ready for their sister's big day, a cigarette constantly in her hand and her fan going ninety to the dozen.

*

Dr Parker had jogged back to his bedsit in the village and had a quick wash and shave and change of clothes. Looking

436

at his reflection in the mirror, he saw a tired face – but also a happy one.

Hurrying back out into the morning sunshine, he thought of Angie and was pleased her special day had been blessed with such perfect weather. Warm and sunny, with a lovely gentle sea breeze.

The villagers were already out on the street, setting up tables for the VE Day celebrations. The children were running around, excited by the prospect of a party – one of them had already acquired a party hat, and another was stuffing a sausage roll in his mouth, which had obviously just come out of the oven judging by the way he was frantically waving a hand in front of his mouth.

As Dr Parker strode as fast as he could to the asylum, he checked his watch. He was cutting it fine.

The half-mile walk took him just under ten minutes, and then it took another five minutes to walk through the asylum to the west wing, where the staff accommodation was located – where Claire had spent the last two and a half years since starting work here, and where he had also spent quite some time, and quite a few nights, since they had started courting.

He knocked on the door.

'Come in!' Dr Eris shouted.

Walking into the small, one-bedroom cottage, Dr Parker immediately spotted two large suitcases in the hallway.

Dr Eris was packed and ready to go.

'John!' she exclaimed.

'I'm sorry I couldn't get here sooner,' Dr Parker said a little breathlessly.

'Don't worry, I knew you were in theatre until the early

437

hours. I rang the hospital and they told me. You must be shattered.'

Dr Parker nodded, although he didn't feel at all shattered. He felt quite energised. Buoyed up by the decision he'd made.

'So,' Dr Eris said, 'are you still absolutely sure about the choice you've made?'

'Yes, I am,' said Dr Parker.

*

Helen had her fingers crossed the sun would stay out for the entirety of Angie and Quentin's wedding day. Glancing up at the clear blue sky, she thought the odds looked good.

She was pleased she had been tasked with making sure all was well with the reception and had agreed to be on call for any last-minute emergencies. She was glad of the distraction. She did not want to think about John and his departure from her life. She had tried telling herself to buck up, but it was easier said than done.

Driving back over to Ashbrooke to Lily's, Helen had seen the town in high spirits. Everywhere she looked, people were smiling and chatting. Side streets were no longer passable as the residents had dragged tables out and were making preparations for an all-singing, all-dancing street party – she had even seen a piano being carefully carried out of someone's front door.

Helen wished she could feel the euphoria and lightness of being she could see all around her, but it was no good. Her heart was as heavy as stone.

Turning into Tunstall Vale, Helen reprimanded herself for being so miserably self-indulgent. Poor Angie. It was her wedding day – and not only had her mam done a bunk with her fancy bit, Helen now had yet more bad news to impart.

Dorothy had asked Helen if she could check that Angie's father had been released from his overnight stay at the local cop shop and was on track to meeting them all at the church. All he had to do was step into his hired suit and be there on time. The church was only a few minutes' walk from the house, so it shouldn't be too much of a problem.

If only life were that simple.

Helen had nipped to the police station and had been relieved to find that Mr Boulter had indeed been released. The duty officer she spoke to said that they weren't Brownshirts, and that they'd known his daughter was getting married today, so had freed him first thing.

But after driving to the family home and knocking on the front door, Helen couldn't get an answer. The neighbour had eventually come out and told her she'd have better luck trying the pub. It had taken all of her courage to enter the spit-and-sawdust pub opposite. Angie's father had been propping up the bar. He was unshaven, and already well on his way. He slurred an apology that he wasn't in any state to escort his daughter down the aisle. Helen was in full agreement.

Now she had to tell Angie. This was going to be a double whammy. No mother or father at her wedding. And, by the sounds of it, there had been some uncertainty as to whether Quentin's parents were going to make it.

Helen thought briefly of her own mother.

What was it with parents?

*

439

Just about all the guests were now at St Peter's Church. Some had already gone in and taken their seats, but the majority were still outside, smoking, chatting and enjoying the feel of the sun on their faces.

Rosie, Polly, Gloria, and Martha were all done up to the nines. Polly was wearing a lovely citron-coloured frock, Gloria had treated herself to a floral-patterned dress made of chiffon, and Rosie was wearing a Marlene Dietrich-inspired cream trouser suit. Even Martha had on a new summer skirt and bolero cardigan. They were all, of course, also wearing either a hat or a fascinator. Dorothy had demanded it.

Their significant others were standing a little further way. There was Jack, wearing the same suit he had worn for his wedding, Bobby, looking handsome in his naval uniform, Peter, in his best suit, which looked a little big for him as he had not regained the weight he'd lost during his time in France, and then there was Adam, Martha's 'friend', in a smart suit and tie.

The women had agreed not to leave Polly on her own today as she was the only one without her significant other. She hadn't said, but they knew how much she was yearning to have Tommy back.

'So, Helen's not heard anything from Dr Parker?' Rosie asked.

Gloria shook her head.

'I'm surprised he's not dropped Dr Eris like a hot brick,' Polly said angrily.

'Me too,' Martha agreed.

'Perhaps Helen's right – there's a reason they're not together,' Rosie said, trying to dampen the women's ire.

*

The taxi driver was in a jovial mood as he drove Dr Eris and Dr Parker to Ryhope railway station. Pointing to a folded-up copy of the *Daily Mirror*, he regaled his two passengers with a summary of the front-page news, telling them how British troops had entered Utrecht to a tumultuous reception.

'What a day this is going to be! What a day!' he declared, taking off his cap and waving it at a friend carrying a crate of beer from the Albion. The pub was where John and Claire had gone for many a supper – and which had also been John's regular meeting place with Helen, before Claire had come on the scene.

After they'd pulled up at the station and he had given the driver a generous tip, Dr Parker grabbed a trolley and loaded it up.

A few minutes later, he was standing waiting on the wooden platform with Dr Eris by his side.

When the train pulled in, Dr Parker transferred the suitcases into the luggage rack of the first-class apartment.

He put his hand out to help Dr Eris on board.

*

As soon as Helen told Angie the news about her father's no-show, Lily stepped forward. She had Jemima on her hip. The little girl had become fascinated with the woman with the orange hair and sparkling jewels. She loved being perched on her cushioned hip and feeling the light breeze whenever Lily started to fan herself.

'Well,' Lily said, looking at Angie and trying to gauge how upset she was about the news, 'there's only one thing for it.'

Dorothy, Angie, Helen and the rest of the children, who had gathered round, stared expectantly at Lily.

'*George will do the honours!*' she shouted down the hallway. '*Won't you, darling?*'

Hearing his name, George appeared from the back parlour.

'And what "honours" would those be?' he asked, walking with his stick towards everyone who had congregated in the hallway.

'*You* will have the honour of giving Angie away,' Lily informed him.

George gave his wife and then the bride a puzzled look.

'My dad's too busy getting hammered,' Angie explained. 'He told Helen to say he was sorry – that after everything that's happened, he's not up for it. Sounds like he just wants to drown his sorrows.'

George bit his tongue. *How could any father do this to his daughter on her wedding day? Especially a daughter like Angie. The man should be bursting with pride.*

'If you would like me to walk you down the aisle, Angela, it would most certainly be a huge honour,' he said with the utmost sincerity.

'I'd love you to,' Angie said, forcing back the feeling of bitter disappointment in her mam and her dad. She'd never asked them for anything other than to attend her wedding, and they couldn't even do that.

'Good. That's sorted then!' Lily said. 'Now, George, you better get upstairs and change into your uniform – and make sure you've got your medals pinned on too.'

George looked at Angie – hoping that perhaps she might say he could give her away in his civvies. She didn't. She might be the bride, but she would not go against Lily's wishes, and if Lily wanted him in his military regalia, then that's what was going to happen.

442

'Don't forget, darling,' Lily said, putting Jemima down and pointing towards Maisie and Vivian, who were going into the kitchen, 'it was Angela who discovered your uniform, shoved away in the attic of your flat. It was she and Dorothy who brought it to us – along with your medals, which, for some unknown reason, you seemed determined to hide away. It will have special significance for the bride, won't it, *ma chère*?'

Angie nodded. She looked at George and gave him a sympathetic smile.

'Right, I'd better put my dress on,' she said, giving Dorothy and Helen a hug, and thanking them for everything they'd done. 'You two go now and tell everyone we'll be there soon.'

They made to leave.

'Oh,' Angie suddenly chirped up. 'And tell Quentin I love him, and I can't wait to be his wife!'

'We will,' Dorothy and Helen said at the same time, both with smiles on their faces.

Angie was marrying the man she loved, and Quentin the woman he had fallen for the moment he'd first clapped eyes on her.

The day was about them.

And that was all that really mattered.

*

As soon as they arrived at St Peter's Church, Dorothy went off to find Quentin to pass on Angie's message – and also to tell him about the change of plan with regards to who was giving his bride away. She thought she saw a look of relief on Quentin's face.

443

'Well, that makes it even on the parents' front,' Quentin declared, with no bitterness. 'My dear mama and papa have also cried off. Apparently, Mother has come down with some ghastly ailment, which means that Father can't come either as he will have to stay and tend to her every need.'

Dorothy wasn't surprised. Angie had told her Quentin had thought it unlikely that his parents would turn up. He had guessed there would be some last-minute emergency or illness that would stop them attending their son's wedding.

'Thanks for passing on the message,' Quentin said. 'Good to know Angie's not having any pre-wedding jitters.'

Dorothy laughed. 'Far from it, Quentin. Apart from me, you're the best thing that has happened to Angie.'

Quentin chuckled.

'And Angie is by far the best thing that has *ever* happened to me,' he said.

Seeing Henrietta arrive with Dr Bernard, Helen was glad her grandmother had taken the plunge as she had promised she would and had come to the wedding. Watching them walk down the pathway to the church, Helen thought how well matched they were. She smiled her welcome.

'Oh good, Henrietta's made it,' Mrs Evans said, suddenly appearing at Helen's side.

Reaching her granddaughter, Henrietta opened her arms and kissed her on both cheeks.

'You look absolutely fabulous – as always,' she said, although she knew that inside Helen was suffering. It was one of the reasons she had forced herself to come today. She wanted to be there for Helen – to support her in any way she could. She'd had a rotten twenty-four hours. The love of her life was leaving town today with the woman he was going to marry – and that morning she had seen her mother carted off to the asylum. Now here she was at a wedding – a celebration of love – without a consort, and with no prospect of love in the near future. She knew it would take a long time before Helen found someone to love the way she loved her doctor – if ever.

'What a gorgeous day for it,' Henrietta said as she took Mrs Evans's hand and squeezed it. 'Is Ethan here?'

Mrs Evans looked around and saw Mr Emery chatting to Lily and George, who had decided he was the man to take on all their legal work now they were a legitimate business. Well, legitimate up north, at any rate. The London bordello was thriving – and as many of the clientele were from the upper echelons of the Met Police, Lily had no worries about it being raided.

Mrs Evans waved to Ethan and watched as he said his apologies and made his way over. When he reached them, he greeted Helen, as he always did, with a handshake.

'We have a proposal to put to you,' Mrs Evans said to Helen.

'A proposal?' Helen queried, looking at Henrietta, Mrs Evans and Mr Emery. 'That sounds intriguing. Tell me more.'

'Well, my dear,' Henrietta said. 'I'm afraid, whether you like it or not, I have transferred all of your grandfather's estate into your name. The "hard cash", as they say, has been deposited into your bank account.'

Helen looked shocked. She'd had a sense her grand-mother had been up to something, as Mr Emery and Mrs Evans had been at the house yesterday, but not what.

'But that's madness, Grandmama! The estate is yours,' Helen argued.

'It's the sanest thing I've ever done,' Henrietta batted back. 'You're actually doing me a favour. I don't want to be bothered with stocks and shares and bank statements.'

'Well, thank you, Grandmama,' Helen said, still looking taken aback.

'No, *thank you*, my dear. You're taking a burden off my shoulders.'

Helen exhaled, not knowing what to say.

'We did, however,' Henrietta continued, 'want to ask you if you would be happy to hand over the Glen Path house to us so that we can convert it into a home for unmarried mothers.'

Helen widened her eyes. 'What a brilliant idea!'

'We'd like to call it "Grace's House",' Mrs Evans said with a sad smile.

'That's wonderful,' Helen said.

'We just wanted to check that you didn't want the house – or had a desire to live there?'

Helen shook her head vehemently. 'No. Definitely not.' She looked at Mr Emery. 'Just tell me what I have to do and sign, and I'll do it.'

'I'll need to apply to the council for a change of use, but I can't see that being a problem,' Mr Emery said.

'Oh, and the venture will include Agatha,' Mrs Evans said, looking at Henrietta and back to Helen. 'We feel she has made amends for her past behaviour. Is that acceptable to you?'

'If you both feel she has put right any past wrongs, then I'm guided by you both,' Helen said. 'Just say how much you need – it's really your money, after all, Grandmama.'

Henrietta shook her head. 'No, my dear, it is yours now to do with as you wish.'

'Well,' Helen declared, 'the first thing I will be doing is financing Grace's House. It's going to help so many women.'

'That's what we hope,' Henrietta said, smiling at Mrs Evans.

'Right,' Henrietta said, looking around to find Dr Bernard. 'Now we've settled that, it's time for you to introduce my escort and I to anyone we don't know.'

Chapter Fifty-Four

Angie was ten minutes late to her wedding. She had warned Quentin that she would be as she hadn't wanted him to worry. Dorothy had told her that every bride had to be a little late, which meant Angie had to be as well.

'Look!' Gloria said.

'Here comes the bride!' Dorothy tried hard not to shriek.

They all looked to see George's MG driving towards the church.

After the car pulled up outside the entrance, they all crowded round while Georgina took a shot of the bride, looking stunning in her ivory silk wedding dress, being helped out of the car by George, who was dressed in his smart khaki uniform, complete with medals and peaked cap.

Helen looked round to see Jack and Bobby ushering the rest of the guests into the church and to their seats. It had been agreed that Helen, Dorothy, Rosie, Gloria, Polly, Martha and Georgina would be the last to go in as they wanted to see Angie before she walked up the aisle. They had wanted to be particularly supportive due to the lack of any kind of parental presence.

'You look amazing!' Polly told her.

'*Amazing!*' they all agreed.

'And you, too, look very handsome, George,' said Rosie, smiling.

Another buzz of agreement.

George frowned and put out his arm for Angie to hold.

'Right, come on – give the bride a few moments to collect her thoughts,' Dorothy ordered, ushering everyone to the church entrance as though herding sheep into a pen.

'Good luck!' Martha called out over her shoulder.

'Enjoy!' said Gloria.

'And remember, nice and slow down the aisle – no galloping!' Dorothy reminded both Angie and George.

Angie touched her tiara and beamed back at her friends.

As they hurried into the church through the front porch, Jack was holding the door open with Hope by his side. Helen caught him and Gloria exchange looks. Helen knew why. Gloria had told her how they had met here in secret before their affair had been discovered and Jack banished to the Clyde. Helen glanced down at Hope, looking adorable in a pretty pink dress. At least, Helen thought, all the hardship and heartache her father and Gloria had endured had been worth it to have what they had now. It must be a wonderful feeling.

As Helen walked into the church, she smiled at Kate, who was waiting just inside the entrance, ready to make sure the dress was perfectly in place, as well as the tiara and train, which was the same one Polly had worn for her wedding to Tommy.

Lily, she saw, was waiting at the top of the nave with Angie's brothers and sisters – the girls looked as pretty as a picture in their ivory bridesmaid dresses, the boys very dapper in their smart morning suits. Maisie and Vivian were checking them over, flattening down hair and reminding them what they had to do.

As Helen walked down the aisle to take her place near the front, she saw Quentin chatting to the vicar. He looked very handsome in his tailcoat, grey-striped trousers and silk cravat. He kept looking around. He was clearly nervous, but no more so than most grooms awaiting the arrival of their bride.

When everyone was settled, Helen saw Dorothy nod to the vicar, who in turn nodded to the elderly organist, who then dramatically raised both hands before plunging them onto the tiered keyboard, starting off the ceremony and filling the small church to the rafters with the vibrating sound of the Bridal Chorus.

Everyone turned to watch Angie being escorted down the aisle by George Macalister, former captain of the 9th Battalion of the Durham Light Infantry. Angie's brother and sisters followed, occasionally looking at Lily for reassurance, which she gave them by way of a big smile and a nod towards the front of the church to show them they had to look where they were going, for they were treading dangerously close to Angie's long train.

Helen noted the relief on Lily's face when they all reached the altar.

Handing Marlene, the elder girl her wedding bouquet and silver horseshoe, Angie then pointed them towards Dorothy, who was sitting in the front pew with Bobby.

Helen knew Dorothy had opted not to be a part of the wedding procession, primarily because she hadn't wanted to wear a bridesmaid's dress, but also because she felt there was something special about it being just Angie and her siblings.

Looking at them now, Helen thought she had made the right decision. On top of which, Dorothy looked stunning in a figure-hugging navy blue dress that matched Bobby's naval uniform perfectly. The coordination made them an even more striking couple.

As the vicar gave his words of welcome, Helen glanced across to the pews on the other side. Dr Bernard was whispering something in Henrietta's ear. Helen had noticed he'd barely left her grandmother's side, knowing that attending the wedding was a huge step for her. The more Helen got to know Dr Bernard, the more she liked him.

Next to Henrietta sat Mrs Evans. Helen was sure that she must be thinking how she would have loved to have seen her daughter married. Charles Havelock had deprived her of so much. At least 'Grace's House' would go some way to putting right a terrible wrong.

Major Black was near the front due to him needing space for his wheelchair, and next to him sat Agnes and Dr Billingham, who were holding hands, their courtship now out in the open.

Behind them sat Beryl with Audrey and Iris, who had been allowed to wear make-up, and were now looking like young women.

Helen's attention was directed to the front of the church again when the vicar cleared his throat loudly and started his introduction.

'A wedding is one of life's great moments,' he began. 'A time of solemn commitment as well as good wishes, feasting and joy.'

Helen looked at Angie and Quentin as they stood at the altar. She could just make out their faces every now and again when they glanced at each other and exchanged tentative smiles.

'A man and wife should love and support each other in good times and in bad,' the vicar declared in robust tones.

Helen couldn't help but think of John and how he had showed her love and support in her times of need.

And how in just four days it would be John and Claire standing at the altar, exchanging their vows.

'I now declare you man and wife.'

A gentle murmur rippled through the congregation.

'You may kiss the bride.'

Quentin bent his head and kissed Angie gently.

As he did so, a ray of sunlight shone through the stained-glass windows, creating a rainbow of light that fell on the couple. It was a picture-perfect moment.

There were a few *aahs*, then Angie's brothers and sisters started to clap, much to everyone's amusement.

*

It had taken Tommy two days of travelling to get back home. He had managed to cadge a flight back with some SOE agents. It had been a hairy journey – *give him a rough sea any day* – but he'd made it. It had been followed by another bumpy journey in the back of an army truck, but at least he was on terra firma. Then a train back up north.

Walking out of the station and into the daylight, he felt a surge of adrenaline. It had been almost two and a half years since he had seen Polly. He craved to feel her in his arms again. To feel her soft skin on his. To kiss her.

He felt a slight rush of nerves, though, when he thought of Artie. Although he had seen a photo of his son, there had been no recent ones. Artie was now twenty months old. Polly had written to tell him that their son had started walking and was saying the occasional word.

Would Artie know that he was his father?

He reminded himself not to expect too much.

He just had to be thankful that he was here now – and unlike so many, he was alive, and well, and about to be reunited with his family.

*

When the organ struck up to fill time while the marriage certificate was being signed, Helen, who was sitting in the front pew, was trying her hardest not to imagine John and Claire's nuptials on Saturday. Listening to the music and watching Angie and Quentin sign the marriage certificate with Dorothy and George as witnesses, she felt a tear trickle down her cheek and quickly brushed it away. She could cry as much as she wanted when she was on her own later this evening, by which time, she swallowed back more tears, John would have arrived in Northallerton. Ready to start his new life with Claire.

*

Tommy had arrived at St Peter's Church just after the start of the ceremony. He had not wanted to disturb Polly or Artie, who he was sure would now be seated. More than anything, though, he didn't want his reunion to have to be made in a hushed whisper. He wanted to pick Polly up and swing her around, hear her happiness, and hold his son and tell him that he was his dad.

The next forty minutes had felt like hours as he'd waited impatiently. He'd walked to the river's edge and looked out over the Wear, breathing in the familiar smell of the river and the North Sea, so different to that of the Mediterranean.

He looked across to the south docks and could just about make out the Diver's House where he had lived with his grandfather. And where he had proposed to Polly.

He would miss Arthur. But he knew he had been lucky to have him so long – and that his death, by all accounts, had been a peaceful one. And one, he thought, Arthur had expected and welcomed. He knew his grandfather would have been glad to finally be with his beloved wife, Flo, once again.

Hearing the church organ strike up the Wedding March, Tommy walked to the side of the church, so he would not be spotted. He didn't want to spoil Angie and Quentin's day – or in any way take the limelight away from them.

He watched from his vantage point as the newly-weds came out of the church, followed by the congregation. There was much chatter and laughter. He thought of his own wedding day and smiled. It had been perfect, although tinged slightly by the knowledge that he would be flying back to his unit the following day.

Keeping his eyes trained on every person as they came out of the church entrance, he took in each face, his heart thumping with anticipation.

And then he saw her.

His heart went to his mouth.

She looked even more beautiful than he remembered. Her yellow dress seemed to highlight her vibrancy. Motherhood suited her. He saw her smiling at the bride and groom, before bending down to chat to Artie.

He could only see the back of his son, but suddenly he

caught his profile as Artie looked at his mother. Tommy saw his son's love for his mother, a smile appearing on his cherubic face as his mammy pointed to the bride and groom.

Tommy walked up to Polly. As she stood up straight, he gently put his hands across her eyes.

'Guess who?' he whispered into her ear.

Polly spun round.

'Tommy!' she cried out. 'Oh, my goodness. Tommy! You're back!'

And then they kissed. And laughed and kissed again. Tears trickled unashamedly down Polly's face.

Wiping her cheeks with her hands, she looked down at her son, who was staring up at them both.

'Artie,' she said. 'Look who's here.' She bobbed down so that her face was close to her son's. 'Remember we talked about him?'

Artie looked blankly for a moment.

'Remember I showed you a photograph of him?' Polly cajoled.

Suddenly the little boy's face lit up.

'Dadda!' he said, pointing his finger at Tommy.

Tommy's smile stretched wide, his eyes glistening with tears of pure happiness.

'That's right,' he said, stretching out his arms and reaching down to pick up his son. 'I'm your daddy.'

Tommy raised his son in the air and watched as his face broke into excited cries of excitement and joy as he was spun around.

Polly looked at father and son. She would never forget this moment.

Tommy looked at Artie, entranced by this little boy who

was his son. He caught himself in the boy's smile and he saw Arthur in his eyes.

In this little boy he saw the past and the present and the future.

A future that was bright and filled with hope and possibilities.

And as he looked at Polly, her eyes brimming with tears, he knew it would also be a future filled with love and happiness.

*

Dorothy and Helen – along with most of the other guests – watched Polly and Tommy's reunion. Helen naturally thought of John and how it must feel to hold and kiss the man you loved after such a long time. It was this, as much as the reunion, that brought tears to her eyes.

After Georgina had taken a photo of Polly, Tommy and Artie – the first of the Watts family together – she turned her attention back to the bride and groom, manoeuvring them into position outside the church porch and ordering the guests to refrain from throwing any confetti until she'd taken her shot of a very radiant Angie and Quentin.

It had been agreed that Dorothy and Helen would go ahead to the reception venue to ensure everything was ready for when the newly-marrieds arrived.

Luckily, they didn't have far to go as the distance from St Peter's Church to Thompson's was only a few hundred yards.

Dorothy was still thrilled with herself that she had thought of having the reception at the yard. She'd been even more thrilled when she'd seen Angie's face on hearing her sugges-tion. She'd said it was the best idea Dorothy had ever had.

Quentin, who had always admired Angie and her friends for choosing to work in a shipyard during wartime, also thought it was 'a perfect location' – a way of celebrating both their marriage and the hard work the women had done for the war.

Helen and Dorothy were pleased to see that the yard's huge metal gates had been decked out with bunting, ready to welcome the new Mr and Mrs Foxton-Clarke. As they walked into the yard, they saw Rina coming out of the canteen with a tray of sandwiches. Harvey was holding the door open for her. Vera followed with two large plates piled with slices of corned beef and potato pie. It had been decided to have food peculiar to the area. Vera had been down to the south docks that morning and bought a load of crabs, winkles and fish, which she had cooked in the café with all the windows open to try and reduce the smell. Fishcakes, crab sandwiches and crab 'nippers' formed part of the extensive buffet.

Everyone's fingers had been crossed for good weather so that the reception could be held out in the yard, but if it had rained or been too windy, the celebration would be enjoyed in the canteen. Thankfully, the day was sunny, dry and with a surprisingly genteel breeze, and looked set to stay that way.

'Good ceremony?' Rina asked.

'Wonderful,' Dorothy said, inspecting the table and smiling her approval.

'I hope everyone's hungry,' Vera huffed as she made her way back to the canteen, which had also been decorated with streamers and balloons, ''cos we've got enough here to feed the five thousand.'

'I'm sure they will be,' Helen said as she and Dorothy followed Vera back into the canteen.

As soon as they were inside, they were hit by the smell

of home cooking. Vera and Rina had worked hard from first light. Helen knew they would be well rewarded by Quentin, but she also knew they would have done it for free, if the newly-weds did not have deep pockets.

Looking over at the canteen, they spotted Muriel, a pinny over her best dress.

'All right there, Dor, Miss Crawford?'

'Yes, thank you, Muriel!' they both replied.

'All shipshape 'n ready to go.' Muriel nodded at the tea urn and the rows of cups and saucers.

'Thanks, Muriel,' Dorothy said. She also wanted to thank her for being such a gossip and spreading the word about 'Our Martha – Star of Thompson's Shipyard' . . . 'Heroine' . . . 'The Woman Welder Who Knows No Fear'. There had hardly been any mention of Martha's infamous mother.

'How'd it go?' Pearl popped up from under the long table that had been transformed into a bar, where there were crates of beer as well as soft drinks.

'Perfectly,' Helen said.

'And Tommy's just turned up,' Dorothy added.

'That's brilliant news!' Bill appeared from the kitchen with another crate of booze. Helen reckoned they must have cleared out the pub.

Pearl stood back and surveyed her make-do-and-mend bar. She looked pleased with herself.

'Right, we're ready for the rush, aren't we, Bill?'

Bill put an arm around Pearl's waist and pulled her close, giving her a kiss on the cheek.

'Ger off, yer great lummock,' she said, pushing him away. It was obvious, though, that Pearl didn't really mind. Her grumpy façade no longer fooled those who knew her.

Helen looked at Pearl and Bill and inwardly she had to let out a bittersweet sigh.

Even Pearl had manged to find love.

Content that everything was in order, Dorothy and Helen went to the main gates to greet the newly-weds.

They only had to wait a few minutes before they saw Angie and Quentin walking hand in hand, chatting and smiling at each other. They looked relieved and totally relaxed with one another. There was no doubt in anyone's mind that, despite the couple being polar opposites in so many ways, they couldn't be better matched.

As soon as they arrived and walked into the yard, Angie and Quentin let out a gasp of amazement at the rows of tables, all covered with white cloths and adorned with vases of wildflowers and jam jars with candles flickering in them. There was a huge Union Jack hanging from one of the smaller cranes, and a large dance floor had been marked out with chalk, while wooden pallets with rugs and cushions had been pulled close for people to relax on as the day wore on.

'Congratulations!' Dorothy said, handing them each a glass of champagne. 'Helen's going to give you the grand tour . . . And I'm going to welcome the guests.'

'It's amazing!' Angie said. 'Thank you.'

'I'll second that,' Quentin added, his eyes taking in the beautifully festooned tables and colourful decorations – all contrasting with the backdrop of the grey and metal of a shipyard.

It was almost surreal.

Chapter Fifty-Five

At Sunderland train station, Kate, Maisie and Vivian were making their way down to the southbound platform along with Lily, George, Rosie, Peter and Charlotte. They had left after the church service, as soon as Georgina had allowed them to throw their confetti. They knew they were cutting it fine, but they'd made it with five minutes to spare.

As they all hurried down to the main platform, Maisie and Vivian walked to the front carriages of the locomotive and flung open the door to the first-class compartment.

'We're travelling first class?' Kate asked.

'Of course, what other class is there?' Vivian drawled, posturing, hand on hip.

'Although you'd never think it,' Maisie said, looking around. 'Where's the porter?'

Just as she spoke, a young boy who looked barely out of short pants arrived, out of breath. 'Would you like a hand getting aboard, miss?' the boy asked Maisie. He looked at Vivian and blushed. 'And you too, miss?'

'Sweetie, I can get myself on board, but your muscle would be appreciated in hauling our luggage up.'

Again, the young lad blushed. He had worked here for eight months but had never come across a movie star – or rather, movie stars. For the two women were most certainly famous.

Maisie and Vivian said their farewells. Lily whispered to Maisie that she was to ring as soon as they had arrived and got settled. The young lad loaded the luggage with great care, making sure none of the leather cases suffered even a scuff. When he was finished, he stood at the open door to the carriage, waiting for Kate to board.

Lily waved him over, pushed a note into his hand and told him to skedaddle. The young boy's face lit up like a beacon. 'Thank you, madam. Thank you.'

Lily shooed him away with a smile.

'So, the time has come.' Lily looked at Kate. Glancing at Rosie and George, she saw they were clearly trying to keep their emotions in check.

Kate stepped forward and threw her arms around Lily. Once again, she was a street beggar. Back then, when she had arrived at the bordello and had been fed and watered and shown to a warm room with a soft bed in it, she had wanted so much to wrap her arms around this wonderfully eccentric woman with the orange hair and big bosom who was offering her salvation, but she didn't. Now she could – felt free and able to do so. And she wanted to say so much to her, tell her how much she loved and admired her – how thankful and indebted she was to her. To her and to Rosie. The two people who were responsible for saving her life. A former working girl and the madam of a bordello. She smiled as she wiped away her tears. *And society would claim that they were the ones who needed saving.*

'Don't you be sad,' Lily said. 'This is the beginning of a great new adventure for you.' She cupped her hands around Kate's face. She was so pretty, but the sadness she carried within, and which, ironically, made her so brilliant at what she did, still showed and probably always would.

'And you know your room will always be there for you when you come back to visit.' Lily forced herself to say the words with conviction, although she believed that once Kate started her new life, she would not return. 'But if, in the meantime, Rosie or anyone else should bring a little waif and stray to the door, then I shall let them have temporary use of your little attic bedsit.'

Kate smiled. 'Of course – always the one for waifs and strays,' she said, tears in her eyes.

'And don't you be sad about leaving me,' Lily said. 'I'm already planning my next trip to London. Give it a few months, when you're the toast of the fashion world, and I'll probably have to make an appointment.'

Kate looked at Lily, who was blinking back her own tears.

'Come soon, won't you?' Kate said, suddenly consumed by a wave of panic and loss.

'I will,' Lily promised.

'And I will too,' Rosie said, cocking her head towards Charlotte. 'This one here is already nagging me about a date.'

'And I've told *this one here*,' Charlotte deadpanned, 'that it's exactly five weeks until the end of term, and that it would be best if we were to book a ticket for the day after I break up.'

Kate chuckled. Charlotte would, she was sure, get her way. It made her feel a little less anxious.

The train let out a blast of steam.

'Come on, get on,' George ordered, waving his stick at the door to her carriage. He could see Maisie and Vivian sitting by the window, watching the farewells. He was glad they were going with Kate. They would see her settled in. And make sure she was safe.

462

Kate flung her arms around George, Peter and Charlotte, then Rosie and, finally, once again around Lily.

'I don't have to say how much I love you all, do I?' Kate said.

'Of course you do,' Lily said. 'You know my ego needs constantly stroking – well, that's what George keeps telling me.'

Kate stepped on board, shut the door and pulled down the sash window.

'I love you all, so much. So very much.'

And just as the tears started to drip down all their faces, the stationmaster blew his whistle and the train slowly pulled away.

As they all waved their goodbyes through the dense fog of steam billowing up from the train's undercarriage, Lily thought that she had never felt so sad and yet so happy. Her little sparrow had mended her broken wings and was flying off – up, up and away to a new and exciting future.

*

As they drove back to the reception, Peter and Rosie looked at Charlotte, who was staring out at all the revellers. The street they were due to drive down had been cordoned off for the purposes of a street party. Several kitchen tables had been pushed together and covered with white sheets. The women were bringing out plates of sandwiches and bowls of trifle. Rosie didn't think she had ever seen so much bunting and so many Union Jacks.

Charlotte caught them looking at her and she smiled.

'I've made up my mind,' she suddenly declared.

'About?' Peter asked, as if he needed to. They all knew that Charlotte had been chatting to her form teacher about her options once she finished school. She'd been told she had the pick of the bunch, no matter what she wanted to study.

'About what I'm going to do with my life,' Charlotte said, staring at them both intently, wanting to see their reaction. She had planned to tell them today – it seemed the perfect time to do so.

'And?' Rosie asked.

Lily shuffled around in the passenger seat. Her face expectant.

'I've decided I'm going to study law,' Charlotte announced.

'Well, I think that's an excellent choice,' Peter said.

'I couldn't agree more!' George shouted from the front, although he was keeping his eyes glued to the road. He'd already had one partygoer who looked slightly the worse for wear stagger off the pavement and onto the road.

'That's tremendous news, *ma chère*!' Lily said, her eyes flicking across to Rosie. 'And have you decided which university is going to be lucky enough to have you?'

Charlotte chuckled. Lily always talked as though she were the brightest and best student in the country.

'Durham!'

'Good choice!' Lily clapped her hands. She looked at Rosie and saw the relief on her face. *They could keep an eye on her – make sure she didn't go off the rails.* Lily tutted to herself. *Who was she kidding?* She and Rosie were relieved because neither of them could bear the thought of Charlotte being any more than twenty miles away. They were both going to miss her terribly. Another fledgling was going to leave the nest.

Chapter Fifty-Six

Arriving back at the reception, Charlotte could not contain her excitement at Angie and Quentin having their wedding reception at the yard.

'It looks amazing!' she said, taking in the scene.

Lucille was playing skipping rope with Angie's sisters. The boys were playing tag and whooping with laughter. Occasionally, one of the children grabbed the hooter, which had been left on the pallets, and gave it a squeeze. It was still a novelty to be able to make loud noises – another sign that the war was over.

Seeing Charlotte, Gloria waved her over. They all wanted to hear how the send-off had gone.

As soon as Rina spotted Rosie, she hurried towards her. 'Such an enchanting wedding, wasn't it?'

Rosie agreed.

'And such an unusual venue for the reception,' Rina added.

Rosie chuckled. 'I know! You'd have thought Angie would have had enough of the place.'

Rina put her hand in her pocket and pulled out a letter. Rosie could see instantly it was airmail.

'From Hannah?'

Rina nodded. The smile on her face told Rosie all was well.

'I thought you might want to show it to the women. Give them all an update.'

'Oh, they'll be over the moon,' Rosie said. She looked at Rina. 'You missing her?'

'Terribly,' Rina admitted. 'But I'm keeping myself busy.' She glanced over to see Vera appearing from the canteen with a tray of vol-au-vent. Seeing Rina, she creased her brow and cocked her head towards the kitchen.'

'Talking of which, it looks like I'm needed.'

*

'All right, Ma?' Bel asked as she reached the makeshift bar with Joe and Lucille. It felt strange to be back at the yard. She had spent many an hour in the canteen, but although she had enjoyed her work with Marie-Anne in admin, she did not miss it. Besides, her real reason for working at Thompson's had been to find out about her parentage.

'Port and lemon?' Pearl pre-empted.

Bel shook her head. 'No thanks, Ma. Just a lemonade, please.'

'Not drinking?' Pearl queried. She had noticed her daughter had ordered just a lemonade yesterday when she'd popped in the Tatham with Joe.

'Thought I'd give it a rest for a while,' Bel said nonchalantly.

Pearl looked at Joe, who was shuffling about, looking a little awkward. She then gave her daughter a piercing look. She had not been the best ma in the whole world – quite the reverse – but she did know her daughter. Could read her like a book.

'How long a rest?' Pearl asked, giving Bill a sidelong glance. He, too, was now looking at Bel and Joe.

'A while,' Bel said. 'Just a while.'

'A nine-month while?' Pearl asked.

'Might be.' Bel gave a half-smile. Nothing got past her ma.

'Fingers crossed, eh?' Pearl said.

Bel nodded.

'Fingers crossed, Ma.'

As Joe took the tray carrying the drinks, he cast a look back at Pearl. She had a big smile on her face.

Realising that she was smiling, she stopped.

Bill nudged her. 'Good news, eh?'

''Bout time,' Pearl grumbled.

Inwardly, though, she was chuffed to pieces. Her daughter had been desperate to have a child with Joe and now, it would seem, she'd been granted her wish.

As Pearl asked the next guest what they would like to drink, her mind wandered.

How her life had changed since she'd tipped up at the Elliots' shortly after Teddy had been killed more than four years ago.

Gradually, she had mended her tattered relationship with Isabelle.

And she'd found the daughter she'd had to give up as a baby – *or rather, Maisie had found her.*

She had gone to battle with Charles Havelock.

And lived to see him die.

She'd met and married Bill.

And become the owner of a pub.

She now had three grandchildren, with another on the way.

Life really couldn't get any better.

Not that she would admit that to anyone else, of course.

*

'To the woman who has brought so much light, love and happiness into my life – to the woman I adore.' Quentin raised his glass and looked with love at Angie. 'To my amazing wife.'

Everyone cheered and clapped and sipped their drinks. Angie smiled self-consciously and blushed.

Just before they returned to their conversations and food, Angie stood up, much to everyone's surprise. Not only because it wasn't convention for the bride to make a speech, but because Angie was probably the last person they would expect to want to make a speech.

'I just wanna say thank yer to everyone for making this day so wonderful,' she said. They were all quiet, their attention focused on the bride in her beautiful dress, which they all knew had been designed by the town's own 'Coco Chanel' and was made from parachute silk. The smattering of crystals that had been sewn into the fabric, and which were also in her veil and tiara, were sparkling in the sunlight.

Angie turned to Dorothy, who was sitting next to her.

'And a special thank you to my best friend, my maid of honour 'n all-round top wedding organiser – Dorothy Williams.' She smiled and forced herself not to get teary. It was difficult, though. The past two days had worn down her hard edges and left her feeling emotionally exposed.

'Dorothy, yer the best friend anyone could ever want.'

Angie raised her glass, and everyone smiled at Dorothy, who had started to blush. Bobby put an arm around her shoulders and squeezed her close, knowing that his sweetheart only liked being the centre of attention when she chose to be. She could be surprisingly shy.

'And just so yer knar, Dor,' Angie said, putting on a

schoolmarmish tone, 'yer gonna keep being my best mate even when yer off travelling the world!'

At the thought of leaving Angie and the rest of her friends, Dorothy felt the sting of tears.

'I will. I promise,' she mouthed.

Angie looked at Quentin, sitting next to her.

'And Quentin and I have also got some news to tell everyone.'

She paused, enjoying the looks on the faces of their guests.

'No, it's not what yer think,' she chuckled.

'Quentin 'n I have had a chat.' She looked at her siblings, who were being surprisingly well behaved. 'And my brothers and sisters are coming to live with us in the country.'

Four excited, rosy-cheeked faces beamed back at her.

'As well as our neighbour, Mrs Kwiatkowski – who, you all know, was the one to originally introduce me to Quentin.'

Angie, Quentin and Mrs Kwiatkowski exchanged amused looks. The old woman's short-term memory might be going, but she well remembered Angie's first words to her future husband, which had been loud and accusatory, in her belief that he'd been up to no good.

Angie looked at Quentin, who raised his glass to the children and then to Mrs Kwiatkowski, who raised her glass of Polish vodka.

'We've certainly got the room!' Quentin declared. And probably even more after his parents decided to move out – something he had a strong feeling they would do. The house – or rather, mansion – was officially his, having inherited it when he'd turned twenty-one. Something for which he had his beloved grandfather to thank.

Everyone clapped, then raised their glasses. Rosie caught

Angie's eye and she raised a glass to her and smiled, hoping it conveyed the words she would have liked to say – that she and Quentin had made an incredible sacrifice. They were starting their young married life with four children and an old woman to care for. But looking at the gloriously happy faces of the newly-weds, she saw that they in no way saw it as a burden. Angie, she knew, would become a mother to her brothers and sisters, like Rosie had become a mother of sorts to Charlotte. And just like Rosie had done, she knew Angie and Quentin would make sure they were properly schooled and given the best start in life. The boys would no longer be destined to a life down the pit like their dad. And her sisters would know they had options.

She wondered if Angie would want to have her own children. That was presuming she could have children. Rosie took nothing for granted. Life, she had learnt, was lacking in certainty, and sometimes it ended up sending you down a different route to the one you had intended or wanted to take. Sometimes, Rosie mused, looking at Peter and Charlotte, those unexpected turns in life led to something rather special.

Subconsciously touching the light feathery scars on her face, she thought of the sacrifices she had made – and how she had been repaid tenfold.

For sitting here now, with Peter and Charlotte, Lily and George, and all her friends, she could not want more from life.

As everyone started chatting, and the children went back to their games, Bobby took hold of Dorothy's hand.

'Are you still sure about travelling – about leading "an unconventional life"?' he asked, quoting Dorothy. 'You don't

want to follow in Angie's footsteps and have all of this . . .'
He looked at Bel and Joe with Lucille, and Agnes and Dr Billingham, looking very much in love as they kept the twins entertained.

Dorothy smiled. 'Nope. I want adventure rather than marriage and babies.'

'Good,' Bobby said. 'I'm more than happy with that. Now we just have to pick our first destination.'

'We'll have another look at the map tonight. See where we'll be able to go first.'

Bobby laughed out loud. 'How could a man refuse such an offer!'

Dorothy scowled at him – then kissed him.

'I love you, Bobby Armstrong.'

'I love you too, Dorothy Williams. And always will. Married or not.'

*

After the women walked down to the ferry landing to give Stan the ferry master a drink and a plate of food, Rosie gathered everyone together so that she could read Hannah's letter out loud. Smiling at Helen, Rosie thought she was putting on a good show. They had all commented quietly to each other that they knew she was feeling rotten. Dorothy had said she could see the heartbreak in her eyes. And for once, Rosie thought Dorothy was not being dramatic. Helen, she could tell, *was* heartbroken. She had loved Dr Parker for a long time.

'Here goes . . .' Rosie began, holding the letter out in front of her.

They all listened to Hannah's description of her work,

and how she had still not found her parents. She admitted it seemed unlikely that they were still alive after what she had learnt since being over there, but she was still glad she had volunteered. She felt that she and Olly were doing some good and helping those who were still alive.

Olly's pen-and-ink drawings, she added, were incredible. She was very proud of her 'husband'.

The women all agreed that getting the letter today and reading it together had made it feel as though their 'little bird' was here with them in spirit – a part of this special day.

*

Dorothy clinked her glass to get everyone's attention and declared, 'The Prime Minister!'

Everyone quietened down and without further ado, Dorothy switched on the wireless.

Turning the volume high, there was silence as the perfectly articulated and very excited voice of a BBC presenter announced Churchill's appearance on the balcony of the Ministry of Health in London.

The bells of St Martin could be heard ringing out, followed by a huge cheer as Churchill gave his famous V-sign.

'He's wearing his boiler suit – his famous boiler suit,' the presenter couldn't contain his surprise and joy, 'and he's had the audacity, should I say, to put on his head his famous black hat – no one can say it goes with a boiler suit, but you heard what a cheer it raised from the crowd.'

There was more cheering before the crowds quietened down.

'This is your victory!' Churchill declared. 'Victory of the cause of freedom in every land.'

The guests all cheered – obliterating the cheers of the crowds coming through the wireless.

Bobby looked across at his mam. Gloria caught his eye and smiled. Their thoughts were with Gordon, whom they would see soon. He had written, telling them that he had been given leave.

Agnes looked over at Beryl, who had Iris on one side and Audrey on the other. She knew Beryl would be thinking of her husband, who was presently languishing in a Burmese POW camp, and praying that the war beyond Europe would also end in victory soon.

'In all our long history we have never seen a greater day than this,' the Prime Minister continued.

More cheering.

Major Black shuffled around in his wheelchair and looked at Joe, whose walking stick was propped up against the edge of the table. The sacrifices they had made – and the life Joe's brother had forsaken in this battle against evil – had been worth it.

'Everyone, man or woman,' Churchill spoke slowly and deliberately, *'has done their bit.'*

The women welders glanced at each other and smiled.

'None has flinched. Everyone has tried. Neither the long years, nor the dangers, nor the fierce attacks of the enemy have in any way weakened the unbending resolve of the British nation.'

Everyone started to clap loudly. Proudly.

'God bless you all!'

The band struck up 'Land of Hope and Glory'. Along with the crowds in the capital, all the guests joined in the singing. At the end there was a huge cheer – not just in London, or Thompson's shipyard, or in 'the biggest shipbuilding town in

473

the world', but across the length and breadth of the country. This was not just a victory over the enemy, but a victory for humanity. It was a momentous occasion. One no one would forget for as long as they lived.

When the radio was switched off, Martha, as directed by Dorothy, put a record on the gramophone. As Vera Lynn's voice crackled into life singing 'There'll Always Be an England', Dr Billingham whispered in Agnes's ear, 'Life is so short, and we should enjoy it now.'

Agnes looked across at Polly and Tommy and counted her blessings that her son-in-law had returned in one piece. She thought of Teddy, who had not returned. Then she looked at Joe with Lucille on his shoulders, and Bel chasing after the twins, who were toddling around with surprising speed.

She looked back at Dr Billingham. 'I thought that's what we'd been doing?' she asked with a half-smile, gently taking his hand in hers.

Dr Billingham felt her touch and smiled too.

'Marry me,' he said simply. 'Marry me, Agnes Elliot.'

Agnes took in his words. She did not seem shocked.

Instead, a mischievousness crept into her eyes.

'Well, Dr Billingham, if you put it like that, how can I refuse?'

And with that, Dr Billingham sealed the deal with a kiss.

Chapter Fifty-Seven

Dr Parker sat and looked out of the window at the passing scenery. He loved this part of the country, with its double bounty of lush green countryside and beautiful coastline. He smiled at the young child who was holding a Union Jack in her hand. She had been waving it at a herd of cows, but now, bored, she was focusing her attention on her fellow passenger.

Dr Parker kept on smiling even after the little girl's attention was diverted back to her mother, who had kissed her cheek and was pointing to some horses grazing on a hilly bank.

Looking out of the carriage window again, Dr Parker felt as though he truly knew the meaning of the expression 'on cloud nine'. He felt like a bird soaring up into the clear blue sky. Completely free. Full of joy. He had been in seventh heaven since Claire had told him of her deceit yesterday. Of course, he'd been astonished by what Claire had told him. And angry. Angry for so many different reasons. She had lied to him. Manipulated him. She had threatened Helen, and in doing so had threatened Helen's friends. Claire had sworn blind that she would never have followed through with her threats, but he wasn't so sure.

The anger, though, didn't last for long, for all he could really think about was Helen.

She loved him.

Was in love with him.

And with that knowledge had come the greatest feeling of elation he had ever experienced. True euphoria, which had blotted out any feelings of outrage and resentment towards Claire.

He had told her straight that the wedding was off. They were no longer engaged. He had forced himself to listen to her arguments that they would make a wonderful couple. They could have a good marriage. A brilliant life together. He had been forced to hold his tongue when she had inferred that he and Helen were not suited and would not last.

Again, he had told her that he could not be with someone who had tricked him so. There had to be trust in a marriage – in a relationship – and that could never be the case between them.

Claire had not wanted to give up, though. He knew she was being truthful when she said that she really did love him. That she had fallen in love with him – eventually. But he also knew that her fight to keep him was mainly because she did not want the humiliation of suffering a second cancelled wedding.

She had asked him to think about it – that she would wait until the very last minute before she had to leave for the station.

When Dr Parker had left Claire, he had wanted more than anything else in the world to go to Helen right there and then, take her in his arms, look into those emerald eyes, tell her he loved her, and then kiss her for a long, long time.

When he'd returned to the hospital to pick up his belongings, the new receptionist had caught him and told him of the emergency. She must have seen the look on his face because she'd told him in the same breath that she couldn't get hold of any other surgeons and it really was a matter of life and death.

He had managed to pull himself together and calm down. When he'd put on his surgical gown, he'd put all thoughts of Helen aside, although it had been hard.

By the time he'd come out of theatre, it was the middle of the night. His body was exhausted, but his mind had been jumping about like a first-class athlete, full of boundless energy. He was surprised he had managed to sleep.

He didn't want Claire thinking he might have changed his mind overnight. And if he was honest with himself, he didn't want her missing her train and continuing to argue the case that they should be together, so he'd gone round there and endured the ride in the taxi and the wait for the train to arrive.

When he had kissed Claire chastely on the cheek and said goodbye, he knew that he would never see her again. It would be highly unlikely, anyway, unless professionally their paths crossed, but he doubted it somehow.

As soon as the Northallerton train pulled out of the station, he had seen another hissing its way into the station, bound for Sunderland. He had run like the clappers over the wooden bridge to the platform opposite. He had even vaulted the turnstile, much to the stationmaster's vexation, shouting back that he would pay on the train.

He had managed to jump into the first available carriage just as the whistle sounded and the train started to move.

Looking at his watch, Dr Parker willed the train to go faster.

He still had something he wanted to do before he went to Helen.

*

477

Dr Parker was forced to spend much longer in town than he'd intended due to the huge crowds of people in the centre. Everyone was in high spirits, chatting, laughing and singing. Someone had set up a gramophone and people had started to dance on the corner of Athenaeum Street, near the south entrance of the railway station.

There was the unmistakable feel of a street carnival. Dr Parker had never seen so many people. Nor so many flags draped out of just about every window. The shop windows had been decorated – all in celebration of the victory in Europe.

At one point, he couldn't move in any direction. He was jammed like a sardine in a can. He guessed there must have been thousands of townsfolk in Fawcett Street alone. They seemed to be crowding around the town hall. He heard some snatches of conversation and realised they were waiting for the Prime Minister's speech to be broadcast to the nation.

It was amazing – and wonderful to see – but also very frustrating. He just wanted to grab what he needed and get over to see Helen at the wedding reception. But it was taking much longer than he'd anticipated. He just hoped the shop-keeper he had spoken to this morning would keep his word and would wait for him, even though he was running late.

When he finally made it to where he wanted to go, he saw the owner walking to the back of the shop, having turned the sign to 'Closed'.

Dr Parker started banging so hard on the glass front door, the proprietor couldn't hurry back to open it fast enough, afraid the glass would break.

*

'So,' Rosie said, 'it looks like I'll be losing most of my squad when our boys come back home.'

'Most?' Dorothy said.

'Yes, you, Angie, Gloria, Polly . . .'

Polly opened her mouth to object. But as she did so, her eye was caught by a figure squeezing through the narrow opening of the iron gates.

She squinted hard.

She looked at Helen, who was standing in front of her. She had her back to the yard's main entrance.

Out of the corner of her eye, she saw Gloria jolt. She, too, was looking at the figure who was now striding towards the wedding party.

Seeing that Gloria and Polly were staring at something, Dorothy followed their gaze.

She let out a gasp and grabbed Angie's arm.

'Aw, Dor!' Angie said, looking down at her best friend's hand clamped on to her bare wrist.

'Look!' Dorothy said, releasing her grip.

Helen looked at the women, and then at Martha, who was standing next to her.

'What are you all gawping at?' Martha said, starting to turn round.

Helen saw a smile spread across Gloria's face.

'Oh my goodness, look who it is!' said Georgina.

Helen turned around. The sun suddenly came out from behind the clouds and partially blinded her.

She blinked, but all she could see was a small crowd of wedding guests walking across to the canteen.

And then she fixed eyes on him.

At first, she thought she was hallucinating – that she

so desperately wanted John, her mind was fabricating this vision of him walking towards her with a wide smile on his face.

God, she'd be joining her mother at the asylum at this rate.

She continued staring as he got nearer.

No, she wasn't going mad.

It *was* John.

It was John!

As Dr Parker walked across the yard, it was as though he had tunnel vision. All he could see was Helen. She looked gorgeous, as always. She was staring at him, but it was as though she didn't recognise him.

He slowed down a fraction and smiled.

And then he saw it. A light clicked on in her eyes, which had until that moment looked a little sad and doubtful.

But no more.

Now they were sparkling and seemed to reflect the love and happiness that he, too, was bursting with.

'Helen!' he said, reaching her.

'John!' Helen said, her smile widening. She wasn't sure whether she wanted to laugh or cry. 'What are you doing here?' she asked. 'I thought you were going to Northallerton today?'

Dr Parker shook his head.

He glanced at the women, who were all quiet, full of expectation.

'I'm guessing Gloria didn't tell you?' He briefly dragged his vision away from Helen to look at Gloria.

'Tell me what?' Helen asked. She scanned the women's faces, but no one said anything.

'I know everything,' Dr Parker said. 'Everything Claire did. The threats she made—'

'How?' Helen asked.

'Claire told me,' said Dr Parker.

Helen was surprised. 'Really?'

'Well, I believe she might well have had her arm twisted a little.' He looked at the women.

Helen narrowed her eyes at her friends. 'Did you go and see her?'

'Rosie drove,' Martha volunteered.

'Rosie drove?' repeated Helen.

'That might be up for debate.' Polly laughed.

Rosie tutted.

'I'm learning,' she told Helen.

'But only Gloria went to see Dr Eris,' Angie explained. She and Dorothy had demanded they tell them every word of what had gone on. They had been miffed they had missed being a part of it, but also a little glad there hadn't been space in the car.

'You talked to her?' Helen asked Gloria.

'I did.'

'And?' Helen asked, still processing everything she was hearing.

'I simply told her that she had to be truthful with Dr Parker,' Gloria explained.

'Otherwise, we would be!' Dorothy blurted out.

Helen looked at her friends, her eyes starting to well. She wanted to thank them, but was too choked with emotion to speak. She would tell them later.

'I think we need to check on the guests,' Rosie said, looking at the women and nodding her head away from Helen and Dr Parker.

'Definitely,' Dorothy said as they all turned and ambled off.

Dr Parker looked at Helen and gently took hold of her hands.

'There's so much I want to say – to talk about,' he said, raising her hands to his mouth and kissing them. 'But for now, I just want to tell you how much I love you.'

He smiled on seeing Helen smile.

'How much I am *in love* with you – and always have been.'

He looked at Helen and leant in to kiss her softly on the lips. She closed her eyes and lost herself in the feel of his mouth on hers. She had wanted this moment for such a long time. And it felt better than she could ever have imagined.

Feeling his hand gently touching her cheek, Helen opened her eyes.

'I love you, Helen Crawford. More than anything and anyone,' Dr Parker told her.

Helen smiled.

'Oh, John.' She leant forward and kissed him.

She kissed his cheek and then his neck.

'And I love you too.'

And then she kissed him again.

'I think this is the happiest day of my life.'

Dr Parker looked at Helen, entranced as always by her emerald eyes.

'I know this might seem a little hasty.'

He paused.

'But I feel we know each other so well. I was thinking how close we have become these past few years.'

Helen nodded. 'We have.'

'We know everything about each other,' Dr Parker said.

Helen smiled. 'We do. The good and the bad.'

'Because of that . . .' Dr Parker hesitated again '. . . and because I know I want to be with you for the rest of my life . . .'

He pushed his hand into his trouser pocket and pulled out a small velvet box.

'I wanted to ask you if you, too, would want to be with me for the rest of your life?'

He opened the box to reveal the most beautiful emerald engagement ring.

Helen gasped in amazement.

'It's gorgeous,' she said, her eyes still glued to its beauty.

Dr Parker was quiet.

Helen looked up at him.

'You are the best thing that has ever happened to me, John,' she said.

'Can I take that as a yes?' he asked tentatively.

Helen smiled and kissed him.

'Yes.' She kissed him again. 'Yes, yes, yes.'

And then they didn't speak any more as Dr Parker pulled Helen into his arms and they lost themselves in each other's kisses.

Georgina had been watching from a little way away and just at that moment had quickly managed to raise her camera, focus and snap.

She got the perfect shot. It would be one for her portfolio, and also a perfect wedding present.

Because she was sure there would be a wedding – and it would be sooner rather than later.

Chapter Fifty-Eight

Dorothy nodded over to Martha, who was in charge of the gramophone that had been loaned by George, along with his record collection. As instructed, she lifted the needle off the record that was playing, which in turn had the desired effect of getting everyone's attention.

'I do believe it is time for the bride and groom to have their first dance!' Dorothy announced to the wedding party.

She looked over to Angie and Quentin.

'And I suspect the new Mr and Mrs Foxton-Clarke will have this particular song imprinted on their memory – as it was this record that was playing when Quentin proposed to Angie.' Dorothy paused. 'A proposal, it has to be said, which ended up not quite going to plan – but was still lovely all the same.'

Everyone chuckled. They'd all heard the tale of how Quentin had accidentally dropped the engagement ring on the dance floor, only for Angie to find it and Quentin to propose while she'd still been holding it.

'"Only Forever" by Bing Crosby!' Dorothy announced.

Quentin offered his hand in true gentlemanly fashion to his new wife as Martha carefully put the needle on the spinning vinyl record and the velvet tones of Bing Crosby filled the air.

As the newly-marrieds started to dance, Dr Parker gently

pulled Helen close and kissed her neck. The two had not left each other's side since they had finally acknowledged their love for one another. If they weren't holding hands, then Dr Parker had his arm around Helen's waist, or hers was around his.

'I can't wait for us to have our special song.'

'Me neither,' Helen murmured as she watched Angie and Quentin dance, the look in their eyes evidence that this marriage was destined to be a happy one, a very happy one.

'Why don't we make the next song to be played "our song"?' Dr Parker suggested. 'It will remind us of this day for ever. This moment.'

Helen looked at him with sparkling eyes and a smile on her face that proved to Dr Parker just how wrong he had been: Helen loved him – and not just as a friend.

'I think that's a wonderful idea,' Helen agreed.

Dr Parker gave Helen another quick kiss – wanting it to be much more than quick.

The wedding guests watched as the newly-marrieds danced a perfect waltz, then cheered and clapped at the end when Quentin gave Angie a kiss.

There was a brief pause while Martha quickly changed the record.

Dr Parker and Helen looked at each other, waiting to see what 'their song' would be.

There was a brief crackle before the sounds of the orchestra filled the air and once again Bing Crosby began to sing – it was another of his most famous love songs, entitled, simply, 'I Love You'.

Helen looked at Dr Parker as though to reassure herself that this moment was real, for it felt almost too perfect.

Dr Parker stepped aside and held out his hand.

'May I?'

'You may,' Helen said, giving him her hand, on which she was now wearing her engagement ring.

'I can't wait to be your husband,' Dr Parker said, pulling her towards him and holding her close as they started to dance. A slow, intimate dance on the far corner of the makeshift dance floor.

'And I can't wait to be your wife,' Helen whispered into his ear, thinking how long she had wanted to feel his arms around her as a lover and not just as a friend.

And so they danced to 'their song', revelling in the feel of their bodies pressing together, losing themselves in the music.

They had waited so long for this moment.

A moment they had believed would never happen.

But it had.

Finally, it had.

'I don't think I've ever felt this happy in my entire life,' Helen said.

She felt her future husband's hold on her tighten.

'You took the words right out of my mouth.'

Chapter Fifty-Nine

As Angie and Quentin's wedding day started drawing to a close, Rosie went to the canteen and poured out nine glasses of champagne. Walking back out into the yard, she spotted Helen and Dr Parker chatting to Gloria and Jack and Polly and Tommy. 'Women only,' she called out, nodding over to the quayside where they usually enjoyed their packed lunches when the weather allowed.

Today it allowed. The sun was still shining and there was very little wind – just a light breeze coming in from the North Sea. It had been a perfect day for a wedding – a perfect day for them all.

Within a few minutes they were all there – Rosie, Helen, Polly, Gloria, Dorothy, Angie, Martha and Georgina.

'Grab a glass,' Rosie said, holding the tray.

'Yer've got one too many,' Angie said.

'Ah, that one's for Hannah,' said Rosie.

Everyone smiled.

'She'd like that,' said Martha.

'Yeah, even though she doesn't really drink,' said Dorothy.

Polly suddenly chuckled. 'Remember when she went through that stage of drinking Guinness?' Everyone laughed.

'She believed that advert,' said Gloria.

' "*A help to women, bringing new strength to tired limbs*",' Dorothy and Angie chanted together.

Rosie looked at the women, thinking of when they had all started at the yard. She looked at them now and felt so incredibly proud. There hadn't been time for proper training or for them to do an apprenticeship, but they had learnt fast, worked hard and honed their skills as they went. They had proved that they were as good as the men.

'I just want to say something first, if you don't mind?' Helen asked.

'Go on,' Rosie urged.

Helen took a deep breath and smiled. She had been smiling so much the past hour or so, her cheeks ached. Not that she minded. Not one bit.

'I just want to thank you all for what you did,' she said. 'It might sound dramatic, but you've helped change the course of my life – and made me the happiest woman on the planet.'

She looked at Angie.

'Apart from the bride, of course.'

'I think we owed yer,' Angie said simply.

'And we wanted to,' Gloria added.

'Well, I'm going to be eternally grateful that you did – and for having such wonderful friends. So, thank you all.'

She raised her glass and took a sip.

Everyone followed suit.

'Cor, champagne's nice, isn't it?' Angie said. 'I think I prefer it to port.'

'See! I always knew there was a posho underneath that rough exterior,' Dorothy laughed.

Angie tutted.

They all looked at each other with a mix of happiness and

sadness because they knew that after today all their lives would change.

In the past five years, they had all found love – and more importantly, they had found each other.

'So,' Rosie said, 'we've got to promise each other that we won't lose the friendship we have – now the war's won?'

'Agreed,' said Gloria.

'Even when you're halfway around the world, Dorothy, you've still got to keep in contact – and come back and see us occasionally,' Rosie said.

'Yes! Promise, Dor!' Angie demanded.

'I promise,' Dorothy said, suddenly having a flash of just how much she was going to miss her friends.

'And Angie, you've got to promise to leave your stately home and come and hobnob with the hoi polloi every now and again.'

Angie laughed. 'Dinnit worry, I will.'

'And Gloria, you've got to leave your nice new home with your little garden and new neighbours and come and see your old workmates . . . Same goes for you, Polly.'

Polly laughed. 'You'll be sick of the sight of me. I'll be bringing Artie to see his dad during his lunch break. He's got a lot of time to make up.'

'And you, Georgina?'

'I will,' she said solemnly.

'Good!' Rosie smiled.

Everyone looked at Martha as she had been missed out.

'Oh, Martha doesn't have to promise to stay in touch,' Helen declared. 'Because Martha's not going anywhere. She's staying right here with me and Rosie.'

Martha's face lit up. 'How come?'

Helen chuckled, casting a look in Georgina's direction. 'As you are now a local celebrity, there's no way the bosses would let you go – even if you wanted to leave!'

Martha's smile was immediate. 'Thanks, Helen.' She knew it wouldn't have been quite that easy, despite the article, and that there was a good chance Helen would have had to argue hard to keep her on.

'I did wonder, however,' Helen said, 'if you'd like to try your hand at riveting? Rosie is going to be training the new apprentices, and as you know, Jimmy, is desperate to have you in his squad.'

Martha nodded enthusiastically.

'And what about you, Helen?' Rosie asked. 'Are you definitely staying? You're not going to run off to London with Dr Parker?'

'No, we've already chatted about that. John was never that keen about moving to London in the first place. We're staying put.'

'Good to hear!' Rosie said.

The seagulls screeched above their heads, and everyone looked up.

For a moment they were quiet as they looked out at the River Wear.

'So,' Rosie said, drawing everyone's attention back to each other. 'This might be the closing of one chapter, but it is also the start of another. A chapter that begins with the promise to keep in touch. To remain friends, no matter where we all are.'

The women chorused their agreement.

'To friendship!' Georgina said.

'To the future,' Angie added.

'To happiness.' Polly held her glass up to the blue skies.

'To love,' Gloria said, thinking how much love she had been gifted since starting work here at the yard.

'To the women welders,' Helen said.

'To *us all*,' Rosie counteracted.

'Three cheers to us!' Martha raised her glass and gave a wide, gap-toothed smile.

'To the Shipyard Girls!' Dorothy declared, looking round at her workmates' faces.

'Three cheers for the Shipyard Girls!' Rosie felt herself fill with pride.

Hip hip hurrah . . . Hip hip hurrah . . . Hip hip hurrah.

Epilogue

Helen and Dr Parker married not long after VE Day. They saw no reason to wait. They both agreed they had waited long enough.

Helen continued climbing the career ladder at Thompson's, her eye always on the next rung. Dr Parker was approached by the head of a new department at Newcastle General Hospital that had been set up to work alongside the Artificial Limb Program, which was to be run in tandem with an American governmental agency created in response to the influx of Second World War veteran amputees.

Dr Claire Eris became head psychologist at the Ontario Hospital for the Mentally Ill (formerly the London Asylum for the Insane). She decided marriage was not for her and instead focused on her career, occasionally taking a lover whenever the opportunity presented itself.

Dahlia ended up getting her man after accidentally-on-purpose falling pregnant. Matthew Royce did the gentlemanly thing and married her, but not because he had been duped by the oldest trick in the book – Matthew was far too interested in his own welfare to worry about others, even if that person was going to have his child. No, his decision to marry Dahlia was made after learning that she actually came from an incredibly well-off aristocratic Swedish family. When he'd asked her why she had kept her wealthy background a secret, Dahlia had told him that her reason for doing so was because she had wanted to ward off any gold-diggers. Matthew decided to refrain from enlightening her about his own family's dire financial situation until after the wedding.

Rosie and Peter continued to live happily at Brookside Gardens. Rosie kept working at the yard, training apprentices, but in her free time she developed her property portfolio. Peter returned full-time to the Sunderland Borough Police, eventually replacing Chief Constable Metcalf on his retirement.

As promised, on their wedding anniversary they went to Paris and walked along the River Seine and across the Pont des Arts, considered to be the city's most romantic bridge. They also enjoyed a long weekend away at Wanborough Manor, where Peter had trained with the SOE, and which was now a B & B.

As planned, Charlotte went to study law at Durham University and ended up specialising in criminal law. It was her way of getting justice for women like Rosie and putting men like her uncle Raymond behind bars.

Polly stayed on at Thompson's until August, when the Second World War ended throughout the rest of the world. There had been a slim possibility that she might have been able to keep her job, but when she felt the subtle changes in her body just a few months after Tommy's return, she knew there was no way she could work at the yard and be a mum to a toddler and a newborn. Besides which, Agnes would have had her guts for garters.

*

493

Gloria, Jack and Hope moved out of the flat on Borough Road and into one of the new prefab houses in Nookside, in a part of town known as Grindon. It had a little front garden, and the area had a lovely sense of community. Ironically, it was not far from the home she had shared with Vinnie, but her life with Jack and Hope could not have been more different. Not a day went by when she did not thank her lucky stars she had trooped to the labour exchange at the start of the war and been given a placement at Thompson's.

Because of her time there, she was now happier than she had ever dreamt possible.

Martha started her new job with Jimmy's squad of riveters and took to it like a duck to water. She continued to 'step out' with Adam the tuba-playing miner.

Angie blossomed in her new role of wife, guardian to her four siblings and manager of the estate. The workers adored her as she was the most down-to-earth, hands-on employer they had ever known. She could drive a tractor with the best of them, and, of course, if there was any welding to be done, she was the person they were told to call on. She had kept her overalls and welding mask from Thompson's and liked nothing more than to slip back into the attire of her former life.

Dorothy and Bobby left for foreign shores as soon as it was safe to do so. They were both adept at turning their hand to any kind of work to get by, but after a year of seeing all the places Dorothy had dreamt of, they fell in love with America and settled in New York, where Dorothy started working for a women's magazine and Bobby got a foreman's job at New York Harbor. They did get married, but only for practical reasons.

And Dorothy did start to mention to Bobby that having a family might not be totally out of the question.

Dorothy and Angie, of course, remained best friends, regardless of the miles that separated them. They spoke every week on the phone and were both avid letter writers.

Hannah and Olly were given official jobs with the Red Cross. Hannah as a translator, and Olly as an artist. His drawings of the scenes he had witnessed at Belsen were lauded and printed in publications all over the world. The pair came back home regularly to see their family and friends.

Hannah's aunty Rina and Vera became joint owners of the café – something those who knew Vera well could never have imagined her even considering before Rina turned up on the scene.

Georgina was promoted to news editor. Her ambition was to become the paper's first female editor. The women were in no doubt that she would fulfil her dream.

And so, the women welders' friendships continued – as did their love and care for one another. No matter if their new lives had taken them off in different directions or to different places, they all stayed close.

Helen, Rosie, Gloria, Polly, Martha and Georgina would meet up every Friday night for a catch-up in the Tatham. Martha would bring any letters sent by Hannah and Olly.

Angie would drive the ten miles from the estate every fortnight and regale them with stories about Dorothy.

The bond they had all formed during their years as Shipyard Girls remained as strong as the many welds they had forged – and the many ships they had helped to build.

Welcome to

Penny Street

where your favourite authors and stories live.

Meet casts of characters you'll never forget,
create memories you'll treasure forever,
and discover places that will stay with
you long after the last page.

Turn the page to step into the home of

Nancy Revell

and discover more about

The Shipyard Girls...

Dear Reader,

It is with a bittersweet heart that I pen this final letter to you all as *The Shipyard Girls* series draws to a close.

When I was thinking about what I wanted to write, it suddenly dawned on me that I have been immersed in the world of *The Shipyard Girls* for the same amount of time the women welders have worked at J.L. Thompson & Sons. And like my beloved characters, I now find myself feeling sad that this period has come to an end – but like them, I, too, also feel very excited about what's on the horizon.

So, it might be farewell to Rosie, Helen, Polly, Gloria, Dorothy, Angie, Martha and Hannah, but it is not goodbye from me as I hope you will join me in my future endeavours.

Until we meet again.

With Love,

Nancy
x